heartbreak town

ALSO BY MARSHA MOYER

The Second Coming of Lucy Hatch

The Last of the Honky-Tonk Angels

heartbreak town

A NOVEL

MARSHA MOYER

THREE RIVERS PRESS • NEW YORK

This is a work of fiction. Names, characters, places, and incidents either are the product of the author's imagination or are used fictitiously. Any resemblance to actual persons, living or dead, events, or locales is entirely coincidental.

Published in the United States by Three Rivers Press, an imprint of the Crown Publishing Group, a division of Random House, Inc., New York.
www.crownpublishing.com

THREE RIVERS PRESS and the Tugboat design are registered trademarks of Random House, Inc.

Library of Congress Cataloging-in-Publication Data
Moyer, Marsha.
Heartbreak town : a novel / Marsha Moyer.
1. Country musicians—Fiction. 2. Country musicians' spouses—Fiction.
3. Texas—Fiction. I. Title.
PS3613.O93H43 2007
813'.6—dc22 2006032554

ISBN 978-0-307-35154-8

Printed in the United States of America

Design by Chris Welch

10 9 8 7 6 5 4 3 2 1

First Edition

For Andrew and Gabriella Moyer,

who put words into my youngest characters' mouths

so much more eloquently (and comically)

than I could have done on my own

acknowledgments

A number of people are responsible for making this book happen—so many that to try to recognize them all would be impossible. Those whose contributions I cannot fail to single out are Allison McCabe, my editor at Three Rivers Press, for breathing new life into Lucy and company; my agent, Barbara Braun, for her ongoing support and faith in me; and my friend Ben Rehder, who read and commented in detail on a very long and convoluted early draft of the manuscript and helped me begin to shape it into the book you now hold in your hands—and loaned me Billy Don Craddock, to boot. Thank you all.

heartbreak town

prologue

You can die of a broken heart. I never knew that, but it's on *Good Morning America,* so it must be true. A Kentucky soldier got killed overseas, the tank he was riding in blown up by a mine, and one week later his wife back home dropped dead in her kitchen, right in the middle of making pancakes, gone before she hit the floor. I stop pouring water into the Mr. Coffee to look at the TV. Her brother's the one telling Diane Sawyer about it, a heavyset man in a brown suit, his face unshaved and sagging, hard luck and sorrow pulling everything south. "She always said if anything happened to him over there, she'd just up and die," he says, his voice as cracked and rough as horsehide, "and danged if that in't what she did."

"So you're saying, Mr. Oakley, that she died of a broken heart?" Diane Sawyer asks in her low, creamy voice. She's wearing a sweater the same color as her eyes, and I quit thinking about that woman on the kitchen floor just long enough to wonder how Diane Sawyer manages to get tricked out like a million bucks at an hour when most of us are still in our nightclothes with our teeth unbrushed.

"Know it for a fact," the brother says, and nods his chin hard, one time, like he's daring her, or God, or us watching at home, to argue.

I shiver, pulling my robe tight around me, and switch on the coffeemaker. I can see it all so clearly—that lady staggering into her kitchen, her hair a mess and her sweats mismatched, taking out the batter bowl and the Bisquick, wanting even in her haze of grief to do something ordinary, to try to get back a piece of her old, normal life. Did she feel it, I wonder, the splitting of her heart, like a chisel cracking rock, cleaving in two the heavy purple muscle? Or did it just sputter once or twice and then give out, like the battery in an old radio? I see her hand rising to her chest in surprise, her head turning one last time to look at the sun slanting through the curtains, the carton of eggs on the counter, the icebox door covered with to-do lists and kids' artwork and a snapshot of her husband wearing his uniform and a shaky grin, a promise—*I'm coming back to you, baby, nothing can keep us apart*—that maybe even as the shutter clicked he knew he wouldn't be able to keep. Did she understand what was happening? Was she sorry? Or was it a relief, knowing that the work of getting on with her life, minute after minute, one slow, heavy footstep at a time, was over? I admit it, for the space of a heartbeat I envy that lady who, if you believe in such things, is at peace now, reclining on some pearly cloud with her husband and Jesus and the angels. But part of me despises her just a little bit, too. Dying of a broken heart is the easy way out; the rest of us just build cages around the wreckage, shoring up the ruined bits with ropes and scaffolding, pulling ourselves upright, stumbling on.

A face appears, filling up the screen, chubby and smiling under a bad home perm. The lady's name, Diane Sawyer says, was Lucy Grubbs, and she was forty years old. For a second it takes my breath—she has the same first name as me, and we're the same age exactly.

Outside my kitchen window a bar of sunlight crests the trees and angles through the glass, dividing the table like a golden sword. I can hear the dogs rooting around on the screen porch, wanting breakfast. The water and ground beans I fed into the Mr. Coffee start to drip, filling the glass pot with hot, fragrant liquid. In the next room, my son is awake and singing to himself: *I'm a honky-tonk man, and I can't seem to stop.*

Rest in peace, Lucy Grubbs, I think, and switch off the television. The rest of us have work to do.

chapter one

"Jude, are you up? Because if you are, you need to come in here and eat your breakfast." "Honky-tonk Man" stopped as suddenly as it had started. "Jude?"

"I want waffles!" I could hear the squeak of the box spring as he started to bounce.

"We haven't got time for waffles. You'll have to settle for Cocoa Puffs." No reply, just more squeaking. "Did you hear me? Come on, now, or we'll be late."

It got quiet for a minute and then my son appeared in the kitchen doorway, jamming a fist into one eye. His Spider-Man pajamas, brand-new not one month earlier, were already too tight in the chest, riding two inches north of his ankles. He had my brother Bailey's coloring, the same rusty close-cropped hair and gold-rimmed eyes, but his features, his half-cocked smile, were purely his daddy's.

"Tomorrow's Saturday. We'll have waffles tomorrow, okay?" I took a bowl out of the cupboard and set the cereal box in the middle of the table. I was opposed to Cocoa Puffs on general principle, but in the real world, general principle didn't always have the final say.

He took his time dragging out a chair from the table and crawling onto it, dumping a heap of brown pellets into his bowl. I stood at the window sipping my coffee and pretending not to watch him. If he thought you were trying to do something for him, he'd throw on the brakes and start to whine, or pitch a fit. The first whole sentence he'd ever spoken, at sixteen months, was, "I do it myself!"

"Did you hear all that commotion last night?" I asked, watching him splash milk out of the carton over his cereal and onto the tabletop. "Did it wake you up?"

He nodded, picking up his spoon. "That was a *big* truck," he said.

Having a conversation with a six-year-old, I'd come to learn, was like riding a runaway horse; you had to hang on, throwing your weight from side to side to keep your balance, and who knew whether you'd arrive at your destination in one sure shot or go careening off in some direction you never expected.

"I was talking about the storm," I said. It had moved through about 4:00 A.M., waking me with flashes of lightning dancing jaggedly on the ceiling, the rumble of thunder, rain falling gentle at first and then hard and long, hammering the metal roof. I'd thought about getting up to watch the storm or check on Jude, but he could sleep through a typhoon, and anyway my bed felt too cozy; I'd just pulled the blanket up to my chin and gone back to sleep.

"Yeah," he said. "And then the truck. It was almost as loud as the rain!" He inserted a spoonful of cereal in his mouth.

"I don't know what you're talking about, baby," I said. "Did you have a dream about a truck?" He shook his head, chewing thoughtfully. "Well, listen, I need to go get dressed. Can you finish eating by yourself? Don't dawdle, now. You've still got to feed the dogs, don't forget." They were fickle, and just as likely to wander off to the neighbors if you made them wait too long for their breakfast.

I carried my coffee into the bathroom, where I set it on the edge of the sink while I washed my face and ran a brush through my hair. The medicine-chest mirror had a crack in it, courtesy of a prior tenant, and so the face I saw was bisected, uneven, though on second thought, maybe it was my true one, possibly even superior to the original. I'd never been any good at judging my looks. I was pretty when I got married the first time, and the second, when I was almost six months pregnant, I was beautiful. People would gawk at me in public, whether I was driving the flower van or in the grocery store across the produce bins and the dairy case. Maternity made my skin glow and my eyes shine, made me look almost otherworldly, like I'd been pumped full of juice. "Juicy Lucy," Ash had called me. He couldn't get enough of it, making us both late for work in the mornings, coaxing me home for lunch. Then Jude was born, and I became ordinary again, and we went to Nashville and it was Ash's turn.

I wasn't looking so juicy this morning, though, at least according to the bathroom mirror. There were shadows under my eyes, little fan-shaped lines at the outer corners that I couldn't remember seeing before. The divot over my upper lip looked deeper than it used to. Once upon a time Ash had claimed that baggage was what made a person worth knowing, but I wondered if that still held true when you started to carry it on the outside. There was a shoe box of old makeup under the cabinet, and I dug it out and rubbed Erace under my eyes, brushed some blush-on from a crumbling compact onto my cheeks. I couldn't in all honesty say the result was an improvement.

I rooted through the bedroom closet looking for something to wear. When Jude and I came back to Mooney, my boss at the flower shop, Peggy Thaney, not only gave me back my old job but promoted me to assistant manager, and I tried to make an effort to dress like I thought a businesswoman would dress, even if that woman lived in a town of under a thousand in far northeast Texas and had to make most of her fashion choices at Wal-Mart. I found a plain navy skirt and a white blouse with no stains and a minimum of wrinkles, and slid my feet into flats. Assistant manager or no, I was on my feet all day, and drew the line at heels.

I finished my coffee, brushed my teeth, and swiped on some pink lipstick from a tube my stepdaughter, Denny, had left behind half a dozen summers before.

"Jude!" I called. "Did you finish your breakfast?"

I found him in the front hall, still in his PJs.

"Baby, what did I tell you? We need to get a move on. Miss Kimble will be very unhappy if you're late, and you'll get a yellow square. You don't want another yellow square, do you?" He shook his head. "Did you feed the dogs, like I asked you?"

"I forgot."

"Well, hurry and get your boots on. It's muddy out there."

As Jude struggled into his galoshes, I went into the kitchen and put the cereal and the milk away, mopped up the table, and rinsed his bowl and the coffeepot and set them in the sink. When Ash first built this house, he'd been a longtime bachelor, and I guess he never thought about putting in a dishwasher. We always meant to add one, but we didn't live in the house that long together, and when we left for Nashville, it never in a million years occurred to us that any of us, under any circumstances, might be coming back.

I went to the pantry where we kept the forty-pound bag of Purina and filled a big metal scoop. Ordinarily this was part of Jude's job, but if we planned to get out of here anytime in the next half hour, I knew I was going to have to ease things along.

He stood with his nose pressed against the screen door, his pajama cuffs bunched around the tops of his rubber boots, staring dreamily across the porch. A cool breeze drifted in through the screen, like last night's rain had blasted everything clean behind it, leaving the sky as smooth and blue as a Wedgwood plate.

"Jude." I held out the scoop.

"See?" he said.

"See what?"

"It's just like I told you."

I closed my eyes and counted in my head, to five and then back. "What is?"

"The truck."

I opened my eyes and followed his gaze. Sure enough, smack-dab in the middle of our front yard, parked nose-to-nose with my Blazer, was a big, shiny, super-duty Chevy pickup. Brand-new, from the looks of it, still wearing dealer's plates, the upper half was as white and glistening as a spaceship, but from the door tops down it was spattered and caked with wet, red East Texas mud.

"Where'd it come from?" Jude asked. "How did it get in our yard?"

"I don't know." The hair on the back of my neck started to prickle. Nobody we knew had a truck like this, much less a reason for parking it in our front yard. I set the dog-food scoop on the floor. "Wait here."

I opened the door and stepped out onto the porch, then reached back inside and let my hand close around the first thing it found, a golf umbrella with a heavy wooden handle. "It's not raining, Mama," Jude said. I put my finger to my lips and, gripping the umbrella in both fists, went down the steps and into the yard.

I approached the truck slowly, the mud from last night's rain threatening to suck off my shoes with every step. A few weeks earlier there'd been a story in the *Cade County Register* about a rash of vehicle thefts in the area, work trucks and SUVs mostly, taken from homes and places of business and winding up later in the craziest places, stripped of their wheels, stereos, even their batteries and carburetors. But this truck, though filthy, was in possession of all four tires and fancy hubcaps, and as I approached from the rear I could hear music playing, which put to rest any question about the stereo and the battery.

"Is it ours? Do we get to keep it?" Jude came goose-stepping his way around the tailgate, lifting his legs high in the rubber boots.

"Jude, for goodness' sake! I told you to stay on the porch! We don't know—"

I swung the umbrella in front of me, aiming it like a weapon, and threw out my other arm to keep Jude back.

"What? What is it? I want to see!"

The rear door on the passenger side was open. Out of the cab floated the voice of Hank Williams, high and thin and far off, like he was singing from another galaxy, and jutting from the back-seat, toe toward heaven, was a scuffed-up black cowboy boot.

"Lord Jesus above," I said.

"Should I call 911?" Jude asked excitedly. I ignored him and, still wielding the umbrella, crept forward. The boot's heel was worn down on the outer edge, the sole leather as soft as a whisper from age and wear. I knew this boot well, just like I knew its mate, with its hole in the instep the size of a dime. Topping them was an old pair of Levi's, one leg sticking straight ahead, the other bent at the knee and resting on the seat, and above that, a faded gray T-shirt, arms flung upward to expose a couple of ribs so pale and prominent they looked like they belonged to a doctor's-office skeleton.

Lightly, with the tip of the umbrella, I touched the toe of the sticking-out boot. Ash had always hated mornings, and I watched as he sighed and shifted, squeezing his eyes shut, fighting as long as he could to keep the day at bay. For months now, I'd gone over and over my laundry list of grievances, rehearsing what I'd say if and when this time finally came. Now that it was here, part of me wanted to take the umbrella and whack him into next week and part of me wanted just to stand there, watching his lids flicker and his chest rise and fall, wondering at this feeling in my own chest, like a flint striking against rock, the unexpectedness of its small but steady flame.

"Who is it, Mama?" Jude called. "Are they dead?"

I waved at him to hush. The pickup still had that new-factory smell, the dashboard glinting with Armor All, the leather seats giving off a soft glow like they'd been buttered, but the floor was a mess of empty bottles and fast-food wrappers and clothes, and jammed into the console was a Rand McNally road atlas folded to expose the south central United States, a crooked, dark red line like an artery linking northeast Texas to Tennessee.

Ash let out a low groan, twisting his head one way and then the other.

"Ash," I said quietly, trying out the sound of it. I hadn't seen him face-to-face in nearly eight months, hadn't heard his voice—not counting the radio—in three.

With a grimace he pushed himself up onto his elbows, scraped his hair back from his face with one hand, and gave a dry and rasping cough. He opened one eye, squinted at the dome light overhead.

"What," he said, and then, "Aw, shit. Not again."

"*Ash*."

He swiveled his head toward me and opened the other eye. His face had a fuzzy look, its hard planes and angles softened by the pink morning light. It was a look I knew well, this pulling himself hand-over-fist toward consciousness. I tightened my grip on the umbrella and watched him settle back into himself, his features taking on their old familiar edges as his gaze came into focus and a gradual awareness dawned behind it.

Slowly, one corner of his mouth crooked up.

"Lucy Hatch," he said. "I must be dreaming." He stretched his arms over his head; I heard his neck pop. A week's worth of silver stubble peppered his jaw.

He reached down and scratched his exposed rib cage, leisurely and deliberately, the way you'd scratch a cat. I couldn't help noticing he was still wearing his wedding band. "Aren't you gonna say something?" he asked.

"I'm trying to think where to start."

"How about, 'Hey, babe, it's good to see you'?"

"That's not what comes to the top of the list."

"Is it still raining?" He eyed the umbrella in my hand.

"This isn't for weather. It's for self-defense."

"Man, that was some storm last night, huh? I thought I could beat it, but it caught me up near Texarkana, and by the time I hit Atlanta, I didn't think I was gonna make it. It was coming down so hard I damn near missed the turn onto Little Hope. Tried to hook it at the last minute and spun off in the ditch. Lucky thing I bought four-wheel drive is all I can say. Good old Chevy." Ash smacked the upholstery with the flat of his hand. "Like a rock."

Suddenly Jude was standing beside me, saucer-eyed. "Daddy!" he gasped, then ducked behind me and buried his face in my hip.

"Hey! Who's that I see hiding back there? Get on up here, buddy, and let me take a look at you."

Jude glanced up at me. I nodded, and he sidled forward and climbed onto the running board, then froze there, smiling dizzily, his face a tangle of desire and confusion.

"Lord a mercy," Ash said. "Is this Jude Farrell?"

Jude stared. The smile blinked on and off, like a traffic signal.

"Ash. Don't tease him."

"But it can't be! Last time I saw Jude Farrell, he was a little boy. This is a great big, strapping young man!"

"It's still me!" Jude blurted out. "I'm the same me, only bigger!"

"You don't say." Ash pretended to ponder this. "How about me? Do you remember me?"

Jude looked uncertainly at me, then back at Ash. He nodded.

"Well, in that case, how about a hug?"

Jude hung back for barely a second before throwing out his arms, and Ash reached down and hoisted him into the truck, where they collapsed in a heap on the backseat, wrestling and laughing.

"You smell yucky, Daddy!" Jude shouted, hysterical with excitement as Ash held him and stroked his hair.

"Yeah, well, you don't smell so great yourself."

"You smell like a horse!"

"You smell like a hamster."

"You smell like a big fat hippopotamus!"

"You smell like a polecat."

They grinned into each other's eyes. I felt the day unraveling in front of my eyes like a ragged sweater.

"You smell like a ferret."

"You smell like a brontosaurus!"

"All right, Jude, that's enough," I said. "You need to get dressed now. I mean it. School starts in"—I looked at my Timex, automatically subtracting a quarter of an hour—"ten minutes."

"I don't have to go to school today!" Jude cried. "Daddy's here!"

I shot Ash a look—*Help me out here*—and prayed against all odds that at least a trace of our old telepathy was still there.

"Do you want to see my Hot Wheels Turbo Blaster?" Jude was saying. "I've got dinosaurs, too! And an aircraft carrier, and a Captain Hook pirate ship."

"Run do like your mama says, buddy," Ash said. "I'll check out your stuff later, I promise."

"Don't go away," Jude ordered, sliding out of Ash's lap onto the chrome step. "I'll be right back."

"He's in school?" Ash said in amazement as we watched Jude make his way toward the house, feet flapping in the clumsy rubber boots.

"Kindergarten. Since September."

"I swear to God I was just holding him in the hospital. It seems like a week ago."

"Your sense of time has always been lousy."

Ash slid to the edge of the seat, tugging the tail of his T-shirt down over his middle. "What the hell, Lucy. After all I went through to get here, the least you can do is act glad to see me."

"Do I have to *be* glad, or do I just have to act?"

He smiled and massaged the back of his neck. "You're something else, you know that? Looking good and talking sass at, what—six in the morning?"

"It's seven-forty-five. You see? Look around you. The sun is up. People are up and about, getting on with their lives."

"Is that supposed to be a metaphor? I seem to recall you like those."

He leaned between the front seats and switched off the stereo, then took a plastic Coke bottle out of the cup holder, twisted off the cap, and poured a gulp into his mouth, swished it inside his cheeks for a few seconds, and swallowed. "Sorry," he said. "I guess I'm a little rough around the edges. But it was a long drive, and I hadn't planned on sleeping in the truck."

"I don't get it."

"It was raining like a son of a bitch when I got here. I just planned to stretch out for a few minutes in the backseat and wait for it to let up. I guess I must've been tireder than I thought."

"That's not what I— What is the meaning of this, Ash? What is your intent?"

"My intent?"

"We haven't seen hide nor hair of you in eight months. You haven't called since Jude's birthday. And now you land in the front yard in a rainstorm in the middle of the night in a brand-new truck, no warning, no explanation, and I'm supposed to just, just drop everything and welcome you with open arms?"

"That'd be nice, but I'm getting the feeling it's not gonna happen." He'd started rummaging on the floor and under the seats, pulling out various balled-up pieces of clothing, a wrinkled copy of *Nashville Scene,* a sneaker. I'd never known Ash to own sneakers in his life.

"Denny said you were checking into some rehab place in Nashville. A thirty-day inpatient program."

"Yep."

"So?"

"So, what?"

"That was two weeks ago."

"What can I say? They let me out early."

"Early? What for?"

"Good behavior?"

I closed my eyes, pressing my fingertips to my temples. "You left, didn't you? You picked up and walked out and nothing is any different than it was before."

"Meaning what?"

"Meaning you're still a drunk."

"Correction. A drunk is somebody who has a problem. Who can't control himself. That doesn't apply to me."

"You can control it? Since when?"

He took another swig of Coke, then inched forward to the edge of the seat. "Look, I'll tell you everything you want to know, okay? Let me just pull myself together a little bit here, get a shower, a couple of cups of coffee in me, and some breakfast. Hey, how about mixing up some of your famous waffles, huh? How's that sound?"

"Ash."

"Yeah?"

"I need to ask you something."

"I'm telling you, this'll go a lot better once I've got some caffeine in me."

"Do you remember the night I left you?" I said.

He sighed, twisting the top back onto the soda bottle. "Sure, I remember."

"No, do you *really* remember? Do you remember why I left? Because you're acting like you just, just went out for a newspaper and got hit on the head by a brick and forgot how to get home again. It's April, and I haven't seen you since August! Do you think I've just been sitting down here all that time, all damp and dewy-eyed, waiting for you to show up and pretend like nothing happened? Did you think you could just waltz into town and find everything blown over, like some, some middle-of-the-night thunderstorm?"

"Lucy. Listen to me." He reached for my hand, but I jerked it back. "Let's go in the house. Let me clean up a little, make us a pot of coffee, and we'll talk."

"I can't go in and talk! I've got to take Jude to school, and I've got to work. I got promoted," I said. "I'm assistant manager at Faye's."

"Is that a fact."

"Today's the Easter party at Golden Years, and we've got flowers for the church, and a big anniversary bouquet for Loretta Mackey. . . . Is something funny?"

"Faye's Flowers. Golden Years. Mrs. Mackey. Damn, I've missed this place. Nothing ever changes."

He slid out of the truck onto his feet. The sudden proximity caught me off guard, the solid shape and heat of him, and as he raised his arms over his head to stretch out the kinks, the smell just about knocked me sideways: road-ripe and unwashed, rained on and slept in. But underneath it all was another note, sweet and dark like raw honey, a note I recognized the same way a bee must recognize the one hive out of a hundred it calls home.

The screen door slammed, and Jude came running into the yard wearing a pair of camouflage pants with his rubber boots and his Spider-Man pajama top under a bright orange reflective hunting vest.

"You're wrong," I said. "Everything's changed."

But Ash was leaning in to the bed of the truck, lifting the lid on a big Marine ice chest. "You like crawfish, right?"

"Excuse me?"

"I stopped along the side of the road in Arkansas and bought a mess. Thought maybe we could boil 'em up, have some folks over for a little get-together."

"You want to have a crawfish boil?"

"Well, forty pounds is too much for you and Jude and me. Hasn't your aunt got one of those big propane cookers?"

When I didn't answer right away, he turned and looked over his shoulder at me. My mind spun like a whirligig, around and around on its point, all its energy aimed at the simple act of staying upright. I opened my mouth, then closed it. There were too many questions. I couldn't begin to know where to start.

"Hey, you okay?" Ash said. "Come to think of it, you look a little peaked. Maybe you ought to call in sick."

Jude scuttled over and attached himself to Ash's leg. "Daddy, will you take me fishing? I've got a rod and reel. Uncle Bailey's been teaching me!"

"Get in the car, Jude," I said. "We have to go."

"Not today, buddy. I think you better do what your mama says."

"But you just—"

Wordlessly, I snapped my fingers and pointed to the Blazer, and Jude detached himself from Ash and dragged himself over to my car, where he stood dawdling beside the rear door, fooling with a flap on his vest.

"I don't have my backpack!" he yelled. I told him I'd get it.

"Crawfish," I said to Ash. He shrugged, smiled. To look at him, you really might think he'd just run across the state line to buy a bunch of mudbugs and gotten caught in the rain.

I went inside, grabbed my purse and Jude's backpack, and set out the dogs' food.

"Here," I said, sliding my house key off the ring and handing it to Ash. "You might need this." He let his hand close over mine. I slipped my fingers free, tucked them under my arm. "I had the locks changed."

"Another metaphor?"

"Don't push me. I'm not in the mood."

He laughed, reaching into the backseat of the truck. He pulled out a plaid flannel shirt, examined it for a second, held it to his nose and sniffed it.

"Don't worry about me!" he called as I climbed into the Blazer and fired up the engine. "I'll just make myself at home!"

Or, I thought, he might just disappear again as mysteriously as he'd landed, blasting off into outer space in his shiny white pickup, leaving nothing behind but a few ruts in the yard and a cooler full of crawfish. Pulling out onto Little Hope Road, watching my husband get smaller and smaller in the rearview mirror, I couldn't say for sure which prospect I was more afraid of.

chapter two

I thought I was marrying Ash Farrell with both eyes open and both feet flat on the ground. True, I was five months pregnant at the time, had known him a grand total of five months and two weeks. True, my late first husband of fourteen years had only been late—that is, dead—since February. True, Ash was wild and handsome and talented, getting ready to go off to Nashville and be a big country-western star, whereas I had never lived more than an hour's drive from my hometown in my life. But, in the way of people in love, I didn't see those things as challenges; they seemed to me more like interesting novelties, fun and quirky tidbits with which to eventually paper our own long and colorful marital history. Nothing seemed impossible to me then; I had a glut of energy and optimism along with all the estrogen pumping through my veins, and what other people might have seen as warning lights just looked to me like those mirrored balls that hung suspended from the ceilings of the dance halls where Ash sang and played, steadily turning in time to the music, casting our lives in an endlessly revolving shower of radiance. We shone, it seemed, from the ends of our hair to the tips of our toes. I thought we had everything going for us. I thought we couldn't lose.

I PULLED UP in front of Mooney Elementary with no recollection of having driven there, the last ten minutes lost in a cotton-candy haze. The dashboard clock said two minutes past eight, and I could see Jude's teacher standing at the entrance the way she did every morning, scouting for latecomers.

"Hop out quick, baby," I said. "Let Miss Kimble see you're here."

He muttered and squirmed in the backseat, struggling to undo his seat belt. I unbuckled my harness and leaned over the console to help him, but he pushed my hand away. *I do it myself!*

I looked up nervously. Sure enough, here she came, a wide-hipped, frizzy-headed woman, maybe thirty, in a denim skirt and a red cardigan and those thick, clunky sandals the kids called Jesus shoes, heading down the walk toward us with a purposeful stride.

"Mama?"

"What, Jude?" I asked, silently urging him to hurry. I didn't know why Miss Kimble made me so antsy. She was always nice. Even when she was admonishing us for being late and explaining to me about the yellow squares, she was nice.

"Can I bring Daddy for show-and-tell?"

"We'll talk about Daddy later."

I sent the window whirring down and pasted on a bright smile for Miss Kimble.

"Morning!" I called in my best PTA voice. "Here we are! Right on time!" It was a tactic Ash had taught me: Lie in their faces and dare them to contradict you.

"Actually, Mrs. Farrell, the bell rang a couple minutes ago." The fact that Miss Kimble called me by my married name made it apparent she wasn't a native of Cade County. To the locals, I was and would always be Lucy Hatch.

"Really? Hear that, Jude? The bell already rang!"

Miss Kimble ignored me and poked her head through the open window. "Morning, Jude," she said. "Having a little trouble there?"

Jude gave a loud grunt. "Goddamn seat belt!" he said. "It's stuck!"

I think I gasped. Miss Kimble, bless her, just opened the back door, reached over, and unclicked the two halves of the metal clasp, like a genie saying, "Open, sesame!"

"There we go!" she said. "All set."

"What do you say to Miss Kimble, Jude?" I said.

"My daddy came, Miss Kimble! He came in a truck in the rain!"

"Is that right?" She was clearly used to hearing children babble all day and filtering out their fantastical delusions, because she breezed right on ahead. "So, are you excited about the party today? Ready to dye some eggs and eat some cupcakes?"

"Jesus died for our sins," Jude informed her somberly.

Miss Kimble glanced at me. I gave her an unapologetic shrug. I didn't want my son growing up thinking Easter was only about bunnies and candy. Anyway, my mama had worked hard to put the fear of Jesus in me, and I felt obliged to pass it along to the next generation.

"Well, that isn't the kind of dyeing we're going to do here today. Today's about the *fun* side of Easter!"

"They nailed Him to a cross," Jude said. Miss Kimble was starting to look upset, so he tacked on a disclaimer. "But it was a long time ago. In a galaxy far, far away!"

The second bell—the tardy bell—rang. I pictured Jude's chart on the wall behind Miss Kimble's desk, a solid line of yellow like a highway divider: *Stay back. Do not pass.* Was it possible to flunk kindergarten?

"I'll see you this afternoon, baby," I said. "I'll come by Dove's and pick up you and Lily, and you can go with me to the party at Golden Years."

I started to power the window up, but Miss Kimble waved, and I let it down again. "Yes?"

"Cupcakes, Mrs. Farrell."

"Yes," I repeated, like I knew perfectly well what she was talking about. I admit I wasn't giving it a hundred percent of my concentration. I was thinking about Ash and his new truck and his forty pounds of crawfish; I was thinking about his raw-honey smell, and the swath of skin between his Levi's and the hem of his T-shirt. I was thinking about how you could threaten to pull out his tongue with a pair of pliers and he still wouldn't admit he'd done anything that needed apologizing for.

"You *did* get my note, didn't you?" Miss Kimble said.

"Note."

"About the cupcakes."

So many details. Nobody warns you about it at prenatal classes, and it's not in Dr. Spock. Having a child is an endless procession of paperwork, of certifications and immunizations, of progress charts and permission slips. Who could keep track of it all?

"Is this about the sugar thing? Because I know some of the parents are up in arms about it, but honestly, as far as I'm concerned, it's not a problem. Jude can have all the sugar he wants! Well, not *all* the sugar. I mean, I don't want him making himself sick! But, hey, it's Easter, isn't it? What's the point of Easter, if not sugar? Except for Jesus on the cross, that is."

Miss Kimble leaned over and said something to Jude I couldn't hear, then gave him a pat and sent him up the walk toward the building. I watched him go, his backpack bouncing off his hip, his orange vest glowing radioactively. As he reached the door, he turned and gave me a brave little salute, then disappeared inside.

I looked at the teacher, who was watching me with what I recognized from long experience as a pitying expression. *Screw you, Miss Kimble,* I wanted to say. *Screw you and your yellow squares and your ugly shoes. Give me back my boy and we're outta here.*

"Today was Jude's turn to bring cupcakes, Mrs. Farrell. I handed out the schedule at the beginning of the semester, remember? And I sent a reminder note home last week."

"Oh!" My throat felt swollen. My eyes burned. "Oh, hell. I didn't . . . I don't . . ." I turned to the windshield and blinked several times, telling myself to get a grip.

"Mrs. Farrell? Excuse me for asking, but is everything all right?"

I laughed. "Am I going to get a yellow square?"

"I only ask because, well . . ."

Don't say it, I willed her silently. *You only ask because I look like I'm at the end of my rope, and if you say it out loud, that will make it true, and it can't be true, because I need my rope. I need it to hold my family together. Or, if not that, to hang myself.*

"What time is the party?"

"Ten o'clock."

I gritted my teeth and threw the Blazer in gear. "I'll be back in half an hour."

THE FOOD KING didn't have much in the way of Easter goodies. They didn't have much in the way of anything else, either, unless you counted cramped aisles, grimy displays, wilted produce, and sullen employees. Frankly, I was amazed the place was still a going concern. Nobody in Mooney in their right mind or with the means to go elsewhere shopped there; it was hot in summer and freezing in winter, and sparrows roosted indoors in the rafters, a problem no amount of effort or brainpower on the part of the management seemed to be able to fix.

If there'd been time, I'd have driven the eighteen miles to the Super Wal-Mart up near Atlanta with its wide, bright aisles and acres of parking, its mind-boggling assortment of merchandise, a bakery department where a request for Easter cupcakes would be greeted with something other than a head shake and a scowl. Instead, I had to settle for two dozen plain white cupcakes with gummy pink frosting, decorating them myself in the backseat of my car with a bag of stale-looking jellybeans and a jar of little candy sprinkles. While I worked, I told myself that if I'd gotten Miss Kimble's note—or if I'd gotten it and then bothered to read it—I'd have baked these cupcakes myself, maybe not from scratch but at least from a Duncan Hines mix, would have made up frosting in different pastel colors and garnished the tops with little sugar bunnies and chicks. Now it was too late for beauty, for freshness and creativity; I had to cross my fingers and pray that nobody chipped a tooth on a jelly bean or broke out in an allergic rash from Red No. 2 dye. I cleaned my hands with a wet wipe and sped back to the school. Luckily, Miss Kimble's class was outside playing kickball when I got there. I left the cupcakes on her desk like a prankster's trick, and ran.

If there was anybody in Cade County, Texas, you could count on to be not just out and about but at full typhoon force at eight-thirty on a weekday morning, it was my aunt Dove. As I pulled up to the curb in front of her house I could see her, a straw hat trimmed with a red bandanna on her head, bent over her spring garden.

Dove's garden was the talk of the county. Teeming with every vegetable and annual native to East Texas, it was also a kind of multicultural shrine that she'd decorated with tiny statues and prayer stones and amulets and religious medals, the way most of her neighbors set out plastic geese in ladies' bonnets and cast-iron donkeys pulling wheelbarrows. Hardly a day went by, especially in summertime, that folks didn't stop, sometimes driving quite a distance, to look over the place, and some felt moved to add their own trinkets to the mix, so that in among the rosaries and miniature Buddhas, you just might find an Elvis Presley key chain or a shot glass from the Isle of Capri casino in Bossier City. Dove didn't really care if you wanted to pray to Jesus or Krishna or Santa Claus or the almighty dollar; one thing was as sacred as the next, as far as she was concerned, and "live and let live" was her motto, though I can't say that it was the prevailing one in Mooney, Texas, population 990, about nine hundred of them hard-shell Baptists.

"Some folks is up early," she said as I came through the gate. "Then again, some folks's been partyin' all night."

She showed me the saucer in her hand, where fifteen or twenty slugs floated in a shallow pool of liquid. "Last call for happy hour," she said, her blue eyes glinting. Tufts of white hair like goosedown escaped from the brim of her hat. She wore a T-shirt featuring an iron-on likeness of Porter Wagoner in full pompadoured and sequin-suited splendor over the block-printed slogan, WHAT WOULD PORTER DO?

I bent to the dish and sniffed. "Beer?"

"You know, I been doin' this for I don't know how long, but I always thought it was somethin' in the brew that killed 'em. Come to find out it ain't the alcohol—they just fall in and drown. I sure wish I'd a figgered that out sooner, I could've saved me a piece of cash over at the Pak 'n' Sak. That boy runs the register acts like he's fixin' to turn me over to Liquor Control." She jiggled the dish contemplatively. "Must've been some bash. There's more of 'em over there. Looks like they invited all their friends. It's a wonder they didn't keep me up all night, singin' and dancin' and gettin' in fistfights."

"What's with the shirt?" I asked.

"You like it? Me and Rowena thought 'em up." Rowena Sheppard was Dove's oldest friend and cohort in the Cade County Garden Club. "I was over at her house last week and she had that CMT on the TV and, I swear, you'd a thought we was watching *America's Most Wanted* on the Fox channel—all them boys with big old baggy pants and scraggly beards and sunglasses, looking like they been sleepin' under a bridge somewhere, holdin' up gas stations and smokin' who knows what. Goodness sakes, I says to Rowena, is this what things has come to? Whatever happened to the days when country music was so fancy and proud, when the ladies had gowns and hair up to there, and the men wore them beautiful suits with all the beads and spangles? It was Rowena blurted out, 'Yeah, what would Porter do?'" I laughed. "We're thinkin' of havin' a batch of 'em printed up and sell 'em at Market Days downtown," Dove said. "Then, if that goes good, maybe branch out, get set up on the Intranet. Start us a reg'lar campaign."

"Hm. Maybe I ought to get in on that."

"So, how about it?" She held out the saucer full of little bloated bodies. "You here to help me round up the casualties?"

"No, thanks. I've seen enough slugs floating facedown in their beer to last me one lifetime." I picked up a little metal Matchbox car with Dale Earnhardt's Number 3 on it, squeezed in between Saint Francis and a Chinese Foo dog.

"Any particular slug on your mind?" Dove asked as she tipped the dish's contents, bugs, beer, and all, into an old coffee can. "Or is there some other reason you're standin' in my front yard at the break of day looking like you got the devil on your heels?"

"I look like I've got the devil on my heels?"

"Well, maybe not just anybody'd think so. But I ain't just anybody." Thirty-some-odd years before, when my daddy, Raymond Hatch, walked out on my mama and brothers and me, Dove had taken the boys and me under her wing, been more of a mama to us than our own mama, her sister Patsy, ever was, and except for my brother Bailey's wife, Geneva, she knew me better than anybody.

"Ash is here."

She looked up, glanced past me toward the Blazer, back to me again.

"He's at the house, I mean." Dove jiggled the coffee can a time or two, then set it on the sidewalk. "He came last night, during the storm. I found him when I went out to feed the dogs this morning, sound asleep in the backseat of a brand-new pickup. Said he fell asleep waiting for the rain to let up. He acted like this was a regular thing—like he'd been gone two, three days, tops. He couldn't seem to figure out why I wasn't falling all over myself to see him. When I left to take Jude to school, he was getting ready to go inside and take a shower. Just like it was any old day."

"Well, I'll be. What happened at that dryin'-out place up in Tennessee?"

"He said they let him out early. He said he's got things under control."

Dove snorted and gave the brim of her hat a yank. "Well, I'll tell you this—if he shows up here, I mean to sit him down and give him a piece a my mind."

"I think you can count on it," I said. "Guess what he had in the back of the truck? Forty pounds of crawfish. Says he wants to have everybody over for a crawfish boil. He's talking about borrowing your cooker."

We looked at each other, then started to laugh. Dove shook her head.

"If that ain't Ash, through and through."

I nodded. "A little food, a little drink, a little music, and pretty soon we forgive him all his trespasses."

"So, you goin' along with this plan?"

"Have I got a choice? We're still married. The house is still his, half of it anyway. And Jude was so happy to see his daddy, Dove! I could barely pry them apart to get him to school."

"Well, all I can say is, everbody's gotta face the music sometime," Dove said. "Even if their name is Ash Farrell."

"Try telling that to Ash. He's got his own rules." I looked at my watch. "I've got to run. If I hurry, maybe I can get to work before the news breaks."

"I wouldn't count on it."

"Anyway, I wanted to give you a heads-up. So if he comes breezing in your back door, he won't give you a heart attack."

"Let him come a-breezin'," she said with a sly smile, and waved as I drove off.

I wasn't officially due in to work till nine, when the shop opened, but I liked to get in early and get a jump on the day. Some days I beat Peggy in and some days I didn't. Since making me assistant manager, she'd been going around telling people she was semi-retired, but all that meant was that she could run out to meet her friends Alene and Mary Dale for coffee at the DQ whenever she wanted, maybe go home early and watch *One Life to Live* if things were slow.

To be frank about it, business in a small-town, home-grown flower shop was not so brisk that Peggy had to be underfoot all the time. I took care of the books and the ordering now, and we had a Voc Ed student from Mooney High who came in from eleven to three to help with chores and delivery. But Faye's had been Peggy's mama's shop before her—that's where it got its name—and it had helped her keep her two kids in clothes and school supplies and put supper on the table, especially after Peggy's husband, Duane Thaney, passed on. What was she supposed to do, she said, now that her kids were grown and gone—sit around the house and watch herself shrivel up and get ready to die? There was enough of that in Mooney as it was, according to Peggy, and she wanted no part of it.

She'd had a scare a while back that had something to do with it. When I first went to work for her, Peggy had been the size of a parade float, bumping gently around the shop in her bright flowered muumuus. But about five years before, she'd gone in to see the doctor about some shortness of breath and tightness in her chest, and next thing she knew, she was in County General with an emergency triple bypass. Over the months that followed, recovering from the surgery, she'd lost sixty pounds. When she got on her feet again, she took up power-walking and lost another eighty, and now she was a hale and muscular figure who could be seen marching through the streets of Mooney in her Spandex bike shorts, hand weights pumping, her hair pulled through a saucy little cap. A lot of women her age spent their days shuttling from one neighbor's house to another, eating coffee cake and playing bridge, but Peggy took pride in calling herself the exception to the rule.

I pulled in next to her Pontiac and took out my key to let myself in the back door. I'd barely inserted the key in the lock when the door jerked open, flying backward on its hinges. I gave a little shout and dropped my purse. Not even eight-forty-five in the morning, and already my nerves were shot.

"Lord, Peggy! Are you trying to scare me to death?" I knelt and started gathering up the spilled contents of my purse: loose change, cough drops, a rubber figurine from a McDonald's Happy Meal.

"Lucy!" she cried. "I can't believe it!" She had on a hot pink smock over khakis, and she looked terrific.

"Believe what?"

"Ash is here!"

I jerked up my head and looked around.

"Oh, not *here,* here. But here! In Mooney, his hometown!" I stood and squeezed past her into the shop. She followed me into the showroom, where I tossed my purse on the counter. "I guess I don't have to tell you, I've been praying for this day a long time."

I walked over and poured myself a cup of coffee. Peggy and I liked our coffee the same way, Louisiana style, strong and dark and laced with chicory.

"I'm afraid to ask how you found out." It had barely been an hour since I'd come upon him fast asleep in his truck in the front yard, and the only person I'd told was Dove. The grape-vine in our hometown was a mighty thing, but this had to be a record, even for Mooney.

"He called."

"Ash? Called here?"

"Not five minutes ago!" Her face was flushed, eyes shining.

"What did he want?"

"Oh, I—something about books or towels or some such. I was just so excited to hear his voice! I guess my brain flew right out of my head."

I sipped my coffee. It was black and scalding in a way I found deeply satisfying, like penance.

"Aren't you going to call him back?"

I set my cup on the counter. "Am I hallucinating? Am I the only one around here who doesn't think it's perfectly okay for a person to fall off the face of the earth for eight months, then just show up one night like nothing's happened, like it's the most ordinary thing in the world? He can't be bothered to check in and let me know he's alive since Christmastime, and now he's calling about *towels*?"

"I just knew this would happen! I was telling Alene, someday that boy will wake up and see the error of his ways! I—oh, my goodness. I'd better run over and tell Burton at the café. Why, the pot's probably up to a hundred dollars by now!"

I started to go after her, to tell her that she hadn't even heard the facts yet, such as they were, but I stopped myself. Facts were far down the list of considerations for the crowd at Burton's café, well behind intrigue, propaganda, and wild speculation. Since the day I met Ash Farrell, we'd been the object of some kind of pool or another; as far as I could tell, the town was pretty neatly divided, fifty-fifty, between those who thought Ash and I were soul mates, fated for life, and those who hadn't thought we'd ever get together in the first place, weren't surprised when I left him in Nashville and came on home, and wouldn't believe now we'd find a way to piece things back together.

I picked up the phone and dialed the house, but the line just rang and rang. Maybe Ash was in the shower. Or maybe he'd already turned tail and headed on down the road, his white truck rocketing along the highway, trailing broken promises like a string of cans on the back of a honeymoon car.

I'd no more than set the receiver in its cradle when it rang again. I answered, bracing myself. "Faye's Flowers, Lucy speaking—how may I help you?"

"What time is it there?"

"Denny?" I felt a soup of mixed emotions, relief and anxiety and joy and irritation, at the sound of her voice. "Where are you?"

"Elko, Nevada. Isn't that wild? Ty booked us some rodeo gig. I thought I'd seen it all, but man, those bull riders know how to *party.*" She sounded hoarse and happy. By now I was used to these calls from all over the country, as well as her more-or-less permanent confusion about what time zone she was in. It was 6:50 A.M. in Elko, Nevada, and my guess was, she was just rolling in.

"Is everything okay?" I asked.

"With me, you mean?"

"Who else am I talking to?"

"Oh, I'm fine. In fact, I'm great." For a beat or two there was silence on the line. "I met a guy."

"Not on the back of a bull, I hope." My brother Bailey had rodeoed for a while after high school, and I knew bull riders were as wild as they come.

She laughed. "Not even close. He's the new bass player in my band."

I clapped my hand over the mouthpiece to keep from screaming. If there was anything worse than a bull rider, it was a professional musician. Hadn't her daddy taught her anything?

"His name's Will Culpepper. He's gorgeous. I'm totally in love."

I closed my eyes to conjure a picture of my stepdaughter, the way she looked in the eight-by-ten photo that hung over the bar at the Round-Up—the same one I had on my bureau and Aunt Dove kept as part of the family shrine on top of her TV—with her torn jeans and beat-up boots and flame-colored hair the same shade as her Fender guitar, aiming her feisty smile at the camera. But my mind kept going back to the day she'd first showed up to stay with Ash and me, a chunky, stringy-haired fourteen-year-old with a chip on her shoulder and a gift none of us, least of all her daddy, could've imagined. I missed that girl. She'd needed me in a way nobody, not even my son, had before or since. I don't care who you are or what kind of job you've done, it's hard to see somebody you've had a hand in raising take off out the nest, to stay behind and watch her fly.

"I can't wait to meet him," I said. I wondered if Ash knew this Will Culpepper. I wondered if he'd greet him like a comrade, or just go ahead and have him killed.

"But, look, that's not why I called," Denny said, her voice going suddenly solemn. "There's something else. Something I think you need to know. I got a message yesterday on my cell phone. That is, I got the message this morning, a few minutes ago. But the call came yesterday." She paused. My throat felt like it had been sandpapered. "It's Daddy," she said. "He checked out of the rehab place. Left, I mean, without being discharged. He just took off. They don't know where he is."

I started to laugh.

"Lucy?" Denny said. "Did you just hear what I said?"

"Sorry. It's just that I know all this already."

"You mean they called you, too?"

"No, I mean he's here. He showed up last night. In a truck, in the rain."

"Well, I'll be a— Is he okay?"

"I'm not sure. I think he may have had a lobotomy."

"What?"

"Or maybe it's just selective amnesia. He knows Jude and me, all right. But he acts like we just saw each other yesterday and things were swell. When I left for work he was getting ready to take a shower."

"His old self, in other words. King of Denial."

"He had a cooler with him, full of crawfish."

"Crawfish?"

"Forty pounds. He said he bought it off the side of the road in Arkansas."

"I don't get it. Is that supposed to be some kind of peace offering?"

"You tell me. I mean, I like crawfish just fine, but I'd rather have a straight answer out of him."

"Good luck."

"And you should see this truck. Great big shiny four-by-four, crew cab, leather seats, satellite radio, the works. It had to have cost forty thousand dollars. It still has the dealer's plates on it. I was too scared to ask him where he got it."

"I guess this means the rehab thing didn't take."

"I had a hard time getting a straight answer there, too. All he'd say about it is that he's got it under control. You know your daddy—he could be standing in the middle of a tornado and he'd be saying things are under control."

"Yeah, with a beer in one hand and a shot in the other one while he was saying it." Both of us mulled that one over awhile. "So, are you gonna take him back?" she finally asked.

"You mean, let him park in the yard and use the shower? Or let things start up where we left off back in Nashville? Right now I can't even think straight. It seems to me there's an awful lot of muddy ground in the middle."

"Well, you sound like you're handling it okay."

"I don't think it's really sunk in yet. But Jude's bound to be telling it all over school, and Peggy just ran over to the café to spread the word. I imagine it'll be a three-ring circus around here in no time."

All of a sudden she gave a yelp. "Hey!" she said, and then there was laughter and muffled conversation on her end. It made my heart hurt. From a mother's perspective, I wanted her to be happy, but woman to woman, what I felt was pure, smoldering envy.

"Lucy?" Her voice was suddenly clear again, bright and breathless. "You still there?"

"Let me let you go," I said quickly. I hoped she wouldn't want to put Will on. I didn't think I could stand it, not today. "Listen, try not to worry about your daddy and me. I'm sure this will all make sense in a day or two." I didn't really believe that, but what else was I supposed to say? Leave Elko, Nevada, and Will Culpepper and your Fender guitar and get on down here and give me a hand? She'd have done it, and I knew it. I had to remember an old promise I'd made myself, that I'd never get in the way of my kids' dreams, not unless it was life or death, and this wasn't, at least not yet.

"You sure?"

"I'm sure."

"We're heading down to Vegas for a show tonight. But I'll call you later, okay?"

"Denny. Don't worry."

"Hey—don't tell me what to do." More muffled talk, a giggle or two, then she said, "I've got to go. Are you really okay?"

"I really am. Tell Will I said treat you right or I'll sic your daddy on him."

"I'll do it. Give Daddy a kiss for me. Wait—on second thought, just tell him I sent my love. Jude, too. Y'all behave. Don't make me come down there and straighten you out."

"Don't be silly," I said, like that wasn't exactly what I'd been hoping.

"Love you. See you soon."

chapter three

I said I loved her, too, and slowly hung up the phone, then refilled my coffee mug and carried it to the front of the shop and stood looking through the door glass at the street. Things were quiet at this hour on Front Street, but then, things were almost always quiet on Front Street. We were half a block off the main square, away from the bustle of the courthouse and the bank and the café, and unless you specifically wanted flowers, there wasn't much reason to come by here. I can't say it didn't appeal to me on some level, this sense of being off the beaten path, several steps removed from the mainstream. I caught myself and smiled. Ash was right; I was a sucker for a good metaphor.

The front door rattled, and I looked out to see Mrs. Florence Binder standing there with a panicky look on her face. I guess the sun was reflecting off the glass because she didn't see me; she frowned at the CLOSED sign, then looked worriedly at her watch. It was still five minutes till opening time, but I stepped forward anyway and flipped the dead bolt. With business the way it was lately, more folks every day buying their flowers at Wal-Mart or off the Internet, we couldn't afford to miss a customer.

"Oh, Lucy!" Mrs. Binder exclaimed, rushing past me into the shop. "Thank goodness you're here. I came just as soon as I heard!" She looked a little crazy, her blue-rinsed hair neatly curled and styled on one side and mashed flat and slept-on-looking on the other. Her blouse was buttoned wrong, and she sported pink terrycloth bedroom scuffs with plaid Bermuda shorts, a look that would get you ridiculed even in Mooney.

"Alene Worley called me, after Susie Castle called her. I told Alene it couldn't be true, but I live the closest, so she told me to rush right on over here and find out for sure. Straight from the horse's mouth."

"I'm afraid it's a fact, Mrs. Binder." I couldn't for the life of me think why Mrs. Florence Binder was so wrought up about Ash coming back to town. Maybe she'd lost a bundle over at Burton's café.

"But—how? I don't for the life of me understand how a thing like this could happen."

"I'm not sure myself," I said. I wondered if it would save time if I just made up a flyer and had it Xeroxed over at the Copy Shoppe. I could include a small photo, like a wanted poster, along with the pertinent data: Last night, a truck, the rain.

"But it's the same order we've had for the past fifteen years—why in heaven's name would we change it now?"

"Excuse me?"

"We want *lilies.* Not carnations. Not roses or daisies or daffodils. Lilies! It's Easter, for goodness' sake!"

I started to laugh.

"Well, I'm glad you think this is funny, Lucy Hatch!"

"I'm sorry, Mrs. Binder, but I don't know what in the world you're talking about."

"I'm talking about this, this *plot,* or whatever you want to call it, to change our order for Easter lilies to carnations! Why, if that isn't the most outrageous thing I've ever heard! The Methodist Flower Guild has a reputation to uphold!"

"Yes, ma'am. I know you do."

"This is all that new woman's fault—that Kay Dotson, from Avinger. Ever since she and her husband moved here last June, she's been trying to take over the Guild. But our parishioners expect a certain, well, elegant and *traditional* style of floral decor. I don't think I have to tell you, there is nothing elegant about carnations. Carnations are cheap and tacky and the Methodist Flower Guild will not have them!"

"Yes, ma'am. I couldn't agree more."

I beckoned Mrs. Binder to follow me. At the rear of the shop, I threw open the cooler door, then stepped back and invited her to look inside. Four dozen Easter lilies sat in their foil-covered pots, the plastic webbing still in place to keep the blooms from opening and drooping too early.

"Are those ours?" She sounded skeptical, like a bunch of Baptists might rush in and seize them at any moment.

"Two dozen," I said. "The rest are for the shop and the Easter party at Golden Years."

"No carnations?"

"No, ma'am."

"Were there ever any carnations?"

I shook my head.

"Kay Dotson didn't call here?"

"Not to my knowledge."

"The whole thing was a rumor, then."

I smiled. "Imagine that."

"I'm sorry, dear." Mrs. Binder took off her glasses, wiped them nervously on the hem of her blouse, put them back on again. "Alene said that Susie said that somebody else called her and *swore* Kay Dotson had changed the order." She gave a lady-like snort. "Like we'd ever give somebody from Avinger the authority to do a thing like that."

"It sounds like the kind of thing somebody from Avinger *would* do."

"I've lived in this town my entire life," she said as I walked her to the door. "You'd think by now I'd know better than to believe every old thing I hear."

"It's a pretty common affliction around here."

"We need those lilies over to the sanctuary by five," she reminded me, stepping out onto the sidewalk. "Good Friday service starts at seven, but Major Weatherby wants to get in there early to rehearse the choir."

"They'll be there."

I looked up the block as a white Chevy pickup turned the corner. It was possible there was more than one truck like this one in Cade County, Texas, but I doubted it. It looked sparkling, fresh-washed, and I could hear Hank Williams from two hundred feet away.

"Sakes alive, will you look at that," Mrs. Binder said as the truck pulled up to the curb in front of the shop. Behind the tinted windshield, the driver raised a hand in greeting. Mrs. Binder raised hers hesitantly back. "Now who can that be?"

"Mrs. Binder?" I said. "Pardon me for saying so, but your blouse is on crooked."

"Oh! Oh, goodness me." She glanced down. "I ran right out the door the minute Alene called. I must look a fright!" With that, she turned and scuttled off in the opposite direction, her pink scuffs slapping against the sidewalk.

I walked over to the truck as the driver's-side window went buzzing down and Hank Williams stopped in mid-yodel.

"You can't park there," I said. "It's a fire lane."

"I'll keep the motor running." Ash's hair was damp and combed straight back off his forehead, though there was still several days' stubble on his cheeks. He was wearing a pair of expensive-looking mirrored sunglasses.

"You're out early," I said. "The package store doesn't open till ten. But then, with all the trips you made there over the years, I'm sure you remember."

He lifted the sunglasses and looked at me, then lowered them again across the bridge of his nose. "I see you haven't lost your edge."

"I've had lots of time to work on it. It's nice and sharp by now."

"I called here earlier."

I decided not to say that I'd tried to call him back. "Were we out of your favorite soap? I'd have stocked up, but I wasn't expecting you."

"What the hell happened at the house?"

"What do you mean?"

"I mean, where is everything? My books are gone, and all my old LPs. Even the dishes and the towels are different. About the only thing I recognized was the blanket on the bed."

"The renters took it."

"What?"

"Or hauled it to the dump, pawned it, something."

"You mean those people Shirley Tinsley at the real estate office picked out, that she said would be the perfect tenants? Speakes or some such? They cleaned us out?"

"They got mad when Shirley told them I wanted to move back. Maybe we messed up their bootlegging enterprise or something. I guess this was their way of paying us back for kicking them out. I was just glad they left the furniture."

"Well, son of a— Did you call the sheriff?"

"Of course I did. But people like that don't leave forwarding addresses, Ash. They just kind of melt into the woods, like leaf rot."

"Jesus! I'd had those books, some of 'em, since high school! What the hell would a bunch of Speakeses want with the likes of Faulkner and Hemingway? I doubt they can read anything more complicated than a Lotto ticket. And my records—do you know what those records were worth?"

"Fine. Hire a PI and a lawyer. Spend hundreds of hours and thousands of dollars looking for people who can't be found so you can sue them for money they haven't got. Be my guest. I haven't got the time or the energy."

"I'm not talking about the money! I'm talking about the, the sentimental value. My whole life was in that house! What gives a bunch of goddamned rednecks the right to haul it all off in a cardboard box?"

This from a man who was currently living out of the back of a pickup. "I'm glad to see you've got your priorities straight," I said.

"What are you talking about?"

"Nothing. Never mind." I hated those sunglasses. All I could see when I looked at them was myself, all my spiked and gleaming edges.

"This wouldn't have happened if you'd let me sell the place, like I wanted."

"If I'd let you sell it, I wouldn't have had a place to come back to."

"Well, maybe that wouldn't have been such a bad thing."

Suddenly my eyes filled, and I turned my head. How, I wondered, had what we'd had turned into this—a competition to see who was sharper, who had the upper hand?

"Ash, I can't . . . This isn't . . ."

"What? It isn't what?"

"I don't know! I can't think. Could you please take off those glasses?"

He yanked them off with a flourish and set them on top of his head.

"Thanks," I said. "You reminded me too much of a cop or something."

That made him smile. "I. Remind you of a cop."

"I told you I couldn't think."

"Can I come back later? Buy you lunch?"

"I don't think that's a good idea."

"You got another date or something?"

"It would serve you right if I said yes."

"Yeah," he said, nodding solemnly, "it would."

"Just give me a little time, okay? I'm still trying to get used to the idea that you're here."

He held up his hands and opened the palms wide. "Ladies and gentlemen, Ash Farrell, live and in person. Spreading joy wherever he goes."

I smiled, thinking of what Dove had said earlier: *If that ain't Ash, through and through.*

"I stopped by Dove's this morning," I said. "I told her some fool showed up in my yard talking about borrowing her crawfish pot."

"I'll go see her. Maybe at least one person in this sorry town'll be happy I'm home."

"I almost forgot—Denny called," I said. "Do you know anything about a fellow named Will Culpepper?"

"I've seen him around. Shifty-eyed tomcat. What about him?"

"He's sleeping with your daughter, that's what."

Ash's face went stupid for a second, then quickly resumed its former expression. "She told you this?"

"She's madly in love with him, were her exact words."

Ash scoffed. "I give it a week. Two, tops."

"And then what?"

"And then I hunt him down and wring his goddamned neck." His hands flexed on the steering wheel. There was something scary in his eyes, something flinty and cold. It reminded me of the old Ash, the one I'd last seen one August night in Nashville, storming down the driveway behind my speeding pickup, his face contorted by whiskey and rage. It gave me a chill, but in a way I was grateful for the reminder. I hadn't spent eight months honing my hard edges for nothing.

He sighed, turned loose of the wheel, sat back, and raked a hand through his hair.

"Forget it," he said. "Forget I said that. She's twenty-one. Free to screw up her own life like the rest of us."

"Denny's got a pretty good head on her shoulders," I said. "Maybe she'll do better than we did."

From the direction of the courthouse I saw Peggy headed in our direction, carrying a box of what I knew to be lemon-filled doughnuts. It looked like she'd managed to pick up a few hangers-on along the way.

"Better get your game face on," I said. "Here comes your fan club."

Ash tilted the side mirror and looked into it. "Who's that? The one up front, in the pink?"

"You mean Peggy?"

"Peggy Thaney? Your boss? No way! Peggy's big as a house."

"Like I tried to tell you," I said. "Not everything's the same as you remember it."

"Reckon I can make a run for it?"

I turned and waved to Peggy, who broke into a trot. "I wouldn't, if I were you. Seems to me you need all the fans you can get."

As I stepped away from the curb toward the shop door, I saw Ash glance at himself in the rearview mirror, his eyes for just a second as blank as a deer's in headlights. Then he notched his mirrored sunglasses back in place, and by the time Peggy and her crew caught up with him, he had on his old, well-worn skin again: live and in person, spreading joy wherever he went.

"YOU MEAN HE was here in the shop and I missed it?" Audrey cried when she came in at eleven. "Oh, man, I am so bummed!" We were loading up the van to deliver the party goods to the old folks' home.

"He wasn't *in* the shop," I corrected her. "He was out front, at the curb. Could you take these, please?"

I handed her a bunch of balloons and wrestled open the van door. After all these years, we were still driving the same old Econoline as when I first came to work for Peggy. It had been elderly and unreliable then, and the intervening years had not done a thing to improve its condition. The only consolation was that it was impossible to go too fast in the thing, since it would buck and shimmy wildly anytime you tried to push it over fifty. Audrey had had four speeding tickets in her Dodge Charger since getting her license the year before, so I counted this as a blessing.

Audrey slouched against the side of the van and pouted. Or maybe it was just an optical illusion, caused by the silver stud sticking through her bottom lip. The hem of her T-shirt rode up to expose a little roll of flesh above the waistband of her jeans. YOU WISH, the shirt said in baby-blue script across the chest. Audrey was seventeen and had style to burn, if style is what you call youth and beauty and the complete disdain it took to try to disguise it with dyed-black hair and raccoon eyeliner and jewelry inserted through various unorthodox pieces of skin. She had a lanky, sleepy-eyed boyfriend named Joe who worked for the cable company, and they smelled like pot and sex and patchouli oil, separately and together and constantly.

"I can't believe it," she said. "I live my whole entire life in the most boring town on the face of the earth, and then the one time something exciting *does* happen, I'm in fucking Spanish class and I miss it."

"Watch your language," I said, without any real reproach or conviction. I knew that under the skin, where it counted, Audrey was, like me, a hometown girl. In spite of her edgy appearance and mouthy attitude, she couldn't hide her basic sweet and earnest nature. In an hour or so, at Golden Years, she'd be passing out the cake and corsages, getting the ladies and gents all lined up with their wheelchairs and walkers, and it wouldn't faze her a bit when Mrs. Mundy got so excited she dropped her punch, or Mrs. Virgil kept thinking Audrey was her long-lost sister. I could send Audrey to funerals or the hospital, and in two minutes flat she'd be holding hands and passing out Kleenex and helping visitors find the bathroom. It wasn't part of her job description, but it was worth its weight in gold. Folks always appreciate a hometown girl when they see one.

"There," I said, shuffling the lilies around in the back of the van, making sure they wouldn't tip over in transit. "Is that everything?"

"I don't get it. How can you be so cool? If my ex showed up in town for the first time in a hundred years, I'd be a basket case."

"In the first place, he's not my ex. And it hasn't been a hundred years—not quite."

"Lucy! This is Ash Farrell we're talking about!"

"So?"

"So he's the biggest deal to ever come out of this shitty town."

"Now there's a glowing compliment."

"My mom used to hear him sing at the Round-Up. She said he was the hottest thing on two legs around here."

I shook my head. People always think it would be so great to hook up with somebody they see on a CD cover or on TV. I guess they believe those guys really are the way they seem in front of the camera, that their lives are just one long music video. I used to think that, too.

"So how long's he sticking around for, anyway? You think I'll get a chance to meet him?"

"I don't know, Audrey. Maybe you'll luck out and he'll invite you to his crawfish boil."

"Huh?"

"Never mind. Have you got the keys?" She held them up and dangled them. "I'll meet you there, okay? I've got to run by Dove's and pick up the kids. Miss Jeanrette will help you unload if you get there before me."

"In this thing?" Audrey kicked the van's right rear tire affectionately. "You could drive to Houston and back and still beat me."

I WASN'T SURPRISED to find Ash's new truck parked in Dove's driveway. I pulled in behind him and sat looking across the garden at the house. The front door was open, and the sound of the B-52's poured through the screen, down the sidewalk, and into the street. As I unlatched the gate, I could hear Jude and Lily yelling at the top of their lungs:

Love shack bay-bee
Love shack baby!

I opened the screen door and let myself into the front hall, where I stood for a minute at the living room threshold. The couch and two wing chairs had been pushed back, and Ash was lying in the middle of the rug with a can of Mountain Dew propped on his stomach, the two kids leaping and pogoing in a ring around him, waving their arms and hollering over the blare of the music. They threw up their arms and shimmied, then spun in circles and collapsed, scrambled up and started dancing again. *Funky little shack! Funky little shack!* they screamed. It looked like some kind of bizarre cult ritual, a ceremony to appease a mad and irrational god. We'd been dancing to "Love Shack" since before he could walk, Jude and me, since I'd had to stand him on his chubby baby feet and swing his little hands. I tried not to let memory rankle me, but I admit I wasn't having much luck.

"Mama!" Jude shouted, spying me at last, and he and Lily ran to me, their faces lit from inside, a sight that never failed to smooth over any stray potholes in my soul. I knelt and pulled them to me, relishing the feel of their small, solid bodies against mine. Their hearts beat wildly; Jude smelled like puppy sweat and Lily like cookie dough.

"We're doing the Love Shack, Mama!" Jude said. "Lily and Daddy and me!"

Ash sat up and switched off the stereo. He smiled at me and hoisted his soda can.

"Well, you guys had better get a move on if you want to come to Golden Years with me. The Easter party, remember?"

"We had an Easter party already, Aunt Lucy," Lily said. "At school."

I ran my hand over the silky black bowl of her hair. There was something rare and luminous about Lily, a gleam she gave off that was partly her own and partly because of how long we'd waited for her. I never could look at her without thinking about how Geneva and Bailey must have felt walking into the orphanage in Changzhou and seeing their daughter for the first time, knowing that of all the babies in that room, that country, the world, this was the one who was meant for them—like she'd just been waiting for the Hatches to show up and take her home to Texas, where she'd always belonged.

"Was it a good party?" I asked.

Lily bit her lip. "The cupcakes were funny."

"Yummy?" I said hopefully, feeling my stomach sink.

"They were gross. They were *pink*."

"*I* thought they were yummy," Jude said. "Yummy, yummy, yummy!" He ran over and took a swig of his daddy's soda.

"Well, I'm pretty sure the party at Golden Years will be better," I said. "We'll have singing, and ice cream and cake. And Audrey will be there. You're crazy about Audrey."

Lily eyed me dubiously, like I was some sleazy door-to-door salesman trying to bilk her out of her last dollar. "What kind of cake?"

"I don't know for sure, but I'm betting probably chocolate." She cocked her head thoughtfully, like a little bird. "I could sure use you, Lily Belle. I need you to help me pass out the flowers."

Dove came up the hall, wiping her hands on a dish towel. "I thought I heard somebody."

"It's a miracle you can hear anything," I said. "Your neighbors are probably getting ready to turn you in for a public nuisance."

"Naw, we'll just invite 'em to the party."

Ash stood up and crushed his empty can in his hand. "You wanna go check those mudbugs of yours?" Dove said. "It's prob'ly time to switch the water."

"Sure." Squeezing past us into the hall, he grabbed my hand and did a little jitterbug step. Then he turned me loose and walked off toward the kitchen.

"The crawfish are here?" My hand felt hot where he'd gripped it.

Dove shrugged. "Seemed easier to fix 'em at my place, seeing's how I've got the cooker and all. Anyhow, I thought you might not feel like goin' home this evenin' to a houseful a folks whoopin' it up, after the kind a day you had."

I felt a rush of gratefulness so strong it made me dizzy. I looked at my watch; there was still half a workday and a party for a bunch of senior citizens to fit in. "Come on, kids, we've got to head out," I said.

They ran ahead of me into the garden. Dove and I followed slowly to the door.

"Did they eat lunch?"

"Grilled cheese. Jude had two."

"Who all's coming to this wingding?" I asked.

"Just us. Your brothers and their wives and kids. I reckon I'll call your mama, even if she won't show, it bein' Good Friday. And I thought I'd ask Rowena. She's practically kin."

"Have you talked to Geneva?" I was surprised I hadn't heard from my sister-in-law. She, of all people, I would've expected to drop everything when she heard Ash was in town.

"She's been doin' that continuin' education course all week out at County," Dove reminded me. "I called her up and left a message, though. I figger we should be hearin' from her any second."

"What about Bailey?"

"Your brother had a few choice words to say about Ash and his crawfish. But this bein' a holy day, I don't think I should repeat 'em."

"He'll be here, though, right?"

"Oh, I don't think either one of the boy's'd miss it."

"Maybe we ought to go ahead and call the sheriff now. Tell them to have somebody on call, just in case."

She smiled and squeezed my arm. "You go on and take care of your party," she said. "Let me worry about tonight."

I KNOW OLD folks' homes have a bad rap—dumping grounds for human flotsam, hotbeds of ugliness and abuse—but, not to paint too starry a picture here, I have to say Golden Years was different. It's true it wasn't the most glamorous place; the corridors were papered with gaudy murals and smelled of boiled greens and Lysol. But the staff was kind and cheerful, and you could feel their good-heartedness when you walked in the door, doing its best to lift up the old souls inside and succeeding as often as not. My sister-in-law Geneva had worked there for five years before she went back to her job at the ob-gyn clinic, and she hardly ever found it depressing. Sad, sometimes, and hard; folks were old, after all, got sick and died. But you could do worse than to end up at Golden Years, where beautiful girls with elaborate, towering hairdos and names like Shontalle and LaToya would dole out your pills, wheel you in to dinner, listen to you reminisce about the day you met your first love, bring you a blanket for your feet. I used to think they were just going through the motions, those girls, but then it dawned on me that there was no incentive, no bonus for good behavior beyond a minimum-wage paycheck. They were just nice girls, doing what they knew was right.

The cake turned out to be white with yellow frosting and clusters of gooey sugar roses clumped in the corners, but I put Lily and Jude to work right away so they wouldn't notice, carrying around the corsages to the residents who sat around the edges of the rec room in their best dress-up attire. Many of them were in wheelchairs, but a couple were still proudly, if conditionally, mobile; one, Miss Grace Wick, wore a bicycle helmet to roam the halls, thanks to a tendency to fall without warning and bump her head.

Jude threw himself into the task with his usual verve, but Lily was more reserved, doling out her flowers guardedly, like communion wafers. In spite of the old van's balkiness, Audrey had arrived well ahead of me; the room was fragrant with the scent of lilies, and the clusters of balloons floating near the ceiling did their best to add a festive air.

The administrator of Golden Years, Penny Jeanrette, came zipping in in her Pepto-Bismol-pink skirt and peplum jacket, clapping her hands, and she and I and some of the aides got busy pinning corsages onto the ladies' blouses and boutonnieres on the shirt collars of the handful of men. Mr. Henry Tabor, a retired preacher, stood up and recited a long, rambling prayer. Then we all sang a couple of hymns, "Blessed Redeemer" and "Were You There When They Crucified My Lord." It always gave me a chill to hear the airy old voices raised in song, to try to picture myself or someone I loved in one of those chairs, wearing a corsage and stumbling over the words to the old hymns. I came to Golden Years because it was my job, but partly, too, I believed I was performing a kind of voodoo, making an offering against what might someday come to be.

The aides and I cut the cake and started to hand the pieces around. Jude was over by the aquarium, making faces at the goldfish, but in a quick scan of the room, I couldn't spot Lily.

"Jude, where's Lily?" He ignored me, his cheeks puffing in and out. I grabbed his arm. "Listen to me. It's important. Where is your cousin?"

"Ow!" he cried. "I don't know! You're *hurting* me!"

"Have you seen Lily?" I asked Audrey. She was helping a frail little gentleman make a bib of his napkin, and shook her head. I asked a couple of aides, but none of them knew anything, either.

I reminded myself to breathe and not panic. It had only been a couple of minutes, I was sure, since she'd been here; she couldn't have gotten far. She was only six years old; it wasn't like she could lift someone's keys and hijack a car. And Golden Years was off the beaten path, on a wooded tract well above the highway. Those were the pluses. The minuses were she was only six years old, and Golden Years was off the beaten path, on a wooded tract above the highway.

I did a wild sprint through the building, cursing under my breath, winding up finally outside in the courtyard, where I found her standing small and defiant-looking at the base of a crape myrtle tree.

"Lily!" I resisted the urge to run and scoop her up, to feel her heart beating against my chest like wings. It's hard to explain what a private little person she was, what formidable limits she possessed. My son was the owner of big, messy emotions that he gave vent to freely, like an opera singer. Lily was less excitable; she held things close to the vest. I didn't know if it was her history that made her this way—she was not quite two when Bailey and Geneva adopted her—or if it was just her nature. But I'd learned that the usual reactions, fury and hysterics, didn't work with her. Jude and I would have shouted awhile and then fallen into each other's arms and sobbed like a couple of divas, but I knew I was better off keeping my cool with Lily.

"What are you doing out here, baby?" I asked as my heartbeat gradually returned to normal. "You're missing the party."

"There's a cat," she said, and pointed. I looked up. Sure enough, a ragged-eared red and white tom blinked at us from a limb about ten feet up.

"That's Rusty." He was one of five or six cats who had the run of the grounds and building; it wasn't unusual to see them skulking down the hallways or curled up in a linen closet. "He lives here."

"Why? Does somebody make him?"

"Well, no. I guess he likes it."

She shivered, even though it was a mild and sunny April day. "Can we go home now? I'm scared."

"Of what?"

"The people in the chairs."

I tried to think what to say. I hated lying to kids, mine or anyone else's. Lily's fear was deep and instinctive, and it seemed to me that it needed to be honored.

"They won't hurt you, Lily. They're just old, that's all."

"I don't *like* it. Their hands are cold and they want to put me in the stove and eat me. Just like the witch in the story!"

"Oh, Lily. Nobody's going to eat you! That's just a fairy tale."

"You said the cake was *chocolate*. You said it, but it's not!"

"I'm sorry. I was wrong. Let's find Jude and go back to Aunt Dove's, okay? I bet she's got some chocolate for you, a Hershey bar or some brownies."

I stepped forward and held out my arms, and to my surprise she let me pick her up, even though she was almost too big for that. She lay her satiny head on my shoulder.

"I'm tired," she said. "I've had a long day."

And for a minute I forgot about Ash, the way he was always pulling at me, even from afar, and the old folks inside, like soldiers marching into battle, raising their voices against their fear. I forgot about everything but Lily's hot breath in my ear, her weight in my arms, her sugar-cookie smell. It seemed to me that life at its best was a series of lucky accidents, a random spin of the wheel. Here were Lily and me, two strangers from opposite sides of the world thrown together by fate or happenstance, hanging on to the wheel, and to each other, for dear life.

chapter four

We locked up the shop at five on the nose, and Peggy followed me in her Pontiac over to Aunt Dove's. The street and driveway were crowded; I counted my brothers' and sister-in-laws' trucks in addition to Ash's, Dove's friend Rowena's Chrysler LeBaron, and a couple of vehicles I didn't recognize. There was no law-enforcement cruiser or TV news van, at least not yet. The night was young.

Because Dove's showpiece was her front-yard garden, it was easy to forget sometimes that the rear of the house was a jewel of its own kind. The backyard was narrow but deep, shaded by elms and live oaks and bordered with trumpet creeper and honeysuckle and waxleaf ligustrum. It was always five degrees cooler there than anywhere else in town and smelled like heaven, especially now, in early spring, when all the bulbs and shrubs were in bloom.

But today the usual feeling of peaceful sanctuary had vanished, annihilated by the sheer mass and volume of Hatches. In spite of the fact that most of us lived within ten miles of one another, we were hardly ever all in the same place at the same time, and when we did have occasion to come together, I tended to be shocked by how many of us there were and how much noise we were capable of generating.

It always took me a beat or two to recognize my nieces and nephews, my older brother Kit's kids. Ranging in age from twelve to sixteen, they changed height and weight and hairstyle and color as easily, it seemed, as they changed their clothes. The twins, the babies, were as tall as their mama, but whereas Connie was plump and soft as bread dough, her daughters had the lanky, affected look of fashion models. They stood huddled with their brothers in a corner of the yard, fooling with a portable stereo; every now and then a guitar lick or a thudding bass beat blared out, then vanished in a fuzz of static. My brothers were near the back fence pitching horseshoes, and Connie, Dove, and Rowena sat in lawn chairs with their chins tipped back to catch the sun. Over on the patio, Ash watched over the propane cooker with the help of his assistant and number one fan, Geneva, who'd evidently managed to swing by home on her way from her continuing-ed course at the hospital and get done up for Ash's welcome-home party in Jordache jeans, a body-hugging pink T-shirt, and three-inch open-toed heels.

Dove and Connie hoisted plastic tumblers and waved at Peggy and me.

"Y'all look like you should be on a beach somewhere," I said.

"Oh, right," Connie said. "All that's missing are the water, the sand, the ocean breeze . . ."

"Drag up a chair and join us, you two," Dove said. "We're drinkin' Mind Erasers."

"Good Lord—what's that?" I asked, pulling over a couple of chairs. I waved to Geneva on the patio, but she was laughing at something Ash was saying and didn't see me.

"Vodka, Kahlua, and Sprite," Connie said. "Guaranteed to cure what ails you."

"Or at least make you forget about it for the duration," Rowena added.

"I think I better hang on to my mind," I said. "It might come in handy later."

"I'll have one," Peggy piped up. "What?" she said as I gave her a look. "You're not my mama or my boss, either one."

"Maybe not. But you better not be calling in at nine tomorrow, telling me you've got the flu."

"Tomorrow's Saturday," she reminded me. "I'm off the clock. For that matter, so're you."

"Come on, Lucy," Connie said. "One little drink. It's the weekend, and anyway it's a party."

I shook my head, and she got up to make Peggy's drink. With one ear I listened to the four of them chatter as I watched Ash and Geneva on the patio, the easy way he moved from the cooler to the cooker and back, his movements smooth and economical, with a rhythm remembered from his carpentry days. Geneva bobbed and weaved around him like a moth around a flame. Just like that, it seemed, after years in exile, he'd reclaimed his notch on the Hatch family tree.

"Earth to Lucy."

I looked up as Connie handed me a can of Sprite. "Here you go. A virgin Mind Eraser."

"For your virgin mind," Peggy said. Everybody laughed but me. "Oh, come on," she said. "Where's your sense of humor?"

"Y'all need to go easy on Lucy," Connie said, reclaiming her chair. "This has got to be the weirdest scene imaginable, don't you think? Having to hang out and act normal with somebody you used to be married to? And with your family around! So you can't yell at him or cry or freak out or any of the things you're secretly dying to do."

"Thanks, but it's not that bad," I said. "Anyway, I shouldn't have to remind y'all, but we're still married."

Dove reached over to pat my leg. The five of us had unconsciously arranged our chairs in a semicircle facing the patio, claiming front-row seats for the floor show.

"Ash looks good, don't you think?" Connie said.

"He looks like the 'before' guy on the commercial for—what's that stuff called? That men's hair color," Rowena said.

"Those ads have got it backward, if you ask me. The guys always look sexier with the gray in their hair than they do without it."

"Sexier than we do, that's for sure."

"The crow's-feet look better on them, too."

"Yeah. How come we get wrinkles and they get character?"

"Not to mention cellulite."

We all gazed down self-consciously. I tugged the hem of my skirt over my knees.

"Still. I like the—whatever it is—the grizzled look," Connie said, nodding in Ash's direction.

"I think it's called the broke-out-of-rehab-and-took-off-without-my-shaving-kit look," I said. Everybody got quiet and looked at me. "Denny called this morning and said the hospital told her he checked out. No, wait, that's not right—that makes it sound like he was released, and he wasn't. He left. Halfway through the program."

"Well, honey, maybe he'd had all the rehab he needed," Connie said. "You know there are just some people who don't take to that stuff. They do better on their own. With, you know, Jesus or willpower or whatever."

"Yeah, and there are plenty of people who just keep right on drinking."

"*Is* he drinking?" Peggy asked. "You know this for a fact?"

"All he's said is that it's under control. Meanwhile, here he is, back in town, feeding y'all crawfish, making you ooh and aah over how good he looks and feeling all sorry for him because I walked out on him." I jiggled my soda can. "And look at Geneva. How many Mind Erasers has *she* had?"

Connie reached over and took my hand. "You know what you need?"

"Yeah. A Mind Eraser of the permanent kind."

"No, you need to come by the house and let me do you over." I laughed. "I mean it, Lucy. A little color would do you a world of good right now." Connie was the local Mary Kay representative, known far and wide for her faith in the restorative powers of contour cream and eyeliner.

The back door burst open and Jude and Lily came running out, yelling like wild Indians. Both of them had on makeshift Porter Wagoner T-shirts, several sizes too large; Jude's hung past the knees of his cargo shorts, and Lily had belted hers with one of Dove's old scarves and was wearing tights underneath, like a go-go dancer. To complete their ensembles, Jude wore a rubber dinosaur mask and Lily had strapped on a pair of gauzy angel wings, remnants of last year's Halloween costumes.

"Look at us, Aunt Lucy! We're all dressed up for the party!"

"You look great, both of you." I pulled Jude into my arms. He wedged himself between my knees and grinned up at me from beneath the snarling snout of a *T. rex.* At moments like these I felt no accountability for Jude's character or his future, only an endless ocean of love, blue and deep and skimmed with little whitecaps of good fortune.

"You look beautiful, Mama!" he said, patting my face.

"That's very gallant of you, baby. See there?" I said to Connie. "Somebody likes me just the way I am."

"Gallant, what's that?" Jude wanted to know.

"It's a five-dollar word for 'nice.'"

"So, can I have five dollars?" he asked, grinning again when I laughed, then squirmed out of my arms and went racing after Lily, who'd spied her daddy and her uncle Kit playing horseshoes. I watched her wings bobble in the sun as they ran, the flash of Jude's brown legs like knife blades where only days before, it seemed, they'd been soft and white and boneless. You said it to yourself over and over again: *Don't blink; they'll be grown before you know it.* But still, you did it. You blinked and you missed things and would never get them back.

"How long till we eat, do you think?" Connie said.

"Here comes the cook. You can ask him yourself."

Ash sauntered up, looking exactly like somebody who knows he's the center of attention and isn't one bit worried that he might not come out smelling like a rose.

"Ladies," he said. "What's going on? Y'all about set for a feast?"

"We're erasing our minds," Connie said, lifting her glass. "I'm about halfway there, myself."

"All but Lucy," Peggy put in. "Lucy wants to keep her mind, for some reason."

"Maybe she hasn't got anything she wants to erase," Ash said.

"Ha! Don't get me started," I said.

A cloud passed over Ash's face, one that only somebody who knew him like I did would recognize. His eyes stayed crinkled, the corners of his mouth stayed turned up, but his eyes went black and flat, like the leading edge of a storm. *Stop,* I told myself. Did I really want to do this here, now, in front of my whole family? Didn't I owe him, if not the benefit of the doubt, then at least the dignity of not airing our dirty linen in public?

"How long till supper?" Peggy asked, filling the silence. "I'm starved."

"Maybe half an hour or so," Ash said. "We're just about to start the cool-down." The trick with crawfish was to boil them for just a few minutes, then add ice to the pot, bringing the water temperature down slowly to let the bugs soak up the seasonings. You had to taste them every so often, and depending upon who was making the final call, the process could take fifteen minutes or an hour. But there were vegetables to be cooked, too, and dip to be made. Half an hour, I'd bet, was a conservative estimate.

I stood and smoothed the front of my skirt. "I think I'll run inside and wash up."

I let myself in through the back door into the kitchen. The icebox was open and Geneva stood leaning in, rifling through the crisper, her rear end in the air.

"Where exactly did you say those lemons were?" she said, her voice muffled. " 'Cause I'm finding everything but— Oh. Hey." She saw it was me and smiled. "I thought you were somebody else."

"I wish that was true, for both our sakes."

She closed the icebox and gave me a hug, and I let myself be hugged, losing myself in the bulk and fragrance of her. In Nashville, what I'd missed even more than the smell of East Texas red dirt and pine trees was my sister-in-law's unique and heady blend of Aqua Net hair spray, Cornsilk face powder, and Coty Wild Musk perfume.

"You poor thing," she said, letting me go. "You must've had a hell of a day."

"Well, it's a good thing you're here, to remind us of the power of mascara and a good push-up bra."

She laughed and gave her neckline—if you could call it that, seeing as it was far south of her actual neck—a tug. "I just wanted to look nice for Ash's homecoming."

"And I know he really, really appreciates it."

"So what's the story? Dove said you came out and found him sleeping in his truck this morning." I nodded. "What happened to rehab? I thought he was supposed to do thirty days."

"He left—went AWOL. But he claims he's got everything under control."

"And you believe him? Or you don't."

"I don't know what to believe. I don't know what his idea of 'under control' is. Beer instead of hard liquor, maybe. That's one version I've heard. Or beer before five, the hard stuff after. That's another one."

"I guess he didn't exactly blow into town and sweep you off your feet," she said. She'd found the lemons and the cutting board, and took a knife out of the dish drainer.

"He did invite me to lunch," I said. "But I wouldn't go." Geneva looked at me over her shoulder, raising her eyebrows. "I had work to do. Anyway, I just—I couldn't, Gen. I'm not ready. The whole thing feels too weird to me. He acts so, so offhand about it all, like it's the most regular thing in the world to just drop back into our life after falling off the face of the earth for half a year. But all he seems to care about are crawfish. That and those Speakeses running off with his record collection—he cared plenty about that."

"Maybe he's looking for a way in," Geneva said, the knife blurring as she halved and quartered lemons. "I mean, maybe he's just blowing smoke until he figures out how to say what he needs to say. Did you ever think of that?"

The screen door flew open and Lily and Jude charged in, begging for Popsicles. "No Popsicles, it's almost time for supper," Geneva said. She dumped the cut lemons into a bowl and handed it to Jude. "Here, take this out to your daddy. Tell him I'm in the kitchen trying to keep his ass out of the doghouse."

"Geneva!" I laughed as the kids ran out again. "You know better than to say a thing like that. Those two soak up everything and then spit it right back out again."

"Good. The truth shall set us free. Now, where did I put my drink?" She located her plastic tumbler, swirled it a time or two, then drank down the contents in one long gulp. "Whew! Want one?" she said, reaching for the vodka bottle.

"You know, I think maybe I do," I said. "Mix me up one, okay? I'll be right back."

In Dove's guest bathroom I splashed some water on my face and washed my hands with one of the little seashell-shaped soaps in the dish. No wonder Connie thought I needed help; by the light of the naked bulb over the mirror, I looked like the "before" photo in a magazine makeover story. I was at that age, I suddenly realized, when a woman has two choices: to rally and make a stand, or to give up caring. There was nobody on earth I admired more than my aunt, who cut her own hair with the sewing scissors and had never worn a thing on her face but Noxzema. I wanted to be as carefree about my appearance as she was, but I didn't think I could do it. A little chip had been permanently embedded in my head that kept playing Ash's voice murmuring, "Juicy Lucy," over and over. I didn't think I could get rid of it without major surgery—although maybe a Mind Eraser or two would help.

Walking back through the house, I found the kitchen empty, and Geneva and Ash on the patio tending the pot full of cooling crawfish. Geneva had a tumbler in each hand, and Ash was standing there, easy as you please, his foot propped on the ice chest, drinking a Bud tallboy. I could feel my blood pressure rising as I took a glass from Geneva. I opened my mouth, then thought better of it and decided I'd go pitch a few horseshoes.

The game had broken up, though, by the time I got there, and Bailey and Kit were lounging on the grass in the shade with their own cans of beer. I smiled at the sight of my two good-looking brothers in their jeans and steel-toed work boots and snap-front denim shirts with the HATCH BROTHERS CONTRACTING logo stitched in red on the breast pockets. Kit, big and sandy-haired, looked like he usually did, rumpled and worse for the day's wear, whereas Bailey might have just rolled out the front door fresh as a daisy, his Wranglers creased, his shirt collar crisp.

"Can I ask y'all something?" I said, tucking my skirt under me to sit beside them on the grass. "Who are all these folks? It seems like just the other day we were the only Hatches in town."

"Good question," Kit said. "Those kids over there, for instance. See the tall one, with the ring in his ear? And those two, with the little bitty T-shirts and their bellies showing, like hoochie-koochie girls? Who are they?"

Just then Lily dashed up and clambered into Bailey's lap, taking his face in her hands and pressing her palms together on either side of his mouth, their private cue for him to pucker up and give her a kiss. "My daddy!" she exclaimed, pulling back to give us all a smug look before running off again.

"Her slave, she means," I said. "Mr. Step-and-Fetch-It." Bailey just smiled and tilted his beer to his lips, his expression goofily happy, like a teenage lover's. He'd waited thirty-eight years to become a daddy, and wasn't about to apologize to anybody.

"Just wait," Kit said. "One minute they're hanging all over you, kissing you on the mouth, and the next thing you know . . ." He nodded toward where his brood was congregated around the boom box, the boys shoving each other, the girls acting bored and listless. Still, in spite of the hair gel and the ugly, clunky shoes, there was a homegrown sweetness to them that no amount of costuming or posing would ever cover up.

"Speaking of strangers," Bailey said, "who invited the guy on the patio?" He winked at me over his beer.

"Don't ask me," I said. "I walked out of the house this morning and there he was. Like one of those toadstools that pops up in the rain."

"Kit thinks we need to shake him down."

Kit dug his can into a little divot he'd made for it in the grass. "I just think we ought to find out what he's up to. You know, have a little come-to-Jesus. See what he's got on his mind."

"If it was up to me, we'd of tied him to a tree and horsewhipped him a long time ago," Bailey said. "Anyway, I know what he's got on his mind."

"No, you don't," I said. "If I don't, then there's no possible way you could."

"I thought he quit drinking," Kit said. I shrugged and took an exploratory sip of my own drink. It tasted like it would probably live up to its name, but the process might not be all that agreeable. "Well, hell, isn't that what you go to rehab for? To quit drinking? Looks to me like somebody needs to ask for their money back."

"I don't think you get a refund when you quit the program," I said.

"He quit?"

"Walked out. Or snuck out, broke out, something. I've not been made privy to the actual details."

"And he hijacked a truck and showed up here?"

"Don't forget, he stopped to pick up forty pounds of crawfish on the way."

Bailey and Kit looked at each other. "He can't do that, can he?" Kit asked.

"I don't see why not," Bailey said. "There's plenty of places to buy crawfish up and down the road between here and Memphis."

"Supper, everbody!" Dove called, banging a spoon against a pot lid for good measure.

Kit struggled to his knees. "I'm telling you, we need to shake him down," he said.

"Listen," I said, pouring the rest of my Mind Eraser in the grass, then stood up and brushed off the back of my skirt. "I grew up without a daddy, same as y'all did. For Jude's sake I'm not burning that bridge to the ground unless I know for sure it's the only way. Okay?" My brothers were silent, studying their beer cans like there was some secret encoded on the labels. I smiled. "I'm not sixteen, you guys."

"Maybe we oughta follow him around for a few days. Just to put a little bit of fear in him," Kit grumbled as he and Bailey got to their feet.

Ash had plenty of fear in him already, I thought as we walked across the lawn in the shadows of early evening. But I decided to keep that particular observation to myself.

THE PICNIC TABLE was too small for all of us, so Dove spread a tablecloth on the grass for the kids, and for a while the backyard was quiet as we laid into our feast. The crawfish, I had to admit, were perfect, succulent and spicy. Every now and then somebody would murmur in appreciation, or ask their neighbor to pass the dip.

It wasn't till we'd polished off half the bugs that we began pushing our plates away and the conversation picked up where we'd left off: gossip, discussions of work and weather, not small talk so much as the talk of folks who see each other regularly and can afford to indulge themselves in the trivial details of one another's lives.

Eventually the discussion turned, like it usually did, to Little League. Our town was too small to have separate boys' and girls' leagues, so Jude and Lily were both playing for the Hatch Brothers team that spring, Jude at third base, Lily as star pitcher. As an athlete, Jude was erratic. It wasn't that he couldn't hit or throw, but the rituals of the game, the uniforms and gear, the crowd in the bleachers, the shouts and laughter of the other players, all were so exhilarating to him that he had a hard time concentrating, and was likely to be admiring the stitching on his glove or gazing at some minor drama on the sidelines as the ball sailed past his head and into the outfield, his uncles and teammates screaming to get his attention. Lily, on the other hand, was as cold and focused as a hit man, a bona fide throwing machine; a bomb blast in the stands couldn't distract her when she was on the mound.

"As far as coaching goes, we're a little thin in the outfield," Kit was telling Ash. "Maybe if you're gonna be around awhile, you could give us a hand. Our next game's Wednesday," he added, but Ash just nodded distractedly, contemplating his beer can.

"So, how's things up in Nashville?" Bailey asked, sensing a crack and rushing in. "You must be chomping at the bit to get back onstage. It's been a good long time now, am I right?" Ash shrugged, turning his beer around and around in his hand. "Seems to me you can't afford to take too long out of the, the whatayacallit? The public eye. You stay away too long, folks might forget about you. Move on to something new."

"I guess that's true." Ash looked up. "The thing is, I don't know if I'm gonna keep on doing music. I'm not sure I've still got it in me."

There was a short, shocked pause, and then everybody was talking at once.

"What?"

"You've got to be kidding!"

"After you worked so hard! How can you just walk away?"

Ash let the protests and exclamations die down.

"Look, it's just that things are different now. The stuff I used to think was important doesn't so much seem like it anymore."

"Well, that's the silliest thing I've ever heard in my life," Geneva said. "You're a musician. It's what you *are*! You can't just decide *not* to be anymore, like a, a Baptist, or a Republican."

"Nashville's been your dream your whole life, Ash," Peggy said. "You finally got yourself a toehold. Why would you let go now?"

"And what would you do instead?" Kit asked.

Ash gave a small, self-conscious laugh. "Are the Hatch Brothers hiring? I used to be a pretty good carpenter."

Kit and Bailey looked at each other, then at me. I shook my head. I had no idea where any of this was coming from, if it was dead serious or part of a long, crazy joke, one that had started with a white pickup and forty pounds of crawfish.

"Look," Ash said, spreading his hands on the tabletop, "I'm just hanging out this evening, all right? Just kicking back like the rest of y'all, sucking on crawfish heads, having a good time, enjoying the company. I don't want to have to think about Nashville, or work, or any of the rest of it. There's plenty of time for that later. And I promise, when I make up my mind, y'all will be the first to know."

Kit cleared his throat, and Connie picked up the tea pitcher and started pouring refills. "Who wants more slaw?" Dove asked. But the only person who had any appetite left was Ash.

chapter five

"Good old Ash," Geneva said. "You can always count on him to be full of surprises." We were on the patio, scraping plates into a drawstring Hefty bag.

"Trouble is, you can't tell what's for real and what's for show. He never makes a move without thinking about his audience."

"Well, maybe that's why he wants to step aside. Stop performing awhile and just live a little, like the rest of us."

"No," I said. "Ash hasn't got it in him to live a little. He's got to live bigger than everybody else, louder, just plain *more* than everybody else. It would kill him to be like the rest of us."

The bag was full; I drew it shut and tied the strings in a quick, tight knot. Lily and Jude were wrestling in the grass, the big kids had gone inside to watch TV, and the women still sat clustered around the picnic table, sipping tea and talking. There was just enough light left in the sky and from the little electric lanterns strung from the tree limbs to make out Ash and Kit and Bailey near the back fence, flinging horseshoes, the spike nearly invisible in the dusk. From across the yard came grunts and curses and laughter and the occasional clang of metal on metal. It occurred to me that if my brothers really did want to put the fear in Ash, one stray horseshoe would probably take care of it.

"You know, Lucy, it's no secret I had a crush on Ash back in the day, when he used to sing at the Round-Up. But after y'all got together, I never envied you. I always knew the idea of him and the reality were two totally separate animals."

"Well, I wish you'd told me that six or seven years ago," I said. "You could've saved me a lot of grief."

"You wouldn't have heard me. Anyway, regrets are a waste of time, if you ask me."

"That's because you don't have any."

"Sure I do. Mine just aren't as interesting as yours."

As she spoke, Ash came across the yard to the edge of the patio and opened the ice chest and took out three more tallboys. I guessed two of them were for Kit and Bailey, but something inside me started twisting itself in a knot.

"Where do you suppose he plans on sleeping tonight?" Geneva asked as Ash set two cans on the pavement, then popped the tab on the third and took a long drink.

"I've been wondering the same thing myself."

Ash noticed us watching him and cocked his head, looked back over one shoulder and then the other, then pointed to himself with the can and raised one eyebrow and grinned. I couldn't help it; I felt a stirring in my chest, a pinpoint of light in a place where for a long time there'd been none. I didn't want to feel that way; I knew Ash was just being Ash, using looks and charm to smooth over dubious behavior. How many times had he gotten away with it in his lifetime—ten thousand, a million?

"Oh boy," Geneva said as he closed the cooler and set his beer on the lid and headed in our direction. She picked up the Hefty bag. "Not that I'm not dying to stick around, but I think I'll leave this one to you."

Without a word, Ash swept me up and started to dance me across the patio under the glow of the Japanese lanterns, one arm around my shoulders and the other around my waist. *Oh baby don't it feel like heaven right now,* he sang along with the radio, *don't it feel like something from a dream?* Part of me wanted to tell him to knock it off, that he was making a fool of himself and a spectacle of us both, but it felt too good to be up against him this way, to breathe in up close the smell of him, to give myself over to the second-sense movements of our feet and all the rest of it.

"Lord, I've missed this," he said into my hair.

I lifted my head and looked at him.

"Well, it's been right here all the time," I said. "It's not like you didn't know where to find it."

"I think I forgot how it felt to be part of something like this." He gestured with his chin toward the backyard. "Something so good and, well, ordinary."

"You gave up 'ordinary' to go to Nashville," I reminded him. "Nobody put a gun to your head."

"Let me ask you something. When did you figure out you'd made a mistake?"

"About what?"

"About me. Marrying me, I mean, and following me to Tennessee."

"I didn't. Is that what you think I think? That I made a mistake?"

"You saying you don't wish you'd done things different?"

"Sure I do. That's not saying I wish I hadn't done them at all."

We stopped moving and stood looking at each other, a long look, unadorned. He reached up and brushed a stray strand of hair away from my mouth with his thumb.

"We've got a lot to talk about," he said.

I swallowed, nodded my head. In spite of everything that had come to pass over the last seven years, all that water under a very long bridge, I felt the exact same way I'd felt the first time Ash and I ever danced together at the Round-Up, when he'd put his mouth in my hair and asked me if he stopped by my house later, might he find the front door open? I knew what I was signing on for; I'd known then and I knew now, and whether it was love or engineering was nothing but splitting hairs.

"So maybe we ought to go home and get started," he said.

He smiled, and I felt the heat rush to my face. "It's just about Jude's bedtime anyway. I'll go on ahead, get him tucked in."

Ash nodded, his hand lighting gently for a second in the small of my back, sending a ripple along my spine before lifting off again. And then he did something I found sweet but strange. He leaned forward and kissed me on the forehead, right along the hairline. His lips were dry and cool. I felt the grizzle of his unshaved chin against my skin.

He took something from his pocket and pressed it into my hand. The house key.

"I'm right behind you," he said.

I MANAGED TO get Jude into his pajamas in record time, putting him to bed without a bath even though he was streaked all over with dirt and grass. "Don't I get a story?" he asked as I bent over and kissed the top of his head.

"Not tonight. It's way past your bedtime." I switched off the light.

"I want Daddy to read me a story!"

"Tell you what," I said. "You lie here nice and quiet with your eyes closed, and when Daddy gets here, we'll see." Backing out of the room, I crossed my fingers and hoped he'd be asleep before

Ash came home. I wasn't about to come right out and tell my son that I had other plans for his daddy.

I ran to the bathroom, throwing off clothes as I went, and jumped into the shower, sudsing myself and swiping a razor over my legs, the whole time keeping one ear peeled for Ash's truck in the yard. I rubbed lotion into my skin, all over, and put a squirt of Calvin Klein Eternity behind my ears. I remembered when Ash had given me the bottle, a few days after Denny first arrived to stay with us and I'd just found out I was pregnant with Jude. The gift had struck me as funny then—both the perfume itself, when I'd never been much of a perfume girl, and the name, which seemed so optimistic, so unlike the rough-and-tumble future that seemed to lie ahead of us. Little did I know how inconsequential those troubles would seem someday, how small and transient. I spritzed a little in the crooks of my elbows and behind my knees. If Eternity was forever, then, technically speaking, it was never too late.

I rifled through my bureau drawers, quickly concluding that sexy underwear wasn't an option; I'd left all my good stuff back in Nashville, and when it came time to buy new, I'd stuck to whatever I could get at Wal-Mart that was plain and cheap. I hadn't been thinking about sex then anyway, just survival, hardly imagining a time when the pendulum would swing back the other way. I slipped my white terrycloth robe on over clean, bare skin, and hoped that whatever God gave me would be enough for Ash.

In the kitchen I switched on the light over the stove hood and filled the kettle with water. I didn't really want tea, but it was something to do, something to take my mind off what was keeping Ash.

Not that it was time to worry, not yet; less than an hour had passed since that funny little kiss on the forehead on Dove's patio. Still, I had to admit it stung a little, knowing that the object of my desire was somewhat less burning in his desire for me.

Maybe, I thought suddenly, I'd gotten his signals wrong. No, it wasn't possible; Ash could be maddeningly cryptic about some things, but about this one, we'd always read each other loud and clear. Had one of my brothers smacked him upside the head with a horseshoe after all? Or maybe the local deputy, Dewey Wentzel, had pulled him over on the farm-to-market road. I had an awful memory of the first time I'd sat home waiting for Ash, the night of that first dance and the unlocked front door. I'd waited hours, and he never came, and then finally, at three in the morning, he'd called, claiming to be in jail. I'd hung up on him in a rage, my image of myself as a woman of the world in tatters, only to learn the next day that he truly had gotten arrested, the target of an irate not-quite-ex-girlfriend, and had spent the night locked up in the jail on the top floor of the courthouse. It was Dewey Wentzel who'd hauled Ash in that night, and from that day on, till Ash left for Nashville, there'd been no love lost between those two. For all I knew, Dewey had spent the whole evening lying in wait, sitting back in the pines off Little Hope Road with the cruiser lights off and the radar on, just waiting for Ash to go rocketing by and bust him.

I turned on the burner and took down a canister of chamomile tea. Chamomile was supposed to be good for the nerves. When the kettle whistled, I poured steaming water over a tea bag, then sat down at the table and wrapped my hands around the mug, watching the minute hand of the clock crawl forward. How many times had I sat here, just this way, holding a cup of tea between my hands and brooding about Ash? How many nights of my life had gone down the drain, worrying about things I knew I had no control over, spending my fury and my tears on things I couldn't fix? Over the past eight months my sharpest feelings about Ash had gradually boiled off, the way you boil off a roux. I'd forgotten what it was like to be this angry, to hurt so bad it was physical, a sharp pain every time I breathed in. Or maybe *forgotten* is too drastic a word; I'd suppressed it, stuffed it down inside me the way I'd stuffed that old shoe box full of makeup under the bathroom counter. The tubes and compacts might be sticky or crumbling, but it was surprising, after all those years, how well they'd held their color.

I washed and dried my teacup and set it in the dish drainer, then walked through the house, turning out lights as I went. In the bathroom I scrubbed my face and my teeth, shucked my robe, and got into my ratty old nightgown, a cotton rag left behind in a bureau drawer, too decrepit for even a Speakes to bother with. For good measure, I locked the front door, feeling a little twinge of satisfaction as the dead bolt slid home.

I didn't think there was any way I would sleep, but I dropped off within minutes, into a strange dream about the Sistine Chapel. I'd never been there, not in real life, but I'd seen pictures, and a special once on TV. In my dream, the figures painted by Michelangelo all those centuries before came down from the ceiling and were walking around in my front yard, some in brilliant robes and tunics, some of them as naked as jaybirds, their muscles rippling and glistening like silk. I stood inside the screen door watching them, thinking, *Why are you here? What do you want?* One woman in particular, wearing a blue shawl, kept looking back over her shoulder at me with wide, worried eyes, like she knew a secret but wasn't sure she should let me in on it. I just stood and watched them wander around, muttering among themselves. They seemed to be waiting for something, but I couldn't figure out what, or make out what they were saying. I tried pleading with my eyes with the woman in the shawl: *Tell me.*

For a long time she gazed back at me. I watched her mouth move, but I still couldn't hear her. I shook my head. She beckoned me closer. I could feel the heat of the bodies now, the smell, not of paint, but of real flesh. I was scared. I knew they were perturbed, but why? What had I done?

The woman's lips parted. *You said it was chocolate!* she said. *You said it, but it's not.*

I woke sitting upright in bed, my heart skittering in my chest. Headlights swung across the front of the house, slashing a bright arc across the bedroom wall. The dogs were barking. I waited with held breath for a swirl of red and blue light, a blast of radio static, the news I'd been waiting seven years to hear.

The lights went out, and I heard a door open and close, a voice speaking to the dogs, silencing them. Not Dewey Wentzel, then; those dogs wouldn't have stopped barking for Dewey, or anybody in a uniform, under any circumstances short of him shooting them.

Then footsteps on the porch, the screech of the screen door hinges that I knew but kept forgetting needed WD-40. I threw back the sheet and slid out of bed and ran down the hall in the dark just as Ash started to pound on the locked door with his knuckles.

I turned the dead bolt and yanked open the door, flipping the switch for the porch light before I remembered the bulb had burned out and I'd never gotten around to replacing it. I stepped out onto the porch, pulling the screen door shut behind me.

"What the hell," Ash said, backing toward the porch rail. I could only make out the shape of him, silhouetted against the night sky, but I could smell him; it came off him in waves, sweet and sickening, his breath, his pores, maybe even the platelets of his blood. It was a smell I hadn't smelled in months, but it threw me right back to that last night in Tennessee. "You're a damn sight less friendly than you were last time I saw you," he said.

"That was three hours ago."

"Three hours? No shit." There was real wonder in his voice, that his deeds could have strayed so far from his original intentions.

"Where have you been? You said you were right behind me."

"Well, now, let's see. First I helped Dove put up the cooker and rinse out the coolers. Seemed like the least I could do, seeing's how the party was my idea in the first place. Then I got a big old bag full of crawfish and drove it by your mama's."

"You—what? You went to see my mama?"

"I felt sorry for her, having to miss the party, 'cause of church and all. I wasn't sure she'd be too glad to see me, and she was in her robe already, but she asked me in and gave me a Coca-Cola. She seemed pretty happy to have the crawfish. She asked me to come by in a couple days and change out a bathroom washer for her."

"I'm not believing this."

"You know, Lucy, she isn't getting around like she used to. That hip of hers is pretty bad."

It was scary how normal his voice sounded, how silky and cool. When you hear *drunk*, you think of some guy weaving and slurring, passed out in a ditch. But with Ash, the more he drank, the smoother he got, the more charming and courtly. His hands didn't shake, he was hardly ever sick. He could frame a window drunk, play the guitar, drive, make love. The only snags were a troublesome tendency to black out, to lose track of time and have to scramble to cover his tracks, as well as a nasty streak that could spring up and out at you without warning, claws bared, like a cornered cat. It was the smell more than anything that gave him away, that and his eyes, black and opaque, a one-way mirror. I was glad it was dark and I couldn't see them.

"Then, let's see . . . I decided to make a quick stop by the Pak 'n' Sak, and you'll never believe in a hundred years who I ran into there."

"Elvis?"

"My old buddy Isaac King! He was on his way home from his job at the hospital, picking up a gallon of milk. How come you didn't tell me him and Rose had another baby?" I'd only seen Isaac a handful of times since I'd come back to Mooney, and then only from afar. I kept hoping I wouldn't run into him face-to-face so that I wouldn't have to explain what had happened. "He talked me into riding out to the house with him, to see Rose and the kids. I ended up staying a little longer than I intended. But here I am, finally. All of a piece."

"You're a piece, all right. Where'd you get the whiskey?"

"The what?"

"Give me a break. Did you buy it, or did Isaac give it to you?"

"I might've had a beer at Isaac's."

"Ash, you're stinking," I said. "Did you really think I wouldn't be able to tell?"

"Uh-oh," he said. "Here it comes. Mr. Shit, meet Mr. Fan."

"Do you even remember what you said to me earlier, on Dove's patio? You know, for such a slick talker, you sure know how to go the other way in a hell of a hurry."

"I can explain everything, Lucy, if you'd just calm down a minute and not go off half-cocked every time I try and talk to you."

"I don't understand any of this, Ash. What are you doing?"

"You mean, what's my *intent*?"

"Don't make fun of me! You've been here all day and I've yet to get a straight answer out of you. Why did we spend the whole evening sitting around my aunt's backyard eating crawfish? Then, just when it seemed like we were making a little bit of headway, you go off and get lost for three hours! You haven't got any more scruples than a rat in the gutter. If somebody dangles a bottle in front of you, you're gone."

"If we could just go inside and sit down—"

"No," I said. "You're not setting foot in this house, not in the shape you're in."

"You're trying to tell me I can't come inside my own house?"

"You slept in the truck last night, you can do it again. Or go find one of your fan club. To hear you tell it, the whole town's full of folks just waiting for Ash Farrell to show up and ring their doorbell. Jesus, Ash! I feel like I, I don't even know you anymore! You walked out of rehab, but you're still drinking, and talking crazy about quitting music. . . . The only reason I can think of for you to've showed up here is that you've finally run out of places to run. How's that supposed to make me feel? How am I supposed to trust you again?"

"Mama?" Jude's voice floated through the screen. "Who's yelling?"

"Nobody. Go back to sleep."

"Is Daddy here?"

"Hey, buddy." Ash pushed off the porch rail and moved toward the door. "What are you doing up? You oughta be asleep by now."

"I was waiting for you."

"Well, here I am."

"Can you come in and read me a story?"

"It's way past story time, baby," I said. "Run on back to bed now. There'll be plenty of time for all that tomorrow."

"Tomorrow's Saturday," Jude said cheerfully.

"That's right."

"And we're having waffles, right? And cartoons! Daddy, will you eat waffles with me and watch *Power Rangers*? And then maybe later we can ride in your truck."

"That sounds great, Son. We'll see what your mama has to say about it in the morning."

"Get on back to bed, Jude," I said, but he hovered there, a nervous little ghost in the dark. "Can you tuck yourself in?"

"Only if you guys promise, no more yelling."

We promised, our voices subdued, and Jude faded silently up the hall. The night that had earlier been moonlit and plump with promise seemed to flatten around us. Low clouds scuttled overhead, and the woods smelled damp and rotted, like a grave. Neither Ash nor I spoke for a long time. I wanted to think he was considering the magnitude of our situation, but I knew he was really just working on his defense.

"I could sleep on the couch," he said finally. "Just for tonight."

"No," I said. "I left Nashville to get away from this. I'm not letting it start up again."

"So what am I supposed to say to my son when he wakes up in the morning and finds me out here in the truck? How am I supposed to explain that?"

"I don't know, Ash. How do you think I've felt the past eight months? It's hard to know what to tell him when you won't even admit yourself you've got a problem."

"I'll say I've got a problem! You want me to sleep outside in the cold, like a damned dog!"

"It's sixty-five degrees out here, easy. Anyway, you've got all that alcohol in you to keep you warm." More stashed in the truck, too, I bet. "Oh, why am I even trying to talk to you? You won't remember this conversation in the morning anyway."

"I remember a lot more than you give me credit for."

"If that's really true, then maybe you ought to think about it." I reached for the door handle. "Do you want a blanket?" I asked. But he'd turned to face the yard, and didn't answer me.

I stepped inside and latched the screen, then shut the door and turned the dead bolt. I went back to bed, where I lay gazing at the ceiling, turning my wedding band around and around on my finger and waiting for the sound of Ash's truck firing up and pulling out, or his fist or his foot battering the front door. But the only thing I heard, somewhere around four in the morning, was a mournful snatch of Hank Williams, his voice so reedy and faraway-sounding he might have been singing from the Great Beyond: *So lonesome, I could cry.*

chapter six

The room grew furry around the edges with light, and I rolled over and looked out the front window. For the second morning in a row the pickup was there, shimmering under a film of dew.

I got up and put on coffee in the dark, a ritual I knew by heart. While it was perking I splashed water on my face and brushed my teeth. Then I slipped on my garden clogs and an old field coat over my nightgown, poured the biggest mug we had full of French Market brew, and carried it out into the yard.

It was chilly out, dawn a crimson band below the tree line, the moon a pale thumbprint in the dark blue sky. I took an experimental sip of coffee, black and steaming in the cool morning air. Ordinarily I loved this time of day, everything still ahead, a blank scroll of possibility. Maybe Ash and I were doomed from the start, one of us preferring to get up early, the other one ducking in just ahead of the sunrise, like a vampire. Every bedroom in our house in Nashville had blackout shades on the windows, and the first thing I'd done when I got home to Texas was take down all the curtains. I didn't want to miss another minute of daylight.

I stood for a while watching Ash curled on his side on the backseat of the pickup under an old army blanket, one arm over his head and his mouth ajar. There was a trace of tenderness, one lingering note, but mostly what I felt was a wave of bereavement, bone-crunching and soul-sapping. Something I loved had been lost. I didn't know if I would ever find anything to take its place, whether I had the heart or the guts anymore to try.

I opened the door and poked my finger into the hole in the sole of Ash's boot. He woke with a start, jerking his head up and looking around wildly. He looked awful, bleary-eyed and puffy-faced, as he sat up shivering, pulling the old wool blanket tight around him.

"I don't guess that's for me," he said, spying the mug in my hand.

"It was. But while I was waiting for you to wake up, I drank it."

"What ungodly hour is it, anyway? Four? Five?"

"Almost seven."

Ash groaned. "Decent people are asleep at seven."

"Decent people don't get shit-faced and have to sleep in their trucks," I said. "Anyway, it's Saturday. Jude will be out here any minute, wanting waffles and cartoons."

"I suppose you came to rub that in my face, too."

"No. I came to see if you'd care to join us."

"Let me get this straight. You kicked me out of the house last night, and this morning you're inviting me to breakfast?"

"Well, yes. Except that I didn't actually kick you out, since you weren't in the house to begin with."

Ash shook his head. "I can't keep up with you. It's too early. Besides, I've got a crick in my neck from sleeping in the goddamned truck."

"Better not think about it too much," I said. "You're just lucky I woke up in a generous mood."

"Funny," he said, throwing off the blanket, "I don't *feel* lucky."

"Come in and have some coffee, and maybe you will."

I poured us each a mug full, and Ash carried his to the bathroom while I got out the flour and Crisco. A few minutes later he was back, his face scrubbed and his hair combed back from his forehead, wearing a different shirt than the one he'd slept in. He walked over to the Mr. Coffee and topped off his cup, then pulled out a chair at the table.

"You always fix breakfast in your jacket and your yard shoes?"

"Sorry. I left the fringe and sequins back in Nashville."

He smiled. "That's okay. I never was big on sequins at breakfast."

We were quiet as we sipped our coffee and I mixed up the waffle batter. I couldn't remember the last time Ash and I had spent a peaceful five minutes this way, without a phone ringing somewhere or a terse word tossed out by one or the other of us, a remnant of a fight that had no beginning or end but just seemed to play continually, a loop that had become the background music of our lives. Most of my happy memories, I realized, were right here in this kitchen, before Nashville, before we'd gone and ended up running everything that was sweet and good between us into the ground. I glanced up at him as I measured out baking soda and salt, but I couldn't tell what he was thinking, if he had his own memories, or if it was all he could manage just then to keep his eyes open and his head upright. Whatever was the matter with him, I knew better than to think a plateful of waffles was going to fix it.

"Can I ask you something?" I said. "What you said to me last night at Dove's, about realizing when I'd made a mistake marrying you—what was that about?"

Ash lifted one shoulder and dropped it again. "I don't know. I guess I was trying to figure out how something can be just fine one day and then all of a sudden you turn around and it's gone to hell."

"Are you talking about us? Or are you talking about something else?"

"I'm talking about pretty much everything."

"Look," I said, turning to him, setting down the measuring spoons. "I didn't ask you in here to harangue you. But can't you— How can you be sitting there looking like a whipped dog and not know the answer to that question?" His eyes skidded sideways, away from me. "You're sick," I said, "and you need help. Till you admit that, we can sit in this kitchen till kingdom come and nothing will ever change."

"I hated that fucking hospital," Ash said, shoving his coffee mug to the middle of the table. "You never heard so much high-flown bullshit in your life. The doctors were worse than the patients. The whole thing was nothing but one big circle-jerk."

"There are other places," I said. "Maybe you just need—"

"Maybe I *need* everybody to just get the fuck off my back and let me handle it my way."

"You mean because you're doing such a good job on your own? My Lord, Ash—have you looked at yourself? You're living in a truck!"

"That truck cost more than some people's houses."

"I've been meaning to ask you about that."

"I thought you said no haranguing."

"I said that's not why I invited you in. I didn't say I'm not capable of it, should the need arise."

He looked at me for a minute, then laughed and picked up his coffee. "You're too much, Lucy, you know it?"

"I'm going to act like you meant that as a compliment. Would you mind getting Jude up? I'm about to put the waffles on."

You'd have thought Santa Claus was in town to hear Jude holler when he opened his eyes to see Ash at his bedside. As I poured the first batch of batter into the waffle iron and added a few of the blueberries Jude loved, I could hear him and Ash carrying on in there, tussling and grunting, doing the things men do to demonstrate their affection for each other.

I served them the first pair of waffles hot off the griddle, with butter and a jug of Blackburn's syrup. Jude polished off three waffles in an eye-blink, but I noticed that Ash was only picking at his.

"Eat," I said, nudging him with the handle of my spatula. "You need some meat on your bones."

"After this, we're gonna watch cartoons for seventeen hundred hours," Jude said happily, swirling his fork through a puddle of syrup and melted butter.

"Not quite seventeen hundred, baby," I said. "Remember, you've got baseball practice today."

"You can come, Daddy!" Jude said. "You can watch me catch the ball!"

"I could watch you catch the ball all day long," Ash said with a smile.

"I'm not too good," Jude said. "But Uncle Bailey says it only counts how hard I try."

"Your uncle Bailey's a smart man."

"Who wants more waffles?" I asked, holding up the batter bowl.

"Me, me!" Jude waved his fork in the air. Ash shook his head, but I served him one anyway, then sat down beside them to eat a couple of my own. Outside the kitchen window, between the pines, pink and white dogwoods were blooming, scattered among the green like the edges of a lace handkerchief. I couldn't help musing about what might have happened if we'd stayed in Mooney, if Ash had just gone on remodeling kitchens and singing at the Round-Up for fifty bucks a night on weekends. Would Saturday mornings at the breakfast table, cartoons and baseball practice, have been a regular thing for us? It worried me that Jude would grow up thinking of his daddy as some glamorous stranger, somebody who dropped in from time to time with his fancy gifts and his city ways. Of course, that was better than a hungover daddy who slept in a pickup.

"Is it time yet, Mama?" I knew what that meant: *Power Rangers* or *Transformers,* Jude's current favorite cartoons.

"Not quite. But I think *Clifford*'s on now."

"*Clifford*'s for babies."

"Why don't we run you a bath while you wait? You've still got grass all over you from playing in Dove's yard last night."

"No bath!" he announced, climbing off his chair. "It's Saturday and I can be dirty if I want to."

I made a grab for him, but he was too fast for me, scooting around the table and into his bedroom. "Come in here, Daddy, and see my toys!" he called.

"Go on, if you feel like it," I said to Ash, getting up to rinse the plates in the sink. "Just don't forget to remind him when *Power Rangers* comes on at eight, or you'll never hear the end of it."

He tipped back his chair and reached for my hand. Mine was damp from the dishwater, but his was dry and warm, the tips of his fingers ridged with calluses from years of playing guitar. No, Ash could never have stayed in East Texas when Nashville called. Those calluses reminded me of that, like an athlete's muscles, proof of the thing he'd spent his whole life training for.

"Where's your ring?" he asked, turning my hand over in his. I still wore my plain gold wedding band, but the three-carat diamond he'd bought me with his first check from Arcadia Records had seemed too flashy for Cade County. More than that, it felt like a billboard for something I wasn't sure I could advertise anymore, the strength and brilliance of my marriage.

"Bank," I said. "Safety-deposit box."

"I thought maybe you'd hocked it."

"Not yet."

"I'm gonna put that down as a check mark in my favor. Not a big one, but I'll take what I can get." He squeezed my fingers, in no hurry to let go. "Thanks for breakfast," he said.

"You didn't eat ten bites of it."

"But I appreciated every bite."

"Daddy!" Jude shouted. "I'm setting up my dinosaurs!"

Ash pushed back his chair and stood up. We were face-to-face, as close as we'd been in the past eight months, not counting on Dove's patio the night before. It was too late to wish I'd done something about my bird's-nest hair and naked face, just like it was too late to stop myself from thinking about all those Nashville girls who probably slept in blusher and false lashes. But this was my kitchen, my husband, my life, still.

From the other room came a loud mechanical roar.

"What the hell was that?"

"*T. rex*," I said. "He sounds pretty mad."

"Just what I need, on top of everything else. A pissed-off dinosaur."

T. rex roared again, followed by a bloodcurdling human scream.

"Jesus," Ash said, letting go of my hand and moving in the direction of Jude's room. "Do I need weapons for this?"

"Just patience. And a sense of humor."

I took advantage of the dinosaur battle to dress in my usual Saturday uniform of jeans and a T-shirt, pulled my hair into a ponytail, and swiped on some sunscreen and lip balm. Then I gathered up a load of towels and put them in the machine, and washed and dried the breakfast dishes. If Ash could act like everything was normal while all the evidence said otherwise, so could I.

At eight o'clock he and Jude moved into the living room and turned on the TV, and the cartoon racket started to blare. I used to be totally opposed to all forms of electronic entertainment, until Jude started toddling and I figured out what every parent eventually learned, that videos and cartoons were a way to buy myself a few uninterrupted hours on weekend mornings to get my chores done or just sit and enjoy a second cup of coffee. If my son turned into a social deviant because of *Spider-Man* or *Toy Story*, well, then, I guessed I'd have to accept the responsibility.

I was sitting at the table, enjoying the sunlight and trying not to think about much in particular, when Ash came in, rubbing his eyes with the back of his hand.

"Had enough already?" I said.

"Mm. A little of that stuff goes a long way."

He poured himself a fresh cup of coffee and stood at the sink drinking it and looking out the window.

"This place is like—I guess I'd forgotten how pretty it is," he said. "Or, not forgotten exactly. But just sort of put it out of my mind."

"Tennessee's pretty."

"Not like here. You can hear yourself think here. In Nashville it's just go, go, go all the time. Even up in the country, you can still feel that hum."

"Well, you must've had some idea what you were getting into when you went up there in the first place," I said.

He shook his head. "You know, I think I had this notion that because country music had these sweet, humble beginnings, the business would be like that, too. Just one big, happy family, picking and grinning on the porch. But you take away the guys with five-hundred-dollar Luchesses and bad comb-overs, and you might as well be in L.A."

"So you decided to get out. Just quit doing the thing you do better than anything else, that you spent twenty, twenty-five years working for, because of a few guys with fancy boots and bald spots?"

He shrugged without looking at me. "It's a long story."

"There's plenty of coffee," I said.

"Arcadia canceled my contract."

I set down my mug. "What?"

"You heard me. They dropped me."

"But you— I thought you had a deal for two more records!"

"I did."

"They can't just call it off, can they, just like that?"

"You know what Tony said to me? It's nothing personal. Time to thin the ranks, give some new folks a start. Let them try to figure out how to swim with the sharks."

"But Tony signed you! He drove down to Texas, twice, just to convince you to move up there and throw your hat in the ring! How can he say it's not personal?"

"Easy," Ash said. "He's got a job, remember? Professional ballbuster."

I held out my cup, and Ash poured me a refill.

"How long have you known this?"

"Since—let's see. I guess day before yesterday. He called me at the rehab. How's that for a nice touch? I get out of group therapy, all these sniveling idiots whining about their boring personal problems, and I get paged to the phone, and bam! All over but the shouting."

"I can't believe it," I said. "There has to be something you can do. Talk to a lawyer, something."

"I already did. Or, rather, I talked to Vern, who called *his* lawyer. He said he'd look into it, but he wasn't real encouraging. Neither was Vern, for that matter. Contracts have loopholes, you know, for cases like this. There's all kinds of mumbo-jumbo in there. Have you ever heard of force majeure?" I shook my head. "It means forces beyond your control. The labels use it as a sort of escape hatch. Artists hate it, but lawyers love it, because it's damned near impossible to prove. Or, I guess I should say, disprove."

"But isn't it Vern's job to stand up for you? Isn't that what managers do?"

"Vern's got a lot bigger fish to fry."

"I don't care," I said. "He made a commitment when he took you on. Are you trying to tell me that now he can't be bothered because you're not big or important enough?"

"I think that pretty much hits the nail on the head."

I'd never liked Vern Bellamy; as far as I was concerned, he was one of the fancy-boots-and-comb-over guys. But he was a big wheel, and Ash had been thrilled when he'd offered to represent him, too scared to turn him down. And there'd been a good first couple of years—two records with Arcadia, radio airplay, videos in heavy rotation on CMT, an opening slot on one leg of a big Alan Jackson–George Strait tour.

I'm not sure I can pinpoint when I first noticed that what once looked like an upward arc, infinitely ascending, had turned south and started plummeting back toward earth again. Ash was struggling with writing and recording his third CD, sleeping on the couch at the studio, or so he said. The times I did see him, he stomped around the house in a black cloud, consuming cases of beer and fifths of Jack Daniel's and complaining about Tony and Vern riding him, trying to bite off and chew up little pieces of his soul. The record, when it finally came out, was beloved by no one, not its creator, its distributor, or the fans, and the lone single, along with the CD, sank like a stone. Ash toured and toured, but the venues, instead of growing, started shrinking. He went from arenas to theaters back to dance halls and county fairs, small-town Corn Festivals and Azalea Parades. He even came back home to be grand marshal at the annual Cade County Dogwood Days celebration, where he'd sung with his old band on a platform on the courthouse square and the mayor had given him a key to the city and a plaque proclaiming him MOONEY'S FAVORITE SON. We had an ugly fight afterwards in Bailey and Geneva's guest room that woke up the whole household, and Ash drank so much on the flight back to Nashville, one of the flight attendants had to help me get him off the plane.

For a while he threw himself into the dark romance of the thing: the beleaguered artist, the tragic, misunderstood genius. He'd wander the house with George Jones or Hank Williams blaring from the speakers accompanied by the clink of bottle to glass, the pop and hiss of a beer can opening, the slow gurgle of liquid being poured, swallowed, poured again, getting stoked and congratulating himself for being in such fine company.

Then the music stopped. I'd come upon him sitting in some shadowy corner, his face a mask, eyes dead, a glass in his hand, and no amount of threatening or coaxing on my part could talk him out of it. I once took Jude and left for a weeklong visit to Mooney, hoping to shake Ash out of his funk, but when we got back to Tennessee, he was still sitting in the same chair wearing the same shirt he'd had on when we left, looking for all the world like he hadn't moved a muscle in six days.

Still, your mind can tell you one thing and your heart something else completely, and in those days I was still listening to my heart. I loved Ash—not the same way I'd loved him when I met him, all his big talk and razzle-dazzle, but in ways that were deep and tangled, roots below the surface. More than anything, I loved the man I'd first seen onstage in our old hometown, the one he'd been on the verge of showing the world, but that somehow, for the past couple of years, seemed to be running through his grasp like water, like music, like love, something you felt but couldn't hold.

All this went through my mind as I sat at my kitchen table and watched Ash stare out the window, his shoulder blades rigid under his T-shirt, a muscle jumping in his unshaved jaw. He was still a handsome man, with his fine-carved cheekbones and swept-back silver hair, but he was starting to look blurry around the edges. I wondered if that was how he felt, too, like a cartoon character half-erased, beginning to fade away.

"After Tony hung up, I just stood there with the phone in my hand," he said. "There were these two people having a fight down the hall in the day room, something about which game show to watch, and a counselor came along and broke it up. One of the aides walked by, pushing a cart loaded with lunch trays. She looked at me and smiled and said hi. And I was thinking, How can everybody be acting so normal? My whole net is gone—my job, my wife, my kid, the whole nine yards—and these assholes are bickering over TV and chicken à la king."

"So you left."

"Nothing much they could do about it. I'd checked myself in, so they couldn't hold me. Not that they didn't try. I'm stuffing shit in my duffel bag, and this poor little girl with a B.A. in psychology is standing there the whole time wringing her hands and giving me the twelve-step creed like her life depended on it. You never heard so much cockamamie bullshit in your life, about one day at a time and working your program.

"I hiked out to the highway and stuck out my thumb and got a ride back to Nashville with a guy in a work truck. I got him to drop me by the Chevy dealership, that big one on the south end of town. I figured I'd better make a deal quick, before the word got around that I was Mr. Has-Been."

"What about your Jeep? Wasn't it still back at the house?"

"I didn't want to go back to the house."

"You mean you bought a brand-new, forty-thousand-dollar truck just because you didn't want to go home?"

He smiled. "Want to know what one of the little psychology girls at the rehab told me? She said I have a problem with impulse control."

"And you decided to play right along. Jesus, Ash!" I stood, slamming down my coffee cup so hard the syrup bottle in the middle of the table tipped over.

"No yelling!" Jude yelled from the living room.

I sat down again, placing my hands flat on the table, and stared at them until I felt steady again. I wanted to yank off my wedding ring and bury it, or make Ash swallow it. That'd teach him a thing or two about pain and suffering.

"You know, this might come as a surprise to you, but plenty of folks manage to make it in the music business without flaming out or cracking up."

"Little late for that. I'm already out of the music business, apparently."

"You know why Tony let you go," I said. "It isn't because you don't have the talent. It's because you seem hell-bent on living out this, this Hank Williams fantasy."

"I've already outlived Hank by a dozen years. Anyway, plenty of folks drink. Hell, look at George Jones—he drank for fifty years."

"Till he drove off a bridge and just about died! Is that what you're going for? The longest-drinking-man-in-show-business award? You trying to trounce George Jones? Or are you waiting for something big enough to stop you? Because if losing your job and your wife and your kid aren't enough to do it, then maybe a bridge is the only way."

"I'm telling you, Lucy," he said in a taut voice, "I can handle it."

"Well, I can't."

He pushed himself away from the counter and started to cross the room.

"Wait," I said. "I'm not finished."

"What's left to say? You've made yourself pretty goddamned clear."

"Sit back down," I said. "Just for a minute."

He looked skeptical, but he pulled out a chair and sat, hooking one ankle over the other, and folded his arms across his chest. I could just see him sitting this same way in group therapy, limbs stiff, jaw twitching, mouth set in a smirk. How could you get through to somebody who'd already made up his mind? If Jesus Himself had walked in wearing a gold halo and offered Ash His hand, it wouldn't have convinced him to give up his shield.

"Look, I know you must feel—"

"You don't know how I feel."

"Okay. But I *think* you feel like you've been hung out on the line and left there, twisting in the wind. And I'm trying to say it's not true."

"Is this the speech about letting go and giving over everything I have to a Higher Power? Because if it is, I've heard it already, so you can spare me."

"No. This is the speech about how I want to try to make things right with you again. But I can't do it unless you meet me partway."

He held up his hands, palms open. "I'm here, aren't I? Isn't that partway?"

"But it took you eight months to get here! Have you got an explanation for that that you can make me understand? Because I'm having a hard time coming up with anything that doesn't involve Miller High Life and Jack Daniel's."

Ash sighed, uncrossed and recrossed his ankles.

"You know, I've been thinking a lot, Ash, over the last few months. And for the longest time I tried to excuse you. I mean, I can only imagine how it must be, having people throw things at you right and left—money, power, drugs, themselves, whatever. It would go to your head, right? To anybody's head. But at some point it stops being fun and games and it turns into a habit. And when it gets to be a habit, it starts to be, I don't know, dehumanizing. Didn't you respect yourself more than that? Why would you sell off everything, all your talent and your career and your family, just so you could snort coke out of some bimbo's cleavage? I mean, every now and then, weekends and holidays, I can understand. But every chance you got for five years? I'm not talking about what you did to me; I didn't even feel like it was about me. What I want to know is, why did you start hating yourself so much?"

He pushed back his chair. "Are you done?"

"Not quite. You keep telling me you can make me see how things got the way they did, even though I haven't seen any proof so far that you can. I want to give you a chance. But all this, this slamming in and out and pointless arguments about stuff we've been over time and again—this is why I left Nashville. I can't live this way, and I won't have Jude in the middle of it, either. I haven't given up on you, even if you think I have. But whether you admit it or not, your drinking is behind everything that's happened to you. I'm not the only one who feels that way—ask Tony, ask Vern, anybody. Till you get a grip on it, I can't live with you."

"You can't keep a man out of his own home. It's not legal."

"I can call the sheriff and get a restraining order. Is that the way you want to play it?"

"What the hell am I supposed to do?" His face was tight, furious.

"I don't know. Check into a motel, sleep in the truck, go back to Nashville, whatever. But if you want to stay with me and Jude, you have to start sober."

He turned back toward the door. "Is that all?"

"Forget about you and me for a second. Don't you remember what it was like, being a little boy with no daddy? Do you think it's right to keep doing what you do to Jude, ducking in and out of his life like a criminal?"

Ash looked away, rubbing one eye with the heel of his hand.

"I hope you'll come to his baseball practice this afternoon," I said. "It would really mean the world to him." I got up and set my cup in the sink. "One o'clock, at Old Settlers Field."

I turned to rinse out the coffeepot, listening to Ash go into the living room, his and Jude's voices mingling with the Transformers. Footsteps retreated up the front hall. The screen door squealed and slammed. The truck roared to life and pulled out. I thought about Lucy Grubbs, the woman who'd died in her kitchen of a broken heart, of how smart she was to get it over with all at once like that, instead of an inch at a time, in bits and pieces.

chapter seven

"At first I felt really good, for saying what I should've said a long time ago," I told Geneva. "But then I started feeling awful. I mean, you should've seen his face. It was like kicking a dog that's already down."

We pushed our carts side-by-side up the frozen-food aisle at the Super Wal-Mart. Try doing this at the Food King back home and you'd have needed the Jaws of Life to separate you, but here you could go two and three wide with the ease of a big-city freeway.

Ash had shown up for Little League practice, right on time, but he'd headed straight out onto the field to join my brothers, and he was still there when Gen and I left on our weekly grocery run. Bailey and Kit had offered to take the Hatch Brothers team for pizza after practice, so Geneva and I were enjoying a kid-free shopping experience, which meant the luxury of one-hundred-percent adult conversation as well as the possibility of reaching the checkout with at least a halfway decent ratio of fruits and vegetables to cookies and chips and sugar-coated cereals.

"Tell you what," Geneva said, reaching into the freezer case for a bag of broccoli. "Bailey showed up in our front yard for the first time in eight months without an excuse, I'd be tearing him a new you-know-what. And when I say 'excuse,' I mean watertight—like unconscious and tied to a tree in Bora-Bora. With video and signed depositions to prove it."

"Well, Ash had the unconscious part down, at least. He might have been tied up, too, for all I know. He probably would've liked that." We piled bags of frozen french fries into our carts, although the way our kids ate them, we should probably have just had truckloads delivered to our front doors wholesale. "You don't think I was too hard on him?" I said.

"Ha! What was that business about his self-respect, how it's not about you? Hell, yes, it's about you! He may not have been sitting around thinking, 'How can I hurt Lucy?' But he was just doing whatever he wanted, whatever made him feel good. He *wasn't* thinking about you, not for a minute. If that's not disrespecting you, I don't know what is."

"So you're saying my marriage is a sham and a lost cause."

"No, I'm not saying that. Y'all still love each other, for one thing. Any fool can see that." I sighed, slumping over my cart. "I just think you need to keep laying down the law. Either Ash is gonna toe in, or he's gonna keep on heading downhill until he finally hits something." I thought about George Jones and that bridge. "You just have to remember, it's his call. You know what Dove always says." Geneva stopped to check out a sale on Lean Cuisines, three for seven dollars. "I wonder if Bailey would eat pork lo mein."

"Dove says she wonders if Bailey would eat pork lo mein?"

Geneva put the package back and closed the freezer door. "Dove says all you can do is make sure you're standing where they can see you, holding out your hand."

We left to take our groceries home after agreeing to meet at Pizza Rita's to join our families. I got there first and found Bailey sitting among the ruins of several pizzas, sipping a beer and looking cheerfully exhausted. Jude and Lily were in an adjoining room playing video games, but Kit and everybody else had gone home. There was no sign of Ash.

"How did he seem to you?" I asked Bailey, reaching for a wedge of cheesy crust and biting off a hunk. Nothing like an hour's worth of shopping for healthful food items to work up a craving for greasy junk.

He shrugged. "Same old Ash. Maybe a little lower-key than usual. Did y'all have a big blow-out or something? He wanted to know if he could spend a couple nights at our place."

I set down my pizza crust. "What did you tell him?"

"I told him that if there was something going on between y'all that had him looking for a place to sleep, then I felt like it was probably in my best interest not to put myself in the middle of it. He just kind of stared at me and said, 'I guess that's a no.' Then he walked over and said something to Jude, and got in his truck and left."

I sat back, watching my son in his red-and-white Hatch Brothers shirt and matching cap, firing an imaginary Uzi at a screen full of bad guys while his mercenary little cousin egged him on. Ordinarily I tried to steer Jude away from the more violent games, the ones with bleeding bodies and blazing weapons, but some biological imperative seemed to keep pulling him in, and today I was too beat-down to put up a fight. Sometimes everything you did as a parent felt like a losing battle, that the whole point of having kids was to let them wear away at your principles until you gave in and let them turn into the natural-born psychopaths they really were.

Just then Geneva arrived, and I watched my brother's face light up at the sight of her, watched him set his beer bottle on the table and get up and fold her in his arms like they'd been apart for months and not hours, like he'd just gotten back from some long and tortuous journey to Bora-Bora. Any time I started to doubt the basic decency of humankind, especially the male half, all I had to do was look at my brothers. They'd never come home from a long weekend in Vegas with bite marks on their necks and their wallets missing. They'd never walk out of rehab and spend $40,000 on a pickup; they'd never be in rehab in the first place, because, while they liked a good time as well as the next guy, they also understood the meaning of moderation.

"What did Daddy say to you earlier, at the ball field?" I asked Jude as we were driving home. He'd pitched a fit about not being allowed to go back to Lily's, like he usually did on Saturdays, but I wanted him to have a bath and an early supper and bedtime tonight. We'd promised to go to Easter sunrise service with my mama, which meant getting up at five the next morning.

"He said to keep my head down."

"What?"

"He said that's why I can't throw the ball where I'm looking. 'Cause I don't keep my head down."

"I meant later on. When he was getting ready to leave. Did he say 'See you later,' or anything like that?"

"He said for me to be good and the Easter Bunny would bring me a surprise."

Visions of extravagant foolishness raced through my mind: a child-sized Easter basket brimming with stomach upset and tooth decay; thirty-foot inflatable plastic rabbits or, God forbid, a cage full of regular-sized live ones.

"Mama?"

"What, baby?"

"Jason Marchman said there's no such thing as the Easter Bunny. He said it's just your mama and daddy hiding things in the night."

"Well, what do you think?"

"I think Jason Marchman smells funny. Like when Aunt Dove cooks cauliflower."

I smiled, and Jude started to laugh, a big, openmouthed, machine-gun laugh. He loved to crack himself up; nothing made him so happy as being the life of the party.

"It's like Granny says," Jude said, serious again. "Just because we can't see Jesus doesn't mean He's not there. Same with the Easter Bunny, right?"

I thought about trying to explain the difference, but the more I thought about it, I wondered what the difference was, especially if you were six years old. What was faith, anyway, but belief in a thing for which there was no proof?

"Mama?"

"Yes, Jude."

"How come the Easter Bunny brings us presents, but Jesus doesn't?"

"Well . . . Jesus gave us the gift of Eternal Life." I shuddered at how much I sounded like my mama.

"What's that?"

"It means you go to heaven when you die."

Jude made a face in the rearview. "I'd rather have candy."

I suppressed a smile, flipping on my signal for the turn onto Little Hope Road. "Better not let your granny hear you say that."

"I bet Daddy will bring me some," Jude said excitedly. "I bet the Easter Bunny will give lots and lots of candy to Daddy for me. I bet he's waiting at my house right now!"

He wasn't, though—not the Easter Bunny or Ash, either one. He didn't come for supper, or for Jude's bath or prayers or his bedtime story. It was all I could do to persuade Jude to let me turn out the light at eight-thirty. He kept insisting Ash would be there any minute, that we just needed to read one more page, to stay up a few minutes longer.

He'd had a big day, though, and the pull of sleep was too much for him. I sat beside him for a few minutes in the dark, my hand resting lightly on the blanket, listening to his breathing deepen and slow. Once I was sure he'd drifted off, I went and straightened up the kitchen, made myself a cup of tea and drank it. I laid out my dress for the next morning. Just before turning in for the night, I went out and stuck a new bulb in the porch light—a hundred and fifty watts, bright enough for any lost soul to see, should one happen by in search of shelter. All night long it shone in my bedroom window, until I rose at five the next morning and shut it off. It was still dark out, but I knew by then nobody was coming.

I WOKE JUDE and we put on our best dress-up clothes and went to sunrise service at First Baptist with Mama. We weren't regulars, like she was, but it *was* Easter, and Jude liked it if nothing else for the sheer spectacle of the thing, the pews jammed with folks in suits and rustly dresses and fancy hats, the rousing organ music, Reverend Honeywell in his white-and-gold stole, his yellow hair like a crown, holding up his hands and exhorting us to go therefore and make disciples of all nations, baptizing them in the name of the Father and the Son and the Holy Ghost.

Afterwards we crowded into the fellowship hall for cookies and punch with our fellow worshipers. "Lucy, dear, how *are* you?" I must've heard it a hundred times, all those church guild ladies sidling up to grip my hand moistly between theirs and peer into my eyes. Like I didn't know what they were really up to: trying to see if they could tell by looking at me whether Ash and I were truly together again, in the biblical sense.

Then we went back to Dove's. Geneva and Bailey and Lily came by after services at their own church, and the kids hunted for Easter eggs in the backyard, and we all sat down together at the dining room table for roast lamb and new potatoes and lemon pound cake.

It was midafternoon before Jude and I finally got home. Ash's truck wasn't in the yard when we pulled in, and I was glad. I knew I was supposed to feel all pure and righteous because Christ was risen, but the past couple of days had worn on me, and all I was wondering was how I could get Jude to entertain himself for an hour or two so I could lie down and take a nap.

I was hanging up my dress when I heard Jude hollering from the back porch. "Mama! Come look! The Easter Bunny's been here!"

I walked through the kitchen in my slip, anticipation and dread making my head pound. Even so, I had the breath knocked out of me by what I found: a travel trailer sitting in my backyard.

A shiver moved up my spine. I remembered a story I'd heard in town the week before, about a botched drug bust over in Morris County. The deputies and the feds had been staking out the operation for months, a couple of brothers known to cook up a particularly potent form of methamphetamine out of an old trailer deep in the woods on the Cade County line. But after hundreds of hours of surveillance and paperwork, when the law finally showed up to take the brothers down, not only were they gone but the trailer was, too, literally overnight, nothing left but a clearing and a set of tire tracks. Every neighbor within ten miles was questioned, but nobody'd seen a thing, or would admit to it, anyway. For all intents and purposes, that trailer had vanished into thin air.

Jude unlatched the screen door and ran down the back steps and into the yard, still wearing his church pants and his clip-on tie.

"Stay away from there, Jude!" I called.

"But I want to see!"

"Don't touch anything! We don't know whose it is or how it got there!"

I went into the hall and picked up the cordless phone.

"Nine-one-one. What is your emergency?"

It was an excellent question, one I should probably have thought about how to answer before I'd dialed.

"Hi, Luther," I said. "It's Lucy Hatch. Farrell," I added.

"Oh, hey, Lucy. How's it going?"

"Pretty good. And you?"

"Oh, you know—can't complain."

"I saw your mama in church this morning. She sang the solo."

"Yeah, she's been practicing for weeks. How'd she do? She was worried about hitting the high notes."

"No, she did fine. It was real inspiring."

"Good, good, that's good." A silence fell. "You called nine-one-one to talk about my mama?"

"No. I—well, I don't know how to describe this, exactly."

Luther's voice dropped into a professional register. "Everything you say here is strictly confidential."

"There's a trailer in my yard."

"A traitor?"

"Trailer. A travel trailer. Like—you know. Those two brothers over in Morris County were staying in."

"You mean the meth trailer? The one that disappeared?"

"Well, I don't know that it's the exact same one. But I—"

"How'd it get there?"

"I'm not sure," I said, although I was beginning to have a sneaking suspicion. "I just got home from church and found it."

"Is there anybody in it? Did you look inside?"

"Well, no, Luther—that's why I called you."

"Hey, Marjo!" Luther called out. "Guess what? The meth trailer done showed up in Lucy Hatch's yard!"

I heard a flurry of conversation on the other end, and then the sheriff came on the line, her voice gruff and businesslike: "Lucy? Marjo Malone here."

I was beginning to regret my haste in calling the law. "Hey, Marjo. I'm sorry I bothered y'all. This is probably a bunch of fuss about nothing."

"Well, look—is there a trailer in your yard or isn't there?"

"Yes. Yes, there is."

"And it's not yours?"

"I think I'd know whether I owned a trailer or not."

"Can you describe it for me?"

"Hang on." I carried the phone to the back door, covered the mouthpiece with my hand. "Jude! What did I tell you? Get away from there!" I went out onto the step and squinted. "I don't know," I said to Marjo. "It looks like a travel trailer. I guess eighteen, maybe twenty feet long? It's kind of off-white. Or maybe it's just dirty. I don't know what else to tell you." What kind of distinguishing marks were we talking about, anyway—moles, scars, maybe a Japanese dragon tattoo?

"Have you gone inside?"

"I have not and will not. Look, I have a feeling I know who's— "

"Dewey and me'll be there in fifteen minutes. Just leave things the way you found 'em—we might need to preserve evidence."

"Evidence?" I said.

But she was already handing the phone back to Luther. I heard her tell him, "This I gotta see."

MARJO MALONE HAD been sheriff in Cade County for three years, ever since her predecessor, Bill Dudley, retired. The gossips at the DQ and the café were of two minds as to how she got elected: either ability and experience outpaced eccentricity with voters, or her opponent for the position, longtime deputy Dewey Wentzel, really was that universally and deeply reviled.

To be fair, Marjo wasn't a true eccentric, not in the time-honored, Deep East Texas tradition. What she was was pushing fifty, tall and square-shouldered with a white skunk-stripe in her dark hair, given to wearing bright red lipstick and earrings shaped like little silver pistols dangling from her pierced ears. Marjo had never married, which would in itself have made her suspect, even without her bone-rattling voice and hard stare and Marshal Dillon swagger. But she was the daughter and granddaughter of Texas Rangers; it was her granddaddy's Colt revolver swinging in a leather holster off her hip that, when push came to shove, carried more weight with the citizens of Cade County than the rumors that she'd been seen sipping beers in a roadhouse with a good-looking female gym teacher from Mount Pleasant. In three years Marjo had done more than Bill Dudley had in ten to clean up the drug labs in and around Cade County. She loved to go on the TV news and talk about throwing the book at drug dealers, to peer into the camera with her flinty eyes and talk about locking them up and throwing away the key. She'd done it, too, personally sending at least a dozen small-time dealers to county lockup and one or two on down to Huntsville. There was nothing better to whet Marjo's whistle on an otherwise quiet Easter afternoon than the prospect of a good bust. As I watched her climb out from behind the wheel and stand adjusting her holster in my side yard, I was torn with relief that she'd showed up and would take control, and feeling like I'd better have something here that would make the trip worth her while.

"It's back here," I said, leading Marjo around the side of the house while Dewey stayed out front to radio for backup. "There," I said, pointing, like she couldn't see perfectly well with her own eyes what was in the middle of my yard.

"Huh," she said, her hand still riding lightly on her holster. "It's a trailer, all right."

The back door of the house opened and Jude came pounding down the steps in his shorts and bare feet. "Look what the Easter Bunny brought me, Sheriff Marjo!" he called.

He started to dart past me, but I reached out and grabbed his arm and pulled him to me as Marjo approached the trailer.

"Is that it?" I called. "Is it the meth trailer?"

She held up her hand and with the other rapped on the metal door. It was a reach, even for a tall woman. Somebody, however, had taken the time to lay a couple of cinder blocks as makeshift steps, and she climbed those and knocked again, then reached for the knob and turned it. The door swung open easily.

"Huh," she said again, and spoke into her two-way radio. Then she leaned inside, sticking her head and shoulders over the doorjamb. "Hey!" she called. "Hello? Anybody home?"

Dewey came scuttling around the side of the house on his stubby little legs, puffing and drawing his gun. "I got you covered, Marjo!" he yelled. You could tell he'd been waiting his whole twenty years in law enforcement to do that. She disappeared inside the trailer. Dewey crept forward, his gun trained in front of him but wobbling so bad that if something had jumped out from the doorway, he'd have fired right into the cinder blocks.

Then Marjo reappeared, holstering her gun. "Put that away," she said to Dewey. "The place's empty. Where's your flashlight? My dang battery's dead."

He handed his over and they went inside together, following the wavering beam of light. Marjo came out finally, scowling and shaking her head.

"It ain't the one we're lookin' for," she said.

"How do you know?"

"Serial number," she said, and showed me a little notebook she carried in her pocket. "But I knew soon as I walked in we wasn't talkin' about no meth trailer. This one's old, but it don't stink. Meth stinks, you know—it ain't somethin' you can cover up with a can of Lysol. Plus the folks that cook it ain't usually too big on housekeeping." She stuck the notebook back into her pocket. "The bad news is, whose is it and how'd it get here?"

A white Chevy pickup turned the corner of the house and pulled into the yard in a plume of red dust.

"Actually," I said to Marjo as Ash alighted from the truck with a spring in his step, sipping from a can of Pepsi, "I've got a pretty good idea."

"Daddy!" Jude shouted. "The Easter Bunny came, just like you said!"

"You like what he brought you, buddy?" Ash said. "I told you it'd be a surprise."

"I can't believe you," I said. "You moved a trailer in here, in my backyard, without even asking me?"

"Well, now, Lucy," Ash said mildly, "I didn't see much point in asking you, seeing's how you'd have just pitched a fit and told me no."

"I *am* telling you no! You need to get it out, right now!"

"Hold up a sec, folks," Marjo said. "Somebody want to clue me in here?"

"This is Marjo Malone," I said to Ash. "The new sheriff."

"Ash Farrell," he said, sticking out his hand. "Pleased to meet you."

"I know who you are," she said. "We got a file downtown on you this thick." She held up her thumb and forefinger.

"Down—? Oh, right. Speak of the devil. It's Deputy Dawg."

Dewey emerged from the trailer, his hand on his gun belt. "Hey, Farrell," he said. "I heard you was back. I took a call on a stolen truck last night, matches the description of the one you're driving. You got proof of ownership?"

"Look, y'all want to stop the pissing contest and cut to the chase here? You know something about this trailer?" Marjo said.

"Yeah, I know something about it," Ash said. "It's mine. I bought it."

"You bought it where?" I said. "From who?"

"Ed Ruscheka's place, out on 1841. Paid four thousand cash for it. See? Here's the bill of sale." Ash produced a slip of paper from his jeans pocket and handed it to Marjo, who skimmed it and handed it to me.

"Well, I don't care if you did buy it fair and square," I said. "You can't just haul it out here and set it up in my yard without asking me. He can't, can he?" I asked Marjo.

"Depends. Who owns the property?"

"I do," Ash said.

"We both do," I corrected. "Texas is a community property state. That means what's half his is half mine. Right?" I looked to Marjo to confirm this.

"Well, yeah, but it works both ways. What's half yours is half his. So he's pretty much got just as much right to put a trailer on the property as you would, if you'd thought of it first."

"I wouldn't have thought of it first! I don't want it there! It's ugly and it—well, you can't just set up a trailer without electricity and water and all. What were you planning on doing about that?"

Ash looked smug. "Matter of fact, there used to be a trailer right here, in this very spot. I lived in it for a year and a half while I was building the house. There's already wires for the electric, and I can run a pipe out to your septic. It'll take me a day, maybe two, to get everything hooked up, and I'll be good to go."

"I don't believe it," I said. "There's got to be a zoning law, something."

Marjo shook her head. "You could go over to the county tomorrow and look up the plot records, but I'm doubting it. A spread this size, what, five, six acres? Rural, mostly wooded—outside the city limits? Gonna be pretty tough to put restrictions on it."

"You mean I could put whatever I wanted out here and it would be okay? I could build a meth lab or a whorehouse, and there'd be nothing you could do about it?"

"Drug labs and whorehouses is against the law," Marjo said. "But if you wanted to open, say, a tool-and-die shop, or an antiques barn, we'd have no say in the matter. Same goes for your living arrangements. You could build a whole dang trailer park out here, invite all your friends and relations. Long as what you're doing ain't hazardous or illegal, or it ain't disturbing the peace, it's your business."

"Don't give him any ideas," I said. I stared angrily at Ash, who gazed benignly back.

"You're the one said I couldn't sleep in the house," he said. "I'm just playing by your rules."

The sheriff gave a gut-deep sigh, a sigh that said she knew where this was headed and what's more, she'd heard it all before. "Y'all want to do me a favor? Wrangle this out on your own. I'm gonna head on back to town and get me some supper."

"What about the paperwork on that truck?" Dewey Wentzel said, but Marjo motioned at him with her head, and he gave Ash one last, fuming look and followed her off around the house.

Ash scooped up Jude in his arms. "Looks like it's just you and me, buddy," he said. "Everybody else is pissed off."

I turned and went into the house, letting the screen door slap shut behind me, took a can of Coke out of the icebox and popped the tab, then stood for a second at the kitchen window, holding the can against my forehead. My favorite view, of the woods beyond the house, was gone, replaced by a hulking metal box on wheels. Lord only knew what the inside was like; I pictured peeling linoleum, flimsy paneling, faulty wiring, raw sewage floating in the yard. Worst of all, I pictured Ash coming and going, living his life by his own rules not fifty feet from my back door, and not a thing on earth I could do about it.

Well, there was one thing. I marched down the hall to the linen closet and rummaged around until I found an old baby blanket of Jude's, then took a hammer and some tacks from the kitchen drawer and nailed it over the window.

I climbed down from the chair, eyeing the makeshift curtain with its absurdly cheery pastel colors and border of little marching ducks. It wasn't much of a screen, and the satisfaction of pounding in the nails was already wearing off by the time I heard Jude come in the back door and start tossing things around in his bedroom.

"Jude!" I called, but he didn't answer me. I put the hammer back in the drawer and walked to the door of my son's room. He was on the floor stuffing things willy-nilly into his backpack. I watched plastic dinosaurs go in, a couple of Hot Wheels racing cars, his Spider-Man pajamas. "What are you doing?" I asked.

"I'm going to live in the trailer with Daddy!"

"You are not."

"Yes, I am. I can sleep in his room. He said so!"

"Jude, listen to me. Daddy doesn't— Well, first of all, there's no lights or water in the trailer. That means no way to cook supper, or take a bath or wash dishes. . . ." I saw I needed to take another tack. "No TV to watch cartoons on. And how will you see to play or read your books?"

"We'll have fire," Jude said. "Like in olden times!"

"You can't build a fire in a trailer," I said. "I bet there's no air-conditioning, either. Did you think of that? Summer'll be here before you know it."

"Air-conditioning's for sissies," Jude said. He sounded so much like my brothers, I would have laughed if I hadn't been so mad.

I left him there, happily packing for his adventure, and went out the back door and across the yard to the trailer. The door was wide open. I stuck my head in, but couldn't see much. Even with all the windows open, it was dark and stuffy in there.

"Ash?" I called.

"Back here."

I made my way down a short hall to the bedroom. The place had a musty, ghostlike feel, something I couldn't put my finger on, like bits and pieces of all the lives that had played out between these walls had been left behind, covering everything with a sheer glaze of hopelessness. There wasn't a lick of furniture, nothing but a bedroll and a red plastic milk crate inverted to serve as a table.

"Welcome to my humble abode." Ash had emptied the contents of his duffel bag on the floor and was sorting things into piles: clothes, toiletries, a gold frame with a picture of me holding Jude as a toddler, both of us smiling in the Tennessee sun.

"You know, I bet I can get somebody out here to certify you," I said. "If this doesn't qualify as insanity, I don't know what would."

"Go on ahead. Maybe you'll have better luck than you did getting me arrested."

"Don't think I've given up," I said. "I plan to be at the courthouse when they open, first thing in the morning."

"You heard what the sheriff said. Show me a legal document that says I can't do what I want on my property, I'll get off." He shook the wrinkles out of a shirt and dropped it on a stack. "Of course, if you'd just let me in the house in the first place, we wouldn't be having this conversation."

I stuck my head into the tiny bathroom: toilet, lavatory, a showerhead, and a drain in the middle of the floor. "Ash, what are you doing?"

"Looking for that red flannel shirt of mine," he said. "I could've sworn I had it when I left Nashville."

"That's not what I'm talking about."

"Oh." He smiled. "You're talking about my *intent*."

"Don't bullshit me. It's bad enough, you just dropping in out of the blue after eight whole months without any kind of rational excuse. But this"—I waved my arm around the room—"this is taking it to a whole new level."

"Let's just say I'm reassessing my priorities," Ash said. "Is that rational enough for you?"

"Meaning what?"

"Meaning that my life's turned into a country-western song. I lost my job, I lost my wife—"

"And you're drunk and living in a trailer. Congratulations. Except for prison, I think that covers all the bases." I looked out the back window. My old view of the dogwoods and pines was Ash's now. "So if you're not playing music anymore, what? You're just going to sit out here in the woods and stare at your belly button?"

"I wouldn't be the first. Ever hear of a guy named Thoreau?"

"Did you tell Jude he could move in with you?"

"Not in so many words. I said he could stay with me whenever he wanted."

"Well, for the record, he can't."

"Hey, I'm gonna get the place cleaned up good. Get a little furniture. And once the electric and the plumbing are hooked up—"

"This isn't about lights and water, or sleeping in a bedroll. It's about your drinking. I won't have Jude living with it—not in Nashville, not in my house, not in a trailer in my backyard. I've done the best I could the past few years not to turn him against you, but every day you keep this up, you're pushing me further and further." Ash seemed to be examining a particularly fascinating whorl in the fake wood paneling. "He thinks you hung the moon, Ash. Why can't you live up to that? Why won't you even try?" I turned and let myself out of the trailer and back into the yard.

On the screen porch I met Jude coming out dragging his backpack, which was too heavy to carry.

"Hold up a minute," I said. "We need to talk."

"I can't," he said. "I'm going to Daddy's."

"Well, that's what I want to talk to you about, see," I said. "He's not quite ready for you out there."

"That's okay," Jude said. "I can sleep on the floor."

"Jude, listen to me. Daddy and I have a deal. And until Daddy holds up his part of it, then he can't have any company in the trailer. Understand?"

"No," Jude said. "What kind of deal?"

"I can't tell you that. I'm sorry. It's just between him and me."

Jude's eyes welled with tears. He dropped the backpack.

"But he *said*!" he wailed, his voice quavering up and down like scales on a piano. "He said I could come whenever I wanted!"

"But he forgot to ask me first."

"I don't like you!" Jude shouted, running off down the hall. "I think you're very mean, and Daddy thinks so, too!" He slammed his bedroom door. Then, for good measure, he opened it and slammed it again.

I did what I often did in times of stress, which was to close my eyes and picture myself at Faye's. I breathed deep, filling my lungs with the imaginary, comforting scents of roses and gardenias, hyacinths and lilies, eucalyptus, raffia, the deflated Mylar balloons stacked on the counter waiting for a turn at the helium tank to send them airborne. Truth be told, I felt grounded at Faye's in a way I never did in quite the same way anyplace else. There I could still conjure a remnant of who I used to be, the widow who'd walked in that door seven years before and asked for a job like she did it every day, who'd let herself be watched and wooed in front of the whole town by a handsome carpenter in a white pickup truck. I'd had nerve then, or at least a kind of energy that passed for nerve, and now I missed that person. I missed her innocence, her dumb hope. I wanted to pull her aside and warn her about the long and heartbreaking list of things she didn't see coming. Oh sure, I'd tell her, right now it's all slow dances and sweet whiskey kisses. But someday there will be lost weekends, raised voices, doors slamming in the night. Someday there'll be a trailer in your yard.

chapter eight

The trailer, it turned out, was only the beginning. When I got home from work on Monday, there were also a backhoe and a pumper truck. I stood on the screen porch watching Ash and a man I didn't know supervise the backhoe operator, who had excavated part of the septic tank and several lengths of PVC pipe, along with a three-foot-high pile of red dirt.

The septic work took two full days, though I had only Jude's sketchy narrative for details, since I was avoiding questioning Ash directly. The third evening, when I arrived home, the hole in the backyard was not only filled in but neatly graded over—we'd never had any grass to speak of in the first place, thank goodness—and inside the trailer, lights burned in every window.

"Well, I'll be damned." As I watched out the kitchen window, Ash wrangled an orange vinyl dinette chair off the tailgate of his pickup and up the cinder-block steps.

Geneva elbowed me aside so she could get a good view. Bailey had taken the kids to Little League, and, against my wishes, she'd come out to the house bearing a big care package for Ash full of nonperishable foodstuffs and secondhand dishes and household supplies.

"Hey, he's still my brother-in-law," she said. "Anyway, Lucy, aren't you dying to see what he's done with the inside?"

"I've *seen* the inside. Trust me, the best way to improve it is to take a torch to it. Or a pickax. Did you bring one of those?" I poked around in the cardboard box. "Easy Cheese," I said. "Now there's a wholesome dietary essential."

"Fine," she said. "I'll go check things out, bring back a full report. On second thought, maybe I'll just keep it to my— Hey. Who's that?"

I set down the canned cheese and moved back to the window just in time to see a willowy figure coming out Ash's front door in Levi's and broken-down boots, tossing back a hank of long, black hair like she was cracking a whip. Ash, in the bed of the pickup, handed down a second chair to the woman, who hoisted it smartly.

"Jesus Christ," Geneva said. "It's Heather Starbird."

Heather Starbird was one of those tough, sexy girls who looked like they should be driving a forklift or wrestling a live crocodile on the Discovery Channel. She and her boyfriend, Tripp Redmond, had moved to Mooney while we were living in Nashville, two or three years before, but they'd quickly become minor local legends, and so, when I came back to town, I became aware of her by reputation, would see her drive by in her old wood-paneled Buick wagon and think, *Oh, there goes Heather Starbird,* even though I'd never had occasion to meet her. Heather cleaned houses and commercial buildings for a living, while Tripp had a lucrative business repairing air-conditioning in automobiles until an even more lucrative sideline in marijuana farming brought him to the attention of Sheriff Marjo, who sent him off on a two-year, taxpayer-sponsored vacation to the Department of Criminal Justice in Cherokee County. Without Tripp, everybody expected Heather to disappear quietly, but she'd stuck around, looking vacant and mysterious as she drove her wagon from one job to the next, her ropy black hair flying out the window. There were all kinds of stories about her, that she was one-quarter Cree Indian, that you could see old needle tracks inside her arms if you looked hard enough, that she was just hanging around waiting for the right time to try to break Tripp out of prison.

"What's she doing here?"

"Moving furniture?" Geneva said.

"How old is Heather Starbird, anyway?" I said. I couldn't help noticing the delineation of her triceps, the tanned ribbon of skin between her jeans and her green tank top as she carried the chair up the steps.

"I dunno—thirty?"

"You're sweet," I said, "but there's no way that girl's a day over twenty-five." We watched as Ash carted a small table from the pickup and in through the front door. He met Heather coming out, and they did one of those laughing after-you, no-after-*you* tangos.

"Well, you know how it is. Skinny girls look older."

"Right." Heather stood on the cinder blocks, twisting her hair into a knot at the back of her neck, her long legs planted shoulder-width apart.

"I mean, look at her! Those hipbones are like doorknobs."

"Is this supposed to be making me feel better?" I said.

"Come on, Lucy. There's not a chance on God's green earth Ash has got something going on with Heather Starbird. It's right in your backyard, for heaven's sake!" It sounded like Geneva was trying to convince herself as much as me. "Maybe he hired her to do some cleaning for him."

"That must be it."

"Well, I'm not standing around here guessing. Give me that box."

"You can't go out there!"

"Why not? It's a free country."

I stood at the window watching Geneva cross the yard, watched Ash greet her with a kiss on the cheek, watched him take the box from her and set it on the step and introduce her to Heather, who immediately went back indoors, leaving Ash and Geneva out front to chat for a minute or two before she, too, followed Ash inside.

I turned and went into Jude's room and started picking up dinosaurs and putting them in his toy box, even though I knew I'd catch an earful from him when he got home and found I'd moved them. Then I went back into the kitchen, took a package of hamburger meat out of the freezer, and set it on the drain board. Through the window I saw Heather sitting on the tailgate of Ash's truck, swinging her legs and smoking a cigarette. Ash and Geneva came outside, and Heather flicked her butt into the dirt and stood up, brushing her hands on the seat of her jeans as Geneva walked back toward the house.

I hurried down the hall to my bedroom. "Lucy?" Geneva called as she came in the door.

"Back here!" I grabbed a pile of dirty laundry off the chair in the corner to make myself look busy.

"You don't fool me for a minute," Geneva said, coming into the bedroom. "I saw you standing there with your nose up against the kitchen window."

"Don't you need to run along?" I said. "Your family will be home any minute."

"I was right," she said, taking a seat at the edge of the bed. "She's cleaning the place for Ash. The guy he bought the trailer from gave him her name." And even if he hadn't, Ash would have found her anyway. A sexy, black-haired girl with track marks, a boyfriend in prison, and a pot farm—they probably broadcast satellite signals to each other, something beyond the range of the ordinary human ear.

"The furniture came from one of her clients," Geneva went on as I started sorting the laundry. "Ash happened to mention his place wasn't furnished, and Heather told him about this lady she works for down near Kildare whose renter moved out and had some stuff she wanted to get rid of. Ash got the whole lot for thirty bucks—a couple of chairs, an end table, a chest of drawers, even a mattress."

"Good for him," I said. "Looks like he'll be needing it."

We heard Ash's truck start up, and Geneva and I moved over to the window and watched it roll slowly past the house on its way out to the main road, Ash at the wheel, Heather in the passenger seat, smoking and staring out at nothing. "Must be Happy Hour," I said.

Geneva turned to me and shook her head. "Don't you ever give anybody the benefit of the doubt?"

"Anybody, yes. Ash, no."

"Want to let Jude sleep over tonight? It'll save you a trip back to town."

I put his pajamas and a clean set of school clothes in a shopping bag, and Geneva took them and drove away. I stuck the hamburger back in the freezer. Without my son to tend to, I had the whole evening to do whatever I wanted. I could scramble an egg for my supper, clean house, balance my checkbook. Better yet, I could lie in the tub eating Rocky Road ice cream and reading *Cosmopolitan* till I turned into a prune. I stood gazing out the kitchen window at the lights burning from the windows of the trailer, and saw that Ash had left Geneva's box sitting on the cinder-block steps. It would serve him right, I thought, if I went over and decorated his new place from end to end with Easy Cheese.

I poured myself a glass of iced tea and carried it out onto the front step. The evenings were getting longer, and the air had a sweetness to it, a blend of pine and sun and good red dirt. There's a saying in Texas that springtime is nothing but two or three mild days between winter and summer, but when it was here, it had a way of tricking you into believing it would be endless. Or maybe I knew better, but wanted to believe it anyway. If I hadn't had a problem with wishful thinking, I wouldn't have been where I was in the first place. A bird cried out in the deep woods, and I thought about Hank Williams and his whippoorwill, his midnight train whining low. Maybe it was true that some lights were meant to burn brighter but shorter than others, and the rest of us were left to go on fumbling in the dark as best we could. I had to admit, I missed that light. I wondered if Ash had come back to East Texas because he missed it, too.

A vehicle turned in off the FM road, headlights bobbing and twisting through the trees toward the house. I thought if I kept still, Ash might not see me sitting there, but the lights, instead of heading around the side of the house, swung into the front yard. There was enough daylight left to see that this wasn't Ash's truck, but a sleek black sports car, a low-slung two-seater.

The engine died, and a man climbed out of the driver's seat, swiping a hand through his long, dark hair. Something about the gesture gave me goose bumps.

Then the passenger door opened, and I jumped to my feet, spilling my tea. When Denny was off in Nashville, or tooling around the countryside with her band, I couldn't stand to think about her sometimes because it made me miss her so much. But now, as I ran down the steps and pulled her into my arms, I let my feelings for her rush over me, warm and pure and restorative, like bathwater. I never gave a thought to the sports car or the squinting, handsome man. I was only thinking that she was here, making good on her promise to come down and straighten us out.

I stepped back and held my stepdaughter at arm's length, trying to see past who she'd become to what she'd once been. If there was a ghost of that teenager, it was buried somewhere inside this supple young woman with the fire-engine-red hair and skim-milk complexion, the faint spattering of freckles. She had on jeans and fancy hand-tooled boots and a cut-off T-shirt that read, IF YOU'RE NOT SORE, YOU HAVEN'T BEEN RIDING IN VEGAS. She looked good as a redhead. We were almost exactly the same height. Through some weird kismet, she'd come to look like she could be my real daughter, by birth and not just happenstance.

It wasn't just the hair, though, that made her look different. I couldn't put my finger on it until she stuck out her left hand and I saw the diamond band winking there like a miner's headlamp. Then I knew. It was love that had changed her, that lit her up like candles inside her skin.

"Oh, my Lord! You're *engaged*?"

"Guess again."

"Not . . ."

Denny turned and motioned to the man, who came loping around the car, and hooked her arm through his.

"Say hello to Mr. and Mrs. William Butler Culpepper the third!" She laughed, her cheeks flushed, her dark blue eyes burning. She looked a little unhinged to me, not just with love but with a recklessness I recognized from Ash's end of the gene pool. "Will, this is my stepmom, Lucy Farrell."

"Pleased to meet you," Will said in a low, pulled-taffy voice, blinding me with his teeth. No wonder Ash wanted to kill him. It was probably like looking into a mirror, like seeing the reflection of your own snakeskin heart.

"Well—my goodness!" I took the hand he extended. "Welcome to the family. This is so sudden!"

"We had a few days off in Vegas, so we, well, we just did it!" Denny said breathlessly, her words tumbling over each other. "I mean, when it's right, why wait? You know yourself what that's like."

I started to say that I hardly thought my situation was a shining example. But Denny was gazing at Will like his face was a magnet, something she couldn't tear her eyes away from. I could have stood there yammering till I was blue in the face and she wouldn't have heard me. It was too late for that; the damage was done.

"Where's Daddy?" Denny asked.

"It's a long story."

"What else is new?"

"Come back here and let me show you something."

I led the way around the side of the house, Denny's arm linked through Will's like a tow chain, chattering a mile a minute: about how they'd been playing craps at the casino at Caesar's Palace and Will had started winning and then kept on winning, and when the pot got to eight thousand, they'd cashed in and run over to Harry Winston and bought the ring, then hopped in a cab and gone straight to the Happy Together wedding chapel. I had to admit, it did sound madcap and romantic. But then, I knew firsthand all about madcap and romantic.

We rounded the corner into the backyard and Denny pulled up short, stopping her narration in midsentence. "What the hell is that?"

"Looks like a trailer," Will drawled. I glanced over at him to see if he was being funny, but there didn't seem to be an ironic bone in his body.

"I can see *that.* What's it doing here?"

Just then, the sound of another engine could be heard making its way up the road. As Ash's truck appeared around the side of the house, Denny threw up her arm and waved, and he pulled in next to the trailer and cut the engine.

He got out carrying two oversized plastic bags from Wal-Mart, dropping them on the running board as Denny hurried forward to give him a hug.

"Oh, Daddy," Denny said. "What are you *doing*? This is just so, so *crazy*!"

"I might ought to ask you the same thing, baby girl."

"I've been so worried about you! The people at the rehab called me when you took off. Didn't you ever stop to think about that? Couldn't you have just called and told me what you were doing?"

He smiled at his daughter and smoothed her hair. "You mean you were so worried about me, you drove all the way down here to check on me? Looks like you'd have more important things to do than that."

"Well, no, I . . . We just wanted to tell you in person."

"Tell me what?"

"Daddy, you remember Will." Her voice quavered a little.

"Be hard to live in Nashville any length of time and not know Will Culpepper." Ash looped his arm around Denny's neck and together they walked toward us, Ash giving Will the full brunt of his gaze. "I hear you're playing in my daughter's band now."

Will's Adam's apple rolled. "Yes, sir."

"Well, good. Maybe you can keep an eye on her for me. See, we have a deal, Denny and me. I made her swear on her life she'd never get mixed up with a musician. I promised her if she did, I'd have no choice but to chase him down and cut off his—"

"Daddy! He's kidding," Denny said to Will, slipping her arm through his again. "He's just trying to scare you."

"It's working," Will said, giving us all a shaky smile. For a second nobody said anything, and then, to my surprise, Ash laughed.

"Go ahead, lay it on me," he said. "Whatever it is y'all came down here for. All the way from—where?"

"Vegas," Denny said, and thrust out her hand. In the fading daylight, the diamond winked like a strobe.

"So I guess this means y'all are going steady?"

"We got married, Daddy," Denny said. "Day before yesterday, in Vegas."

Ash looked from Will to Denny to me, back to Will again. A blue vein pulsed at his temple.

"Well, hell. I wish she'd waited another twenty, thirty years, but since it's a little late for that . . ." He stepped forward and stuck out his hand. "You're a lucky dog, Will Culpepper. I hope you know it."

"Yes, sir."

"And you know who you've got to answer to if you don't treat her right."

"Yes, sir. I do."

Ash nodded, then turned to Denny and opened his arms. "I hope you're happy, baby girl," he said as they hugged. "You've made me feel about a hundred years old."

"I *am* happy, Daddy. You don't know how much." She broke free of Ash's embrace, dabbing her eyes with the back of her wrist. "So, we brought champagne, and we want to take everybody out honky-tonking. Tonight's Round-Up night, isn't it? I've been telling Will all about it. I thought we could all sit in."

Ash looked at his feet, then off toward the trailer.

"What?" Denny said. "What's going on?"

"Your daddy's taking a leave of absence from the music business," I said.

"Oh, bull," Denny said. "That old band of yours really used to tear things up. You know they'd be thrilled to death to see you."

"There's a little more to it than that," Ash said. From the look on his face, I wished I'd kept my mouth shut.

"Hey, remember Curly's?" I said. "Out at the lake, where we used to go for chicken-fried steak? They've got a great jukebox, and it's not so loud and crazy there. We'd have a chance to sit and get acquainted."

Denny stood scowling at her daddy. She knew something was up, but because of Will Culpepper, I guessed, her old antennae weren't working right and the signals were scrambled. "That sound good to you, Will?" I asked. "Could you go for a cold beer and a chicken-fried steak?"

Half an hour later we were in my Blazer, with the champagne in a paper bag under the seat, headed for the lake. Ash rode silently in front beside me and Will in back, while Denny leaned forward between the seats and talked: about Will, their wedding, the tour, Will again. I kept my eyes on the road and now and then made some vague comment, but I don't think she even noticed. Her face swam in the rearview, rosy and animated; she gave off happiness in waves, like a furnace. I couldn't help thinking about the summer she'd first come to stay with Ash and me, how some days you could barely pry five words out of her with a crowbar. It wasn't twenty miles to Curly's, but by the time we got there, if I'd had a dollar for every time she'd said Will's name, I could've bought a chicken-fried steak for everybody in the place.

"You call this a honky-tonk?" Denny said to me over her shoulder as we followed the hostess to a table. She and I had changed into dresses back at the house. Hers was short and loose, of flowered cotton, a sort of sexed-up *Little House on the Prairie* look, and her red hair switched in front of me as we crossed the room.

Curly's wasn't much to write home about, it's true, a prefab building with tables at one end and a jukebox and a linoleum dance floor at the other, a banner over a tiny platform announcing, KARAOKE TONIGHT! For years the place had been nothing but a rundown burger shack, but when the new owner, Roger

McCool, took over a few years back, he'd put in a bar and installed the karaoke machine to try to bring in a drinking crowd, which for the most part was a lost cause. Not that there weren't plenty of folks around who liked their whiskey and beer; but the locals tended to be farmers and blue-collar workers, who as a rule weren't the kind to stand up and belt out Whitney Houston tunes to a room full of their neighbors no matter how many sheets to the wind they got. Strictly speaking it was a private club, which meant you couldn't buy alcohol unless you had a membership, but anybody could get one at the door for five dollars, or you could bring your own bottle, like we'd done. Will opened the champagne, a pricey brand I remembered from our early, upwardly mobile days in Nashville, like a pro, twisting off the wire cage and easing out the cork with his thumbs and a gentle pop.

"Y'all celebrating something special?" the hostess asked as she brought a tray of glasses. Denny showed her ring, and the woman slipped an arm around Denny's shoulders and gave her a squeeze, even though they'd never seen each other in their lives and likely never would again. Will poured the bubbly and passed it around. "To happy ever after," Ash said, and cut his eyes at me. "Amen to that," Will seconded, and we clinked our rims together and drank. The fizz went up my nose and I sneezed, and everybody laughed. The hostess came back around with menus and a basket of cornbread and a round of Budweiser, on the house. We ordered chicken-fried steak plates, salads with ranch dressing, mashed potatoes and cream gravy.

"Man, I miss eating like this in Nashville," Will said as he buttered a square of cornbread. "Things there've gotten so uptown, seems like there's nobody left remembers real country cooking."

"Where are you from, Will?" I asked.

"Mississippi," he said, pronouncing it like a native, without the second syllable. "Little dot on the map called Hub. Not famous for much of anything, unless you count all the people like me who couldn't wait to get out."

"Your folks from there?"

He nodded. "My daddy used to run a cotton gin. Him and Mama retired a few years ago, moved to Gulfport."

"How long have you been playing music?"

"Pretty much all my life, I guess. I picked up my uncle's guitar when I was eight or ten. I wasn't that good, though, so I switched to bass when I was in junior high."

"Will writes songs, too," Denny said proudly.

"Have I heard anything of yours?" I asked. In Nashville, everybody was a songwriter. You'd be standing in the buffet line at a party and fall into conversation with some mousy-looking guy who, it would turn out, had written four number one hits for George Strait, or last year's Grammy Award–winning tune for Martina McBride.

"Not yet," Denny answered for Will, who was picking at the label on his beer bottle with his thumbnail. "But you will. The next record will have a couple of Will Culpepper originals."

"*Your* next record, you mean?" Ash said. We all looked at him. It was practically the first thing he'd said all evening.

"Will hasn't got his own deal yet," Denny said. "But all that's gonna change when folks hear what he can do." Ash opened his mouth, then glanced at me and shut it again.

"Speaking of music," I said, "why don't y'all see what you can find on that old jukebox?"

Denny and Will slid off their chairs and crossed the room and stood scanning the playlist on the old Select-O-Matic, their hands resting lightly on each other's waists in a way that gave me a pang. Will dropped in a handful of coins, and a few seconds later a velvety voice started to sing "A Rainy Night in Georgia," and the two of them moved out onto the dance floor and fell into a clinch. Ash and I sat silent for a while, watching the newlyweds.

"I don't know what kind of songwriter he is," Ash said, "but he's a hell of an actor."

"Maybe he's not acting," I said.

Ash flicked his eyes at me. "Trust me. He's gonna break her heart."

"And you know this how? Oh, right, I forgot. Takes one to know one. Isn't that what they say? Like you and your new friend Heather Starbird."

This time Ash's eyes fixed on me and stayed there.

"Look, you're the one who kicked me out of the house. Seems to me you gave up your right to criticize the company I keep."

We were interrupted by the waitress, who slapped down platters of meat and potatoes and gravy.

"Never mind," I said to Ash as she walked off. "Forget I said anything. I just want this to be a nice evening for Denny."

"I don't think you have to worry about that," Ash answered. Denny and Will continued to sway, melded into a single comma, on the dance floor. "Think we should tell them their supper's getting cold?"

"He's awfully good-looking, I'll say that for him," I said. "Not that that's necessarily a recipe for happiness or anything. I mean, look at you and me." I took a sip of champagne, but it was warm and flat. "Next time I think I'll just marry some fat old bald guy."

Ash smiled a half-smile. "Last I heard, you already had a husband."

"A piddly little detail."

Denny and Will came back to the table, flushed and sweaty-looking. For the first time it occurred to me to wonder where they were going to sleep that night. The only double bed in the house was mine, but the thought of the two of them together in my bed, married or not, made my stomach queasy.

Will ordered another round, and we ate and made small talk. The alcohol went straight to Denny's head, making her giggly and more talkative than ever, while Will drank steadily but silently, with no apparent effect. After the first beer and the champagne toast, Ash had switched to iced tea, which surprised me. Maybe he really was determined to prove he could control things, like he said. Or maybe he was saving up for later. I wanted to relax and enjoy myself, to bask in Denny's good mood, but I didn't like the way Ash kept staring at Will Culpepper across the table, the way Will kept his eyes down and didn't look back.

The waitress cleared our places, and Denny got up to use the ladies' room. A few minutes later I saw her over at the bar, talking to the owner. I'd gotten to know Roger McCool a little bit the last few months, ever since the first time Jude and I had stopped in for supper and he'd seen the karaoke setup. It was early, the place more or less empty, and Roger had been more than happy to demo the system for us, performing a soulful rendition of Charlie Rich's "Behind Closed Doors." Jude was exhilarated, and had to get up there and try it for himself that very minute. Ever since he could talk, almost, he'd had the ability to hear a song once or twice and remember every word and inflection, so the fact that he was too little to read the words off the monitor didn't faze him a bit; he climbed up on the platform and sang, "I'm a honky-tonk man and I can't seem to stop," like a veteran of the Grand Ole Opry. "Your boy's really something," Roger said to me as he delivered Jude along with two catfish platters to our table. After that, Jude begged to go to Curly's every time we left the house, but I tried to be careful about overindulging him. For one thing, he was impossible to live with afterwards, sulking and flouncing around like a runner-up on *Nashville Star.*

Suddenly Denny's amplified voice came through the speakers at the far end of the room, making the rest of us jump. "Testing one two," she said, and tapped the mike with her thumb, the sound reverberating in the small, high-ceilinged room.

Will Culpepper spun around in his chair. "Uh-oh," he said. Sure enough, Roger McCool was fooling with the controls of the karaoke machine, and Denny stood on the platform in her little prairie dress, swaying and grinning under a row of colored spotlights.

"Hey there," she said into the handheld mike. "How's everybody out there doin' tonight?" The only people present besides us were the staff and maybe half a dozen folks lingering over the remains of their supper, but Denny seemed to be under the impression she was onstage in Vegas.

"Y'all go on ahead with your business," she said. "I just thought I'd get up here and sing a song to my brand-new husband, Will Culpepper, who's made me feel like the luckiest girl on earth."

A few people clapped uncertainly. Denny tossed back her hair and nodded at Roger, and a prerecorded track started up, the old Otis Redding song "That's How Strong My Love Is."

She started out soft, almost tentative; but as the verses spooled out, her voice, like I'd heard it do so many times before, began to take on a force of its own. It was too much, really, for such a sweet little song; it was too big, not just her voice but what she was feeling, too big to be trapped inside pretty words about sunshine and rainbows. She didn't sing it like a love song, but like a sort of lament, laid out raw and bloody, stripped bare. It tore at my heart, hearing her; I wanted to run up and grab the mike out of her hand, to lead her outside and sit her down and say, "Now listen here. Don't give yourself up this way. No good will come of it. Save a piece back for yourself." But I, like the rest of the people in the room, sat listening, mesmerized.

When it was over, everybody applauded like crazy. Under the pink and blue lights, Denny stepped back and bowed. Then she took the mike again. "How 'bout another one? Any requests out there? Hey, maybe my daddy will get up here and join me. What do you say, folks? Can y'all give it up for Cade County's own Ash Farrell?"

More applause; faces swiveled in our direction.

Ash's chair scraped on the linoleum as he got to his feet. But instead of making his way toward the stage, he dropped his napkin on the table and turned on his heel and quickly strode across the dining room and out through the front door.

Will and I exchanged a glance, and wordlessly he got up and he headed for the stage. I could tell he was trying to talk Denny down and that she didn't want to hear it, that she was ready to stay up there and sing all night, with or without her daddy.

Eventually he succeeded in leading her back to the table. Her good mood had evaporated; she was red-faced and cranky.

"Y'all are nothing but a bunch of party poopers!" she said, pawing through the bottles on the tabletop, looking for one that still held a swig of beer. "I thought we were going honky-tonking!"

"Sit down a minute, sweetie," I said, and pushed a glass of water toward her. "Take a break."

"I don't want to take a break! This is supposed to be a party! Where's Daddy?"

"Denise. Sit down."

My use of her given name got her attention. "You, too, Will," I said. I felt a little bit sorry for Will Culpepper. I wondered when he'd hopped into that limo with Denny bound for the Happy Together wedding chapel if he'd had any idea what he'd be getting into.

"Look," I said. "It's probably not my place to be telling your daddy's business, but I think you ought to know. He lost his record deal. Tony Amate called him in the rehab and told him they're dropping him from the label."

"What?" Denny screeched. "They can't do that! It's—it's criminal!"

"I think so, too. But it *is* legal—some loophole in the contract. At least that's what Vern Bellamy says. He's supposed to be talking to his lawyer, but he didn't sound too hopeful."

"Vern Bellamy's a dickhead," Will said. "Everybody in Nashville knows that."

"Daddy's just got to find another manager and another label. Forget Arcadia and start over from scratch," Denny said.

"He says he doesn't want to play music anymore."

"Oh, right. He's gonna do what instead? He can't just lounge around a trailer in East Texas for the rest of his life." Denny seemed stone sober now. "Where'd he go, anyway?"

"He took off when you called him up onstage."

"Shit," she said. "He's probably halfway back to Mooney by now." She pushed back her chair, throwing her hair over one shoulder. "I'm gonna go find him. See if I can talk some sense into him."

"I don't think that's a good idea."

"Why not?"

I sat looking at her, trying to think where to start. Her daddy's love for her was only one point of a triangle along with pride and envy, and tonight, I knew, the talent and ambition he'd bequeathed her had already scraped a nerve.

"Because it's your honeymoon," I said instead, and stood up. "Y'all stay here, feed some more money into the jukebox, dance a little. I'll go see about your daddy."

chapter nine

I found Ash slumped against the front fender of my Blazer, one ankle crossed over the other, his eyes on the ground. He had to have heard me crunching toward him across the oyster shells, but he didn't look up till the last minute, till I was standing right in front of him.

"You all right?" I asked. It was a clear, cool night, a quarter moon along with a handful of stars tossed as carelessly as gamblers' dice across the dark blue sky.

He kicked a stray pebble with the toe of his boot.

"What are we doing here, Luce? Why, after everything we had going for us, are we sitting in a fucking karaoke bar in the middle of nowhere, listening to our daughter blow the roof off the joint for some asshole who doesn't even know what she's worth?"

"You don't know that. Why won't you give Will a break, for the time being, at least? They've only been married two days." Ash shrugged. "I don't think this is really about Denny and Will," I said. "This is about you."

He laughed sourly. "I guess I'm still trying to figure out how something I wanted so bad and worked so hard for for so long could turn out to be so different from how I expected it to be."

"How's that?"

"You really want the whole sad story?"

"Yes. I do."

He pulled in a breath, held it a second, then let it out again. "Okay. I always knew I had the goods. That I could write good songs and sing them the way folks wanted to hear them. I just thought the rest was automatic—that once I got to Nashville and got signed, I'd get a chance to put my music out there and I'd learn what I needed along the way, about all the stuff I didn't know, the business.

"But I guess I was dumb, or maybe just unlucky. It was like the train left the station without me. I mean, I could see my face up there on that train, but I never felt like I was in the driver's seat, you know? And by the time things slowed down enough for me to look around, I couldn't get my bearings anymore. It seemed like the farther along we went, the harder it got for me to recognize the territory."

He lifted his head and looked at me. "Go on," I said.

"It's like, on the one hand, all of a sudden you've got about five thousand new best friends, telling you how you're the greatest thing they've ever heard. Then at the same time there's all these other folks—the record company guys, the promoters—and they're smiling, like everybody else, and shaking your hand, but at the same time they're running these little calculators they have in their heads, tallying up their score sheets. It's like they're talking out of one side of their mouths but you never really know what they're saying.

"It got so I didn't know who to believe. On the one hand, I had a couple good records that did okay, got some good press.

And the live shows always went great, lots of folks coming out and having a big time, rocking the joint, singing along.

"But at the same time I felt like Arcadia was—I guess the word is 'disappointed.' Not that they said it, not in those words. There was just this sense of, of their not being in my corner anymore, of my having let them down. Because, for whatever reason—maybe I wore my hair parted wrong, maybe Tim McGraw or some other top dog put out a record the same day—I hadn't met their expectations. I went up there thinking I was gonna be the next big thing, and instead I turned out to be just—well, a pretty good songwriter with two good records and a few thousand fans."

"But that's something, isn't it? Isn't that how you build a career?"

"You'd think so, wouldn't you? That they'd take a chance on a new guy, bring him along, give him a chance to learn the ropes? And maybe in the old days, they used to. But it's not like that anymore. Now they want you to come roaring right out of the chute with the songs, the looks, the buzz . . . If you ain't got it, there's twenty guys right behind you who do, and one of *them* might be the one. It's not personal. Hell, it's not about *you* at all. It's about—" He pantomimed pulling the handle of an old-fashioned cash register.

"But look how much you accomplished!" I said. "Don't you know how many folks try to do what you did and don't have one-tenth that kind of success?"

"I didn't *want* one-tenth the success," he said. "You know me—I'm an all-or-nothing kind of guy."

"Why didn't you tell me?" I asked. "How was I supposed to know what was going on without your talking to me about it?

"You remember when we were just starting out, you and me, how I used to tell you it didn't matter whether you had the guts to do something, just so long as you could play the part? That acting like a thing's a fact is the first step toward making it come true?"

I nodded. "I just couldn't stand for you to know how far off track I'd gotten. Here I'd up and yanked you and Jude up by the roots and dragged you to Tennessee . . . It got so it was hard for me to be home after a while. Seeing you so sad, so homesick—don't try to tell me you weren't. Every time I walked in the door you had the phone glued to your ear, talking to your aunt or your sister-in-law. It just seemed like the harder I tried to figure out where I'd screwed up, the further from the truth I got."

We stood quiet for a while, listening to the wind in the trees, the sound of a powerboat on the lake across the highway.

"So you've decided to hang it all up?" I said. "To let go of everything you worked so hard to build up all these years?"

"I just don't think I've got what it takes anymore."

"Are you talking about the desire? Or the gift? Because the gift is still there, Ash. A bunch of assholes in suits can't take that away from you." He just shook his head and wouldn't look at me. "You know, this isn't like you at all. You've always been the most single-minded person I know. You set your sights on something and you went after it hell-bent. How can you let something like this knock you all the way off track? How did you get so cynical?"

"Have you heard one goddamn thing I've said? I feel like Tony ripped my guts out and left me twisting in the wind! Don't you think I'm allowed to feel a little bit *cynical*?" He bit down hard on the word, spat it out.

I didn't have an answer for him, though I knew what he meant. I remembered how I'd felt right after Mitchell died, how I'd gone through the early days of widowhood feeling like two people, like one of me was floating up near the ceiling and watching the other, a shadow of her old self, washing dishes, making beds, going through the motions down below. I'd felt it again when I'd left Ash in Nashville and come home to Mooney, waking up sometimes in the middle of the night with my head spinning, wondering, *How did I get here? Where did my old, good life go?* I never had Ash's grand ambition, but I knew how it was to feel adrift, all the usual touchstones gone.

The front door of the restaurant opened, and a couple came out with their arms draped around each other's waists, their voices low and laughing as they made their way toward a blue sedan.

I heard Ash's breath hitch, and without thinking twice about it, I turned toward him and put my hand to his face, cupping his jaw, feeling the chafe of week-old beard against my palm. I smelled the clean cotton of his T-shirt, the soap he'd showered with, his breath warm and whiskey-sweet, even though I hadn't seen him drink anything but beer.

His palm slid down the length of my arm, brushed my hip. A car pulled into the parking lot, its headlights capturing us briefly in its glare, and we stepped apart. I felt dizzy, whether from longing or relief or the champagne I'd drunk earlier, I didn't know.

"Don't ask me to go back in there, Lucy," he said. "I can't do it. I just can't."

"Wait here," I told him. "I'll get Denny and Will."

I WOKE THAT night in Jude's bed from a wisp of some forgotten dream, muddleheaded and cotton-mouthed, not sure at first where I was, and sat up, groping around in the dark, banging my hand against the nightstand as I reached for something, anything, familiar. It was Jude's smell that finally brought me back to earth, and I managed to locate the glowing face of the Big Ben clock beside his bed. A quarter to twelve; I'd only been asleep for an hour or so, after getting Denny and Will settled in my room. I'd drifted off still wearing my going-out dress, and could feel my hair tangled around my shoulders, eye makeup gluey under my eyes. I sat at the edge of the mattress for a minute, trying to remember what had woken me, but whatever it had been, real or imagined, it was gone.

I got up, letting the stiffness work slowly out of my joints, and moved into the kitchen without bothering to put on a light. I turned on the tap and ran cold, clear well water into my hand, drinking from my cupped palm, patting the last drops against my cheeks. Outside the window, the moon was hidden behind gossamer clouds, the trailer a pale shape against the dark woods. The thought of Ash, footsteps away but lost to me in some way I couldn't understand, made my chest ache. Why, I wondered, didn't we fight harder to hold on to the things that mattered? We tossed away human beings as casually as we threw out old newspapers, replaced them just as casually with the next day's version. How did our heart's desire, along with everything else, get to be so disposable?

Beyond the window, something moved. I blinked, lost it, then found it again—a ribbon of white, floating in the silvery light. My heart stuttered for a second. Just down the road from our house was an ancient cemetery, a tiny, fenced-in plot of tumbledown headstones more than a hundred years old, and even though Ash and Denny claimed to love it there, communing with spirits, the notion of one slipping over the fence and rambling around our property at midnight never failed to fill me with dread. It wasn't that I didn't believe in their right to coexist with the living; I just didn't particularly want to entertain one in my own backyard.

I made my way on tiptoe down the back hall and eased open the door. From inside the screen, I held my breath as I watched the white-clad shape move to and fro across the yard. As my eyes adjusted to the dark and I recognized the shape, it crossed my mind that it might have been easier dealing with a ghost than with the specter of who my living, breathing husband had become.

I pushed open the screen door and walked barefoot down the steps.

"Ash."

He turned at the sound of my voice, faceless above his white undershirt.

"I'm lost." His voice seemed to come from some hollowed-out place inside him.

"Lost?"

"I want to go home."

I moved closer, near enough to catch the smell of him, sweat and liquor and fear. "But you are home," I said. "This is where you come from. Right here."

"I can't feel myself, Lucy." He stretched one hand in front of him. "See this? I know it's mine, my hand, right there. But it doesn't feel like it belongs to me."

"Don't be silly. Of course it's yours."

"Yeah? How do you know for sure? I mean, did you ever wonder sometimes if maybe you died and you just don't know it? Maybe this is heaven, right here, right now."

I stepped toward him, took his hand in both of mine. It felt cold and stiff, and something flipped over inside me, like what he'd just said, crazy as it sounded, might be true.

"I don't know what to do. I want so bad to get back home, but I can't see the way. Everything's dark. It's so dark."

He bowed his head over our clasped hands, pressed them to his face, his tears running between our fingers, into my palms. The only time I'd ever seen Ash cry was when Jude was born, and never like this, like something huge and terrifying was coming up out of him, wave after wave, knees bent, shoulders heaving.

"Ash," I said. "Look at me." I took his face in my hands and tried to lift it, but his head, his pain, was too heavy. "*Look* at me."

Slowly he straightened, throwing back his head. This face—eyes swollen, grooves as deep as plow tracks at the corners of his mouth—wasn't the Ash I'd married, the handsome devil I'd watched grinning into spotlights from stages all over the country. But what hit me hard wasn't the strangeness of it, or the awfulness, but the blunt, unexpected truth, the realization that I was seeing past the surface to the real Ash, one I knew in some deep and unexplainable part of me, in my blood and my bones.

I looked into his eyes and felt something opening up in me, a channel of light, blooming in my chest and traveling down my spine, into my arms and legs, fingers and toes. He stretched out his hands toward me the way a child might reach for something irresistible, magical. Could he see it, the light in me? His hands settled lightly on my hips, and I slid my arms around his waist and let him pull me close, wrapping his arms around me as I pressed my face against his throat, breathing in the scent of him, feeling his breath in my hair.

Then my arms were around his neck and I raised my face to his and he was kissing me and I was kissing him back, our mouths closed at first and then open, tongues twining and teeth clacking against each other's as what had been forgotten became familiar again. I wasn't sure I trusted myself, if what I was feeling was pity or forgiveness or the pure intoxication of skin on skin.

We pulled out of the kiss for a second, looked at each other, then fell back into it, greedily this time, like conspirators who know exactly what they're up against, what's at stake. He drew me against him, the full length of our bodies pressed thigh to thigh as he ran his hands down my back in my dress, over my hips and my arms, his pelvis arched hard against mine. He seemed breakable, I thought, the bones in his face sharp, shoulder blades jutting beneath the taut casing of his skin. But the core of him felt as real, as solid, as it ever had. Ash had his own convoluted needs, things that were greater and part of a wider world than I could ever hope to understand. But this, for me, was the center of the universe. How had I forgotten that? How could I have let it go?

We stumbled backward in a clumsy lockstep, landing against the side of the pickup, my back against the wheel well and the hem of my dress rucked up over my hips as Ash leaned into me with all his weight and I pushed against him with all of mine. The scrape of his beard against my face and my neck was raw and thrilling, the familiar coarseness of his palms and calloused fingertips as he ran them up the insides of my thighs. A thousand warring thoughts flew through my mind, but none of them was able to penetrate the web of pure desire that spun itself around us, a tight-woven lattice of limbs and mouths, heat and breath, my legs coiling around Ash's hips as he hoisted me into his arms and carried me, in a matter of seconds, up the cinder blocks to the trailer, through the front door, and down the hall to the bedroom.

We fell onto the bare mattress, reaching inside clothes to wrangle with hooks and zippers. I was conscious of nothing but urgency, momentum, that to lose it would break the spell, and I willed myself to stay inside the feeling, to let go and take what I needed, to take Ash back to me. I managed finally to get my dress over my head, and lay back in bra and panties against the mattress as Ash moved over me, running his mouth from my jaw to my collarbone and the tops of my breasts, lifting them in his palms. With one thumb he hooked a bra strap off my shoulder and rolled the nipple free of its cup, bending to touch its hard tip with his tongue, sending a bolt of electricity through all my nerve endings; I made an animal sound deep in my throat, and pulled his head to me with both hands, holding it there, the ends of his hair sweeping my breasts as he nipped and sucked. It had been more months than I could count since Ash and I had made love, and I couldn't even remember the last time we'd been together this way, without any remnants of our messy history working its way in, just giving ourselves over to sensation, our bodies meshing together like ghost dancers who'd been doing this particular two-step since the beginning of time.

He sat up to skin his T-shirt over his head and peel off his jeans, then lay back beside me. I bent over him, kissing my way from his chest to his stomach, letting my hands roam his skin the way I had the first time I'd ever touched him, when, after fourteen years of marriage to a shy and modest man, such brazen nakedness was still a marvel to me.

He reached for me and hoisted me over him to straddle him, his hips arching under me, against the thin membrane of my panties. I sat up tall, tossing back my head, unhooking my bra and letting it drop beside the mattress. Pewter light streamed through the window, and in it I saw myself, breasts thrust out proudly, my hair falling loose around my shoulders and down my back. I looked, I thought, like some Nordic goddess on the prow of a ship. The thought made me laugh out of pure, foolish joy.

"What?" Ash asked, looking up at me.

"Juicy Lucy," I said, and laughed again at finding what I'd thought was a memory instead still real and alive, just waiting to be resurrected.

He smiled and slipped one finger, then another, inside the elastic of my panties, into the wet warmth there. "Ah," he murmured, pulling my face back to his with his free hand. And he kissed me again, his tongue in my mouth, his fingers moving inside me with the rhythm of his hips, gently at first, then more determined.

"Ash," I whispered, pulling back. "Wait, we— This isn't going to work."

"Baby, everything's working just exactly the way God meant it to."

"You know what I'm talking about."

He groaned, his head dropping back against the mattress. "Look, they gave me every test in the book when I checked into rehab. I'm as clean as a whistle, I swear."

"It's not that," I said. "It's—I don't want to get pregnant. We can't take the chance."

He sighed and rolled out from under me, off the mattress and onto the floor. A lump rose in my throat as I stared at the hard knobs of his spine, the beautiful twin dimples in his lower back as he knelt facing the window in a wash of light. I knew in my head that regret was a waste of time, but my heart wanted nothing so much but to go back, back before marriage and Jude and Nashville, to when what Ash and I needed from each other was so straightforward, the future nothing but a sweet, diaphanous weave of possibility. This, when you got right down to it, was the big difference between us; I liked my dreams safely contained, like lightning bugs in a Mason jar, where I could sit and muse through the glass on their teasing, winking light, whereas Ash never could wait to unscrew the lid on that jar, turning his dreams loose in the world, running after them full tilt as they flew off into the night. How had I let myself believe that we could just pick up where we'd left off years before, leaving our troubles like muddy boots at the door? No matter how bad we wanted to believe it or how hard we tried, we weren't those people anymore.

Then he turned back toward me, a small cardboard box lying across his outstretched palm. I knew what Trojans were, even if the last time I'd seen one had been in the backseat of Tommy Rupp's Firebird when I was sixteen. But if Ash was living the whistle-clean life he claimed, what was he doing with these?

"Now, don't go getting all bent out of shape on me. I bought these the other night at the Pak 'n' Sak. After the crawfish boil at Dove's, when you asked me to follow you home. Look here," he said, tearing open the box and removing one of the foil-wrapped packets. "It's got your name on it. See?" He held it up. "'Exclusive property of Lucy Hatch. Use by any unlicensed party is strictly prohibited.'"

"Farrell," I said, snatching the packet from his hand. "Speaking of licenses, my name is Farrell."

"Believe me, I haven't forgotten."

"You're too much, you know that?" I said as he sprawled beside me on the mattress. "I don't know what I'm doing with the likes of you."

"Yeah, you do," Ash said, sliding down the length of me. He touched his lips lightly to my right instep, then ran his beard up the inside of the corresponding calf, knee, thigh. "You know exactly what you're doing."

It was everything I remembered and so much I'd forgotten, a path we'd traveled who knew how many times together over the years. We seemed to keep losing, then finding, then losing our rhythm again, like a radio that keeps going in and out of tune. I could still recall the song, though, that was the main thing; it still played in me with a steady beat as I pulled him down on top of me. I bit the inside of my lip, tasting blood and salt as Ash thrust himself inside me, too quick, the angle wrong at first, painful. He heard me gasp and lifted his head, but I clasped my legs around his hips, pushing myself upward against him like I could climb right through him, and with a small, sudden cry he slid deeply and fully into me, our pelvic bones grinding against each other's like two flints trying to make a flame.

We raked at each other's bodies, bit and tasted each other's flesh, breaking skin, leaving marks. He rolled onto his back, pulling me on top of him, plunging up into me as I rose and fell to meet him, throwing back my hair as I sat back on my heels and watched us move together in the gauzy light. My climax felt like a slippery thing, darting close and then away again, just out of reach as Ash moved beneath me in a single-minded rhythm, his eyes fixed on mine, black and burning. It scared me a little, the look in his eyes, the way our bodies banged and bruised together. The air was ripe with our sweat and breath, mingled with those of all the strangers whose lives had played out before us between these walls. How many people had done just what we were doing, in this sad little room? How much love and rage and pent-up hunger had been spilled out on this broken-down mattress? It seemed fitting, somehow, that this was how Ash and I would find each other again, much like the way we'd come together the first time, in a narrow iron bed in a tiny rent house, the springs sagging and the floorboards groaning underneath us at the slightest motion. We'd had no idea why we were doing what we were doing then, and we had no idea now—only that it had been and still seemed necessary, a way to save our own lives.

Ash gripped my hips with his hands, his fingers digging into my skin as I leaned toward him, my breasts crushing against his chest, my hair falling in a curtain over our faces, making a tent for our shared breathing. He said my name, raw and hot against my face, under the tent of my hair, and the sound of his voice went right through me, like a switch had been flipped, and I started to come, gradually at first and then stronger, waves of heat moving through my womb and outward, like my skin was lit from inside with liquid mercury. Ash flipped me onto my back and lifted my knees with his hands, pressing them apart as he drove into me, his cry of release buried in my hair as his body convulsed, the muscles in his back and his thighs rippling, and he let out a long, shuddering breath and collapsed beside me.

We lay side by side on the mattress, watching the changing patterns of cloud and moon as they drifted across the ceiling. After a few minutes Ash got up and crossed in the dark to the bathroom; I heard water running, the toilet flush, and then he was back, smelling of Listerine. He stretched out alongside me, his shoulder just touching mine, laying his palm lightly on my belly. I had a vague urge to pee, but I didn't want to move, didn't want whatever had to happen next to happen. I just wanted to lie there and breathe in our combined smells, to listen to our breathing slow and then match each other's. An old Eddy Arnold song popped into my head—"Make the world go away"—as clear as if somebody in the next room had switched on a radio. Tears dammed up in the base of my throat, but I held them in. I held on to all of it, as long as I could, and by the time I finally turned to look at Ash, I saw that he was asleep.

I rolled onto my side and studied him in the half-light. In sleep, all the lines in his face had smoothed out, making him look the way I guessed he must have looked at twelve, or twenty, before the cares of life caught up with him, before his disappointments had begun to etch themselves at the corners of his eyes and between his brows. I watched his chest rise and fall in a slow, even cadence and thought about what he'd said about wanting to go home. The gap between us had been bridged, if only momentarily, bodily, but was that bridge enough to stretch all the way from Nashville to Texas? Maybe, I thought, we could meet in the middle and start over, in a place that wasn't loaded with history. But still, we'd carry all our old baggage with us; it still wouldn't be home.

I got up, stiff and sore in places I hadn't been sore in ages, and made my way to the bathroom, shutting the door quietly behind me before switching on the light. I peed and flushed, then splashed my face with cold water, drying it on a brand-new towel, the Wal-Mart price tag still affixed, that sat in a stack on the edge of the sink. My mouth felt dry and sour, and I opened the mirrored cabinet over the sink to look for the Listerine. I found it, along with a toothbrush and toothpaste, a bottle of aspirin, and a pint of Jack Daniel's, drunk about a third of the way down.

I closed the cabinet and turned out the light, walking quietly back into the bedroom. Ash had turned on his side, away from the window, one arm stretched over his head. I knelt beside the mattress and touched his hip, but he didn't stir. The sadness in me felt huge and immovable, like a rockslide over the road, with

Ash caught on one side and me on the other. I'd been fooling myself. There was no bridge. Making love hadn't changed anything, had only torn open long-held hurts and heaped a whole new set on top of the old ones. I couldn't bring Ash back home, save him from himself. I couldn't even save myself.

Ash didn't wake as I stepped into my panties, hooked my bra, pulled my dress over my head in the dark. The moon was gone and there was a cool spring tang in the air, carrying on it a faint tinge of wood smoke, as I stepped out the door of the trailer and walked barefoot across the yard, hugging my arms across my chest. Letting myself into the house, I took care to shut the screen door quietly behind me. Someone had left on the hood light over the kitchen stove, and there was an empty glass in the sink that hadn't been there earlier.

I stood there as the icebox hummed and the hands on the clock inched past one o'clock, a hollow place like a peach pit lodged between my ribs, thinking about Ash sleeping out there alone on a bare mattress, and Denny and Will drowsing together in my double bed, tangled up together all sated and happy, the way husbands and wives were supposed to. Then I slunk into Jude's room and crawled between the covers, wrinkled dress, dirty feet and all, and lay grasping in vain at the edges of sleep, till morning.

chapter ten

I stood in the kitchen doorway in my rumpled dress and snarled hair, squinting at the clock in disbelief and trying to figure out whether I had a chance of getting to work on time if I pushed it, or whether I ought to just go ahead and put on the coffee, call Peggy and say I'd be late, and generally take things slow and lick my wounds.

I poured water into the Mr. Coffee and shook a scoopful of grounds into the filter, then pulled out a chair and sat down at the table, a table Ash had built himself before I ever knew him, spreading my hands flat on the blond wood surface. I felt flayed, inside and out, even the parts of me Ash hadn't had any direct access to. My head and my bladder ached, and my hipbones felt wrenched sideways in their sockets. I'd already peeked under my dress, seen the bite marks and bruises, the beard burn across the tops of my breasts and thighs. Meanwhile, the house was as quiet as a church; the sun peeked over the window sash with cheerful impertinence, as if to say that the whole rest of the world was grateful and happy, so what was the matter with *me*?

What *was* the matter with me? I'd had sex with my husband, which wasn't immoral or illegal, either one. The only thing I was guilty of was unrealistic expectations. But then there were probably hundreds of women just like me, some of them no doubt right here in Cade County, sitting at their kitchen tables waiting for the coffee to perk and feeling more or less the same sort of thing—an inner letdown, the wretched realization that, sex or no sex, some things were just too broke to fix.

I missed Jude, missed his goofy Spider-Man pajamas, missed listening to him sing as he poured milk all over the table along with his Cocoa Puffs. On the other hand, at least he wasn't here to see me dawdling around the kitchen in my dirty feet and slept-in clothes, wallowing in remorse as nine o'clock drew closer and closer.

The kitchen filled with the fortifying aroma of coffee, and I was trying to muster the wherewithal to get up from the table and pour myself a cup when Will Culpepper appeared, yawning and stretching, his flannel shirt half buttoned and his jeans drooping low on his hips, his black hair hanging in his face. My heart skipped a beat. I'd once seen a photo taken on the day Ash married Denny's mama, and this was just how he'd looked that day, young and slinky and dark-haired, rightful heir to all the bounty life had to offer.

Will swept a forelock off his face. "Hey. I thought I smelled coffee."

"It's just done," I said. "Help yourself. Cups are in the cabinet by the sink. No, the other side."

He took down two earthenware mugs, filled them and placed one in front of me, then pulled out the chair opposite mine and eased into it, setting his own coffee on the tabletop. A Southern boy, coming from money, he'd no doubt had good manners drilled into him from an early age.

I pushed the sugar bowl toward him. "There's milk in the icebox if you want it," I said, but he shook his head and took an exploratory sip of the strong, black brew. My brother Bailey always claimed my coffee had the taste and consistency of 30-weight Pennzoil, but Will Culpepper just sighed, his long bass player's hands curled around his cup, and looked at me with a vague but pleasant expression. He really was criminally good-looking. What spoiled it was the fact that he knew it, knew it and made no secret of it, was obviously used to working it for all it was worth. I said a little silent prayer for Denny, whose hide was thick, but possibly not thick enough for this.

"Did you have a good night?" I asked, then immediately felt myself flush at the unfortunate choice of words. Will's eyebrow quirked up again, along with one corner of his mouth. "I meant, well—how was the bed?" *Damn.* I picked up my coffee and gulped, scalding the inside of my mouth. At least that shut me up for a second.

"The bed was fine." His eyes took me in slowly and fully, from my ratted hair to last night's dress and what was left of my makeup. He sat back in his chair, the barest trace of a smile at the corners of his mouth. "How 'bout you? Did *you* have a good night?"

I didn't have a chance to form any kind of answer, plausible or otherwise, before the back screen door squealed open. Footsteps came rapidly up the rear hall, and then Ash was there, circling the table, parking himself with his back against the counter, his eyes bloodshot, his hair disheveled. I couldn't help noting that his half-buttoned shirt was nearly identical to his new son-in-law's, that his jeans hung on his hips with a similar degree of insouciance.

"Would you like some coffee?" I asked. "It's just made."

"Is something the matter with you?" he said. "Tell me, because I'd really like to know."

"You could at least say 'good morning,'" I said, cutting my eyes toward Will.

"What's good about it? I wake up, sun coming in the window like the first day of creation, and I roll over and the first thing I see—"

"Ash!" I broke in. "This isn't really—"

"The hell it isn't! This is *my* kitchen, my goddamned house. You're my *wife*! What was that last night, Lucy? A mercy fuck?"

I set my mug on the table with a crash. "How dare you!" I pushed back my chair. "How dare you accuse me of, of—"

"Of what? Of using me and then just walking out in the middle of the night, like some kind of sleazy one-night stand?"

"Are you talking about me, or you? Because you haven't got a lot of room to—"

"Lord have mercy!"

Denny stood in the doorway, wrapped in my old seersucker robe, shaking a tumble of hair over her shoulders. "What in the world is going on in here? They can probably hear y'all all the way to town." She bent over and planted a kiss on the side of Will's neck. "Mm," she murmured, breathing him in slow and deep.

"Morning, babe," Will said, circling her waist with his arm and pulling her close. "We're having us a nice little breakfast. Just family."

Ash jabbed his finger in Will's direction. "You keep out of this," he said. "You're walking a thin line already around here, Son, and trust me, I am *not* in the mood."

"Daddy!" Denny said. "What's the matter with you? Why are y'all squalling at each other like a bunch of cats?"

She took note of my appearance, looked at Ash, then me again. "Oh my God!" She laughed, then clapped a hand over her mouth. "Did you guys spend the *night* together?"

"No, as a matter of fact, we didn't," Ash said. "Because, see, Lucy here got up and snuck out in the middle of the night, without so much as a by-your—"

"Ash, shut up. Denny, hon, this is really just between your daddy and me."

"No, it's not," Denny replied. "I mean, seeing's how y'all are having it out right here in the middle of the house and all." She turned to take a mug out of the cabinet. "I *knew* this would happen!" she said as she poured herself a cup of coffee. "You should have seen them right after they first got together, back when I first lived with them, when I was fourteen," she told Will. "They couldn't keep their hands off each other. I remember one night I saw them doing it outside in the front yard! Right up against the side of the pickup, under a big old full moon."

"You *watched* us?" I asked, amazed, at the same time Ash said, "When was that? I don't remember that."

"Y'all used to try and sneak around, but you never were very good at it. I always found out somehow. Remember that time you checked into the Piney View?"

I stood up. "Excuse me, but I am really not comfortable talking about all this in front of—of everybody."

Denny sat down on Will's knee. "I don't get what the big deal is," she went on, sipping her coffee with one hand, the other on the back of Will's neck. "Jeez, you guys are married! And anyway, anybody with two eyes knows y'all are made for each other. Right?" she asked Will, who nodded his chin just enough to seem polite.

"Let me tell you something," I said. "You two are young. You think you invented sex. But wait till you've been married awhile. You'll see. Things get complicated."

They gazed at me out of their languid, sleepy faces.

"Look," I said, "it's not like I'm trying to spoil your visit, or that I'm not happy you're here. But your daddy and I could really use a few minutes in private."

"Whatever." Denny set her mug on the table. "We'll go take a shower. Okay, sweetie?" To seal the deal, she and Will embarked upon a long, full-mouthed kiss, not just mouths but tongues, teeth, the whole nine yards. I wanted to leap across the table and strangle them both with my bare hands.

After they'd disentangled themselves, Ash and I stood staring at each other across the empty table. The bathroom door slammed shut, and moments later came the sound of water rushing through the pipes.

"Great," I said. "Not only have they spent the whole night doing it in my bed, now they're doing it in my shower."

"I've got news for you." Ash took down a cup from the cabinet and filled it with the last few inches of coffee. "Those two may have just discovered sex with each other, but Will Culpepper's been practicing on other people for a long time."

He downed the coffee in one long gulp and set the mug on the countertop. A cardinal alighted on a branch outside the window—red as blood, a male, the ones with all the plumage. "Why did you take off?" Ash said.

"Are you talking about last summer, or last night?"

"Both. Either." I couldn't hold his eye, and looked back toward the window. The bird was gone. "Jesus, Lucy—have I got to nail you to the floorboards? Don't try to tell me last night didn't mean anything, because I know it did, and you know it, too. Why are you forever running away?"

"Because I knew—I know—this isn't going to work."

"How can it work if you won't stay in one spot for two goddamned minutes?"

"I looked in your bathroom cabinet," I said. "Over the sink."

"What were you doing in there?"

"Looking for Listerine." *In all the wrong places.* Oh, why was my head full of this foolishness?

Ash sighed and gripped the edge of the counter. I saw the network of veins in the backs of his hands, a blueprint I'd once memorized and could have described blindfolded, the same way I could've found my way from home to town and back again. Why couldn't I be in the same room with Ash and keep my wits? You'd think after seven years I'd have built up some immunity, but the backs of his hands, the lines around his eyes, the frayed buttonholes on his shirtfront still undid me.

"Look, just because— What you saw doesn't change what happened last night," he said.

"Ever since you got here, you've been telling me your drinking is under control."

"Can we just for once have an honest-to-God conversation between us without it being about my drinking?"

"It *is* about your drinking! I don't understand why you won't admit that! Why can't you just stop?"

"Oh, Luce. Jesus Christ." He let go of the counter edge and scraped his hair back from his face with both palms, closing his eyes, stretching the skin of his face taut.

"I know you think you've got this image to uphold, that you've got to tough it out," I said. "But it's not working, can't you see that? It won't go away on its own."

"Have you heard a thing I've said? This isn't just about me. I mean, yeah, I've got a problem, but you can't keep laying it all on me."

He glanced over his shoulder at the coffeemaker, like a fresh pot might have appeared there by magic, then turned back with a sigh. "Listen to me a minute. Just listen, and don't say anything until I'm through," he said. "I met this priest. Father Laughlin. He runs the AA meetings at the Catholic church down in Jefferson."

"You went to an AA meeting?"

"I think you should go see him. Just drive down there some afternoon and meet him, hear what he has to say."

"About what? I'm not a drunk, and I'm not Catholic."

"And nothing's ever your fault, is it? Lucy Hatch is queen of her own little world, and anything bad that happens, it's off with somebody else's head."

I sucked in my breath, but before I could answer, something stopped me, seemed to rise up like a hand and place itself, gently but firmly, over my mouth. Something—not Ash's voice, not exactly a voice at all, but something small but insistent inside me—told me, for once, to be still.

"I know I need help," Ash said. "I know that. But you've got to own up to your side of it, too, or we haven't got a chance."

I could hear the dogs snuffling around on the back porch, pressing their noses against the screen. Ash pushed away from the counter, opened the pantry door, filled the metal scoop from the big bag of Purina, just like he'd done the very first morning after I'd slept over, just like he'd been doing it every day in the meantime.

"Father Laughlin," he said as he skirted the table and headed for the hall. "St. Jude's, in Jefferson." The screen door shut behind him.

I CALLED PEGGY and asked her to open the shop, told her I'd be in by ten, ten-thirty at the latest, that I'd explain when I got there. After what seemed like an eternity, the shower stopped running, and I waited as long as I decently could before sneaking down the hall and making sure the coast was clear. The bedroom door was closed, and I could hear murmuring and muffled laughter behind it. I guessed, after what Denny had said earlier, it was only fair, given what she'd had to put up with between her daddy and me from the other side of that door a few years back.

I showered quickly—not hard, seeing as there was no hot water left in the tank—unsnarled my hair with a comb and toweled it dry, and grabbed a dress out of the closet in the back bedroom, long and loose and covered with an all-over pattern of little blue flowers. It wasn't as polished as the way I usually dressed, but it made me feel more like the old Lucy again, the one who used to go to work feeling upbeat and hopeful instead of muddleheaded and rundown. Plus, it did a decent job of covering most of the visible damage from the night before. I slipped on my shoes, picked up my purse and my keys, and headed for the door. With any luck, I'd only be an hour late and might not have that much explaining to do.

Denny corralled me on the front porch.

"Lucy! Hold up a minute. I need to talk to you." She was wearing frayed jeans and a tank top, no bra, and with her wild hair and her bare feet with the toenails painted a bright orangey-red, she looked as ripe and ready as one of Aunt Dove's Early Girl tomatoes. Just looking at her, I felt the old, hopeful Lucy starting to fade, started feeling like somebody's worn-out stepmama again.

"What's up?" I said.

"I've been thinking, and I was wondering if you and me could do Girlfriend Night tonight. Remember? Like we used to?"

Of course I remembered. The summer she turned sixteen, the year she'd finally started getting periods and breasts, she'd come up to spend a month with Ash and me and Jude in the new house in Nashville. When Ash was on the road, Denny and I would tuck Jude in his crib upstairs, and with the baby monitor on, we'd retreat to the huge oak-and-marble kitchen, where we popped popcorn and painted our nails outrageous colors and gave each other avocado-and-oatmeal facials, the big-screen TV tuned to an old movie or CMT. Those nights had been some of Denny's and my best times together, but it made me a little sad to think about them now, to recall how sure of ourselves we'd been, how thrilled and awestruck to have wound up in what we thought was permanent Disneyland.

"That sounds like fun," I said. "But what about Will and your daddy?"

"Oh, I was thinking they could go out together, just the two of them. Get to know each other better. Do whatever it is that guys do to, you know—bond."

My ears started to ring as I stared at my stepdaughter, her face as goofy as a month-old puppy's. Didn't she know what men did to "bond"? They drank and picked up women, or, in the case of guys like Ash and Will, sat back and let the women come to them. There might be a little greasy food thrown in, a little televised sports, but the two constants were always there: alcohol and females. Anyway, couldn't she see that her daddy had it in for Will? Did she really think anything good could come from this?

"Have you talked to Will about this?" I asked.

"Not yet. But he'll do anything I say." Denny grinned and held up a crooked little finger. "I've got him wrapped so tight, he can't even holler for help."

In spite of myself, I laughed. It reminded me of a song Ash had played for me once, a long time back.

"Tell you what," I said. "If you can talk them into it, I'm game. Call me later and fill me in, okay? I'll run by Wal-Mart after work and get whatever we need."

"Great," she said happily, then bounded down the steps two at a time into the yard and flung her arms around my neck. "Oh, I'm just so glad we came!"

I hugged her hard, pressing my face into her hair, which smelled like a just-mown meadow. She was as tall as I was, and headed for just as much trouble, and I felt a kinship with her, greater than before, even back when she was sixteen and sitting at my kitchen counter with blue toenails and goop smeared all over her face. We were grown women who had each done something big and irrefutable, and we were going to need each other now more than ever.

THERE SEEMED TO be an unusually large number of Thursday-morning patrons at Faye's when I finally made it in, a few minutes past ten. In addition to Peggy, I counted her friends Alene and Mary Dale, Mrs. Florence Binder, Everett the UPS guy, and an old man I recognized but didn't know personally, one of the feed-cap gossips from the café. Everybody stopped talking as I bent to tuck my purse under the counter. Everett, lounging against the counter with a Styrofoam cup of coffee, gave me a big smile and a wink. The old man turned and started browsing through the greeting cards.

"What was she *thinking*?" somebody, I think Mrs. Binder, whispered. As I was trying to think of a few words in my own defense, Audrey stepped out of the cooler, her arms full of red long-stemmed roses, looking like a beauty contestant from another planet. She wore baggy canvas pants and one of her sawed-off T-shirts with a couple of inches of skin showing in the gap between, and her hair, which the day before had been as black as pitch, was now a shade I'd always thought was exclusive to blonds with too much exposure to sun and chlorine.

I gasped. "Was that an accident?" I asked. "Or did you do it on purpose?"

"Well, the color on the box said 'Champagne and Moonlight,'" she said, "but I think this is a little more . . ."

"Green," I said. "Your hair is green."

Audrey handed the roses to Peggy, who started to arrange them on a sheet of tissue.

"Joe hates it," Audrey said dolefully. "He said I look like a slut. He said it like that was a *bad* thing."

"I could call my sister-in-law Connie for you," I offered. "She went to beauty school. It's been awhile, but I bet she'd know how to fix it."

"You think?"

"Sure. I'll ask her if she can stop by later and take a look."

"Tell her I'll pay her," Audrey said fervidly. "Have babies for her, whatever it takes."

"She's got four of those already," I said. "My guess is she'd rather have the cash."

"What's that on your neck?"

Instinctively I raised my fingers, conscious of seven pairs of eyes on me.

"Other side."

I switched hands, but I still couldn't feel anything.

"Probably a mosquito bite," I said, feeling myself burn from my collarbone to my ears. "We had supper last night at Curly's at the lake. You know how bad they get this time of year down by the water."

"Wow," Audrey said. "Those must've been some pretty big teeth, for a mosquito."

By law I wasn't allowed to smack her, so I had to settle for a sneaky little pinch to the skin above her waistband.

"Hey, guess what, y'all?" I said, since the whole room was listening now, making no bones about it. "Denny's here. She got married."

"Oh my Lord," Peggy said, a hand flying to her chest. "Not to that King boy, I hope! I mean, I like to think I'm as open-minded as the next one, but . . ."

She glanced at Everett, who gazed politely but purposefully back. If he hadn't known it before, Everett knew now that "that King boy," like himself, was African-American. I hated to admit that what Peggy'd said was the truth; in Cade County, she *was* about as open-minded as the next one, which meant, You can cook in my restaurant, mow my lawn, deliver my packages, even drink coffee with my customers, but I'd just as soon you didn't intermingle with my daughter, thank you very much.

"Erasmus is in New York," I reminded her. "Studying at Juilliard. No, this is somebody else. The bass player in her band. His name's Will Culpepper."

They all stared at me, wanting to ask the obvious question they couldn't very well ask with Everett standing there, which was, *What color is he?*

"He's from Mississippi," I went on, which of course didn't tell a thing. "His daddy used to own some kind of factory or something. He's—well, he's real good-looking. In fact, he looks so much like Ash, it's spooky."

The ladies all smiled with relief and nodded at each other. I kept to myself what I wanted to say, which was that I would've been a thousand times happier if Denny had married Erasmus King instead of Will Culpepper. I always thought Erasmus and Denny had found each other too early in life, when both of them were too young and naïve, their feelings for each other too unwieldy to get hold of. Not that I was fooling myself, that any kind of permanent relationship between them would have been smooth sailing. It wasn't just in deep northeast Texas that folks looked askance on mixed marriages, not even in the so-called enlightened twenty-first century. Still, some part of me wanted to believe true love could rise above all that, love and their shared gift for music. But Erasmus had gone to New York and Denny had gone to Nashville; their lives had been growing in separate directions a long time before Denny met Will Culpepper.

"So, y'all went to Curly's to celebrate?" Alene asked. "You and Denny and this, this Culpepper fella?"

"And Ash," I said. "You know—meet the parents and all."

"Great chicken-fried steak at Curly's," the card-browsing old man piped up.

"And *then* what happened?" This from Mrs. Florence Binder, who had such a look of Christian blamelessness plastered on her face that it was hard to believe she had some ulterior motive for asking.

"Nothing special. We ate supper. Drank a little champagne. Denny got up and sang a song on the karaoke thing. Then we went home."

"So did Ash get all chewed up like you did?" Audrey asked, without a drop of compunction. "By those mosquitoes, I mean."

"You know," I said, "I'd love to stand around here all day chewing the fat, but I've got a payroll to get out. So, if y'all will excuse me, I'll be in the back."

"Don't forget to call your sister-in-law!" Audrey sang out as I made my way to the office and collapsed in front of the desk in the swivel chair.

I switched on the computer and sat staring at the screen as it glowed to life and ran through its litany of startup commands, but all I could see was Ash's body moving together with mine, as supple as a pair of sea creatures in the silvery light.

I picked up the phone and called Connie and asked her to drop by and see if she could do anything about poor Audrey's hair. Then I called directory assistance and got the number for St. Jude's Catholic Church in Jefferson.

chapter eleven

"Oh, honey, no, no, *no.*" Connie circled Audrey like a snake, like if she came too close Audrey might coil and pounce. "Hair like yours, you need a double process! You got to lift the base color before you go laying down the blond."

Everett had left to finish his rounds, and Peggy, Alene, Mary Dale, and Mrs. Binder had gone up the street to drink coffee at the café, along, I guessed, with the feed-cap man, no doubt all of them speculating on my mosquito bite and how it factored into the latest poll. I didn't know who'd bought the roses.

"Can you fix it?"

"Well, I'm not saying I can make it look like champagne and moonlight." Connie reached out and fingered a crispy strand. "But I'm pretty sure I can do better than this."

"Hey, I've got an idea," I said. "Denny and me are having Girlfriend Night at the house tonight. Facials, pedicures, all that stuff. Why don't y'all come out and do Audrey's hair there? Say, seven o'clock? We'll make it a party."

"Great! I'll run by Sally Beauty Supply and pick up what we need." Connie was already on her way out the door, waving as she climbed into her maroon minivan.

Audrey let out her breath in a rush and slumped against the counter.

"I don't know how to thank you," she told me.

I brought a bunch of gerbera daisies out of the cooler and took a vase off the shelf. "Look, everybody makes mistakes. Why not try to fix the ones you can, is my philosophy." It wasn't, actually—my own life was proof enough of that—but I thought it sounded like something you'd say to a seventeen-year-old with chartreuse hair.

"So does that mean you and Ash are back together?" I looked up from the flowers. "Well, dang, Lucy," Audrey said. "Everybody knows a hickey when they see one."

"And everybody in town will hear about it now, too, thanks to you."

"You didn't answer my question."

"Listen, I know this is a tough concept for you, but some things are a person's own private business."

"Not around here, they're not."

"What can I say? I'm trying to buck the trend. Do you think you can run these over to Betty Ponds in the loan department at First National?" I pushed the vase across the counter. "It'll serve you right, having to strut that hair on Main Street. Maybe you'll think twice next time about minding your own business."

For the first time that morning, the shop was mine alone, sunny and quiet. After a quick peek at Everett's delivery—some boxes of fancy ribbon Peggy had ordered from a company in California—I took the phone out from under the counter and dialed the number of the Catholic church in Jefferson.

After three rings, a woman answered: "St. Jude's." Her voice was sandpapery, like a smoker's.

"I'd like to speak to Father Laughlin, please."

"Not here right now. Want me to take a message?"

"Actually, I'd— Well, I'd really like to see him. In person."

"You a parishioner?"

"A—? Oh. No, ma'am. I'm not." *I was raised Baptist,* I imagined myself saying, *but I'm not sure what I believe anymore.* "Can I see him anyway? Maybe make an appointment?"

"Well, Father's not real big on keeping a calendar, like regular folks. If I was you, I'd plan on just dropping by. He'll be in this afternoon, between three and five. That's assuming nobody up and dies in the meantime."

I called Dove, who wasn't home, then Geneva, leaving a message on her cell phone about Girlfriend Night, then Bailey to ask if he'd mind watching the kids. I checked the pad on the counter, but the red roses—which, it turned out, had been purchased by Everett—and the bouquet for Betty Ponds seemed to be our only orders for the day. The cooler was fairly neat already, it being Thursday, when the week's stock was low, so I went to work straightening the greeting cards. The old man in the cap had made a mess of them, pulling them out and then sticking them back willy-nilly, the birthday cards mixed in with the baby announcements, anniversary with sympathy.

The front door opened, and I peeked around the card display as Peggy walked in, fortunately alone.

"Hey," I said. "How's everything over at the café?"

"Oh, about like usual," she said. "Buzzing like a swarm of mosquitoes."

We looked at each other and started to laugh.

"That Audrey," I said. "I swear I could skin her alive sometimes. So, did anybody win any money?"

"Dudley Ward. Forty-some-odd dollars and change."

"Well, I'm glad to know some good came out of this for somebody."

Peggy went around behind the counter and picked up the empty coffee carafe. "You don't sound very happy for a woman who got chewed on last night by a big old mosquito."

"I have a favor to ask." She set down the coffeepot again. "I know I was late coming in this morning, but I need to take some time off this afternoon, too," I said. "I guess you could call it mosquito control."

"It's about Ash, you mean."

"I don't know if it's possible to fix what's broke, Peggy. But he asked me to do this. I want to try."

"Then go," she said. "I'll cover for you. It's not like I haven't done it before." She smiled, and I smiled back, remembering how in the old days she'd made it possible for Ash and me to court, how she'd even been in cahoots with him sometimes, running interference, setting up rendezvous.

"Listen, Denny and I are having Girlfriend Night tonight at the house," I said. "Connie's coming out to fix Audrey's hair, and I've called Dove and Geneva. You come, too. Cut loose for once and wreck your diet."

"I'll bring my spicy Velveeta dip," Peggy said happily. "Lord, I don't think I've tasted the stuff in five years."

"Just so long as you don't wind up back in County General."

"Nah. All that plastic they stuck in me, I'll be around till I'm ninety."

"I need to leave around three."

She waved her hand toward me like a fairy dispersing pixie dust. "I think I still remember how to keep this place going on my own."

I LEFT WORK at three and headed across town, then swung south on Highway 59. The afternoon was mild, sunshine drifting in and out amid fast-moving clouds, patterns of shadow and light flickering across the highway.

Twenty miles south of Mooney, I turned off the four-lane and drove slowly through the wide, shady streets of Jefferson. I never could figure out why what looked just plain shabby in Mooney was stately and historic in Jefferson, the aging structures well preserved and tended to, the shopfronts bright and inviting. Every other building, it seemed, was a bed-and-breakfast, and tourists strolled the brick main street, stopping in for pie at the Hamburger Store or Dr Pepper in a bottle at the five-and-dime, buying crafts and antiques, lining up for the riverboat cruise down the Big Cypress Bayou. A ghost was said to haunt the old Excelsior House hotel on Austin Street, but nobody I knew had ever seen it.

I followed the directions given to me by the lady on the phone and, after one or two wrong turns, found St. Jude's, a red-brick building with a white peaked roof set back from the street on a tidy rectangle of lawn, a set of steep concrete steps leading up to the big double doors of the sanctuary.

A sign directed me around the side of the building to the office, and I opened a door and climbed half a flight of stairs till I came to a landing. At the top was a closed door with a cross-stitched sampler mounted at eye level that read, *Do not neglect to show hospitality to strangers, for thereby some have entertained angels unaware.* I knocked twice, but no one answered, so I tried the knob. It was locked.

I stood on the landing feeling a mix of emotions: irritation that I'd driven all this way for nothing, relief that I wouldn't have to confess my sins to a total stranger. A small window overlooked a courtyard garden, and down below I could see a man in a T-shirt and running shorts and heavy canvas gloves tending a crop of rosebushes. I didn't suppose a gardener would know where the priest was, but it couldn't hurt to ask. That way, I could tell Ash in all honesty that I'd done what he wanted, even if I did have to go home empty-handed. Was it my fault this Father Laughlin was too arrogant or too lazy to keep a calendar, like ordinary people?

At the bottom of the stairs I pushed open a side door and stepped out into the courtyard. The little patch of garden seemed too small to hold such an abundance of roses, and yet clearly they thrived here, nodding in the breeze, raising their pink and crimson and salmon and cream-colored heads toward the sun. The gardener didn't see me; he was bent over a scarlet-bloomed plant, humming to himself, a tune I knew but couldn't name.

"Excuse me," I finally said, and he whirled toward me, a pair of shears dropping from his hands and clattering at his feet onto the flagstone walk.

"Heavens!" he said. "You like to have cost me a toe." In spite of the way he was dressed—his T-shirt said MOTOROLA MARATHON 1995, and he wore expensive-looking running shoes on his feet—he was a little on the chunky side, his legs muscular but thick, his belly bowing out above the waistband of his nylon shorts. His arms and legs were covered with dark hair, though there was very little of any sort on his head, despite the fact that he wasn't an old man. In fact, I pegged him at about my age, maybe a year or two older, by the laugh lines around his mouth and eyes.

"What do you think this is?" He stepped toward me, extending one gloved hand. Across the palm lay a handful of green leaves covered with small, dark splotches.

"Black spot," I said.

"No kidding."

"That's what it's called," I said. "It's a fungus. Common to roses, especially in this climate. You spray for it in the spring and again in the fall. I can't remember what the stuff's called, but you get it at the hardware store. My aunt would know. She's the best gardener in this part of the state." Better than this one, that was for sure. What kind of rose grower never heard of black spot?

The man peeled off his gloves and drew one across his sweaty forehead. "I swear, I had no idea roses could be so much trouble."

"You've got to baby them," I said. "There's not just black spot, but thrips, and powdery mildew. . . ."

"You interested in the job? It's yours if you want it." He had a nice smile, his gray eyes disappearing into the creases in a friendly way.

"No, thanks," I said. "I've already got a job. I work with flowers, too, as a matter of fact."

"Oh? Where would that be?"

"Faye's, up in Mooney."

"Hang on a minute," he said. "This famous aunt of yours wouldn't happen to live in Mooney, would she? Lady by the name of Dove Munroe?" I nodded. "I drove by that place once, last summer! Incredible, like something out of a fairy tale. Nobody was home, though, so I didn't go in."

"You should have," I said. "The gate's always unlocked. Folks come from all over and leave things."

"What kind of things?"

"Offerings, I guess you'd call them. There's a lot of religious stuff, not just Christian but Buddhist and Hindu and Muslim, and things from nature, you know, seashells and feathers and such. But there's a lot of cheesy souvenir stuff, too, like key chains and Burger King toys. Just whatever strikes people's fancy, or what they happen to have in their pockets, I guess."

"So it's a shrine, sort of."

"I guess it is. A shrine to everyday life."

"I think that's the best kind."

"I do, too." I leaned forward and held out my hand. "I'm Lucy Farrell."

"Oh my gosh! You're Ash's wife!"

My hand fell to my side. "You know Ash?"

"Didn't he send you?"

"He said I should see Father Laughlin."

"Well, you're seeing him," the man said, bending over to pick up the shears. I'd been expecting a stern-faced old man in dark robes and a collar, and here was this pudgy, sweaty, middle-aged guy in running shorts, wielding gardening shears.

"If you want, we can go inside and I'll show you proof of ID. My diploma from seminary, or my ordination papers. I've even got a picture of me with the Pope." He grinned and held out his hand, and I shook it. "You can call me Punch," he said.

"Punch?"

"I used to box, in prep school," he said. "What can I say? My Christian name's Wesley. Punch fit me better, and it just seemed to stick."

I smiled. He didn't look like an ordinary priest, but for a fact he looked even less like a Wesley.

"Ash asked me to come see you," I said. "I don't really know why."

"Your husband's quite a guy," the priest said. "Not like most of my—what should I call them?"

"Well, he was brought up Catholic, but I don't think he's ever been what you'd call observant."

"Oh, I'm talking about AA, not the church. Most of the drunks around here are more or less run-of-the-mill disillusioned people. You know, office workers, blue-collar types. I'm pretty sure Ash is the only one who ever got as far as Nashville."

"He's still disillusioned, though."

"Yes, on that front, he definitely qualifies." Father Laughlin—Punch—gestured toward a concrete bench, and we sat. "What I'm trying to say is, not many of the folks in our group ever managed to rise very far from their rearing. Ash is probably the only one who managed to break loose. Meaning, I guess, he's had further than the rest to fall."

"I really don't know that much about alcoholics," I admitted. "Or Catholics, for that matter. We haven't got too many of either one in Mooney. Or those that are, keep it to themselves."

"How about you?"

"Excuse me?"

"Your religious beliefs, background."

"Well, I was raised at First Baptist in Mooney, and I still go there sometimes, to keep my mama happy, and so my little boy can learn about Jesus. But mostly I . . ." I hesitated, then shook my head. It seemed too much to try to explain, especially to a man of the cloth, even if in this case the cloth was nylon and synthetic leather.

The Father didn't seem to hold it against me, though. I imagined, between a church and an AA group, he was used to dealing with a good bit of doubt and confusion.

"I'm not really sure what I'm doing here," I said. "I didn't even know Ash was going to AA. He's still drinking, so far as I know. At least he's got liquor in the trailer— Did he tell you he's living in a trailer in our backyard?" The priest nodded. "He's been in and out of rehab, two or three times, but it never seems to take. He always acts like he's above that sort of thing. That he needs to tough it out on his own, to prove he's a man, or something. I don't know. It's complicated."

"Yes, it is. But that's Ash's story, isn't it? What about yours?"

"Mine? I thought I was here about him."

"You left him, am I right, up in Nashville? But now he's back in Mooney, and here you are, talking to me, even if you don't quite know why. That says to me you haven't given up on him—on the two of you—completely."

"We slept together last night," I blurted out, to my instant mortification. I'd spent the past two weeks dodging nosy questions from folks who'd known me all my life, and now, all of a sudden, I was admitting my private business to a total stranger.

"Isn't that what husbands and wives do?"

"Not us. I mean, not since Nashville, not in eight or nine months."

"So, you had a reconciliation."

"Well, I wouldn't call it that, exactly."

The priest and I sat quietly for a few moments. It was an easy silence, and the garden was such a pretty, peaceful place, the breeze light and warm and carrying on it the heady scent of all those blossoms.

"Here's the thing," I said. "Ash fell asleep, after, and I, I sort of panicked. I saw the liquor in the bathroom cabinet, and all of a sudden I started reminding myself all the reasons we're apart in the first place, and all the reasons it can never work. So I left. Left him there, in the trailer, and went to sleep in my own house."

Father Laughlin didn't respond. He seemed to be leaving it up to me whether or not I wanted to continue. "This morning Ash came over while I was making coffee, ranting and raving, saying our problems aren't all his doing, because of his drinking or his carousing, that they're mine, too. That I can't ever stay put long enough to work anything out. I just always up and run."

"Is that true?"

"I guess maybe it is. I mean, I left him three times between the time we met and the time we got married, and that was only six months. Of course, it was just a few miles, those times, but still . . ."

"I don't think the distance is what's important," the priest said. "It's what it says, your leaving."

I gazed at a rosebush just across the walk, its peach-colored blooms the size of salad plates. There was an unpleasant pressure at the back of my throat. I felt the way I'd felt back in grade-school arithmetic class, when it was my turn at the board and everything I'd ever known about addition and subtraction suddenly flew straight out of my brain, like I wanted to just lay my head on my desk and hide my face for a week.

"You know," Punch said, "your husband loves you very much."

The pressure in my throat let loose, and I started to cry. I hated crying, even in front of the folks who knew me well, and it should have been worse in front of this man, this priest in running shorts with a crazy name, but it wasn't. I cried, and Father Laughlin—Punch—put his big red hand on my arm and sat without speaking till I was through. It took awhile. I'd been storing up my tears, it seemed, like an oil field buried deep underground that suddenly comes a gusher. It took a long time to get it capped off. Punch didn't seem to mind, though. He acted like he had folks crying in his garden every day of the week. Considering the business he was in, maybe he did.

"My daddy left when I was six," I said.

Now, where had that come from? I opened my purse and rummaged around until I located a wad of Kleenex, and blew my nose into it.

"Our little boy is that age, exactly," I went on. "Jude. Like your church."

Punch smiled. "Patron saint of impossible causes."

"We thought I couldn't get pregnant. It was a—a surprise."

"Sometimes God gives us answers to questions we didn't even know we were asking."

"Ash grew up without a daddy, too. I don't want what happened to us to happen to Jude."

"Parental bonds are very important. But what about you and Ash? About the two of you? As a couple?"

I twisted the Kleenex in my hands. "I was married before, for fourteen years. Mitchell and I—well, we weren't unhappy, but we weren't exactly happy, either. We just sort of got through the days, doing what had to be done. I thought that was what marriage was about. And I still do think that—at least, I think that's part of it.

"But then he died, and I met Ash, and I—I realized there could be something else. I never really believed in soul mates, or any of that. But from the very start, with Ash and me, there was—something—a recognition, I guess you'd call it. It was like I knew him in some way I'd never known another person before."

"There's a quote I love that I heard a long time ago, when I was just a kid," Punch said. "I have no idea who said it, and I've probably got it a little mixed up, but it goes something like this: 'Love is a gift not to be squandered. But neither is it something to be hoarded.' In other words, what good is it if you don't spend it?"

"Sounds like one of the cards we sell in my shop."

"That's probably where I got it, then," Punch said. "I remember being heavily influenced by Hallmark as a boy."

"So what do I do? I can't just go on pretending Ash's drinking doesn't matter."

"Of course not. But why not let Ash deal with that, and concentrate instead on holding up your side of the bargain?"

"He's coming to your meetings, then?"

"Well, technically, I'm not supposed to say. The name is Alcoholics *Anonymous.*"

"Why's he keeping Jack Daniel's in the bathroom cabinet, then?"

"Sobriety isn't usually an overnight process, I'm afraid. Some folks do quit cold turkey, but most go up and down, back and forth, for a long time before they finally give it up for good. I know, for me, it took almost six years. Even with my faith to lean on, it wasn't easy to let go once and for all."

"You? Were—"

"A drunk? Was and am. In AA, you know, there's no such thing as a recovered alcoholic. We call ourselves 'recovering.' "

"Then how do you know when you're—well, there?"

"That's the thing—there is no 'there.' I'm sure you've heard our mantra: 'One day at a time.' "

I looked at my watch, then gathered my purse and stood. "I'm sorry, but I have to go. I'm having a party at my house tonight. Our daughter—Ash's daughter, my stepdaughter—just got married."

"Congratulations."

"Thanks. And thanks for seeing me. For letting me just drop in like this. Is there— Can I pay you in some way?"

"Sure. Ask your aunt to call me up and tell me what to do about black spot."

"I'll do that." I stepped onto the flagstone walk, breathing in the heavy perfume of the roses.

"Stop by again, if you feel like it," he said. "You know, we have a program called Al-Anon, for the families of alcoholics. If and when you ever feel you're ready."

"Oh, I—I don't know. But thanks. Thanks again."

"Remember," Punch said. "Don't hoard, don't squander."

When I left, he was on his knees between the rosebushes, humming the same tune he'd been humming when I'd arrived.

chapter twelve

At twenty minutes till seven, I found myself racing up Highway 59, the back of the Blazer filled with chips and Cheetos, microwave mini-pizzas and popcorn, two six-packs of beer, one Mexican and one lite. I was hoping against hope to get home in time to warn Denny about the unexpected onslaught of Girlfriends, but I was too late; as I drove into the yard, I saw both Dove's Buick and Connie's mini-van out front, and every light in the house was blazing.

As I was unloading the junk-food stash, I heard Audrey's Charger rumbling up the unpaved dirt road. "Here, let me give you a hand with that," she said, grabbing a couple of sagging plastic sacks with her free hand. In the other she toted a six-pack of Smirnoff Ice.

"Where did you get that?" I asked. "You're not old enough to buy alcohol."

"You think I'm gonna tell you? And get the TABC on somebody's ass? No way, José."

"I didn't expect to be running so late," I said. "Lord, the house is probably a wreck." On the other hand, if it wasn't a wreck before Girlfriend Night, it surely would be after. Anyway, there wasn't one of us who cared more about the cleanliness of our kitchen floors than we did about each other's company—in that regard, I knew, I was blessed.

We found Connie, Dove, Rowena, and Denny sitting around the kitchen table scooping Fritos into a ceramic bowl of onion dip and drinking Seagram's Wild Berry coolers and listening to Loretta Lynn's new CD on the boom box. I dropped my bags on the counter and leaned over to give Denny a kiss.

"Sorry," I murmured into her ear. "I kept meaning to call you. I hope you don't mind, I invited a little company."

"Nah, this is great," she said happily. "It's like old home week or something. Look at Dove's and Rowena's shirts—aren't they wild? I want to take a bunch of 'em back to Nashville."

"Where are the boys? Your daddy and Will, I mean."

"Oh, they took off a little while ago in Daddy's truck. I think they were headed to the Tap to watch a ball game or something."

I couldn't believe she'd talked them into it. I introduced Denny to Audrey as I unloaded the snacks and wedged the beer into the icebox. "Has anybody heard from Geneva?" I asked.

"She called and said she had to stop by the package store," Dove said. "She'll be along directly. Denny, hon, are you sure this here record is by Miss Loretta? I mean, it sounds like her singin' and everthing, but what's with all them weird-soundin' guitars and such? Don't tell me she's crossin' over to the dark side, too."

"Hey, this record won two Grammys," Denny said. "She's my hero. If I ever have a baby girl, I'm gonna name her Loretta." I shot a little glance in Denny's direction, but she seemed to be speaking of some ambiguous future event, not something tangible and imminent. That was the last thing I wanted to worry about right now—her letting Will Culpepper, husband or no, get her in the family way.

I ran down the hall to change out of my work dress into an old T-shirt and cutoffs as Connie went into the bathroom to start mixing up a concoction for Audrey's hair. A few minutes later Peggy showed up, bearing a Crock-Pot full of her famous spicy Velveeta dip. I poured chips into bowls and put popcorn into the microwave, and had just started passing around the beer when Geneva arrived, carrying a bottle of tequila and two of margarita mix.

"Hope you got lots of extra blankets," Rowena said to me. "Looks like we're all gonna be campin' on your livin' room floor tonight."

Denny and Geneva let out squeals at the sight of each other. "Girl, let me hug your neck," Geneva said, and Denny jumped up and ran over to greet her. "Look at you! All married and everything. You look like a million bucks."

I took the blender out of the pantry for Geneva and set about peeling avocados on the drain board. She tried to swipe a bite, but I slapped her hand away.

"These aren't for eating," I said. "Facials, remember? Avocados for dry skin, oatmeal for oily."

"Are you nuts? Connie's got the whole entire Mary Kay product line in the back of her van. I say we let her take care of the facials, and smear those avocados on taco chips, the way God intended."

We decided to put it to a vote, which came up unanimous in favor of guacamole. While Geneva whipped up a batch of margaritas in the blender, I mashed lemon juice and Tabasco and salt into the avocados, and Connie walked back in carrying a bowl of turquoise-colored goo and draped a plastic cape over Audrey's T-shirt. Before long the kitchen reeked of citrus and noxious chemicals, and what with the blender and seven female voices—eight, counting Miss Loretta's—going all at once, you could hardly hear yourself think. Not that thinking was high on anybody's list of priorities, once the drinks started to flow. I wondered if Audrey had considered the wisdom of letting a woman chugging Seagram's apply peroxide to her scalp; but then, I figured, there wasn't much Connie could do, short of decapitation, that would make Audrey look any more dreadful than she already did.

Geneva and I stood propped against the kitchen counter, sipping margaritas and watching Connie work.

"So how'd it go with the priest this afternoon?" she asked.

"Who told you about that?"

She smiled. "A little bird. More than one, actually."

"It was all right. Kind of strange. He wasn't like any priest I ever saw before, that's for sure. He was young and sort of chubby, and he was wearing running clothes. Also, his name was—is—Punch."

"*Punch?*"

"He said he used to box, in school. Oh, and he's a drunk." Geneva leaned back and gave me a head-on glance. "Well, not anymore. But he used to be. In fact, he's in charge of the AA group down in Jefferson. That's how Ash met him."

"Ash is going to AA?"

"Trust me, you can't be any more surprised than I was. I found a pint of Jack Daniel's in his bathroom cabinet last night."

"What were you doing snooping in his bathroom cabinet?"

"Like you wouldn't have been doing the same thing, under the circumstances. Anyway, I had a nice visit with him—Punch—but I'm not really sure what good it did. I thought I was there to talk about Ash's drinking, but the priest just kept saying stuff like I need to let Ash worry about his problems and start holding up my end of the bargain. Every time I brought up Ash, it seemed like, the priest said, 'But what about *you*?' "

Geneva picked up the blender jar and divided the last of its contents between our two glasses. "You want to know what I think?" she said. "I think Mitchell ruined you for real life."

"What's Mitchell got to do with this?"

"Think about it. You were married for a long time to a man who never once rocked the boat. You might have been bored out of your mind, but you never had to learn how to handle the rough stuff. Then he dies, and along comes Ash, and boom, you've got a bunch of great big old sloppy feelings you don't know how to deal with. So, at the first sign of trouble, instead of trying to work things out, you pick up and run."

I stared into the depths of my drink. It occurred to me that the margaritas we were sipping were about the same color as Audrey's hair, or at least the color it had been, before tonight's intervention.

"Listen," Geneva said. "You remember back when we had that trouble, Bailey and me, and I went to stay with Lynda awhile?" I nodded that I did. I'd been pregnant with Jude, and Geneva, heartbroken over a series of miscarriages, had lashed out at me and Bailey and everyone in her path, going so far as to quit her job and move in with her sister up in Atlanta for a few weeks. "Do you think Bailey and I just magically patched things up, back then?" Geneva said. "That the Love Fairy just swung down and waved her wand over us and everything was back to normal?"

"He built you a gazebo," I reminded her.

"Well, yeah, and that was nice, but it wasn't what brought us back together. We talked things out, talked them to death, just about, and we worked to make it good again. And it was *hard* work. It still is, every day. Anybody who says it isn't is either crazy or lying."

"But Bailey isn't a drunk," I said.

"Everybody screws up, Lucy, sometime, somehow. You can't just throw in the towel every time one of you looks at the other one cross-eyed."

She took my empty glass and set it in the sink. "Look, I'm not necessarily talking about you and Ash getting back together," she said. "I'm talking about getting past what happened in Nashville. Not so much for his sake as for yours. So you can just let it go and, well, live your life."

Outside the kitchen window, a pinpoint of light caught my attention, the evening star rising above the trees in a dark blue sky. Here it was, a moment of perfect grace and clarity, courtesy of Mr. José Cuervo—a glimpse into a corner of your life where something that once hovered just out of reach suddenly comes to rest like a small, shimmering bird in your hand. Soon to be followed, I knew, by misery and recrimination and a splitting hangover; but all that was in the future, a blur on the horizon.

"Okay, who's next?" Connie shouted, moving Audrey to a seat at the far end of the table with a clear plastic cap over her head. "Come on, ladies, step right up! Lucy, how about you? A few highlights, maybe? Something to perk you up?"

I glanced at Geneva, who was mixing up another blender full of margaritas. "Go for it," she said, as Audrey and Dove took up the chant.

"You think?" I said. Geneva started making clucking sounds under her breath. "I've never put a chemical on my head in my life."

"All the more reason to do it, then."

Two hours later, Audrey had become a mostly-natural-looking honey blond, Dove's snow-white head was a radiant silver, and my own faded mane, more brown than red since having my son, was shot through with random strands of copper and chestnut and bronze. I stood gazing at my new reflection in the bathroom mirror, ignoring the rattling of the doorknob from the outside. The highlights, along with the eye shadow and lip gloss Connie'd insisted on adding, made me look mysterious and slightly sultry, like someone I could imagine admiring from afar, especially since the mirror didn't reveal my bare feet or torn cutoffs. I didn't feel one bit like me. I puckered up and blew the woman in the mirror a kiss, then laughed out loud.

The knob jiggled again, violently, and I reached behind me and unlatched it.

"Next time you decide to have Girlfriend Night, how about renting a couple of Porta Potties?" Audrey exclaimed, unzipping her jeans as she pushed me into the hall and kicked the door shut between us.

I passed through the living room just as Denny was coming in through the screen door, flipping her cell phone shut.

"Hey," she said. As she pushed her hair out of her face, I couldn't help noticing that her eyes were puffy, her nostrils pink.

"Was that Will?" I asked. All evening long, the thought of him and Ash had been fluttering right at the edge of my consciousness, like a pesky fly that wouldn't go away.

She shook her head, sticking the phone in her jeans pocket. "Can I ask you a question?" she said.

"Sure."

"Come back outside with me," she said, taking my arm. "My head feels funny."

The night air was warm and damp and smelled of pine mulch. I sank onto the top step, pulling Denny down beside me. Low clouds had gathered overhead, and a few stars shone through the milky haze. Behind my temples, the first hint of a headache loomed.

"What was it you wanted to ask me?"

"Do you think it's possible to be in love with two people at once?"

"What brought that up? Who was that you were talking to, just now?"

"You haven't answered my question," she said.

"You haven't answered mine."

"Erasmus," she said. "I was talking to Erasmus."

"I didn't realize the two of you were still in touch."

She closed her eyes, raking a hand through her hair, a gesture that, intentional or not, put me in mind of her daddy.

"We've always been in touch. He was in France over spring break, touring with some hotshot keyboardist. He called me as soon as he got back to New York."

"So, did he know about you and Will?"

"He knew I'd been seeing somebody. But— Let's just say the wedding came as a surprise."

"I take it he's not planning on sending y'all a place setting of china."

"He's threatening to come down here and kill Will, is what he's doing."

I laughed. "Oh, honey. Erasmus wouldn't kill a fly. He isn't about to start messing with Will Culpepper. That's just a lot of bluff. It's what guys do."

"You didn't hear him on the phone just now!" she said. "You didn't hear the things he said!" Tears brimmed in her eyes, spilling over onto her cheeks. "He called me a sellout and a chickenshit."

"What?"

"He said I've always been too scared to admit how I feel about him. That I'm scared of what people think. Because of, you know—the race thing."

"Is that true?"

"No! I couldn't care less about that stuff. It's just— There are too many other things. There always have been. I don't know if I can even explain it."

"But do you love him? Do you love him like you love Will?"

"It's not the same."

"How? You love him less than Will? More?"

She shook her head. "It's just— It's different."

We sat silently for a few minutes, listening to the din inside, the drone of crickets and a hoot owl off in the woods. "I'm about to do something really gross, okay?" she said, then lifted the hem of her tank top and blew her nose on it.

I scooted over and put my arm around her. Through the screen door we could hear Dove and Rowena laughing, the whir of the blender, Miss Loretta singing, "I miss being Mrs. tonight."

"What if he's right, Lucy?" she said. "What if Erasmus is the person I'm really supposed to be with, and Will really is just some, some smooth-talking schmoozer, and I've just made this huge, terrible mistake?"

"Oh, honey. I don't think you can—"

"Girlfriends? Hello!" Geneva's voice floated out through the screen from the front hallway. In a trilling soprano she began to sing: " 'Where have all the Farrells gone? Long time pa-assing . . .' " She elbowed open the screen door and stepped out onto the porch, crooning, " 'When will they e-e-ver learn?' "

Denny and I looked at each other and laughed. "We now come to the musical portion of our program," I said as she brushed away the last of her tears with her fingertips.

Geneva attempted to wedge herself between us on the top step while balancing a full tumbler, but there wasn't enough room for us to go three across, and Denny got squeezed onto the step below.

"It's not nice to walk out on your own party," Geneva said. "What are y'all doing out here?"

"Talking about Jesus and world peace," I said.

"Liar! You're talking about men."

"Denny's talking. I'm just the sounding board."

"What do you want to know, baby doll?" Geneva asked, slapping herself on the thigh. "Ask the expert!"

"I don't think you can help her," I said. "Seeing as you've been married to the same man for a hundred million years."

"You don't think that makes me an expert?"

Denny's cell phone chirruped, and she dug it out of her pocket and flipped it open to check the display.

"God!" she said. She stood up and walked out into the yard, wandering in figure-eights as she murmured into the tiny silver phone.

"So, what's going on?" Geneva asked.

"It seems Denny's not one-hundred-percent certain she married the right guy."

"Shit! Are you serious?" I nodded. "Were our lives ever that complicated?" Geneva sounded a little wistful, the way I guessed only a woman who'd been married to the same man for a hundred million years could.

"Two boys asked me to the homecoming dance once," I said. "Bob Whiting and Leonard Crocker. It was no contest, though. Bob was running back on the football team, all-state, and Leonard was just a nerd with a slide rule and a pocket protector." I reached for Geneva's tumbler and took a swallow.

"I bet you anything Bob's sacking groceries someplace and Leonard's running his own computer empire, flying around the world on his private plane. Hanging out with Donald Trump in Atlantic City."

I laughed. "Probably. But I got all the drama I needed for one lifetime anyhow." I took one last swallow and handed back her glass, which was down to mostly water. "How about you?" I asked as we watched Denny pace, bent over the phone and gesturing with her free hand, like the speaker was right in front of her and not fifteen hundred miles away. "Do you think much about what you missed?"

Geneva didn't answer me right away, and then she stood up. "You know what I could really use right now?"

"A week in Tahiti with Brad Pitt?"

"Hold that thought."

She went into the house and came back carrying a crush-proof box of Marlboro Lights. She shook one out of the pack, lighting it with a cheap plastic lighter, and dropped down beside me again, pulling in a chestful of smoke and then releasing it in a fine, practiced stream. "Want one?" she asked, tipping the pack toward me.

"Why not?"

She passed me a cigarette and lit it for me like I was an old pro. At the first puff my eyes watered and my lungs burned, but I managed not to choke. The second puff went a little smoother, and we smoked awhile in amiable silence.

"So," I said finally, "you were saying . . ."

"What was I saying?"

"Brad Pitt? Tahiti?"

"Oh yeah," she said. "You asked if I ever thought about what I'd missed."

"Well, do you?"

"I don't know, Lucy. We all make our little deals."

"What deals?"

"You know, with God, or the devil—whoever it is you think is running things. They're hard to keep sometimes, though."

I shook my head. Either I'd had too much to drink or not enough, because Geneva wasn't making any sense.

"I thought once we got Lily, it wouldn't be so hard," she said, "not being able to have a baby of my own. But it's been tougher than I thought, letting go."

"That new doctor, in Dallas," I said. "I thought he was supposed to be some kind of miracle-worker." She'd gone up a few weeks before for tests.

"He's a doctor, not a magician," she answered. It sounded like a line she'd picked up somewhere, or had been rehearsing in private. "He said my uterus is an inhospitable environment and it needs to come out. Those were his exact words."

"Jesus! That's the most hostile thing I've ever heard."

"Yeah, he's not much on bedside manner, but he's tops in his field."

"I don't care! I can't believe you'd even think of letting somebody like that cut you open."

"Oh, he won't be doing the cutting. Dr. Crawford will. Next Tuesday morning, six A.M., at County." She dropped her cigarette to the ground and together we watched it smolder. "I meant to tell you earlier. I just— Well, I didn't want to spoil the party."

I put out my own cigarette, half-smoked, and reached for her nearest hand. It was icy, and I held it between both of mine.

"How's Bailey taking it?" I asked.

"He's been after me to do it for a long time. Not just because of the miscarriages. Everybody—Dr. C., the guy in Dallas, everybody—says I'll feel better, be a lot healthier, once it's done. Anyway, Bailey's never been as single-minded about having a baby as I have. I mean, he's got Lily now."

"You've got Lily, too."

"I do. I know." I realized she was trembling all over, like a lightly blown leaf.

"Gen?" I said.

"Just do me a favor, would you? Don't tell me how lucky I am. I am, I know I am, but just don't say it to me right now, okay?"

She inched closer to me on the step and I wrapped my arms around her and we huddled together like Eskimos.

"I want you to promise me something," she said, resting her head on my shoulder. "If anything ever happens to me—"

"Hush," I said. "Don't you know it's bad luck to talk that way?"

"Promise, anyway."

"Nothing's going to happen to you. We're both going to live forever." In my mind's eye I could see us plain as day, two old ladies, as craggy and fierce and gray as battleships, sitting on a porch like this one and watching the sun set, with grandbabies in our laps and dogs at our feet. Jude and Lily would visit, and Denny, of course, bringing us candy and cigarettes and trashy magazines and gossip. Denny would be an old lady by then, too, but a glamorous one, like Loretta Lynn, with bones like scaffolding and a complicated personal life and still, forever, that voice.

Geneva sighed. "Did anybody ever tell you you're a saint?"

"All the time."

Denny shut her phone and started back toward the house. She didn't even blink at the sight of Geneva and me hunched in each other's arms like a pair of cliff-hangers, just sank down on the step below us and wedged her body between our knees, then picked up Geneva's Marlboro Lights, plucked one out of the package, and lit it with expert fingers. She inhaled, then blew out a plume of smoke, peering at me through slanted eyes.

"Everything okay?" I asked, making my voice light.

"Let's not talk about it right now, okay? It's Girlfriend Night." She pulled on her cigarette. She looked agitated and fierce and beautiful, like a warrior princess, and I felt a swell of pride weighted with sadness that, other than my love and my company and my useless advice, she was wholly herself, that there was nothing else in the world she needed from me.

I looked at Geneva, who smiled and shut her eyes and lowered her head back to my shoulder. Denny leaned back against my knees, and I reached down and lifted her hair in my hands. There are so many places mothers can't go; the older kids get, the more ways they find, on purpose or not, to shut you out, and so I knew to take what I could get: the sharp jut of her shoulder blades against my shins, my fingers in her heavy, sweet-smelling hair.

Headlights appeared at the end of the road, rising and falling between the trees. Geneva lifted her head, and the three of us sat up straight as they approached.

"That's not the boys, back already?"

"It better not be," Denny said. "I told them not to even think about coming home before midnight."

But this wasn't Ash's pickup rolling slowly up the unpaved road toward the house. As the vehicle turned into the yard and swung in behind Geneva's pickup, there was no mistaking the light brown cruiser with the Cade County Sheriff's Department seal on the side.

chapter thirteen

I struggled to my feet, feeling like my legs had cotton batting where the bones used to be. The cruiser's door opened and Marjo Malone climbed out, adjusting her gun belt.

"Evenin', ladies," she called. "How's the party?"

Maybe this was a social visit. Maybe Marjo had heard about Girlfriend Night and had decided to drive out and avail herself of a dye job and some spicy Velveeta dip. Or maybe they'd caught Audrey on tape, buying Smirnoff Ice at the Miracle Mart. The possibilities were infinite, but they all seemed to keep circling back to the same, sure center.

Marjo turned and opened the rear door of the cruiser. "Okay, boys," she said. "Climb on out. And no funny stuff, okay? I've had about enough of y'all for one evening already."

"I knew it," I said, grabbing Denny's arm. "I knew this was a bad idea the minute you said it."

Will emerged first, head bent. As Denny and I rushed down the steps into the glare of the cruiser's headlights, I saw that he held a blood-soaked bar towel to his face, and the front of his shirt was splattered as well. The front door of the house opened and women came pouring out, jabbering like a flock of magpies.

"Oh my God!" Denny cried, flinging her arms around Will. "What happened?"

"He broke my fucking nose, that's what!"

"Your fucking nose isn't broken," Ash said from inside the car. He got out slowly, prodding his jaw with his fingertips. There was blood on his shirt, too, though less than on Will's, and his bottom lip was split. "Anyway, you knocked my fucking teeth loose."

"Hear now!" Marjo said. "What've I just been telling y'all on the ride over? We got plenty of empty beds in the jail. I'd be happy to give you both a ride back to town and a night to think this over." Both men stared at the ground like schoolboys after a scolding. "Now I want y'all to cool your jets, work this out like human bein's. And don't make me come out here again, 'cause if I get another call, I guarantee you I'm not gonna be in such a charitable mood." Marjo turned and nodded to me. "'Night, ladies," she said. "Sorry to bust up y'all's good time."

"Thank you," I said, "for not— For bringing them home."

"Like I said—let's work on keepin' it in the family from here on out, okay?" She lowered herself into the cruiser and drove away.

Denny managed to get Will to drop the towel long enough to determine that the blood, while there was plenty of it, had stopped flowing, and even though his nose was swollen and purplish, it didn't seem broken. The ladies fluttered around eagerly, leaning in for a better look at this new husband of Denny's, made all the more tantalizing by his injury, chatting among themselves about what had happened, whether or not he ought to go to the hospital.

I walked over to where Ash stood, working his jaw with his fingers. I stepped up and pried his hand from his face so that I could get a better look, but in the yard light it was hard to see. "Let's get you inside," I said. "Clean you up a little."

"Not in there," Ash said as we watched Denny leading Will up the porch steps, his face still covered by the bloody towel, trailed by a gaggle of females. "He wants to turn this into a circus, let him. I've had a bigger piece of it than I reckoned on already."

"Your place, then." He shrugged, turned toward the trailer. I managed to catch Dove's eye, waved that I was going with Ash, then followed him inside to the bathroom.

As I switched on the overhead light, his reflection leapt into harsh relief, the horizontal ridges of his cheekbones, his busted lip, his eyes pink-rimmed and exhausted-looking. "Here," I said, tilting his jaw toward the light. He winced as I touched it gently with my fingers.

"Tee furt," he said.

"What?"

He pointed with his thumb toward his lower incisors.

"Let's see," I said.

He tipped back his chin and let his mouth fall open. There was no mistaking the smell of beer on his breath, but this didn't seem like the time to make a point of it. I prodded his molars as gingerly as I could. They didn't feel loose, though the gums were red and angry-looking. "I think they'll hold," I said. "That lip looks pretty ugly, though. Have you got anything to clean it up with?"

"Whiskey."

I guessed it would have to do. I grabbed the pint bottle out of the cabinet along with a washcloth and steered him toward the bedroom. Without a word he dropped onto the mattress, tilting back his chin and closing his eyes. I knelt beside him and opened the bottle and touched it to the cloth, pressing it against the cut on his bottom lip.

"Ow," he whispered, but slowly his head fell back and he let go a long, bone-weary sigh. I touched and retouched the lip of the whiskey bottle to the washrag and dabbed it against his mouth.

"Better?" I asked.

"Mm." He lifted his hand and wrapped it around mine, holding the cloth to his lip. How, I wondered, was it possible to harbor such conflicted feelings about someone and not go crazy, to feel so tender and furious at the same time?

"Hair's different," he said.

"What?"

"You did something to your hair. Looks good." He shut his eyes.

"I met your priest today," I said. "Father Laughlin." Ash opened one eye and squinted at me. "You could've warned me," I said. "I wasn't prepared for a fat guy in running shorts named Punch."

"He's not Bing Crosby, that's for sure."

"He was pruning rosebushes when I got there. I thought he was the gardener."

"He *is* the gardener. I think he wears about two dozen hats around that place."

"Well, I hope he knows more about running a church than he does about roses. He'd never even heard of black spot before."

"So what'd you talk about? Besides roses."

"He thinks you're the most interesting drunk in northeast Texas."

"That's not saying much." He squeezed my hand again. "How about you?"

"I don't know any other drunks, so I haven't got a lot of room for comparison."

"I mean, what'd he say about you?"

"He said—let's see. Well, the main thing I recall is that love is a gift. Not to be squandered, but neither to be . . . something."

"You and Punch talked about love?"

"Punch talked. I was just the audience."

Ash lowered my hand to his chest. "What else did he say?" he asked.

"That I need to deal with my own problems and let you deal with yours. But that's what you paid him to tell me, right?"

"Sassy," he said, and closed his eyes again. "Sassy girl."

"How come you hit Will Culpepper?"

Ash shook his head without opening his eyes. "Do me a favor. Lie down here a second, would you?" He patted his shoulder. "Just lay your head right here."

"But there's a party going on over at the house," I said. "I've got guests."

"I hate to tell you, Lucy, but I think Girlfriend Night is over."

I set down the washcloth and the bottle and stretched out beside him, nestling my head into the niche between his neck and his shoulder. He worked his hand into my hair, and I rested my hand lightly on his chest, his bloody T-shirt. In the months since I'd left Nashville, all those nights I'd woken up alone in the middle of the night, I wondered if this wasn't the thing I'd missed most, the rhythm of Ash's heart under my hand. What if we never found a way to make it work and I had to let it go for good, this drumbeat, the guarantee I needed that the world was still turning? Would I ever find anything to take its place? Would I have the heart myself to go on looking?

His breathing grew deep and steady, and gradually mine slowed to match his, and we breathed that way, together, in and out, until we were both half-drowsing. I closed my eyes and turned my face to the side of his neck, inhaling soap and cotton and whiskey and dried blood. Who said everything had to have a reason, or, for that matter, that the reason had to be a good one? Morning would come anyway, regardless. I was dimly aware of voices in the yard, the sound of engines starting up and driving away as I lay breathing in, breathing out, counting the beats of Ash's heart under my hand.

Before I got to a hundred, there came a sharp rap on the front door. Both Ash and I bolted upright, rolled off the mattress, and stumbled to our feet, and I jogged after him up the hall.

Denny stood at the foot of the cinder blocks, barefoot and rumpled, her eyes swollen from crying. "I—we—" She raked her hands through her hair, looked wild-eyed over her shoulder. "I just came to tell you, we're leaving."

"*Leaving?*" I pushed past Ash, into the yard. "But why?" Denny just shook her head miserably. I turned and looked at Ash. "This is your fault, isn't it? There's something you're not telling me."

He spoke over me to Denny. "Baby girl, I think everybody needs to calm down a little. Go back inside and get some sleep. Things will look a whole lot different in the—"

Out front of the house, an engine roared to life: the little two-seater rental car. I reached for Denny's arm, but she stepped backward, out of my grasp.

"Oh, honey, please. What's going on? Can't we just talk about—whatever it is?"

The back door opened and Will stepped out onto the step. "This bus is pulling out!" he shouted. "If you're coming, then come on!"

"Wait a minute!" I moved across the yard past Denny to where Will stood, gripping the handle of their duffel bag in both hands. His hair was wet and combed back, his nose a ripe plum. "What do you think you're doing?" I said. "You can't just take off like this, in the middle of the night, with no explanation! Denny? You're not going with him, are you?" She stood slump-shouldered, weeping. "Look, whatever happened, we can fix it. Just slow down a minute and—"

"We haven't got time for this." Will leaned past me and grabbed for Denny's arm. He wasn't a big man, but for the first time I smelled real danger on him. He stared at Denny, mesmerizing her; I could see her start to sway like a snake.

In an instant Ash had materialized beside me. "You lay a hand on her," he said, "and you're going to be looking at a lot more than a busted nose."

For a minute they squared off, eye to eye. Then Will took a step backward and swung the duffel bag up the steps.

"Fine." He jerked his chin at Denny. "It's your call. You can stand here all night and boo-hoo to Daddy, or you can come with me."

He went up the steps carrying the bag and through the screen door, letting it slam. Denny stood, barefoot in the dirt, weaving and hiccupping. Out front, the trunk of the rental car slammed shut; the motor revved.

"I have to go," she whispered.

"No! You can't!" Something terrible was going to happen; it was one of those gut mother fears, of twisted metal, lights and sirens, the sheriff, for the second time in one night, knocking on your door. I followed Denny up the steps and through the house, but she was pushing away from me with everything she had, batting at me blindly like a swarm of wasps. "Wait!" I called as she crawled into the passenger seat and Will reached across her and slammed the door shut, and the little black car fired up and pulled out, scorching a trail of red dust and rubber I could taste on my tongue as it careened down the road and out toward the highway. I listened to the transmission whine its way through the gears for a quarter of a mile before it finally faded into the night.

Dazed, I wandered back into the house, up the hall to the bedroom, where lights still burned, the bedcovers were disheveled, a damp towel lay on the floor. It didn't seem possible that things could have fallen apart so fast, like Denny and Will had just vaporized into thin air.

I heard Ash behind me, and turned to face him in the doorway, clenching my hands together. "What did you do? Ash, you have to tell me."

He sighed, shook his head "We went to the Tap, right? To watch the ball game, have a couple beers."

"Okay."

"So things weren't exactly going great guns, conversation-wise. I mean, the guy's only interested in one subject, as far as I can tell—Will Culpepper. He didn't even know who the Rangers' pitcher was."

"That doesn't begin to explain how things ended up this way."

"We'd been sitting there awhile, and some guy walks over. Says, 'Hey, aren't you Ash Farrell? My wife and I love your records, man. Can't hardly wait for the next one.' He's sticking this cocktail napkin under my nose for my autograph when Will Culpepper pipes up, 'Well, it's gonna be a long wait.' "

I felt a hollow growing in the pit of my stomach.

"The guy looked at Will a little weird, but he just said thanks when I signed his napkin and walked away. I asked Will what the hell he thought he was doing. 'Just talking truth. It is the truth, ain't it?' he says. 'What business is it of yours if it is?' I ask him. 'None at all. Except that your baby girl thinks you're some kind of hero. How you think she feels about this, you dragging around like a sorry-ass has-been?' " I sat down on the bed. A stray sock lay abandoned in the middle of the mattress, and I picked it up and held it in my lap. "Jesus, Lucy—what was I supposed to do?"

"What *did* you do?"

"Stood up and called him a little shit. He stood up and called me a self-centered asshole. 'You're a fine one to talk,' I said, and gave him a tap. He tapped me back, and next thing you know, we're rolling around like a couple of pit bulls on the barroom floor."

I dropped the sock, stood up, went to the closet, and dug out my old track shoes and sat down to lace them on. I found my purse, my car keys.

"You'll never bring her back, you know," Ash said as I walked past him and out the door. "Not till she wises up to the bastard on her own."

But I hardly needed him to tell me that.

HALF AN HOUR later I found myself at the curb in front of Geneva and Bailey's house in town, the motor of my Blazer running, staring at the kitchen window where, at one-thirty in the morning, a light burned.

A face appeared at the window, and seconds later the porch light came on and the front door opened and there stood Geneva in a fuzzy robe and slippers. I shut off the motor. Somehow I managed to get out of the car, to make it up the walk.

Geneva took my arm and pulled me inside. "What are you doing here?"

"Is Jude okay?"

"Sure. Come see."

I stood at the doorway to Lily's bedroom, gazing at her in the top bunk and Jude in the lower, their sleeping faces illuminated by the faint glow of the night-light. Jude had kicked his covers into a ball at the foot of the bed, and lay sprawled with one arm over his head and one bare foot dangling toward the floor.

I tiptoed into the room and knelt beside him, watching his lashes flutter against his cheeks, his rusty crew cut dark against the pillow. I rested my head beside his, breathing him in. I had to resist the urge to crawl in beside him, to cover his body with mine, curling myself around him the way I hadn't since he was a baby, to snatch him out of bed and drag him out to the car and drive away with him into the night. To tell the truth, I don't know what I might have done if Geneva hadn't put her hand on my arm and, slowly but firmly, eased me to my feet and back toward the door.

"There's coffee, just made," she whispered, leading me up the hall.

"What are you doing up at one-thirty in the morning?" I asked, slumping into a kitchen chair.

"I think that's supposed to be my line."

A magazine lay on the table, the checkout-stand kind with stories about how to spice up your marriage and lose those last stubborn ten pounds. The cover showed a scrawny model in a thong bikini alongside the headline, "How Much Is Too Much? Get the Orgasms You Deserve!"

"I'm glad to see you're improving your mind," I said.

"I guess I'm supposed to be reading some eight-hundred-page Russian novel at this hour?" She took down a couple of flower-printed mugs from the cupboard and filled them from the industrial-size coffeemaker on the counter.

"No, you're supposed to be sleeping next to your adoring husband."

"So are you."

"Last time I checked, I didn't have one."

Geneva handed me my coffee and I started talking. As I described the part where Denny and Will drove off, she got up and took a Sara Lee cheesecake out of the freezer and cut two generous slabs and placed one in front of each of us. When I got to the part where Ash explained what had sparked their departure, she got up again and put the rest of the cheesecake in the middle of the table, and we dug straight into the aluminum tin, carving out jagged pieces with our forks, washing them down with hot black coffee.

"But, Lucy," she said when I'd finished, "it's plain as day, isn't it? He feels threatened."

"Will Culpepper? Threatened?"

"Of Ash. He wants to be the main man in Denny's life, and he's afraid he won't measure up."

"That doesn't make any sense. He's her *husband.*"

"Honey, that's just men for you. I remember when I first took Bailey home to meet my folks, Daddy treated him like a serial killer. Then, our second Thanksgiving together, out of the pure blue, Daddy invited Bailey to go hunting. I don't think I slept that whole weekend. I kept waiting for the sheriff to drive up and say one of them had shot the other one. But all they did was get drunk on peach brandy and fall in a creek and freeze their asses off. And things have been fine between them ever since."

"Well, Will Culpepper scares me shitless. You should've seen how he talked to Denny. But it's like she's so confused she can't see straight. And now they've taken off for Lord knows where . . ."

"I hate to tell you, Lucy, but Denny's a big girl now. So long as she got in that car of her own free will—"

"Funny," I said.

"What?"

"Free *will*?" I repeated. Geneva made a face and shook her head. "Sorry. I guess I'm a little punchy." I sighed, pushed away my plate. "Your turn," I said.

"For what?"

"True confessions. Why you're prowling around the house drinking coffee at one in the morning."

"I don't know. I haven't been sleeping much lately. It doesn't seem fair to Bailey, lying there tossing and turning, keeping him awake, so . . ."

"So, you sit up reading articles about"—I glanced at the magazine—"death by orgasm?"

"No, I sit up and think about what it's gonna be like, five days from now, waking up in County General without a uterus."

"You aren't really scared about the operation, are you?"

Geneva shook her head. "Dr. C.'s done so many hysterectomies by now, he could probably do them in his sleep. It's just that—well, I guess I've been thinking about how this really is the end of the line for me."

"That you'll never have a baby, you mean."

"It's crazy, I know, but I've been thinking about you. How you and Mitchell tried for fourteen years, then he died and you met Ash and just like that . . ." She held up her fingers and snapped them. "Don't look at me like that. I know it means the problem was most likely with Mitchell, not you. Still, I've always had it in the back of my mind . . ."

"What? That you should have slept with Ash a few times, just to be sure?"

"No! But you know what it's like. How your mind gets. I got to thinking maybe there was some weird combination of Bailey's sperm and my egg, something that made me keep losing the babies. That maybe some other guy might have the—what should I call it?"

"The magic bullet?"

She stood up and gathered our empty cups and set them in the sink. "Anyway, I never really would have done anything about it. It's just one of those things that goes through your mind at one A.M., you know? 'What if? What if?' "

"Yeah. I know 'what if.' "

"You want to crash here the rest of the night? The guest room's made up. I can wake you up at six. Give you time to get home and get changed for work."

I stood and walked around the table and opened my arms, and she stepped into them, a big, fuzzy terrycloth presence, solid as a sofa. "I'm sorry," I said into her shoulder.

"What for?"

"That we didn't get everything we wanted. You and me both."

"Nobody gets everything they want."

"Some do."

"Like who?"

I thought for a minute. "Faith Hill," I said. "I bet she doesn't wander around the house half the night thinking about what she'd do over if she could."

"Well, I don't either, mostly. And neither should you. We're the lucky ones. When we're old ladies rocking on the porch together, you'll know that. It's all we'll talk about."

I pulled back, wiped my eyes, nodded, and she looped her arm through mine and led me down the carpeted hall, to where the ones we loved lay dreaming.

chapter fourteen

Luckily, it was a slow morning in the shop, and I was able to sit in the office and pretend to work on the books while Peggy and Audrey gave me a wide berth. At lunchtime Audrey came in and asked if I wanted anything from Dairy Queen, but I just shook my head. Shortly after she left, I heard the doorbells chime out front, and Peggy poked her head around the door frame to say I had a visitor. I didn't have to ask who; it was written all over her face.

"Can't you say I'm trying to finish up the payroll?"

"Oh, Lucy," she said. "He just seems so . . ." She shook her head, like there was no word in her vocabulary to describe it.

"All right," I said, rolling my chair away from the desk. "He's got two minutes."

After three and a half hours of sleep the night before, I was more than a little annoyed by the sight of Ash leaning his elbows on the counter out front, looking as fresh and chipper as if he'd just spent two weeks at a spa. The fact that the last time we'd seen each other we'd been trading recriminations and lame excuses back and forth like tennis volleys seemed to have slid straight out of his memory; he looked bright-eyed, bushy-tailed, damn near born again.

"You had lunch yet?" he asked.

"I'm skipping it," I answered. "Too much work."

"I'll take you up to Willie B.'s. Buy you a rib plate."

"I can't."

"Aw, come on. I want to show you something."

"Something like what?"

He closed one eye, smiling mysteriously. "Gotta take a ride with me and find out."

"Ash, I haven't got time for this. Besides, I'm mad at you. Have you forgotten? You ran Denny off last night."

"Denny ran off because of her cheap-shit scumbag of a husband. That doesn't make it my fault. Anyway, she called the house this morning."

My heart fluttered in my chest. "Is everything okay?"

"They were at some rest stop. Will was inside, paying for gas. She said he hadn't spoken to her for four hundred miles. Sounded like she'd been crying for most of them. But when I said I'd come get her, she said no, that she was sure this was just one of those bumps in the road that all new couples go through. She said she was sure everything would be okay once they got back to Nashville and had some time to talk things out."

I sighed. "What's this thing you want to show me?"

"It's not far from here. Maybe twenty minutes. I'll have you back in an hour."

"Audrey's at lunch, and I don't know if Peggy can cover for me."

"Sure I can." She stepped out of the cooler, where I realized she'd been hovering all along, carrying a pot full of paperwhites as a decoy. "Go. You haven't had a break all day. Audrey and I can run things for an hour without you."

I looked at Ash, who shrugged and smiled as if to say, *There you go.* "I should have known you two would be in cahoots," I said, taking my purse out from under the counter. "This doesn't have anything to do with the Piney View Motor Court, does it?" I asked as I followed him out to the truck.

"We'd need a lot more than an hour for the Piney View Motor Court," he said, opening the passenger-side door for me.

"In your dreams."

He laughed. "Relax. We're just going for a little ride."

We proceeded slowly around the courthouse square out of town, past the Food King and the elementary school, and turned north on farm road 1399. As we passed the city limits sign, Ash pressed the accelerator and the big truck surged forward as the heavy-duty engine kicked in and then leveled out as it picked up speed. He hit a button to send the windows sliding down, and a warm spring wind whipped through the cab, making conversation impossible, especially after Ash slipped a Louvin Brothers CD into the slot and cranked up the volume.

Oddly enough, I felt relaxed for the first time all day, riding next to Ash through the woods, the road a curving black ribbon through a tunnel of pines, breathing in the familiar smells of sun on pine bark and mown hay and cattle. I closed my eyes and leaned my head against the leather headrest, letting the breeze snarl my hair, listening to Charlie and Ira Louvin's sweet, old-time voices singing, *When I stop dreaming, that's when I'll stop loving you.*

I opened my eyes as the truck slowed, and saw that we were approaching the turn to the house. But Ash turned left rather than right off the highway, onto the red-dirt road we called Bates Road, after the family who'd lived there for sixty years, growing corn and sorghum on their two-hundred-acre spread. The old folks, Ruth and David Bates, had passed away when I was just a kid, but their son, Little David, had continued to farm the place until just a few years back, when his wife got cancer and died after a long haul in County General, after which he'd packed up his clothes and sold off the furniture and moved to Florida, to be near his daughter and grandkids. A FOR SALE sign had been nailed to a post next to the highway for so long that the plastic was warped and the letters faded from red to dusty pink. Who was going to buy two hundred defunct acres in this deep, forgotten part of the East Texas Piney Woods? Folks were moving away from Cade County nowadays, not into it, and those farmers who remained were the last of a breed, gradually letting go of any hope of passing along the family business to their offspring, who were heading out of town before the ink on their high school diplomas was dry, bound for the wider world they saw on cable TV and read about on the Internet.

"How long's it been since you've been out here?" Ash asked as he steered the truck slowly over the ruts and bumps in the road.

"Lord, ages. Since Junie Bates got sick, I guess, and I brought over some food. King Ranch casserole, I think it was."

"It's pretty, isn't it?" The fields, once cultivated, now grew wild with tall grass and black-eyed Susans and Indian paintbrush. We rolled past the pink brick ranch-style house, which looked sturdy but haunted somehow, the barn, always Little David's pride and joy, starting to show signs of neglect: a door hanging off its hinges, peeling paint.

"You ever been to the back of the property?" Ash asked as the road narrowed into a thick awning of pines.

"Once, in high school. Norma had a bonfire at Halloween. We were juniors, I think."

"That always cracked me up," Ash said.

"What's that?"

"That the Bateses named their daughter Norma. Like, are they the only people on the planet who never heard of Alfred Hitchcock?"

I smiled. "Poor Norma." It hadn't helped that she was skinny, dark, and twitchy, like her cinematic counterpart. As I recalled it, the bonfire wasn't much of a success; only six or eight kids showed up, and the main form of entertainment had involved a couple members of the track team sneaking off into the woods with a bottle of Mad Dog 20/20, returning there later, presumably, to puke it back up again. It was hard to picture Norma as a housewife in Kissimmee with two sons, but I guessed she was one of the ones who'd managed somehow to triumph over her past, or at least move beyond it.

Sunlight appeared through the canopy and we emerged from the tunnel of trees into a clearing, the sky opening up overhead, as blue as the ceiling of an Italian church. To the right was a field like the ones we'd driven past earlier, overgrown with grass and wildflowers. To the left was a small dog-trot cottage the elder Bateses had once rented out to a man who helped with the crops and other odds jobs around the place, so long back that nobody in town could even remember his name. I doubted it had been lived in for at least forty years, and it showed; the once-white paint had faded to gray, the roof sagged, and a couple of the windows had holes in the panes from unlucky birds or local kids with bottles of Mad Dog in their pockets and nothing to do.

"Look there," Ash said as a body of water came into view. If it had been here when Norma had that bonfire nearly twenty-five years before, I'd either forgotten or hadn't seen it in the dark; or maybe my topography was off, and the party had been on some other part of the property. It was a nice-sized pond, an acre at least, banded with pines and maples and mirroring an irregular blue oval of sky. What was left of a wooden dock tilted from the shore into the water like a drunk stumbling to his knees, and an old rowboat was tethered to a tree on the far bank.

Ash coasted to a stop and cut the engine. "What did I tell you?" he said as we gazed through the windshield. "Pretty, huh?"

"I can't believe I never saw this before. Why didn't the Bateses build their house back here, I wonder? Two hundred acres, and they let the hired man have the nicest piece of it?"

I opened the door and slid to the ground, wandering through the high grass toward the water. It was a balmy day, cloudless and still, but you could feel summer right around the corner, boiling behind that sky like a pot about to lose its lid, turning loose the bugs and heat and humidity. Out on the pond something caught my eye, dark and quick, skimming along the surface—a snake, probably a cottonmouth, hunting for some nice flesh to sink its fangs into. I'd lived in the country more than half my life and, while I didn't have a fear of snakes, exactly, I did have a healthy respect for them.

"Hey." Ash came up behind me through the grass, carrying a can of Dr Pepper. I still had my eye peeled for the snake, but it was gone. "It's great out here, isn't it?" he said. "Can't you just feel the energy?"

"I just saw a water moccasin."

"That's one of the things I love about it. It's so wild. Look there," he said, as a great gray bird soared out of the woods on the far shore, coming in low on one wing like a stunt pilot, and settled itself in the shallows near the rowboat on a spindly leg.

I turned and studied the look on Ash's face, a look I knew well and feared nearly as much.

"What's on your mind, Ash?"

"It's a great spot for a house, isn't it?"

"You already have a house. In Nashville." Not to mention his half-interest in the place I lived in, just across the highway.

"I'm not going back to Nashville."

"How can you say that?"

"I know my mind, Lucy. I knew it before I ever left that place, and I know it for sure now. Here." He nodded toward the water with the pride of some would-be monarch, like this was his birthright, his eminent domain.

"I've got the whole thing already drawn up in my head," he said. "A timber-frame place, maybe four bedrooms, a big stone fireplace in the main room, nice-size kitchen, with a wraparound deck. And this whole side of the house will be glass, so you can look out over the water from every room."

The sun played across the surface of the water, spackling it red and gold. A breeze moved in the grass like a phantom sigh. The gray bird slowly spread its wings and took off, sailing over the trees.

"I remember Little David told me cranes migrate through here sometimes, a couple of times a year," Ash said. "On their way to the coast in the springtime, and back to wherever it is they go in winter. Canada, or Siberia." His eyes stayed fixed on the space where the bird used to be. "They're symbols of good luck, you know."

"I think you'd better get yourself a field guide. That was a heron, not a crane."

"I know what it was. It's too late in the season for cranes. I'm thinking next fall. If we get started pretty quick, the place should be finished by then."

"Who's 'we'?"

"Isaac and me. If the weather holds, we can get it knocked out in a couple, few months."

"Hasn't Isaac got his hands full already, working maintenance at the hospital and taking care of a wife and seven kids?"

"I told him I'd pay him twice what he's making at the hospital."

"How are you planning to finance all this?" Even in deep East Texas, two hundred acres wouldn't come cheap, to say nothing of materials and labor.

"We'd have to sell the place in Nashville."

I took a breath, held it, let it slowly and deliberately out again. "By rights, that place is half mine."

"I know that. You'll get your share. And I'll get mine, to do what I want with."

"And this is what you want? I don't get it, Ash. What are you trying to prove?"

"I need to do this, Lucy. I need something to keep me busy, to make me feel useful again. And I need to do it here, in this place. Don't ask me how I know that. I just do."

We tipped back our heads to watch a jet plane pass by high overhead, leaving a cottony white contrail across the sky.

"Look," he said. "For most of my life, music mattered to me more than anything in the world. But when the whole thing fell apart, up in the rehab, I realized it wasn't music I missed. It was this." We stood quietly side by side, taking in the fields and water and the woods beyond. "All I can tell you is, this feels like where I belong."

"This house you want to build," I said. "It would be for you and Jude?"

"It would be for my family. Whoever that turns out to be."

We stood side by side for a while in silence.

"What about the place in Nashville?" I asked finally. "You think it'll sell?"

"I've been talking to an agent. She's already got an offer. What we paid plus six percent. Cash on the barrelhead." He paused, then added, "I've got the contract in the truck. All we have to do is sign."

"Six percent?" The numbers tumbled in my head, divided by half, along with the thought of not having to live hand to mouth, paycheck to paycheck.

"Let's say I agree to this plan," I said. "You do still get that I think it's crazy, right? You and Isaac out here with your saws and hammers, building yourself a little house on the prairie?"

"You wait," Ash said. "Wait till November. We'll have us a big cookout, and I'll bring you out to see the cranes, and you can call me crazy all you want."

IN A PATCH of shade under the same towering pines where Ash and I had courted seven years before, we sat on opposite sides of a scarred picnic table over Styrofoam plates of pork ribs and potato salad and coleslaw and tall paper cups of sweet tea. Willie had retired from the barbeque business a couple of years earlier, after he had to have his knee replaced, but his son, Lam, still ran the place out of the same metal shed, with the longtime pit man, Marcus Strum, and a young apprentice—nephew or cousin—keeping things smoking out back in the cookers. Ash ate silently but steadily as I picked at my food and read through the real-estate contract. It looked legitimate; everything he'd told me at the Bates's place was there, including the mind-boggling offer price. The buyers were even willing to assume closing costs.

"Will we have to go up for the closing?" I asked, picking up my fork.

"Oh, hell, no. They do everything with fax machines and FedEx."

"What about our stuff? You know, the contents of the house?"

"I can hire somebody to ship it. Or put it in storage, whatever you want."

"Well," I said, letting my eyes roam again over the figures on the bottom line, "whoever it is must want the place awful bad."

"Some young kid who just signed his first record deal," Ash said. "You remember what that was like. You can hardly wait to start proving to the world that you're the real thing."

"You *were* the real thing," I said. "You didn't need a twelve-thousand-square-foot house to make it true."

"Well, I thought I did. But like I told you—things have changed. What I want has changed."

"You know," I said, "you always did your best writing when you were building things. That summer you were remodeling Mrs. Mackey's kitchen, you came up with a new song just about every day."

"Yeah, but there were—what do you call them?—extenuating circumstances."

"Like what?"

"I was in love," he said.

I started to make a joke about how I'd always suspected tomfoolery between him and Loretta Mackey—the way she hung around the kitchen while Ash worked, in her polka-dot blouses knotted at the midriff, offering him hot coffee or cold beer and dropping hints about her husband's long, frequent business trips—but something in Ash's face stopped me.

In spite of how long and how well I'd known him, it seemed to me Ash was always hiding behind something, behind jokiness or charm or anger or the blues. I could probably count on the fingers of both hands the number of times I'd felt he was letting me see him the way he really was, stripped of his mask, his true self laid bare. Our wedding had been one of those times, Jude's birth another. And I'd seen it, I realized, a few times during the years in Nashville, times he'd arrived home from the road or the recording studio exhausted and disappointed; I'd come downstairs in the middle of the night and find him at the kitchen table, his face pale and haggard, and I'd see straight into him, into a place that I had to admit now, to my shame, I hadn't wanted to see, and so I'd either picked a fight, or turned and gone back up to bed. Was it any wonder we'd grown so far apart? I'd used Ash's drinking as the excuse, but the truth was I'd been a coward. Instead of letting myself see how far gone he really was, I'd turned tail and run.

This time, I made myself look. Maybe I knew I'd never be able to live with myself if I didn't, or maybe I was ready now, in a way I hadn't been before. What I felt was the thing I'd felt the first time I'd ever sat with Ash under these trees, the sense that we knew each other in some way that went beyond the here and now, that harked back to old souls, past lives. I'd been raised Baptist, and a lot of the old ways still ran deep in me, but part of me was sure, in a way that went beyond the doors of a church or the pages of a Bible, that there was something else out there. Life was short, and you never knew when you might run into a fellow traveler—a countryman, as Ash liked to call them—but I knew they were rare, and that when you found one, you were bound to him or her, obliged to stand up for each other. Ash and I had failed each other over and over, in so many ways, and yet here we were—again, still—in the only place that felt like home.

I looked at him; I saw. I took him in—not husband or lover, but this fellow traveler, this countryman. I folded open the real-estate contract to the first of many little flags that read SIGN HERE, and asked him for a pen.

THE NEXT AFTERNOON I was picking my way through the bleachers toward Geneva at Little League when, a few rows down, Corinne Jackson twisted around and hollered after me, "Hey, Lucy! Hear you're fixing to get a new neighbor across the road!"

I turned to look at her, along with the other couple of dozen parents in the stands. She jerked her chin toward the outfield, where Ash stood behind third base. I watched Jude race across the field toward him in his Hatch Brothers shirt and cap and throw himself at Ash, who scooped our son into his arms, swinging him to and fro. Even from that distance, I could hear their wild, whooping laughter.

I gave Corinne a tight little smile and slid onto the bench alongside my sister-in-law. She offered me a tall paper cup, and I took a sip: lemonade.

"I'll never get over the way news travels in this town," I said. "It's like the plague."

"Well, I'm a little pissed off about it, to tell you the truth," Geneva said. "Why didn't you call me? How come I had to hear about it from Ash?"

"Ash told you?"

"Honey, Ash is telling everybody. Starting with Bill Larson at the Pack & Post, when he went in to FedEx the papers to the real-estate lady in Nashville. Then, the story is, he went over to the café. Couldn't wait to share the big news."

"He might as well have called the AP wire service," I said.

"But you cosigned the papers, right?" Out on the field, the coaches were putting the players through warm-ups. Hatch Brothers were playing Acme Hardware of Mount Pleasant, and Mount Pleasant didn't stand a chance.

"Yeah. I did."

"And you did it of your own free will? He didn't hypnotize you or drug you or anything?"

"Just with a plate of Willie B.'s pork ribs."

She laughed. "That's pretty powerful stuff."

"I guess I just—I think I understand where he's coming from, at least part of it. It's not that different from when I came back from Tennessee. I just wanted to be home."

"It *is* different, though," she said. "Because you were leaving him. And he's coming back to you." I glanced over at her. "Coming back to where you are, at least. Setting himself up right across the road. You don't make anything of that?"

"I haven't quite figured out how I feel about it. All I know is I'll have some money, once the sale of the house goes through.

Who knows, maybe I'll take off again, go live in France or Morocco or someplace."

"Let's face it, Lucy," Geneva said as we watched our kids take their positions in the outfield, Jude at third base, Lily scaling the pitcher's mound, tugging at the bill of her cap. "You're just like me and you always will be. A red-dirt girl."

As the first batter stepped up to the plate, I thought of the two of us, old and gray, rocking on the porch together. "How are you feeling? About Tuesday, I mean."

"I just have the strangest feeling," she said. We watched Lily wind up to pitch. Strike one. "What if all of a sudden Bailey decides to go find himself some sweet young thing, start himself a brand-new family?"

"Lord, Geneva! What a thing to say."

"Well, why not? Men do it all the time."

"Some men, maybe. Not Bailey Hatch."

She didn't say anything, and I wondered if something was going on between them that I didn't know about, when a beat-up station wagon pulled up to the fence. Together we watched as the door swung open and Heather Starbird unfolded herself from the driver's seat, all legs and wild black hair. I felt a chill at the sight of her sauntering toward the visitors' stands, like the rumors about her practicing voodoo in her shabby little duplex might be true. I thought of what Ash had said to me the afternoon before, at the edge of the pond where his house would stand, when I'd asked him if he was building the place for him and Jude, and he'd answered that it would be for whoever his family might turn out to be. I was a fool, I realized, watching Heather take a seat by herself at the end of the bleachers, crossing one leg over the other and rummaging in her fringed suede bag for her cigarettes. The world was never the kind of place I seemed to think it was, was always throwing me curves. I wondered if it was too late to call the real-estate agent in Nashville, to say I'd changed my mind. Who was to say that Bailey wouldn't run off tomorrow and find himself a twenty-year-old, start hatching babies like rabbits? What kind of person smoked at a Little League game?

"When I get my money," I said to Geneva, "how about you and me take a trip somewhere? Florida, maybe, or Vegas. Just us girls."

She nodded as Heather sucked on her cigarette and exhaled, following the smoke with her eyes as it drifted skyward. It was a warm afternoon, the sky dotted with fluffy white clouds. The smells of corn dogs and popcorn drifted up from the concession stand. The third batter up for Mount Pleasant hit a ground ball to right field and took off for first base, while the Hatch Brothers outfielders went scampering. Parents on both benches rose to their feet, shouting. Heather Starbird took out another cigarette and lit it off the first one.

Meanwhile, I could see it plain, see my son being raised by a black-haired witch-woman with an ex-boyfriend about to be paroled any day. I could see them all sitting out on the deck of Ash's new house, watching the cranes fly in low over the water while steaks charred on the grill and Hank Williams poured from the speakers and empty liquor bottles and syringes and cigarette butts piled up around them. Jude would flunk out of middle school, shave his head, start piercing and tattooing himself in painful secret places, start cooking meth in the basement from a recipe he got off the Internet, or from Heather's ex. The sheriff would let him walk on the first couple of DUIs, but she'd get wise to him finally, and he'd take off in his daddy's pickup and run. They'd find the truck smashed up in a ditch somewhere, empty, and no one would ever see my son again, not till his face turned up on a flyer years later at the post office, or on *America's Most Wanted.*

The game lasted an hour, during which Heather chain-smoked and crossed and recrossed her legs and played with the fringe on her bag and never once gave any sign of interest in what was going on out on the field. When the game ended—Hatch Brothers 6, Acme Hardware 1, practically a rout—Ash shook hands with my brothers, gave Jude a hug, then trotted across the field to where Heather stood waiting. She slid behind the wheel of her station wagon and Ash got into the passenger seat, and they drove away.

From that moment forward, I pledged to myself, I would never let Heather Starbird's name pass my lips, not to Ash or in any other conversation. I'd been holding my head up in Mooney, Texas, for more than half my life while folks talked behind my back; it would take a lot more than a girl with long legs and black hair and a station wagon full of cleaning supplies to make me buckle under. I knew, even if Heather Starbird didn't, what kind of stuff I was made of. Let her see what she thought she could get away with; let them make their bets down at Burton's café. A hundred years from now, there'd be a bronze statue of me right alongside Jefferson Davis at the courthouse. I'd outlast them all.

chapter fifteen

"How long has it been, again?" Bailey asked.

"About two minutes since you asked me the last time."

We'd been in the surgery waiting room at County General since 6:00 A.M. The fluorescent lighting wasn't helping either our complexions or our dispositions, nor were the Styrofoam cups of coffee we clutched.

"Dr. C. said it would take three hours, tops."

"It's been three hours and twelve minutes. I'm sure everything's fine. He'll be out anytime now."

I patted my brother's knee. Beads of sweat pooled at his temples, and he twisted his Hatch Brothers Contracting cap in his hands.

He got up and started to pace, dodging lamps and end tables like they were pedestrians on a city sidewalk. "Why don't you go outside for a few minutes, get some air?" I said. He shot me a look like I'd suggested he buy an airplane ticket and fly to California.

I picked up a magazine and flipped through photo spreads of stars posing with award statuettes they'd won six or seven years earlier, their hair and outfits hopelessly dated. I'd probably already looked at the same magazine a dozen times that morning, but it kept my mind from going down the dark alleys where it really wanted to go. All I could think about was all the Sunday mornings I'd skipped church, all the times my mama had told me she'd pray for my damnable soul. I hadn't eaten breakfast, and my stomach was growling.

At 11:10—four hours and ten minutes after the start of Geneva's surgery—Dr. Crawford came through the door of the waiting room, pushing eyeglasses onto his nose with a forefinger.

"Sorry," the doctor said, "sorry, sorry. Never tell the family you'll be out in a jiff. I know better than that. Y'all must be just about out of your minds."

"Is she okay?" Bailey blurted out.

"Yes, sir. I'll tell you, though, it was complicated. As much scar tissue as I think I've ever seen. It's a wonder she held out so long to get this thing taken care of. She must've been in so much pain. . . ."

"But she's all right now? Everything turned out fine?" I sank back against the arm of the chair, letting the magazine drop onto the table.

"We might have to keep her a day or two longer than we thought, while she heals up. But after that, she'll be as good as new. Better, probably."

Bailey covered his face with his hands. The room seemed to fill up with our expelled breath, our answered prayers.

"I need to see her." Bailey's voice was thick, his eyes swimming.

"She's still asleep, Son," Dr. C. said. "Out like a light."

"I don't care. I just need to see her."

The doctor looked at him a minute, then put an arm around his shoulders. "Okay, my man," he said. "Right this way. But only for a minute, now. After we get her upstairs, you can stay as long as you want. Both of you."

"Call Dove," Bailey said to me over his shoulder as they left the room.

I sat quietly for a minute or so after they'd gone, straightening the stack of magazines with my hands. I didn't care if I never saw another copy of *People* or *Field and Stream* as long as I lived. *Thank you,* I recited silently, *thank you, thank you. I won't forget about this, I promise.* I went to the pay phone in the hall and called Dove and told her everything was all right, and then I went to the cafeteria and ordered a cheeseburger.

Geneva stayed at County General for five days, during which Bailey and I shuttled back and forth between my house and theirs, our jobs and the kids' school and Dove's and the hospital, an endless round of swing shifts and work, meals on the fly and housekeeping left undone. When those five days were over, things would ease up. At least that's what I kept telling myself as I rushed from one place to the next, trying to get flowers ordered and accounts balanced, kids driven from school to Dove's to Little League practice, food on the table, to keep two households from spinning out of control. I'd fall into bed worn to a nub, out the minute my head hit the pillow, then wake up a couple of hours later, wired with a nameless, faceless dread. I'd make myself a cup of Sleepytime tea and sip it at the kitchen table. Outside, Ash's trailer might be dark, or lit up like a Christmas tree. Some nights I had to talk myself out of walking down the hall, making my way brave and barefooted across the backyard to knock on his door. What if Heather was there? What if she wasn't? What did I want from him, anyway? My mind went round and round until it finally reached its limits, wrung itself out, and I could haul myself back to bed to grab a few hours' sleep before the drill started over again.

Later I wondered how I could have been so delusional. In my fantasies, Geneva strode out of the hospital her old self, full of pep and snappy repartee, when in fact she was rolled out in a wheelchair, sore and groggy from pain and medication. The truth was, once home, she needed looking after, too, something that until then we'd had trained nurses to handle for us.

Things, already pointed downhill, started to snowball. Though Bailey was fully capable of getting Lily off to school in the mornings, she played him like a piano, dawdling around until the last possible minute, demanding elaborate breakfasts and wardrobe items that existed either at the bottom of the laundry basket or that she'd seen on some child at school or on TV. She wanted to stay home with her mama, to lie in bed and be waited on hand and foot and watch soap operas and reruns of *Bewitched* and *Gilligan's Island.* That week she got two yellow squares for tardiness, the first of her kindergarten career.

In the late mornings, Dove came over to help Geneva, to fix her something to eat, get her dressed, sit and keep her company. At two she'd drive home again to be there when the school bus dropped off Jude and Lily. The first day, she tried keeping them at Bailey and Geneva's house, but things got out of hand so quickly that she reverted to the original plan, which meant that Geneva was on her own until Bailey or I could get away from work. We were all rearranging our schedules constantly, dropping things half-done to run off and take care of somebody or something else—Geneva's lunch, doctors' appointments, the kids' after-school activities. Some days I was at Faye's for only two or three hours, tops, and would end up coming back in the evenings to take care of paperwork. It got to the point that I dreaded the sound of a ringing phone, and a full night's sleep became a memory.

Finally, one afternoon toward the end of the week, Ash dropped by the shop. I hadn't washed my hair in three days, and it was pulled back with a rubber band into a makeshift ponytail. I'd spilled coffee on my shirt while I was rinsing out the pot. If I'd put on lipstick that morning, it was surely chewed off by now.

But I didn't much care; I was preoccupied, as usual lately, with how I could manage to be in two places at once. Geneva had a checkup in less than half an hour, and Bailey was supposed to drive her, but he'd called to say he was stuck at a job site in the next county. Dove had her hands full with the kids, and I didn't see how I could get away; Audrey had just left on a round of deliveries, and Peggy was down in Marshall for the day, visiting a cousin who'd had an emergency appendectomy. At the sight of Ash standing in my showroom, sunburned and grinning, my first instinct was to rush around the counter and slug him.

Instead, what I did was even worse. My lip started to quiver, and tears pooled in my eyes.

"Hey," he said, laying his hands over mine on the countertop, "hey, hey." I tried to take back my hands, but he got hold of my wrists and pinned them. "What's going on? You look like hell."

"Thanks. I really needed to hear that."

"Here." Reaching into his back pocket, he produced a faded red print bandanna. "Go ahead. You can't make it any worse than it already is, if that's what you're worried about."

He was right. I dabbed my eyes and blew my nose. I tried to return it, but Ash pushed it back.

"Keep it," he said. "Now, you want to tell me what's going on?"

I filled him in on the craziness of the past ten days, about Bailey and Dove and me running ourselves ragged, about the bind I was in just then, with nobody to drive Geneva to the doctor, nobody to keep an eye on the shop if I did.

"Well, hell's bells, Lucy," Ash said when I'd finished blowing my nose again. "Why didn't you say something?"

"To who? We're already doing all we can, and it's just—it's never *enough*."

"To me, that's who. It's not like you don't know where to find me."

I don't *know where to find you,* I wanted to say. *I hardly know anything at all about you anymore.*

"I don't think I'd be too good at running a flower shop," he said, "but I can drive Gen to the doctor if you want. Or—hang on, I've got a better idea. How about if I run over and pick up the kids, so Dove can take her?"

"What'll you do with the kids?"

"What do you think? I'm gonna set them out on the side of the road, let them hitchhike to Little Rock? I'll take them out to my place. They'll be fine." I didn't say anything right away, and suddenly his eyes narrowed and he gave me a faint, ugly smile. "You want me to take a Breathalyzer test first? Is that it?"

"Just go get them, please."

He touched his fingers to his forehead. "I live to serve," he said, and before I had a chance to say something smart, he left, his white truck roaring away from the curb.

I stood clutching his bandanna in my fist, temples pounding, relief replaced by a black wall of anger, at Ash, at myself. Why should I be grateful to him for doing what he should have been doing all along? Did he or did he not consider himself part of this family? Not for the first time, I considered the fact that having Ash living right across the road might end up being more harm than help to Jude. Maybe no daddy at all was, in fact, better than one who behaved like a chameleon, changing color to disappear whenever it suited him, for his own comfort and protection.

There were times, as Bailey was fond of saying, when you had to let go of a thing and take it on faith. I might not know till Jude was grown if I'd done the right thing, might not know till I found myself knocking at Saint Peter's pearly gates. Might never know at all, and was damning my eternal soul to hell or worse, to Purgatory. Not that I believed in any or all of those things, except maybe at those times when I found myself staring wide-eyed at the ceiling at three o'clock in the morning, or in hospital waiting rooms, but they did make me think of Father Laughlin down at St. Jude's in Jefferson. I felt like talking to him right then, though I couldn't have said exactly what about or why. What could a Catholic priest—even one like Punch Laughlin, with his running shorts and his gardening shears—do for a half-assed Baptist like me? Still, I longed for the tranquil courtyard at St. Jude's, the sun on the top of my head, the air sweet with the smell of old roses. If I closed my eyes and let myself, I could almost go there in my mind, and as I did, feeling the real world fall away, I felt a stillness so pure and unexpected, I almost forgot to breathe.

The phone rang. I opened my eyes, my momentary peace evaporating, and answered it. It was Audrey, calling from someplace up on FM 125. The van had a flat.

ASH BROUGHT THE kids back to Dove's at suppertime, the two of them babbling like orphans from some inner-city youth camp about the pond and the old rowboat and a real live raccoon who'd taken up residence in the old handyman's cottage. Their clothes were grimy and they had melted chocolate all over their hands, from Snickers bars Ash had bought them at the Miracle Mart. "We had Cokes, too, Mama!" Jude cried, running circles around Dove's coffee table.

"Thanks a lot," I said to Ash. "He won't sleep for a week."

"Oh, he'll sleep just fine," Ash said. "All that fresh air and exercise. In fact, a dose of it might do *you* good."

"Haven't you insulted me enough for one day?"

"It was an invitation. To ride out and see how things are coming along."

I laughed. "Right. In my spare time."

Dove walked into the living room, followed by Geneva. The sight of her made me gape. For the first time since the hospital, she was in full makeup and fluffy hair, and she wore, in place of her usual PJs or baggy sweats, form-fitting jeans and a sweater. She'd lost weight since the surgery, maybe eight or ten pounds, most noticeable in her face and her hips. Ash whistled between his teeth and she cocked one leg at an angle and batted her eyes at him.

"Wow," I said. "You must be feeling better."

"I feel great. Dr. C. says I'm a walking miracle. He says I can go back to work next week, if I want. Half-days at first."

"That's terrific," I said. Something warm began to work its way up inside me, from my feet to the back of my neck. *My life,* I thought, feeling faint. *I'm going to get my life back.*

"Y'all sit down and stay for supper," Dove said. "You, too, Mr. Farrell. I've got meat loaf, and plenty of those beans of yours, all fixed up the way you like."

"Wish I could," he said. "But I've got someplace I've gotta be."

"Oh, Ash, come on," Geneva said. "What could be more important than Dove's meat loaf and Kentucky Wonders? Anyway, we're celebrating. I'm a walking miracle, remember?"

"Sorry," he said, already moving toward the door. "We'll celebrate another time, I promise. We'll drive out to Curly's and go dancing."

"Say what?" Bailey said from outside the screen door. "You hitting on my wife?"

"You better watch it, bud," Ash said as he stepped out and Bailey came in. "Looks like you're gonna have your hands full."

Bailey turned to Geneva, who threw out her arms and struck a pose.

"Whoa!" he said. "Get a load of *you.*"

"That's right," she said as he walked toward her. "Take a *good* look."

But he wasn't looking; he'd wrapped his arms around her and was holding her as close as he could, murmuring into her hair. Whatever he said made her laugh, low and throaty, like they were the only two people in the room. In the kitchen, Dove was clattering dishes around; the kids had switched on the TV, cartoon animals screeching at each other, cartoon bombs exploding. The warmth inside me slowly leached away as I stepped over to the screen door and watched Ash's truck back out of the driveway, watched his taillights recede down the street, around the corner, disappearing, gone.

A LAYER OF dust covered every surface of my house, and laundry had piled up so high that I'd stopped using baskets for sorting it and had taken to letting it collect on the bedroom floors. Little by little—one room, one load at a time—I worked my way through it all, in the evenings, while the supper dishes soaked in the sink and Jude sat at the kitchen table laboring over his homework, his pencil marking slow, deep grooves in his workbook. Meanwhile, Ash came and went, his trailer like a haunted house in my backyard: phantom sounds of doors slamming, lights popping mysteriously on and off during the night. He was there in the outfield at Jude's games, and every couple of days he dropped by Dove's in the afternoons to take the kids out to his new place, to let them run along the edge of the pond to chase bugs and poke at frogs with sticks, bringing them back grubby and high on sugar and caffeine but exuberant, happy, carefree. Rumor had it that Ash had ordered a timber-frame house kit from an outfit down in Longview, and one day Jude volunteered that "some men in a big truck" had been there, walking around with his daddy, but he didn't offer any more details, and I managed to keep my curiosity to myself.

Then, one late-spring evening, he was knocking at the back door, calling my name through the screen. I wiped my hands on a dish towel and walked down the hall. It wasn't full dark yet, but I switched on the porch light anyway.

Ash shaded his eyes with his hand against the sudden glare. "I just came by to remind you about tomorrow," he said.

"What's tomorrow?"

"We're closing on the Nashville house, remember?"

I'd completely forgotten—lost track of time was more like it. "What do I need to do?"

"Meet me at Shirley Tinsley's office at ten. All we have to do is sign the papers. They'll take care of everything, send it back to the agent up there. The whole deal should be finalized by the end of the week."

"And they'll send us a check?"

"Yep. Then I guess you and Geneva can take off for Vegas."

"Right."

"Listen," Ash said, "I've been wanting to talk to you."

"About what?"

"Jude spending the night. Not every night, mind you, just every now and then."

"So you've quit drinking?" I asked. Ash swiveled his chin, gazing off toward the darkening woods. "We had an agreement, Ash."

"No, we didn't. You laid down the law. It's not the same thing."

"Obviously the answer is no. Why else wouldn't you come right out and say so?"

"Everything always has to be black and white with you."

"Why isn't it black and white? Either you're drinking or you've stopped."

We stood staring at each other through the screen. I could hear Jude singing in the tub at the other end of the house, the whir of crickets in the woods behind the trailer, the faint sound of an engine growing louder as a car made its way up the road toward the house. Headlights swung around the corner, and Heather Starbird's brown station wagon pulled into the yard next to Ash's truck.

"Look." His voice was laced with frustration. "I just want—"

"I'll see you at Shirley's office in the morning," I said, and switched off the porch light and latched the screen door and walked back up the hall, leaving Ash standing there in the dark.

HE WAS WAITING on the front step of the real-estate company the next morning when I got there a few minutes before ten. Shirley's desk was empty, but her young assistant, Betsy Pope, a pretty blonde in a red skirted suit, came out and ushered us into a small conference room, where papers were laid out on a long fake-woodgrain table. She offered us coffee, but we both said no, thank you, so she handed Ash a ballpoint pen and opened the contract to the first of many little yellow flags reading SIGN HERE. We didn't speak, though our wrists brushed occasionally as we passed the pen back and forth, scribbling our signatures again and again above the strange-looking typed names: ASHTON L. FARRELL and LUCY H. FARRELL. *Who are these people?* I thought; I wondered if we'd left them back in Nashville, if they'd ever existed at all.

When we were done, Betsy Pope affixed her notary's stamp and her own signature to the documents, and folded them shut with a flourish.

"I'll get these out by FedEx this afternoon," she said. "The parties up there should have them finalized by the end of the week."

"How long before we get our money?" Ash asked bluntly.

"Oh, it shouldn't take but twenty-four hours once everything's signed. It's a wire transfer, so the funds will go directly into your joint account here at First National."

Ash and I made eye contact for the first time all morning. I'd forgotten we even had a joint account; as far as I knew, there was almost nothing in it, and it hadn't been touched since we'd left Mooney seven years earlier. I felt a little woozy, from the warmth in the room and Betsy's perfume, from all the reminders of the way our life used to be.

"Did you, um, want to make other arrangements?" Betsy asked, her face nearly the same shade as her suit jacket.

Ash looked at me. I shook my head.

"No," he said, turning back to Betsy, "the joint account is fine."

"All right," she said, exhaling with relief. "Then y'all should be good to go. I'll give you a call when the deposit clears."

"Thanks for your help," I said, and turned toward the door. My stomach was doing flips. I couldn't wait to get out of there.

"Mr. Farrell?"

Ash glanced over his shoulder at the young woman standing at the head of the table, all primary colors: yellow hair, red suit, bright blue contact lenses.

"I hate to ask, I mean this probably isn't the time or place, but I was just wondering . . . Well, I've always been such a fan, and if it isn't too much to ask . . . Could I get your autograph?"

"You just got it," Ash snapped. "About two dozen times."

I started at the tone of his voice, and looked at him a second time. He looked bad. It wasn't anything I could put my finger on, exactly—just tired, thin, the grooves etched a little deeper than I remembered at the corners of his eyes.

Poor Betsy looked like she wanted to run out the front door and keep going past the city limits sign. "I'm sorry," she said hoarsely. "I shouldn't have . . . "

"No, it's okay. Sorry." Ash cleared his throat. "Is there something in particular you want me to sign?"

"Um, well . . . " Betsy looked around, but the only paper in sight was our real-estate contract. "Let me just grab something." She ducked out of the room.

"What's the matter with you?" I said. "You didn't have to bite her head off."

"I just don't want to think about that part of my life anymore."

"For heaven's sake, Ash! You can't just walk out of it like an old suit of clothes."

"Want to bet?"

"Look, I've got to get back to work." I turned, hesitating at the door. "I want to hear about it the minute that money hits the bank."

"Don't worry, Lucy," Ash said, loud and clear, as Betsy Pope came back into the room carrying a yellow legal pad, "you'll get your half."

A WEEK LATER we got the call that the funds from the house sale had finally landed at First National. Ash and I made another awkward joint trip, this time to the bank to take care of the paperwork that would split the deposit between his personal account and mine. The rift between us had never seemed greater than it did as we stood on the sidewalk in front of the bank afterwards, gazing at the carbons of the deposit slips in our hands. I guessed this kind of money was pocket change to some of Ash's old Nashville running buddies, but by Mooney, Texas, standards, I was rich. I'd expected to feel elated, but instead I just felt like I needed to go home and soak in a long bath.

"Well," Ash said, looking up finally, "send me a postcard from Vegas." Before I could think of a snappy rejoinder, he was headed off toward his truck, stuffing the carbon into the back pocket of his jeans. I don't know what I was expecting that day I'd stood up in front of God and my family and two-thirds of the population of Cade County and promised to cherish this man till death did us part, but whatever it was, it wasn't this.

chapter sixteen

That night was Jude's first time to sleep over at Lily's since Geneva's surgery, and I had the house to myself. I sat at the kitchen table with a pile of catalogs I'd borrowed from Geneva, dizzy with the thought that I could order anything I saw that took my fancy, but I couldn't quite get into the spirit of the thing. The rug I'd loved at first glance, with further consideration I realized wouldn't fit in the living room or match the couch. The clothes all looked like things either Audrey or the First Baptist guild ladies would wear.

I tried Denny's cell phone, but hung up without leaving a message when I got her voice mail. We'd spoken a few times since the night she took off with Will. Her band was back on tour, making their way along the West Coast, and from the sound of it, the new marriage wasn't all rosebuds and white picket fences. In fact, according to Denny, Will spent most of his free time with the other guys in the band instead of her. It was a scenario I was only too familiar with, and couldn't offer much in the way of comfort, only empathy.

I felt restless, at loose ends. I wandered around the house looking for something to do, but for the first time in three weeks, everything was in its place: floors swept, fresh towels in the bathroom and sheets on the beds, dishes washed and put away, laundry baskets empty. Even Jude's room was as neat as a pin.

I realized I was starved. I'd had a bowl of soup and a sandwich earlier, but this craving was more primal than that, possibly hormonal, like I could devour an entire pan of brownies at one sitting.

I set the oven at three-fifty and got out a pan and my graduated set of mixing bowls, took two eggs and a stick of butter out of the icebox, then opened the pantry and pulled down the flour and sugar, baking powder and salt, vanilla, a bag of chopped pecans. I stared at the items lined up on the countertop. Everything I needed was here, all but one thing. I practically tore the pantry apart, searching behind cans of soup and boxes of Kraft macaroni and cheese, but it was hopeless—no chocolate.

I put back the butter and eggs, turned off the oven, slipped on my flip-flops and grabbed my keys. It was a quarter till nine; if I pushed it, and Dewey Wentzel hadn't set up his Friday-night speed trap on FM 1399, I had just enough time to make it to the Food King before closing.

I screeched into an empty slot in the grocery store parking lot and rushed through the automatic doors, drawing a dirty look from the manager, Kenny Federline, who'd obviously been about to lock up, and Marcel Compton, the lone checker, who spent her time between customers filing her nails to lethal points and appeared ready to jab my eyeballs out with them now. I ran past them for the baking-items aisle, saying, "I'll be out of here in thirty seconds."

I grabbed a box of unsweetened chocolate off the shelf, then decided to pick up a gallon of milk while I was at it. No matter how often I bought it, it seemed we were always running out of milk.

Rounding the corner to the dairy aisle, I saw her: brown polyester pants and a scuffed pair of Keds, a man's cardigan hanging from her shrunken frame, gazing into the milk case like she was hypnotized by the choices there, whole and skim and two percent. There weren't a lot of homeless people in Mooney, but every now and then some poor soul wandered off the main highway, or hitched a ride with a trucker; you saw them sometimes panhandling outside the drugstore or the courthouse until Dewey Wentzel ran them off. Gray hair stood out in a frizzy corona around the woman's head as she began to rummage in a black pocketbook the size of a briefcase. My mama had a pocketbook exactly like that one, with its many compartments and its shiny metal buckle. For one awful second I wondered if someone might have broken into her house and robbed her. Then the woman looked up, meeting my eyes, and another, more awful understanding hit me.

"Mama?" My voice sounded tinny and far-off, like it was coming through speakers in a distant room. Maybe this apparition wasn't really Patsy Hatch after all. When, after all, had Patsy ever left the house without hose and heels, without every hair shellacked into place and her mouth drawn flawlessly in Revlon Fire and Ice?

"I forgot my billfold," Patsy's voice said, jerking me back to reality. "Isn't that the silliest thing you ever heard? Made it all the way to the store with my pocketbook, but I haven't got my billfold."

I approached her hesitantly, trying to remember the last time I'd seen her. Easter Sunday, I decided, nearly six weeks before. A shopping basket at her feet contained a loaf of Wonder bread, a jar of peanut butter, a can of store-brand coffee, two green bananas. Even with milk, it couldn't be more than eight or ten dollars' worth of food. Mama had been shopping at the Food King more than forty years; surely Kenny Federline would let her take her groceries and bring the money by the next day. I looked at her trembling, unpainted mouth, and I knew that she would never ask such a thing, not in a million years. She still had her pride, and she'd hang on to it with fingernails bleeding.

"Go on and get your milk, Mama," I said, reaching past her to open the dairy case. "I'll loan you the money."

She gave a ladylike little snort. "Moneybags," she said, her voice echoing in the bright, empty aisle.

"Excuse me?"

"I guess you're rolling in it now, aren't you? Up to your ears in clover."

I'd forgotten about my newly inflated bank account. Shame flooded through me, and I bent over and reached for her basket.

"Never mind about the loan," I said. "I'd be happy to buy your groceries for you."

She smacked my hand like I was four years old and grabbing for the cookie jar. I reared back, astonished.

"You wait," she said. "You think you're sitting pretty now. But you're all the same, you Hatches." Her voice rose. "Well, let me tell you, Miss High-and-Mighty, you've got another think coming, the whole bunch of you!"

Kenny Federline appeared at the head of the aisle, probably wondering what all the fuss was about. "Store's closing in two minutes!" he called out.

"Come on, Mama," I said. "Let's pay for our stuff and go home. If you've got something to say to me, that's fine, but please, let's not do it here."

She started digging again in her pocketbook. Lord knew what she had in there; the thing was big enough to hide a sawed-off shotgun. "Remember what you always used to say, about not airing your family linen in public?" I whispered as Kenny Federline continued to glare at us, fists on his hips. I was grasping at straws now; Patsy had never said any such thing. She wouldn't have dared to, seeing's how once upon a time she'd been known for running through the neighbors' front yards in her nightgown, trampling the flower beds, crying at the top of her lungs for my daddy, Raymond Hatch, to come back.

"I am not," Mama said loudly, "a part of your family."

"What? What are you talking about?"

"When your sister-in-law was in the hospital, did anybody call me?"

"I—"

"No, I had to hear about it right here in the Food King, from that bigmouth Marcel Compton, of all people. Don't you know *she* was happy to fill me in on all the things not one of my own blood kin bothered to tell me about!" I wished she'd keep her voice down. "And then, when the lot of you were running around town like chickens with your heads cut off, did anybody so much as think of asking me to help? I'm home most all day, you know, except for church and Bible study and prayer circle. I don't get around like I used to, not with this hip, but I think I'm capable of watching a couple of babies for an hour or two, or carrying somebody to the doctor."

"Mama, I'm sorry. We just didn't think—"

"*One* minute!" Kenny Federline hollered, but neither Mama or I budged. I thought nothing in my life could ever equal the humiliation I'd felt when I was six years old and my daddy left us, or when I'd thrown Jude into the back of my truck and driven away from Ash in the middle of the night, but I was wrong.

"That boy you married," Mama said. "He treats me better than the rest of you—you *Hatches*."

Before I could think what to say to that, she turned and made her way slowly, laboriously, favoring her right hip, up the aisle and past Kenny Federline, around the corner, out of sight. I heard the automatic doors whoosh open and shut again.

I bent and picked up her abandoned grocery basket and carried it to the front of the store. "I guess she decided she doesn't want these," I said, handing the basket to Kenny, who made no effort to hide his irritation. Marcel Compton rang up my box of unsweetened chocolate, her mouth a deliberate straight line, even though I knew that when the store opened bright and early the next morning, she'd be telling everybody who passed through her lane about how Patsy Hatch had put her ingrate daughter in her place, right in the middle of aisle 12.

As I climbed into the Blazer, I realized I'd forgotten my milk. But Kenny Federline was locking up behind me, and anyway, I didn't fancy going back to the Food King for a while. I drove home to my empty house and put the chocolate in the pantry. My taste for brownies was gone.

"SHE'S HEAD-TRIPPING YOU," Geneva said the next afternoon as we sat in the bleachers at Old Settlers Field, watching our team get trounced by the visiting White Pine Bulldogs. "Face it, Lucy, she's been doing this to y'all your whole life."

"Yeah, but this was worse," I said. "She was in polyester pants, Gen. And *Keds.* No lipstick, her hair all over the place. And her hip—I think it's bothering her more than she's been letting on. She was limping really bad."

"Dove's been trying to get her to some clinic down in Tyler for months," Geneva said. "Dr. Fisher says she needs a hip replacement, but she won't hear of it. Says Jesus is gonna take care of it."

"I tried calling her this morning, but she hung up on me. Then I drove by her house on the way over here, but she wouldn't answer the door, even though her car was right there in the carport, big as life."

"I'm telling you, she's playing you like an old guitar. Where was she the whole time you and the boys were growing up? And remember how she acted when Mitchell died? Trying to shame you into thinking it was your fault, dragging her preacher into it? Trust me, there's no way on God's green earth you can get on Patsy's good side. I don't even think she's *got* a good side. She's the one who built the wall, and now she wants the rest of you to feel guilty for it."

Dove just snorted when I told her about my run-in with Mama in the Food King. We were at her kitchen counter making her famous tomato, onion, and mozzarella salad for Sunday supper. Through the window we could keep an eye on Jude running loops through the backyard grass, chasing some bug or shadow or imaginary enemy.

"It wasn't funny, Dove," I said. "She stood there looking like a bag lady or something, telling me I was going to hell. That we all are, all the Hatches. Now she won't even pick up the phone or answer the door."

"That mule-headedness is a Munroe thing, not a Hatch thing. She's as bad as the rest of us, maybe the worst of the bunch."

"Geneva said you've been trying to talk her into getting her hip replaced, but she won't listen."

"I haven't been tryin' to talk her into a thing. It's the doctor wants her to have the operation. I just told her I'd drive her down there to get it done. If she'd rather spend the rest of her life gimpin' around like she just got throwed off a bull, let her. I'm not losin' any sleep over it, and neither should you."

"She looked awful, though. I mean, I don't think I've ever in my life seen her without lipstick, much less wearing a baggy old sweater and pants." I set down my knife and turned to Dove. "Oh Lord. You don't think she's . . ."

"What?"

"Going batty again. Like she did when my daddy left."

"Your mama ain't batty, Lucy Bird. She weren't then, neither—just sad and scared. You can't hardly blame her for that. What came after, though—that's the part I can't forgive."

"What do you mean?"

"The way everthing she had goin' for her—you kids, everthing she coulda had ahead of her—she let it go right along with your daddy." Dove scraped chunks of tomato from the cutting board into a big ceramic bowl. "You remember when you first took up with Ash, how I cautioned you about turnin' out like your mama, throwin' your whole life after some man? Well, this is what I was talkin' about. Here she is, closin' in on seventy years old, and she ain't got nothin' to show for it but a whole lotta sadness and meanness. Oh, she gives good lip service to the Lord, but that's just blowin' smoke, far as I'm concerned. You ask me, chasin' after Jesus is the only way she knows to make up for everthing she didn't do in her time on earth."

"Like what?"

"Like doin' right by you kids, for starters. Bein' a proper mama to y'all. She give all that up to sit around chewin' her heart out over Raymond Hatch. Turnin' all that hate and anger in on herself. Do that long enough, it gets so that's the way you see the whole world, through that black cloud. I reckon your mama don't know no different anymore."

"She wasn't like this, though, was she, before my daddy left?"

"No, she weren't." Dove rinsed her hands and dried them on a dish towel. She seemed about to say something else, then thought better of it. I thought of Ash's own daddy, who'd run out on him and his mama when Ash was barely three, and his mama, who, so the story went, cracked up not longer after and turned Ash over to the state, to be raised by a family called Keller. His mama, last I'd heard, was still living in a big, rambling lake house that had belonged to her family in White Pine, not thirty miles away, but Ash hadn't spoken to her in as many years or longer. I wondered why, if I wanted so badly for us to escape the mistakes the ones before us had made, the ones we carried in our blood and bones, we weren't trying harder to do a better job of it.

"So this is all my daddy's fault," I said.

"No, honey. He mighta been the one took off, but it was Patsy chose to let it eat her up, body and soul. That's a fact, and don't you forget it." Dove turned and set the bowl in the middle of the table. "Anyhow, I seen her not four hours ago, headed home from church with her nose in the air, dressed to the nines, like any old Sunday. High on Jesus and no use for the rest of us sinners.

"Now, reach in that icebox yonder and hand me the cheese, and call that youngun of yours in for supper."

IT WAS A Thursday evening the last week of May, the night before the final day of school. There would be a little graduation ceremony the next morning for Jude and Lily's class, launching them from kindergarten into the first grade. It was purely symbolic; after all, the kids attended the same school, Mooney Elementary, from grades K through 6. But Miss Kimble liked the idea of marking the day, and so we would all gather in the school auditorium to watch our offspring march across the stage in their miniature caps and gowns to receive their miniature diplomas, capturing it all on film and video for posterity. Dove was making lunch for the family afterwards. I'd called

Mama two or three times to invite her, but when I finally got her to pick up, she said, in a curt voice, that she was going on a bus trip that day to the outlet mall in Grapevine with the Golden Halo club from First Baptist. It irked me a little, that she'd rather spend the day shopping for cut-rate towels and blouses than watch her youngest grandson mark the conclusion of his first year of school. More to the point, it seemed to me that if I was making the effort to extend an olive branch in her direction, the least she could do was reach out and take it.

I'd bathed Jude and tucked him in early in anticipation of the next day, and after the supper dishes were washed and put away, I poured myself a glass of iced tea and carried it out to the front porch. Summer had snuck up on us almost without my noticing. I was struck, as I sat down on the steps, by how much light the sky still held at nine o'clock, the woods full of the sounds of frogs and birds I'd been hearing all my life but never once seen. I had a sudden memory of myself standing on the front porch of the house I'd shared with my first husband, Mitchell, holding my after-supper coffee and watching night roll in over fields green with corn and sorghum, dotted with cows. Somewhere between the day I'd married Mitchell and the day he died, the sense of contentment I'd felt had turned to a restlessness I couldn't put my finger on, a small but perpetual itch, like a mosquito bite in a hard-to-reach place. If you'd told me back then where I'd find myself tonight, I wouldn't have believed it. If you'd told me, when I met Ash and fell in love with him, that seven years later I'd still be trying to reach that itch, I'd have laughed in your face. One of the troubles of thinking you've got it made is that you can't see beyond your own satisfaction, until one night you find yourself wondering where it all went, or what made you think it was what you wanted in the first place.

Headlights turned in off the highway, rising and falling as they wound up the road through the trees, approaching the house. A small blue Toyota pulled in next to my Blazer. The driver's-side door opened and the dome light came on, just long enough for me to spy a lone figure as it climbed out and slammed the door shut, then stood in the growing dark, studying the house over the roof of the car.

I stood up, setting my iced tea on the porch rail. "Can I help you?"

"Jesus!" a voice yelped. "You scared the shit out of me."

I was trying to decide whether I ought to step inside and get the shotgun, or at least the umbrella, when the voice said accusingly, "Who's there?"

I opened the screen door and switched on the porch light. "I think that's supposed to be *my* question." It was hard to get too worked up about somebody who sounded like Alvin from the Chipmunks. He wasn't much bigger than Alvin, either. In faded jeans and a T-shirt from one of Willie Nelson's Fourth of July picnics, his shaggy brown hair fell over his shoulders and into his eyes, which were magnified behind thick, black-rimmed glasses. He looked like Buddy Holly's long-lost son. Or grandson, probably—the kid couldn't be a day over eighteen.

"Oh my God," he said. "You're Lucy! I feel like I practically know you!"

"You do?" I had a sick feeling in the pit of my belly. I hoped this wasn't going to be one of those made-for-TV moments where I learned that Ash had sired a son he'd never heard of with some one-night stand or old girlfriend.

"You're a legend, aren't you?" the boy said. " 'The Place Love Calls Home'? All that stuff about summer air and auburn hair?"

"It's just a song," I said. "Written a long time ago."

"Are you kidding me? It's a classic. One of the best country love songs ever written. It's an honor to make your acquaintance, Miz Farrell." He leaned toward me and stuck out his hand.

"And you are?"

"Hardy Knox."

I tried to keep from laughing out loud. "Is that your real name?"

"'Fraid so. My daddy had a pretty whacked-out sense of humor."

"And let me guess," I said. "You're Ash's number one fan." Over the years I'd gotten used to groupies of both genders popping out of the woodwork. You found them hanging around every backstage door, the tour bus, hotel lobbies and corridors. Every now and then one tracked Ash down at the house outside Nashville, or managed to get hold of our unlisted number. But I was pretty sure this was the first time anybody had gone to the trouble of trailing him to northeast Texas, a spot so deep in the Piney Woods it wasn't even on the Rand McNally road map.

"Well, yeah. But I'm kind of a colleague, too. That is, I write songs. I'm not quite where he's at yet, but I'm gonna be, someday." I wanted to say I truly hoped he wouldn't be where Ash was now—a burned-out drunk—but he looked so green and hopeful, I couldn't bring myself to do it. "So, is Ash home?" He stood bouncing on the toes of his sneakers, peering around me, like Ash might stick his head out the screen door any second and invite him in for a brew and a hootenanny.

"Ash doesn't live here, actually."

"But I heard he came back down here at Easter. After the rehab thing didn't work out, and his record company dropped him."

"How do you know all that?"

"Those bastards at Arcadia . . . Sometimes I hate Nashville. Every other day I swear I'm never going back." I noticed, as he grinned at me, that he hadn't answered my question. His teeth were slightly too large for his mouth and there were too many of them, but there was something endearing about Hardy Knox.

He looked like somebody you wanted to feed milk and cookies and tuck in with a blanket and a bedtime story. "So, if he's not here, where is he?"

"Well, for the time being, he's living in a trailer out back," I said.

"Y'all haven't split up, have you?"

"Not officially. But we— Wait a minute. Why am I telling you this?"

He grinned again, his eyes glinting behind the lenses. "Because I just drove five hundred fucking miles to save your husband's career."

All of a sudden he looked a lot less endearing. I reminded myself that the word *fan* was short for *fanatic.* Suppose, in spite of his floppy hair and diminutive frame, Hardy Knox was a stalker, a psychopath? For all I knew, there were warrants out for him in all fifty states.

"Well, I'm sorry to have to tell you this, but you wasted your gas," I said. "Ash doesn't want saving. He's given up the music business. Gone back to being a carpenter."

"Give me a break. Guys like Ash don't give up music! He's one of the best songwriters I ever heard."

"You know it and I know it. But Ash doesn't want to hear it."

"I need to talk to him," Hardy said fervently. "I mean, if I could just . . . Will he be back later? Do you think I could wait?"

"I don't think you should get your hopes up."

"I'll take my chances, if that's okay."

I considered him a minute, his skinny frame and scruffy hair, those glasses. "I'm afraid I can't ask you in."

"Oh sure, I understand. I've got my guitar." He gestured toward the car. "Will he be long, do you think?"

"He gets back around dark, most nights. Not always, though. I can't say for sure."

"I just drove down from Nashville, Miz Farrell. You know what it's like there. I'm pretty good at waiting around for stuff to happen."

"Well." I picked up my glass and moved toward the door. "I'm going inside now."

"Sure. Nice to meet you."

I hesitated with my hand on the knob. "Can I— Would you like some iced tea or something, while you wait?"

"I stopped at the DQ in town, thanks." He gazed at me hopefully for a beat or two. "But I wouldn't say no to a beer, if you've got one."

"Sorry. I don't keep it in the house anymore."

"No, ma'am. I can see how you wouldn't."

"Good night, then."

I bolted the door behind me, then went into the kitchen and set my glass in the sink, my heart beating fast. I thought about what, if anything, I should do. On the one hand, calling the sheriff seemed like overreacting; after all, I'd told Hardy he could stay. On the other hand, the world was such a crazy place nowadays. Even here deep in the woods of East Texas, folks cooked meth in trailers, fought each other with knives and guns. Just a month or so before, a man had run over his wife with their pickup in the parking lot at Wal-Mart because she'd bought the wrong brand of cigarettes. And the Klan was still as old and proud and dug-in as the Baptist church, in some corners. I knew what people were capable of.

I stuck my head into Jude's room, where he slept with his face turned toward the glow of the night-light, breathing through his mouth. Crossing to the bed, I touched the edge of his blanket, straightening it. His rust-colored hair was growing out, practically to the tops of his ears now. Since last fall, he'd loved going to the barber every other week with my brothers, but lately he wanted to wear his hair long, like his daddy's.

I double-checked the front door, then went down the hall to my bedroom, where the window was open a couple of inches. Through the screen I could hear the familiar sounds of the woods as full dark came on, the far-off hum of a semi out on the highway: everything the way it usually was, forever and ever, amen. And down underneath it all, as soft as a whispered promise in the dark, the sound of a guitar.

I WOKE TO the sounds of voices, doors slamming. I switched off the lamp and went to the window, but there was nothing out front except my Blazer and Hardy Knox's little blue car. Hurrying through the dark house, I made my way down the back hall and, as gently as I could, inched open the door.

Ash's truck was in the yard, and behind it, against the pale bulk of the trailer, two silhouettes. Through the screen I couldn't make out what they were saying, just voices going back and forth. Then Ash went up the steps, and the door shut with a bang. Inside the trailer, the lights came on.

I crept back to bed, undressing in the dark. As I lay back between the sheets, I heard Hardy's guitar start up again out front. I listened for a while, but it made me too sad to sleep, and finally, I had to get up and shut the window.

When my alarm went off at six-thirty the next morning, Ash's truck was gone, and Hardy Knox was sound asleep, curled in a fetal position on the backseat of his beat-up Corolla. I stood in my robe and watched him through the rolled-down window, his mouth hanging open, his hair over his eyes. His glasses were folded neatly and resting on their earpieces on the console between the front seats, and I noticed he'd taken the time to put his guitar in its case before he'd gone to sleep; it stood at attention, neck up in the passenger seat, like a sentry. For half a second I thought of waking him up and asking him if he wanted some coffee, a bowl of Cocoa Puffs, waffles with blueberries and scrambled eggs, maybe a few slices of buttered toast on the side. Then I remembered what had happened the last time I'd let myself get undone by a man sleeping in the backseat of a motor vehicle. I turned around and went back inside to wake up my son.

chapter seventeen

It would stand to reason that, since Jude had been late to school for nearly two-thirds of his kindergarten career, he'd be late to his own graduation. Luckily, Miss Kimble was so frantic trying to get a dozen five- and six-year-olds into their shiny blue caps and gowns that she barely noticed us slinking in just minutes before the ceremony. I'd had the foresight to wrangle Jude into his costume out in the parking lot, so he was able to sneak into the writhing mass of kids behind the auditorium curtain without attracting his teacher's notice. The last thing I wanted was him getting a yellow square on his very first diploma.

I found my way down a side aisle of the auditorium, excusing myself as I stepped over several pairs of feet to get to the empty seat Dove and Geneva were saving for me. The middle and high schools in Mooney had been rebuilt in recent years, shiny, sprawling buildings full of modern conveniences and technology, but Mooney Elementary was still the old, low-slung brick building my brothers and Geneva and I had attended back in the dark ages, smelling of chalk dust and disinfectant and boiled greens and some other, unidentifiable smell I associated with the fear and exhilaration of childhood. The auditorium was dark and old-fashioned, with rows of attached theater-style seats and a dusty red curtain across the high wooden stage, a stage where I'd watched plays and magic shows and, in sixth grade, the dreaded girls' health lecture.

"Wow," I said as I settled into the seat next to Geneva. "This brings back memories, doesn't it?"

"Now guhls," Geneva said, in perfect imitation of Mrs. Fisk, the longtime school hygiene teacher, who was from Alabama and had an accent even we Texans found exotic, "fuhst you take the belt lahk so." She held her hands a few inches apart, pinching her thumbs and forefingers together. "Then you *slahd* the napkin into the tab, secuhin' it with a little tug." A man in the row in front of us turned around and stared. "Ah know it maht seem lahk a strange and frahtening thang to you now, guhls, but ah assure you, it is only a natchrul paht of the infinite mystuhry of becomin' a *wo*-man."

"Where's Bailey?" I asked, scanning the dimly-lit auditorium.

"Down front, with the rest of the paparazzi." I finally succeeded in picking out my brother from the gaggle of daddies in front of the stage, loaded down with camcorders and digital cameras with telescoping lenses. I was about to ask if she'd seen Ash when the houselights dimmed and Miss Kimble stepped out from between the curtains in her baggy flowered dress and hippie sandals to invite us all to witness this important occasion in the lives of our precious progenies.

The curtains parted to reveal the graduating class in their caps and gowns, giggling and elbowing one another, waving to their daddies down front. Of the whole group, only Lily seemed to be taking this seriously; her mouth was set in a thin line and she gazed straight ahead, focused on some point at the back of the room, ignoring the high jinks going on around her.

Miss Kimble led the class and audience in reciting the Pledge of Allegiance, after which we were treated to a lively choreographed rendition of "Raindrops Keep Falling on My Head," complete with hand gestures and dance steps. Not surprisingly, Jude was the star of this performance, the only one, except Lily, who didn't goof off or ham it up, who never missed a word or a beat, the whole time keeping his eyes trained on the cameras down front. Lily's expression was aloof and long-suffering, like she was the only child up there who understood the indignity of being forced to jump through hoops like a circus animal. The kids paraded across the stage as, one by one, Miss Kimble called their names and presented them with little bow-tied diplomas. For the closing number, they all bunched up again at center stage for a rousing version of "When You Wish Upon A Star."

"That kid of yours got some lungs on him," one of the daddies said to me as the lights came up and we began filing down front to claim our graduates. I was trying to decide whether this was a compliment or not when I saw Ash on the other side of the room, leaning against the wall with his arms folded over his chest. As I met his eyes, he gave his chin a jerk. I pointed toward the stage and our son. Ash shook his head and jabbed his finger at me.

"Would you mind collecting Jude?" I said to Geneva. "Ash seems to have something on his mind."

"Meet you in the parking lot," she said, and I turned and made my way against the tide of parents surging in the other direction. Not a muscle twitched as Ash watched me work my way toward him, tracking me only with his eyes.

"What's up?" I asked, unable to read anything into his body language, the crossed arms and hard stare.

"You told that little pissant where I lived?"

"Excuse me?"

"Hardy Knox."

"I guess you forgot to tell me you joined the Witness Protection Program," I said. "Anyway, he found the house on his own. He acted like he knew you. I never heard of the guy before last night."

"I wish to God *I* hadn't. He's been driving me nuts for two, three years now. Following me all over the countryside, trying to get me to listen to this damn tape of his. I thought once I left Nashville I'd be shed of him. Now I come to find out you're letting him camp out in the front yard."

"I didn't know he was planning on sleeping in his car. He acted like he had business with you."

Suddenly Ash laughed and uncrossed his arms, pushing himself off the wall with one heel. "Hardy Knox, Junior PI. I can't believe he fucking found me. This must be punishment for something I did in a past life."

"Or maybe this one."

"You gotta help me get rid of him, Luce. Tell him I—I got called away on urgent business or something."

"No way. I'm not responsible for covering your butt anymore. Maybe you ought to ask . . ." I caught myself just in time, before I spoke the name I swore would never again cross my lips. "Maybe you ought to listen to his tape, Ash. Hear what he's got to say."

"Forget it. I'll deal with it. Meantime, you watch yourself around him," Ash said.

"Why? He's not dangerous, is he?"

"Nah. But he's got this, this *way* about him."

"What way is that?"

"Just that he can be really—what's the word? *Ingratiating.* Acts all innocent and charming, sliding sideways into your life. Then, next thing you know, he's eating breakfast at your kitchen table."

"Like anybody else I could name?" I smiled, and to my surprise, Ash smiled back. "Listen," I said, "Dove's fixing lunch for everybody back at the house. But if you're too busy entertaining your fan club . . ."

"It just so happens I'm free as a bird." Ash made a sweeping motion with his arm, and fell into step alongside me.

I WAS ON a stool behind the counter at Faye's late that afternoon, tallying up the day's profits on the register, when the doorbells chimed and Hardy Knox walked in, gazing around him with an expression on his face like he'd never seen anything so wondrous as a flower shop before. He was wearing the exact same T-shirt and jeans he'd had on the night before, hanks of brown hair falling over the smudged lenses of his glasses. Behind them, his eyes were a pale, milky blue that reminded me of the old folks at Golden Years. I pushed back my stool and placed my hands, businesslike, on the counter.

"Hardy," I said. "What a surprise."

"Wow," he said. "It smells like Edam in here."

I frowned, confused. "Cheese?"

"*Eden,*" he repeated. "You know—paradise."

I watched him walk around the store, pausing to sniff a pot of hydrangeas, stroking the leaves on a ficus plant, riffling through the greeting cards. "I like this one," he said, holding it up to read aloud: " 'The secret of health for both mind and body is not to mourn for the past, worry about the future, or anticipate troubles, but to live in the present moment, wisely and earnestly.' Buddha said that," he added, like I'd never seen the card myself, like I hadn't been the one to order it. "You know, I'm kind of a Buddhist myself."

"How can you be 'kind of' a Buddhist?"

"I just like the guy's philosophies: 'Be here now,' you know? Sure beats hellfire and brimstone, like I grew up."

"You ought to meet my aunt Dove," I said. I meant it in an offhand way, but Hardy's eyes lit up.

"Yeah? She a Buddhist?"

"No. Never mind. Are you here to buy some flowers?"

"Sure. What's the cheapest thing you got?"

"Well, you're in luck. It's Friday, and those carnations won't last the weekend. I can let you have them for fifty cents a stem."

I opened the cooler for him and he rummaged through the tub of mixed carnations, finally extracting a red one that looked relatively fresh. He placed it along with two quarters on the counter, and I rang him up and wrapped the stem in a sheet of green tissue, tying it with a strand of raffia, just as I would have if it had been a dozen roses. I probably lost more money on the paper and string than I made on the flower, but, like Peggy always said, presentation was everything.

"Here you go," I said, handing him the tissue-wrapped bloom, which he pushed back across the counter at me. "You changed your mind?"

"No. It's for you."

I laughed.

"What?" Hardy said.

"Ash warned me about you."

"He did?" This seemed to please him.

"What do you want, Hardy? I mean, really. Because I'm telling you right now, I don't think I can help you."

"What makes you think I want anything?"

"I know you think I can put you on some kind of an inside track with Ash. But he won't listen to me any more than he'll listen to you."

"See, here's the thing," Hardy said. "I think he will."

I shook my head. "What you're asking—I'm sorry, but I just can't do it."

"Look, Miz Farrell—"

"It's Lucy. Please. You make me feel . . ." I started to say *like your mama,* before I realized that I could, in fact, *be* his mama. "How old are you, anyway? If you don't mind my asking."

"Twenty. In August."

"I don't mean to hurt your feelings, but what makes you think a twenty-year-old nobody showing up out of nowhere can do anything for Ash's career?"

"I'm not nobody."

"So you say. But I don't know you from Adam, and now all of a sudden here you are, sniffing around, trying to find out I-don't-know-what-all about my husband—"

"Relax. I'm not here to pick your brain. Anyway, I've already found out most everything I need to know."

"You have?"

"Sure. He's trying to stay off the sauce, building a house across the road from you. Nice place—I saw it. Water, trees, a regular little sanctuary."

"You've been out to Ash's place?" Hardy shrugged. "How did you find it?"

"I grew up in a small town, too, Miz—Lucy. All you have to do is sit in the DQ for an hour or so, you'll hear everybody's secrets."

"No offense, Hardy, but you're starting to scare me."

"Oh God. I'm sorry," he said, sounding like he meant it. I reminded myself that part of a sociopath's technique is a knack for conning his way into people's lives by making them think he's just as regular as they are. "Listen. Let me ask you something."

"Okay." I wished I hadn't let Audrey go home early. I reminded myself that there were scissors under the counter, the small knife I used to trim stems.

"You're not a musician yourself, right?" he asked.

"I couldn't carry a tune in a bucket."

"But you know music. I mean, you know the real deal when you hear it."

"I guess."

"So you know Ash is it, right? I bet you knew it the first time you heard him sing."

I thought about the first time I'd seen Ash onstage at the Round-Up, and the night he'd driven out to my old rent house to serenade me from the tailgate of his pickup. I thought about the first time I'd heard "The Place Love Calls Home" on the radio, how I'd had to pull over onto the shoulder of the highway and lay my head on the steering wheel as Ash's voice filled the car, a song he'd written on the back-porch steps of the first house we shared, a song about me.

"That's what I thought," Hardy said. "Well, I'm the real deal, too."

"Oh Lord, Hardy. Don't you know that's what everybody in Nashville says? They ought to hand out T-shirts at the city limits sign."

He reached into his back pocket and laid a plain white cassette tape on the counter. "Ask Denny, if you don't believe me."

"You know Denny?"

He turned and started for the door. "Pop that tape in and give it a listen. You'll see what I'm talking about."

"Hardy, wait," I said. He paused with his hand on the knob. "I can't—I'm not promising anything. Understand?"

"Yes, ma'am."

"And you can't go on sleeping in my front yard."

"That's okay. I found a place."

"You mean you're staying? Here in town?"

He smiled and raised his hand. "See you around."

The bells jangled as he pushed his way out onto the sidewalk, leaving the cassette on the counter next to the wilting carnation, like offerings at a shrine.

BUT HARDY KNOX knew me better than I knew myself. By the time I'd locked up the shop and climbed into the Blazer that evening, I could hardly wait to pop his cassette into the deck.

The sound was rich and full-bodied, obviously professionally done. There was only a guitar, a bass, drums, and Hardy's voice. At least I assumed it was Hardy; in contrast to his speaking voice, so thin and reedy, his singing voice was as pure and clear as rainwater. The first song was a sad, slow ballad about growing up in a small town where your choices were, according to the lyrics, to "get out, or stay and die."

I cranked up the volume, trying to match up the yearning in the singer's voice, the poignancy of the lyrics, with the gangly, floppy-haired kid who'd presented me with a red carnation, who I'd watched sleeping in the back of his little Corolla. That tune was followed by a funny, swing-style number about a guy in a dance hall watching his dream girl two-stepping with another guy, starting out all pissed-off and righteous but getting bluer and bluer as the night wore on and the drinks added up, until by closing time the one who'd got away had turned into "the best thing I never had." Then it was just Hardy again, his voice accompanied by a soft, plaintive guitar as he sang about the pain of having to choose between two loves, a girl and his music.

I let the Blazer idle in the parking lot as the song played out. I felt the way I had years before, listening to Ash's voice float in my kitchen window in the dark, like I was being fed a message encrypted in some secret language, and if I just listened hard enough I might be able to figure it out. I wondered now if I'd been paying careful enough attention, or if I'd allowed my mind to wander just enough to let something rare and precious drift out of my reach.

I ejected the cassette as Ash's truck came around the corner, Jude sitting beside him on the front passenger seat. Ash pulled in beside me and opened his door, and Jude scrambled out after him, as brown as an Indian, his hair curling behind his ears.

"Backseat, baby," I said automatically as Jude opened the passenger door and started to climb in beside me.

"Aw, Ma," Jude said. The sound of his voice brought me up short, suddenly so grown-up sounding, so much like Denny's.

"Don't 'Aw, Ma' me. It's the law," I said, giving Ash a pointed look.

"Better listen to your mama, bud," he said. "If anybody knows about laying down the law, it's her." He glanced at the carnation drooping on the seat beside me. "Where'd you get the flower?"

"I work in a flower shop, remember?"

"Huh. Thought maybe you had a secret admirer."

"Maybe I do. If it's a secret, I wouldn't know about it, would I?"

He smiled. "I've got to get on back," he said. "Got a few more hours of daylight left. But maybe Jude can come over this weekend, if it suits you. Now that school's out and Little League's through."

"Sure."

"I'll see you later on then, okay, bud? Give me a hug." He leaned into the backseat and gave Jude a squeeze.

"Pretty soon I'll be too big to hug," Jude said. "Pretty soon I'll be as big as you!"

"Little boys are never too big to get hugged by their daddies," Ash said. "You remember that before you go getting too big for them britches." He pinched the waist of Jude's shorts, and Jude squealed with laughter.

"Ash?" I said as he stepped away and closed the rear door.

"Yeah?" He paused to look at me through the open window. His silver beard was fully grown in now, his arms tan and roped with muscle. I wanted to tell him about Hardy Knox's music; I wanted to hand him the tape, to say, "Here. This is what you're all about. It was once, and it can be again." But I didn't. Ash was the one with the words, the music. My only gift was knowing the real deal when I saw it—not that it had ever done me a lick of good.

"Nothing. See you," I said, putting the Blazer in reverse, backing slowly out of my parking space and heading for home.

"Are you kidding me?" Denny said when she called that evening from a motel room in Bakersfield. "Everybody in Nashville knows Hardy Knox. Hey, guess what?" she said to somebody on her end. "Hardy Knox is in Texas. He followed Daddy down there or something."

"So, what is it that everybody knows about him, exactly?" I asked.

"Oh, there's all sorts of stories. He's a genius. He's a maniac. He's an irritating little prick. Take your pick."

"What's your take on him? He said I should ask you."

"Hardy's okay. He acts kind of like a lost puppy, doesn't he? But don't let him fool you. The boy's got an agenda like you wouldn't believe."

"What kind of agenda?"

"To be the next Harlan Howard. From what I hear, he might even have the goods to back it up. He's always got three or four A&R guys dragging around after him, but nobody's signed him yet."

"How come, do you think?"

"I don't really know. Hardy marches to a different drummer, I guess you could say."

"I already pretty much figured that out. But what's he want with Ash? That's the part I can't make any sense of. I mean, if he's everything you say he is, then why hitch his wagon to a falling star?"

"With Hardy, who knows? Maybe he's got some angle nobody else can see. Then again, maybe he's just doing his Christian duty."

"He told me he's sort of a Buddhist."

Denny snorted. "That boy was raised full-out backwoods Pentecostal. Snake-handling and talking in tongues, know what I'm saying?"

"So, what should I do? Do I need to watch my back, or what?"

"Well, I wouldn't go inviting him to sleep in the guest room. But I don't think you need to call out the sheriff on him, either. If I was you, I'd let Daddy handle him—this is between the two of them, right? It doesn't have anything to do with you."

Except that now it did. How had Hardy Knox understood the quickest way to get under my skin, that by giving me his tape—knowing I'd listen, that I'd be helpless to resist—he'd be sucking me in, creating in me a stepping-stone to Ash?

I went in to check on Jude, to see if he'd managed to get himself into his pajamas like I'd told him, to make sure he said his prayers and to read him a story. I found him splayed sideways across his bed, still in his dirty clothes, sound asleep in a puddle of lamplight with a hodgepodge of toy dinosaurs and army men scattered across the comforter. The thrill of graduating from kindergarten and being outdoors all afternoon with his daddy had done him in. I tried maneuvering him under the covers without waking him, but he wouldn't be budged, and I had to settle for leaving him there, spread-eagled among the little plastic beasts and men.

I flipped through the TV channels for a while, lighting for a few seconds at a time on legal and forensic-investigation series, hip-hop videos, a show where guys in suits and ties were yelling at each other about the economy, a documentary on civil rights. For several minutes I watched Fred Astaire dance on the floor, the walls, the ceiling, as light and easy as a puff of air in his patent-leather shoes. Everybody but me, it seemed, had something extraordinary they could do that set them apart from the masses. Why, if you could write and play music the way Ash could, wouldn't you do it until your voice gave out and your fingers bled? Why wouldn't you, if you had the ability, spend the rest of your life till the day you died dancing on the ceiling?

I shut off the television and wandered out to the front porch to watch the night come on. The sky was deep purple streaked pink with a silvery sheen behind the woods across the road. Heat lightning flickered in the distance and the air smelled of rain, but I knew it was only a tease, a false alarm. It hadn't rained since the night Ash showed up, the night before Good Friday. Everywhere you went you heard folks complaining about gardens needing twice-daily watering, crops and stock tanks drying up in the pastures. I thought about what Ash had said about my fondness for metaphors; the weather, lately, seemed like a pretty good match for what had become my life: parched and listless, withering from lack of sustenance.

I was roused by a nearby rumble of thunder, a sudden shift in the wind. There was a sizzle of lightning, a sharp, metallic smell in the air, and then fat drops began to fall, kicking up puffs of dust in the yard.

I jumped to my feet and opened the screen door, grabbing my keys from the hook inside, and ran to the Blazer, where I'd left the windows down. Inserting the ignition key, I flicked the switch to power up the windows. At the same time, in a flash of lightning, I saw Hardy Knox's tape glowing white in the dash. Without really considering what I was doing, I pushed it into the slot and it began to play, picking up in the middle of the song about the boy whose life was split between his love for a girl and his music.

My throat closed up. I wanted to find Hardy and grab him by the shoulders and shake him. "Go back to her!" I wanted to yell in his face. "Go find her and don't let go!" It wasn't a matter of telling him he couldn't have it both ways; the man who'd written this song understood that. It was the fact that Hardy had chosen, and that the choice would cost him, and he would never get a chance to do it over again.

So caught up was I in the music, I wasn't aware till the last second of headlights slashing through the rain, across my windshield. I slid low in the seat as Ash's truck rolled slowly past, then backed up and pulled to a stop alongside the Blazer. Next thing I knew he was standing outside, beating his fist against the passenger-side window. I contemplated letting him stay out there getting soaked to the skin, possibly being struck by lightning and fried to a crisp, briefly torn between believing things would be easier all around that way and having to explain to our half-orphaned son what I'd done. Finally I hit the button, unlatching the doors. Ash scrambled into the passenger seat, shaking himself like a wet dog.

"What the hell?" he said. "I could've gotten electrocuted out there! What are you doing, anyway?"

I reached for the volume knob and turned it up. "Listen."

Ash sat back in the seat, head cocked. "Son of a bitch," he said after a second. "I can't believe he— That little fucker."

Lightning flashed, and rain blew sideways in sheets across the windshield. He reached across me for the stereo controls, but I grasped his wrist and pushed it away.

"Remember when you asked me to go down to Jefferson and talk to Father Laughlin?" I said. "Well, I'm asking you to keep your mouth shut and listen for five minutes. If you won't do it for you, then do it for me."

Ash sighed and leaned his head against the seat back and closed his eyes. I pushed the Rewind button and held it for a minute, then released it and turned up the volume.

He sat without moving as the tape played and the storm blew and pounded around us. In the dashboard light, the creases in his face looked like the jagged terrain of a strange and hostile country, a place I didn't have a guidebook for, where I didn't speak the language.

When the music ended, I pressed the Eject button, and the cab filled with silence. Slowly Ash raised his head and opened his eyes.

"I don't believe it," he said finally.

"Believe what?"

"I don't believe that's Hardy Knox. It sounds like—I don't know. It reminds me too much of somebody else."

"It's *you*, you idiot," I said. "Who it reminds you of is *you.*"

Helplessly, I felt tears start to roll down my cheeks, and I covered my face with my hands. Ash's fingers brushed my wrist, but I shook him off.

"Why are you doing this, Lucy?"

"I can't believe you'd ask me that. I can't believe you're really that dense."

"Are you getting your period? Is that it?"

"Oh Lord." I rummaged in the console till I found a handful of DQ napkins and blew my nose into one.

"Well, you can't blame me for asking. Practically the only times

I've ever seen you cry, you always claimed it was hormones. I remember when you— Holy shit. You're not pregnant, are you?"

"Why don't you just go?"

"Now? Out in the rain?"

"I mean *away.* Back to Nashville. Or someplace else. Anyplace else. It's just too hard, watching you do this."

"Do what?"

"Not being who you are. Who you were meant to be."

"Look, I went to Nashville, and I couldn't cut it. Do we have to keep thrashing it over and over again?"

"I'm not talking about Nashville. It never *was* about Nashville. You just let yourself get caught up in that, that head trip, that crazy circus. So you couldn't be what some dipshit record company guy expected. So you didn't wind up on the top of the *Billboard* charts or the cover of *Country Weekly.* So what? That doesn't make what you are any less. Don't you get it, Ash? I get it, even Hardy Knox gets it. Why can't you?"

The thunder had moved off, a distant grumble in the east, and the rain had stopped. I took the key out of the ignition, opened the car door, and stepped out onto the damp ground. The air smelled of wet peat and pine, and the temperature had cooled a good ten degrees. Overhead, the sky broke apart into shards of silver and blue, a crescent of moon like a cosmic wink shining through. As I walked toward the house, Ash was still sitting in the passenger seat of my car.

The next morning the air was thick and steamy, the sky a hazy blue. Ash stopped by around noon to collect Jude. Neither of us mentioned the thunderstorm, Hardy Knox's tape, my tears, our conversation. But when I went out to the Blazer to make a run into town for groceries, the tape deck was empty. I looked in the glove box, the console, felt around under and between the seats, but there was no mistaking it; Hardy's cassette was gone.

chapter eighteen

Late the following Tuesday morning, Audrey and I were getting ready for a delivery run when through the front window I saw Ash's truck pull up to the curb.

"If I've told him once, I've told him a thousand times," I said, "he can't park at the curb. It's a fire lane, for heaven's sake. What does he think the red paint is for?"

But when the shop door opened to the usual clamor of bells, it wasn't Ash who walked in, but Hardy Knox. At least I was pretty sure it was Hardy, underneath the dirty jeans and sweat-soaked T-shirt and the sunburn that made him look like an oversize, fresh-peeled shrimp. The only parts of him that were familiar were his thick black-rimmed glasses and his Bugs Bunny grin; I'd have recognized those anywhere.

As Audrey and I looked on, he walked over and opened the cooler door, where he selected one fresh pink rose and placed it on the counter in front of me.

"I hear these are your favorites." He glanced from me to Audrey, his eyes dropping to the front of her T-shirt: TOO HOT TO HANDLE. She smiled crookedly, tugging at the hem of the shirt, which didn't quite hide the strip of flesh between it and her jeans, the little silver ring in her navel.

I pushed the rose back toward him. "I don't need your bribes, Hardy," I said. "And I'm not playing your games anymore."

"It's not a bribe," he said. "It's a thank-you gift."

"For what?"

"For liking my tape," he said. "Don't try to tell me you didn't. I heard all about it. It made you cry." I felt myself flush. "Anyway," he said, "there's something else I owe you for."

"What would that be?"

"My new job."

"Your job?"

"Yep. Ash is letting me help out with the house."

I did my best to hide my surprise. "I didn't know you were a carpenter."

"Oh, I'm not. I mean, it's not like I'm out there hammering and sawing and shit—that's his and Isaac's gig. I'm more like a, a gofer. I fetch tools, and run into town to the hardware store, or to grab them some lunch at the DQ. . . ."

"You mean Ash is actually paying you for this?"

"Well, no, not exactly. But he's letting me stay in the handyman's cottage, for free! Awesome, huh? Hey, listen, I'd better git. I told 'em I'd be back in twenty minutes with burgers and fries. I didn't say anything about stopping off here." He inched the rose once more in my direction. "How much for the flower?"

"Run along, Hardy. The DQ can get pretty busy this time of day."

"I think he really digs my music," Hardy said excitedly as he backed toward the door. "I think maybe we can make something happen."

"Hardy?"

He paused with his hand on the knob. "Yeah?"

I started to say his source was giving out old information, that pink roses weren't my favorite anymore. Give me peonies any day, heavy and blowsy-headed. We almost never got them—only a few weeks every spring when they arrived by FedEx from North Carolina—but when we did, I took them home with me by the armload, stuck them in every available container in big, wild bunches: deep magenta, ivory shading to seashell pink around the edges, and every shade in between. On second thought, Hardy Knox didn't need to know that. Neither did Ash, for that matter.

"You might want to stop by the Sav-Mor and grab some sunscreen," I said.

Audrey and I watched Hardy scale the running board of the truck and ease it away from the curb, looking like an overgrown child behind the wheel.

"Who was that?" Audrey asked as I circled the counter and replaced the rose in the cooler.

"Just some nut," I said. "A victim of Ash's latest pie-in-the-sky scheme."

"He's a musician? Is that what he was talking about, about him and Ash making something happen?"

"Let's go load the van."

"He's sort of cute," Audrey mused as we carried the arrangements out the back door: a mixed spring bouquet for somebody with a new baby in the hospital, a wreath for the funeral home. "In a, you know, geeky kind of way."

"You already have a boyfriend."

"Yeah, but all he does is drink beer and play cards with his buddies and pass out in front of the TV."

I laughed. "Honey, you just described ninety-nine-point-nine percent of the male population. In this part of the world, at least."

"I always thought it would be cool to date somebody in a band."

"Hardy's not in a band," I said. "He's just some guy with a demo tape. Believe me, the bushes are crawling with them."

"Not around here, they're not. Anyway, you *liked* his tape. It made you cry."

I adjusted the wreath and heaved shut the van's door. "If you tell anybody about that, I'll tie a string to that thing in your belly button and hang you up by it till your guts fall out."

"Jeez," she said, "you are so uptight sometimes! What's wrong with crying over music? Isn't that what it's there for? To sort of, you know, keep us plugged in? To God and the universe and each other and shit?"

"Have you got the keys?"

"What are you so scared of, is what I'd like to know," she said. "That somebody might accidentally find out you're human?"

Before I could think up an answer for that, she'd climbed into the driver's seat and slammed the door. A plume of exhaust exploded from the tailpipe as Audrey started up the ignition and wrangled the balky transmission into reverse. I watched the old van buck and shimmy its way out of the parking lot and around the corner. I stood with the midday sun beating down on my head, breathing in gas fumes and hot asphalt and honeysuckle until things started to spin. Then I went inside and turned down the air conditioner a notch and rested my head on the counter until my heart slowed its banging. It didn't pay to loiter in the noonday sun. You couldn't be too careful, exposing yourself to the elements.

A FEW DAYS later I bumped into Isaac King at the Miracle Mart, where I'd stopped on the way home from work to buy Jude a Milky Way to tide him over till suppertime. Ordinarily I didn't fall for that kind of blackmail, but lately the stakes were getting higher; it was hard to compete with a daddy who had his own full-scale, real-life construction set, complete with bulldozers and cement trucks and a bunch of honest-to-God Lincoln Logs. I hadn't been out yet to see for myself, but the way Jude described it, it sounded like one of those TV shows where the crew builds a house from the ground up in five days. I fully expected to hear in a week or so that Ash was getting ready to throw himself a housewarming party, complete with hot-tubbing and grilling on the deck.

"Well, if it ain't Miss Lucy," a voice said behind me in the checkout line, and I turned to see Isaac's friendly face, as dark as cocoa, his pink-gummed, gap-toothed grin. I laid my candy bar on the counter and gave him a hug, breathing in the ripe outdoor smell of him, sweat and sawdust and hard, honest work. I was ashamed to admit how long it had been since I'd seen him face to face. Before we went to Nashville, Ash and Isaac had been best friends, and we'd spent time with him and his wife, Rose, and their ever-growing brood of kids; but I hadn't sought them out when I came back alone with Jude, hadn't seen a way to work the two of us into their life without Ash, our axis, our common core. "Where you been keepin' yourself, girl?" he said, holding me at arm's length. "You look like the world's treatin' you right."

"You look pretty good yourself," I said, taking his arm to pull him aside so that a scowling fat man could pay for his six-pack of Coors Light and a handful of scratch-off tickets. "How are Rose and the kids?"

"Same as ever. Kids growin' like weeds, and Rose, well, I thank Jesus every day for that woman. I married a saint."

"You got yourself a new baby, I hear."

"Yes, ma'am. Ten months old. DeShawn, his name is, but we call him Dumplin', 'cause of how fat he is. I don't believe the boy ever will learn to walk. His mama and the girls, they don't never put him down, just tote him around stickin' goodies in his mouth mornin', noon, and night."

"So are you on your way home now?" I asked, eyeing the two-liter bottles of Dr Pepper and Big Red and Mountain Dew he cradled in both arms.

"Ha! I wish. Ash don't want to quit workin' so long as there's a speck of light left in the sky. Lucky we don't live up in Alaska, he'd be crackin' the whip twenty-four hours a day. No, we're just takin' a break, havin' ourselves a little happy hour."

"That looks like pretty tame stuff, for happy hour."

"Boss man's orders."

"What?"

"Oh yes, ma'am. Ash runs hisself a tight ship these days. I got to say, at first I missed me a beer at the end of the day, but I'm gettin' used to it. And Rose, she sure is happy to have me home sober, come the end of an evenin'. Only one puttin' up a squeak is Hardy Knox. Not much he can do about it, though, 'cept go back to Tennessee, and I b'lieve he'd tolerate pret' near anything not to have to do that."

"What's Hardy doing out there, anyway?"

"I wish I knew. Makin' a nuisance of hisself, mostly. Boy don't hardly know a nail gun from a Skilsaw. Spends mosta his time yakkin' and strummin' his guitar. I can't for the life a me understand why Ash puts up with it, but he won't say. Me, I just try and do my job and keep myself clear of the rest of it."

The fat man finished paying and elbowed his way past us, and Isaac moved forward and set his bottles on the counter.

"We go back, Ash and me," he said. "I figger I owe him to mind my own business and let him mind his. Anyhow, it's good work. Hot and hard, but beats the hell outta moppin' floors at the hospital. Plus, all the Big Red a man can drink. Can't hardly complain about that."

He gestured that I should go ahead of him to pay for Jude's Milky Way, and I stepped forward and handed the pimple-faced teenage cashier a dollar.

"So, when you comin' out to see the Taj Mahal?" Isaac asked as I dropped my change and the candy bar into my purse and turned away from the counter.

"Surely it's not *that* big."

"Oh, I reckon not quite. But it's way more space than one man needs all by his lonesome, for sure."

"I don't imagine Ash will be by his lonesome for long," I said.

"I hope not. Man like Ash, he craves company."

"Tell me about it. I'm sure he'll have the place full up in no time." I squeezed Isaac's arm as the clerk began to ring up his sodas. "It's good seeing you, Isaac. Give Rose my best."

"Yes, ma'am. Don't be a stranger, you hear? Come on out and take at look at our Dumplin'."

I walked out to the car, my insides echoing hollowly. There was never going to be that kind of easy, back-door friendship between the Kings and me again. Too much had changed, and we all knew it.

"What took you so long?" Jude demanded as I unlocked the Blazer and climbed behind the wheel. Despite orders to stay buckled into his safety seat and not mess with anything, I saw right away that he'd cranked up both the air conditioner and the volume on the radio, where Travis Tritt was singing that it was a great day to be alive.

"Didn't I tell you to stay put?" I said, twisting knobs to regulate both the noise level and the temperature. "Didn't I say that right before I got out of the car?"

"Did you get my candy?" I passed his Milky Way over the seat. He took it and began to peel off the wrapper. "Is this the biggest one they had?"

What had become of my baby, the boy who a couple of months before I'd been able to tickle into submission, whose crew cut I'd burrowed my nose against during bedtime prayers, who'd been running through my aunt's backyard wearing a rubber dinosaur head? Who was this dark-skinned, long-limbed creature with hair falling over his ears and the eyes that reflected myself back to me the same way I'd begun to see myself, as a stranger?

I put the Blazer in reverse and swung out of the Miracle Mart parking lot, peeling carelessly onto the two-lane, pressing the pedal down hard. The engine hesitated a second and then surged forward, the tires humming on the blacktop as we sped home in climate-controlled, stereophonic comfort. I found myself missing my old Buick, the one Ash had helped me acquire from Isaac's brother J.D., with its ugly army-green paint job and torn upholstery, its four hundred and twenty-five horses under the hood. It had been, not to put too fine a point on it, a piece of shit, but a kind of magic always seemed to happen when I got behind the wheel; something great always seemed to be emanating from the radio, "Rescue Me" or "Dock of the Bay," and with all the windows down and its big angel-wing fins swooping up from the back, the rush of air through the cab as I sailed down the highway always made me feel like I was on the back straightaway in heaven. It was the first vehicle I'd ever owned on my own outright and, looking back, letting J.D. buy it back for parts when we moved to Nashville seemed symbolic of some other, larger loss, something that had been falling away from me in chinks so small I'd barely noticed until all of a sudden I found that my undercarriage was rusted out, my suspension gone.

At home, I managed to finagle Jude into the tub—he wouldn't let me undress or bathe him these last few weeks, claiming he needed "privacy"—and went into the kitchen to start slapping hamburgers together for our supper. As I kneaded and shaped the patties, I thought about Isaac in the Miracle

Mart with his bottles of soda, the nonchalant way he'd said, "Boss man's orders." If Ash had quit drinking, then why hadn't he said so? Why, the last time the subject came up, had he skirted my question, saying, "It's not that simple"? I kept turning and turning it in my head like the meat I was forming with my hands, but no matter how I fashioned it, it wouldn't come out neat and circular, the way I wanted.

I placed the burgers on a platter and set it in the icebox, washed my hands and dried them on a dish towel, then walked down the hallway to the bathroom. From behind the closed door came sounds of amphibious destruction, objects being dropped into water accompanied by verbal explosions.

I rapped my knuckles against the door. "Jude?" Instantly the bathroom grew quiet. "Everything okay in there?"

"I'm *playing*!"

"Well, I need to go outside for a minute. Five minutes, and then I want you out and in your PJs and ready for supper, all right?"

"What are we having?"

"Hamburgers."

"We had that already this week!"

"Not since Sunday. Would you like to fix supper, for a change?" My voice sounded meaner than I'd meant it to, and Jude's, when it came back muffled by the closed door, was small but still defiant.

"I don't know how to cook."

"Then I guess we're stuck with burgers. Five minutes, you hear me?" He didn't answer, and I knocked again, louder this time. "Jude?"

"All right! Jeesh."

I let myself out the back door and hurried across the yard to Ash's trailer like a thief in broad daylight. I didn't ask myself what I was doing, whether I had a right to know what was going on in his home or whether this might, technically speaking, constitute trespassing. We were still married, after all, which made us legal co-owners of the land and everything that stood on it.

I didn't know whether or not he locked the trailer when he was gone, but I doubted it. What was there to steal but a ratty mattress, a couple of plastic chairs? I scaled the cinder-block steps and turned the doorknob, feeling it give under my hand.

Slipping inside, I shut the door swiftly behind me and leaned against it to catch my breath. Even though all the windows were open, the place was sweltering. I looked around, letting my eyes adjust to the dimness. A neat stack of magazines sat on the fold-out breakfast table, a lone coffee cup was inverted in the dish drainer next to the kitchen sink. I walked over and ran my finger across the surface of the countertop. It came away grime-free and smelling slightly of Lysol. How convenient, having a girlfriend who sold dope *and* kept your house clean!

I tiptoed down the hall, sticking my head into the bedroom. A sheet and blanket lay tangled at the foot of the mattress, and a lamp stood with a small grouping of objects on the inverted milk crate Ash used as a nightstand.

I groped for the light switch, and the items on the milk crate sprang into focus: a glass half-filled with clear liquid, a spiral-bound notebook and an uncapped pen, the small framed photo of Jude and me that I'd seen him unpack on the day he moved in.

I lifted the glass, sniffed and then sipped, tasting the familiar, slightly metallic flavor of well water. Replacing the glass, I glanced down at the notebook. The top page was jammed with Ash's handwriting, small and crabbed, nearly impossible to decipher. I flipped back a page, which was blank but for three words printed in block letters in the middle of the page:

CROW FLY DREAMING.

My heart fluttered, remembering the days before we were married and just after, when words and music poured out of

Ash like breath. He'd always kept a notebook on the bedside table to jot down lyrics that came to him in his dreams; many a night I'd wake and roll over to the sight of his bare back, his breathing soft and quick as he scribbled away in the moonlight. Sometimes the songs came to him fully formed and he had to scramble to capture them whole, like beautiful insects, careful not to tear a wing or a leg. Other times all he got were bits and pieces, a line here, a phrase there.

CROW FLY DREAMING.

It meant nothing, of course, and everything.

"Ma!"

I jumped, dropping the notebook.

"Ma!" Jude hollered again.

Hurriedly, I switched off the light. How was I going to explain what I was doing here? There was no back door, no way I could sneak out and pretend to have been wandering in the woods, nothing I could do but walk down the cinder-block steps in plain sight like the underhanded sneak I was.

I swung open the trailer door, pasting on a big smile.

"Hi, baby!" I said brightly, putting a nonchalant swing in my stride as I crossed the yard. Jude was wearing electric-blue swim trunks and a Hawaiian shirt printed with hula girls. "Did you need something?"

"Phone."

He watched me reproachfully as I walked past him into the house, trailing me down the hall where I picked up the cordless.

"Hello?" I said into the mouthpiece, trying to act like my heart wasn't about to beat out of my chest.

"Help." It was Geneva, sounding like somebody was holding a gun to her head, though I'd heard this tone often enough to doubt that was really the situation.

"What's the matter?" I said. No response. "Is it Lily?"

"Mm."

"Want her to sleep over here?"

"Bless you. You're saving my life."

"No problem. Should we come get her, or will you run her out?"

"I'll bring her. Thirty minutes okay?"

"Fine."

"How about twenty?"

"Tell her we're having hamburgers for supper."

"I owe you big-time," Geneva said, and hung up.

"Guess what?" I said, turning to Jude. "Lily's coming over to spend the night. You want to come set the table for me?"

He followed me to the kitchen, where I opened the cupboard and got down three plates and handed them to Jude, then opened the silverware drawer. When I turned back around with a fistful of forks, he was still standing there, regarding me over the stacked plates.

"I *saw* you," he said.

"Saw me what?" I eased past him and took a set of place mats out of the pie safe.

"In Daddy's trailer."

"I was looking for something," I said. "Something I thought I left over there." I wondered what had happened to my policy of not lying to kids. I guessed it had gone out the window at about the same time my cuddly little boy was replaced by this miniature storm trooper.

"Left there when?" Jude said. "You don't even *go* there."

"It was a long time ago. Put those plates down. Lily will be here any minute."

"You were *spying*!" Jude said. "Like that guy in the movies—James Blond."

"It was just a little thing," I said. "It doesn't matter. Now, do you want that coleslaw Aunt Dove made, or should I fix corn on the cob?"

My son gave me a shrewd look, one that said he was on to me but that his silence could be bought, if I played my cards right.

"Both," he said. "And pie for dessert."

"We haven't got any pie."

"Well, make one."

"It takes a long time to make a pie. Anyway, I haven't got . . ." *The ingredients,* I started to say. *The patience.* But Jude's eyes told the whole story; in color they were his uncle Bailey's, but in the extent to which they could tie knots in my heart, they were all Farrell.

"How about if we go to town after supper and get some ice cream at the DQ?" I said. "You and Lily and me."

He cocked his head—another of his daddy's gestures. "Can I have a banana split?"

I took the plates from him and set them on the table with a sigh.

"You can have anything you want."

chapter nineteen

"What's eating you, anyway?" Geneva asked as we sat across from each other in a booth at the DQ. Since she'd started working three-quarters time, we got to have lunch together every so often, something we hadn't been able to do since I'd moved back to Mooney.

I took my compact out of my purse and frowned at myself in the tiny mirror. "Do I look the same to you?"

"The same as what?"

"Like I did back when things were—you know. Normal."

"You know what your problem is?" she said, reaching for one of my french fries.

"Why bother figuring it out for myself, when I've got you to tell me?"

"You haven't got any direction. You need a purpose. A *cause.*"

"You mean a mission from God?"

"Think about it. You've got a job, a kid, but nothing that really, well, grabs you by the throat and won't let go."

"And you do?"

"No, but I'm not—" She hesitated, pretending to be chewing thoughtfully while she stalled for time.

"What?"

"Now, don't go getting all huffy on me. I just hate seeing you so, well . . ."

"What? Unhappy? You think I'm unhappy?"

"You're putting words in my mouth."

"Tell me what you meant to say instead, then."

"Maybe *aimless* would be a better word. Why don't you take some of that money of yours and do something with it? Like finding yourself a little house someplace exotic. Say Greece. Or Italy! Living among the natives. Learning to cook their food, speak their language."

"Have you been renting *Under the Tuscan Sun* again?"

"Start a little business, then. Something interesting, like a gift shop or a tearoom."

"Oh, right. A tearoom in Mooney, Texas. Number one tourist destination in the state." Geneva had finished her burger and was giving me one of her patented looks, the one that said she knew more about what was good for me than I ever would. "I like flowers," I said. "I'm good with them. In a few years Peggy might retire and let me have the shop for my own."

"Honey, I've got news for you. Peggy's gonna carry Faye's with her to the grave. I don't care what she says now, about taking off to spend more time with her grandkids or whatever. That was her mama's place and she'll never turn it loose so long as there's breath in her body."

I polished off my iced tea. Geneva was probably right, as usual. What's more, I didn't mind if Peggy stayed at Faye's forever. There were some things, like weddings, that still scared the bejesus out of me just thinking about trying to manage alone. Besides, Peggy was my friend. I hoped that, like her mama, she'd die behind the counter, making up a spring bouquet—only not for another thirty years or so.

Meanwhile, my money from the Nashville house was just sitting there, accruing interest but otherwise doing nobody any good. Most of the time I forgot I even had it. I didn't feel like a person with money, or at least the way I thought someone with money was supposed to feel. Every now and then the thought of my bank balance would pop into my head, and I'd get the urge to do something extravagant, like one of those crazy old ladies you'd read about in the paper every now and then who dies and leaves her fortune to her cats or the local poetry society.

But I didn't have cats, Mooney didn't have a poetry society, and anyway, I wasn't dead yet. On the other hand, I didn't have the kind of big dreams and ambitions that everybody seemed to think I should have. I wanted Jude to be able to go to college if he wanted, but otherwise I got the shakes just thinking about something as simple as buying a new couch.

"You know, now that I think about it, I really like the tearoom idea," Geneva mused as we gathered our trash and deposited it in a can by the door. "There's that cute little space next to the Sav-Mor, remember, where Movie Magic used to be?" A few years back, we'd had three video rental stores in Mooney, but the advent of satellite dishes and TiVo had forced all but one of them out of business.

"Catty-corner from the café, you mean? Yeah, I'm sure Burton would love having a tearoom within spitting distance of his place. He'd probably sabotage it before it ever got off the ground. Get somebody to hold back the permits or something. Or, knowing Burton, he'd wait till I'd sunk a bunch of money into the place and *then* screw things up. Poison the chicken salad, or bribe the health inspector to say I had roaches in the deep freeze. Hang me out to dry and stand there laughing over every minute of it."

"Did anybody ever tell you that you are a very, very negative person?"

We stood on the sticky asphalt, digging in our purses for breath mints and keys. "I don't *want* a tearoom, Gen. I don't want to build a business from the ground up, or go remodel a villa in Tuscany. I just want my old life back, the way it used to be."

"Which old life?" she asked.

"Good question."

Back at work, I checked the orders for Monday, straightened the shelves, cleaned out the cooler. The phone didn't ring and not one customer came in all afternoon. I gave Audrey her paycheck and sent her home.

I hadn't been able to get my conversation with Isaac the day before at the Miracle Mart out of my mind. It was about time, I decided, that I saw the Taj Mahal of northeast Texas with my own eyes.

I rinsed out the coffeemaker, locked up the shop, and drove through town, around the courthouse square, out the FM road toward home. There hadn't been a break from the heat or drought since the brief storm the night Ash and I had sat in my Blazer listening to Hardy's tape, and the fields lay scorched bare as I passed the old brick ranch house, the arch of trees and vines overhead thinner than before as I drove beneath it and into the clearing, easing off on the gas behind a bevy of pickups: Ash's shiny white-and-chrome monstrosity, Isaac's old two-tone GMC, and a couple I didn't recognize, banged up with age and hard use. Out of the corner of my eye I saw Hardy's little blue Corolla parked over by the handyman's cottage, which, despite allegedly being occupied, didn't look any less ramshackle than the first time I'd seen it. But I didn't really take it in, struck dumb as I was by what filled my windshield, where a field of long, waving grass used to be. I craned my neck up and up, following the soaring framework, the trusses of the peaked roof, a stone fireplace rising two stories into the air. Not exactly the Taj Mahal, but for Cade County, Texas, a definite contender.

A horn tooted—Isaac, backing up, rolling past me and waving, on his way home. I opened the car door, watching a couple of men crawling around on a wooden platform on the second level. "Not there, Ramon, Jesus," I heard Ash call out from down below. "Look, never mind. *Bastante,* okay? We'll do it tomorrow. Hey, Luce."

He walked up, taking a swig from a bottle of Gatorade. His face and forearms were baked bronze by the sun, his T-shirt soaked through, hair tied back off his forehead with an old blue bandanna. Even though I'd had months to get used to it, the beard still threw me. He wiped his mouth on his sleeve, extended the bottle to me. I shook my head.

"To what do I owe the honor of this visit?"

"Oh, you know—just wanted to see for myself if the stories were true."

"So, what do you think of my log cabin?"

"I don't know what to say."

"Well, you know me. No sense doing things half-assed and then wishing you'd gone all the way."

"Where's Jude?"

He jerked a thumb toward the handyman's cottage. "Just between you and me, I don't think the kid has much future as a carpenter. He'd rather be hanging out with Hardy, learning chord progressions, than how to use a staple gun." Ash shrugged. "Just as well. He's happy, and I don't have to watch him every minute of the day."

"Heaven forbid," I said.

"I only meant it isn't safe to have him underfoot all the time. I thought you'd appreciate that."

"Yes. I do."

"So, come on." He drained his Gatorade and tossed the empty bottle into the back of one of the pickups. "Let me give you the grand tour."

I followed Ash through the bones of the house as he showed me the two-sided wraparound porch, sketched with his hands the kitchen's layout, pointed to where the ceiling of the great room would soar all the way to the second-story roof, explaining the way the furniture would be grouped around the fireplace, the full-length windows on either side that would look out over the deck and the woods beyond. Two Hispanic men came clomping down the stairs, and Ash introduced them to me as Ramon and Jorge. "Lucy," he said, inclining his chin toward me. "My—"

"Ah," one man said, looking at the other meaningfully. "Señora Farrell. *Hola.*"

"*Hola.*"

"You guys can knock off now, okay? See you in the morning."

"Okay, boss. *Mañana.*"

"Where'd you find them?" I asked.

"Come on up," Ash said, ignoring my question, and motioned that I should follow him up the stairs. "Careful. It's just subflooring up here, and there's a lot of junk lying around."

We stepped out onto a wooden platform that extended half the length of the house and would eventually overlook the living area below. "The original plans called for the master suite on the ground floor, but I moved it up here," Ash said. "I'm gonna do this whole wall in windows. I want to be able to sit up in bed first thing in the morning and see nothing but sky and water."

Although the only thing in place was framing, I could see it exactly, the sun coming up behind the pines on the far side of the pond, slanting across the water and into the room as the sky turned from violet to blush to gold. In my mind's eye, a crane soared out of the trees and skimmed across the water, its wings dappled by the early light.

I bit down on my lip to break the spell. As long as I'd known him, Ash had been able to do this to me—weave pictures out of thin air, make something out of nothing but thoughts and words. The last of the day's light filtered in through the rafters, striping his face with broken bars of dark and light. For a moment I felt that old yearning toward him, a pull of something big and mysterious, deep and old. I held on to it for a second or two, the way you might hold to your face the garment of someone you'd lost, breathing in their scent as a reminder that they'd once been here, and real. Then I let it go, watched it sail out through the open rafters and over the pond on wings as wide as an imaginary bird's.

"Listen, I've been thinking." I drew in a breath, let it slowly out again. "I want Jude to stay with you. I don't mean permanently," I added quickly. "I mean he can sleep over with you sometimes. Every few nights or so."

Ash swiveled his chin and looked out over the water. We were quiet, listening to the men loading up their trucks down below, shouting back and forth good-naturedly in Spanish. "What made you change your mind?" he asked as their engines fired up and they drove away.

"He just—he seems so different lately. I don't think I can give him what he needs anymore. Not all of it, anyway."

"You're a great mom, Luce."

"I don't know. Ask me in twenty years. The point is, I think it's time we started getting equal shares."

When Ash finally said, "Thanks," his voice was thick. "Don't think I don't know what this means, because I do."

But he didn't. He thought what I was doing was a fair and generous thing, when it felt to me like surrender, pure and simple. I shut my eyes briefly, but behind my closed lids the images were as vivid as ever. I saw the sun come up over the water, slanting across the bed as Ash sat up, yawned, stretched, blinked into the golden light of a new day. Beside him, a woman slept on her stomach, her face hidden by the pillow. He reached over and slid his hand under the sheet, into the soft, warm hollow of her back.

"Lucy?"

I opened my eyes, laughed a little. "Sorry. Long day."

"So, would it be good if I kept him tonight?"

"Tonight?" Now that it was real and happening, the notion filled me with an upwelling of panic. "Well, all right. But at the trailer. It's still too dangerous out here. I mean, you haven't even got walls or a roof."

"Have you talked to him about this?"

"Not yet."

"Let's go tell him."

We picked our way carefully down the unfinished stairs and through the skeleton of the house. As Ash and I approached the handyman's cottage, we could hear the sound of a stereo tuned low: *When I stop dreaming, that's when I'll stop wanting you,* the same song that had been playing in his truck the morning we signed the Nashville house away.

Stepping onto the front porch, Ash turned to me and touched his index finger to his lips, then eased the screen door open and motioned me inside. The little house was as hot as a stovepipe, despite all the windows open wide and a rickety box fan working hard on the living room sill, stirring up dust. The only furniture was an unmade futon and a particle-board coffee table with three legs, the fourth corner propped up by a stack of books several inches too short, making it hard to tell if it was just the table or the whole foundation that was tilting south.

In contrast, the voices coming from the next room floated cool and sweet, a stream tumbling down through icy mountain peaks, prickling the hair on the back of my neck. Ash stepped aside to usher me ahead of him into the kitchen doorway. They didn't see us at first, Jude sitting on the Formica-topped table, brown legs and bare feet dangling, Hardy facing him in a straight-backed chair with a guitar across his knee, shirtless in faded Levi's, his glasses sliding down his nose, his bare white chest sheened with sweat, their voices twining up and around each other's like morning glory vines, reaching for the heavens. *When I stop dreaming . . .*

"Mama!" For the first time in I didn't know how long, Jude's face lit up to see me.

"Hi, baby."

"Did you hear us? Hardy's been teaching me. It's harmony!"

"It was beautiful. Both of you. I thought you were the stereo."

Hardy stood up, laying the guitar across the seat of the chair, and fumbled a blue cotton shirt off the chair back, jamming an arm into a sleeve.

"Hardy says I could be on the Grand Ole Opry someday," Jude said.

"Yeah, well, that's not really Hardy's call to make," Ash said. All of a sudden the heat seemed to rise in waves from the scuffed linoleum, and the room smelled like sweat and overripe fruit—a reminder of how quickly things could turn. "Hey, buddy," he said to Jude. "How'd you like to spend the night at my place?"

"Really?" Jude looked from Ash to me and then over at Hardy struggling with the buttons on his shirt.

"If you want to," I said. Already I was having second thoughts. What was that old saying that if you loved something you had to set it free? Someone had written a song about it in the eighties that had been a big hit, which just proved how eager folks were to believe the most moronic things. If you loved something you were supposed to keep it tucked up safe by your side, to guard it with your heart and your life. But Jude had jumped off the table and started running around the kitchen, bumping off the counters and the table like a pinball machine on tilt. I was too far out on a limb to go back now.

Finally Ash caught him and swept him off his feet, dangling him giggling and squirming by the shoulders. I had a sudden memory of the morning he was born, lying back on the table with my feet still in the stirrups, stunned by effort and pain, as a nurse handed Ash a swaddled bundle that he cradled to his chest. As he tucked his face close to the blanket, I could hear his voice, soft and murmuring, walking our son across the room, Jude's very first human conversation on planet Earth.

Ash set Jude on his feet. "So, what do you say? Hot dogs for supper?"

"Yay!" Jude said. "Can Hardy come, too?"

"Maybe some other time, dude," Hardy said. "You go on, have a good time with your daddy. Besides, I've got stuff to do."

"But you'll be here tomorrow, right?" Jude asked.

"Same time, same station." Hardy looked at me, flashed a brief, cheerless smile. He turned and started washing his hands at the sink.

"Go get your shoes on," I said to Jude, who dashed off toward the front of the house. "He shouldn't be running around out here barefoot," I said to Ash as the screen door slammed. "When was the last time he had a tetanus shot? I can't remember. Maybe he needs a booster."

"Calm down, mama hen," Ash said. But what did he know? He was the TV daddy who came and went like Santa Claus, bringing presents and good times, while I was the boring, everyday drudge who worried about vitamins and fluoride and fatal diseases.

"Good night, Hardy," I said. "Thanks for the music lesson. I know it's not what you signed on for." He raised his right hand, not bothering to turn around.

I followed Ash back through the living room to the porch. "What *did* he sign on for is what I'd like to know," I said as we watched Jude clamber onto the tailgate of Ash's truck, stuffing his feet into his sneakers. "I thought you couldn't stand the guy, and now he's living on your property, teaching your son to sing harmony?"

"I needed a caretaker," Ash said. "Hardy was handy."

"A caretaker?"

"Somebody to watch the place. Make sure nobody sneaks in at night and makes off with stuff." I laughed out loud. Ash looked at me sharply. "It's no joke, Lucy. Do you have any idea how much all these materials are worth?"

"Sorry. It's just that Hardy Knox isn't exactly my idea of a security guard. What would he do if the bad guys *did* show up? Knock them over the head with his guitar?"

"Don't let him fool you. Hardy's got a lot more on the ball than he acts like."

"Oh, right," I said. "I bet he shot a man in Reno, just to watch him die."

Ash broke into a slow, smoldering smile, then shook his head and laughed. "Lucy, Lucy," he said.

"What?" I was trying not to smile myself, my insides pinging like mandolin strings. *Don't,* I told myself. *Don't even start.*

"Why don't you come over and have supper with Jude and me?"

"Oh, I—"

"How'd you like that, buddy?" he called. "Want to fix hot dogs with your mama and me?"

"No!" Jude shouted back. "Boys only! That's the rule!"

"It's okay," I said. "I've got a ton of chores to do tonight anyway. You guys have a good time. Stop by and I'll give you his bedroll and his PJs."

Ash walked me over to the Blazer and opened the door for me. I got in and turned the key, sent all the windows sliding down. The skin of his forearm on the windowsill glowed golden in the waning light, and I wanted to take it between my teeth, wanted to see if it tasted the way I remembered, of salt and suede, wanted to see if my bite would leave a mark or if it would vanish instantly, like it had never been there.

"I wouldn't take it too hard, Luce," he said.

"What?" I said, switching on the AC. "Take what?"

"It's just a stage he's going through. He'll grow out of it before you know it."

Sure, I thought, *right about the time he's eligible for parole.* Maybe having only one child had been a mistake. Maybe I should have had a spare, so that I'd have at least a fifty-fifty chance of breaking even.

I smiled, sending the windows buzzing up. Ash stepped back and raised his hand in a friendly wave. I turned the Blazer around and headed out the way I came, alone, the only way I knew how to go.

chapter twenty

One day the following week, I came back from picking up lunch at the café to find Ash's truck parked out front of the shop in the fire lane. I'd left Audrey in charge, but when I pushed through the door, the showroom was empty. I set my white takeout bag on the counter and peeked into the office, but it, too, was deserted. The cooler door was open a crack, and I put my ear to it. A stream of cold air leaked out, along with whispers and giggles.

I gave the handle a tug, the heavy door screeching slowly back on its hinges. Audrey and Hardy Knox stood locked in each other's arms like a pair of Shakespearean lovers amid a maze of fragrant blossoms, eyes bleary and mouths bruised from kissing.

Audrey blinked several times, bringing her gaze into focus.

"Hey," she said. "Did you get my tuna melt?"

"What's going on here?"

"Well, duh," she answered. "What does it look like?"

"Not here, not now, no way," I said. "Hardy, would you leave, please? I need to speak with Audrey in private."

"But he hasn't had his lunch yet," Audrey said as they leisurely untangled their limbs.

"He knows where the café and the DQ are," I said.

"I was gonna share my tuna melt. Jeez, you act like we're breaking the law or something."

"Hardy, please." I stepped aside and made a sweeping exit gesture with my arm. Audrey lifted her face to his—not much of a stretch, he couldn't have been more than an inch taller than she was—and gave him a quick peck on the mouth.

"See you later," she said.

"Yep. See ya, Lucy." He sauntered past me and out the door, started up Ash's truck, and peeled away.

Audrey started riffling through the takeout bag on the counter, extracting the sandwiches, lifting the corners of the paper they were wrapped in to see what was inside.

"I don't know why I keep on ordering this," she said as she opened her tuna melt. "I swear Burton could fry up a cow patty and it would taste about the same."

I unwrapped my turkey-on-wheat. "So, are you going to tell me what that was all about?"

"Hardy, you mean?"

"What about Joe? Remember, your boyfriend?"

"Joe and I broke up."

"Just like that?"

"Well, it wasn't pretty, if that's what you mean. He broke a chair. Then he sat down on the floor and cried. It was pitiful, actually. He only had one."

"One?"

"Chair."

I didn't see any point in saying that I didn't think he'd been crying about the chair. "When did this happen?"

Audrey looked at the ceiling. "Let me think. A week ago?"

"How come I didn't know about it?"

She shrugged. "Haven't been paying attention, I guess. It's not like a state secret or anything."

"Isn't Hardy a little old for you?"

"Who're you supposed to be, my mom? Actually, my mom's cool with it," she said around a mouthful of bread. "Hardy met my mom. He liked her. I know," she said when I arched my eyebrows. I'd been in school with Audrey's mother, Johnelle, a sullen, overweight, many-times-married woman who worked as a finisher at the dry cleaner's. It was hard to imagine anybody willingly tolerating her company, much less enjoying it.

"Did you ever stop and think that he might just be after you for—for your body?" I asked.

Audrey reached into the bag for an onion ring. "Sure. Did you ever stop and think I might be after him for *his*?"

"Well, find someplace to carry on besides work, please. If Peggy catches you, we're all dead meat."

"That shows what you know. Peggy knows about Hardy, and she's cool with it, too."

"She does? She is?"

"Oh, you know Peggy. She's just a big old sop. She thinks it's romantic, Hardy being a songwriter from Nashville and all."

Come to think of it, Peggy did have a weakness—or a blind spot was more like it—for that very thing, which had once been rare in Mooney but now seemed to be proliferating like fruit flies.

I opened my mouth, but Audrey cut me off. "Look, save the speech, okay? I know you think you know it all, because of what happened to you. But Hardy's different. He's going straight to the top, and he's gonna stay there. Ash is helping him."

I started laughing and had to set down my sandwich. "Oh,

that's rich. If you want to know how to get to the top and stay there, Ash is for sure the man to ask."

Audrey stared at me with righteous indignation, the kind that comes with the territory when you're seventeen. "As a matter of fact, he *is* the man to ask. He knows all about what not to do, and he's showing Hardy how not to do it."

I coughed a time or two into a paper napkin, then composed myself. "I get it. Like how to win friends and influence people, only in reverse."

"No offense, Lucy, but you don't know Hardy. Anyway, Ash didn't disappear. He's right here in Mooney, building a house and writing songs."

"He— What did you say?"

Audrey was busy rooting around in the bag for more rings. "Him and Hardy are writing songs. Good ones, too. I've heard 'em."

I thought about the scribbles in the notebook at Ash's bedside, the lights in his trailer burning into the night. Hope rose up in my chest like a bird, beating its wings against my ribs, wanting out, wanting to fly. I drew in a breath, feeling a sharp pain in my sternum. There was no bird, I told myself sternly. Hope was a trick, one of those lies in that pot at the end of the rainbow.

"I just hate to see you throw yourself into this and then get hurt."

"But that's what it's all about, isn't it?"

"What are you talking about?"

"It's part of the deal, if you ask me. Like Joe sitting on the kitchen floor and crying. Man, it was so sad, but it was powerful, too, you know? I just kept watching him and thinking, He's so lucky, even though he doesn't know it yet, because he's hurting, but he's *alive.*"

"I'm sure that was a great comfort to Joe. I sincerely hope you shared it with him."

"Oh, Joe wants to kill Hardy. He said so. But, I mean, I'd rather be pissed off or hurting than walking around like a dead person all the time."

I stood up, tossing the uneaten half of my sandwich into the trash. I went into the restroom and shut the toilet lid and sat down on it, gazing at my dark, flat, no-nonsense shoes lined up side by side on the linoleum.

Through the door I heard the phone ring in the shop. There was a rap at the door.

"Lucy? You okay? You haven't got that stomach crud that's going around, do you?"

"No."

"That was Dan Storey on the phone. Today's his wedding anniversary and he totally forgot. He wants two dozen roses carried over to his wife at their house, pronto."

"All right." But still I didn't move. My feet looked so strange down there on the pale green linoleum, like I was viewing them through the narrow end of a telescope.

"Lucy?" The doorknob rattled. "Come on, you're starting to scare me."

"Call Peggy," I said.

"What?"

I stood up and opened the door. "I said, call Peggy. Tell her I need her to fill in for me this afternoon."

I took my purse from under the counter and walked out to the Blazer, backed out of my slot, and started to make my way, on autopilot, across town. At the bypass, I stopped at Orson's Texaco and filled the gas tank, then got on Highway 59 and headed south. It was early afternoon, a weekday; traffic was sparse. I kept the speedometer steady at sixty miles per hour, the divided four-lane threading straight as an arrow through thickets of pine, past trailer houses and cow pastures, gas stations and roadside tomato stands.

At the blinking yellow light in Jefferson, I turned left, snaking my way through shady old neighborhoods. The parking lot at St. Jude's was empty except for a gold metal-flake, beat-to-shit Pontiac with Louisiana plates. I parked next to it and got out, walking past the sign announcing the hours for confession and worship, around to the side door and up the steps. I paused on the landing to look down at the garden below. Despite the drought, the rosebushes were in full bloom, their scent wafting upward through the open window, but it was too hot for any human being in his right mind to be out there.

The door which on my last visit had been closed was open. A woman in a pale blue polyester blouse sat at a computer, her fingers flying over the keyboard. Her gray hair was teased into a wild bird's nest, and an unfiltered cigarette dangled from the corner of her mouth, like a gangster's.

"Whatcha need?" she said without looking at me or breaking her typing rhythm, the cigarette bobbing as she spoke. The desk was a mess of papers and files, a scattering of framed photographs—kids' school portraits mostly, one of a man standing in the hull of a bass boat—and a homemade-looking wood-burned sign that read MRS. IRMA DECKER.

"I'm looking for Father Laughlin."

"He's over to the hospital. Edwina Mueller took sick again. Pneumonia. Poor old girl, they think it might be it this time."

The woman turned in her swivel chair and exhaled, squinting at me through a plume of blue smoke. "I don't know Edwina Mueller," I said.

"You ain't one of them, are you?" the woman said, looking me over head to toe.

"One of who?"

"A parishioner."

"No, ma'am. No, I'm not."

"You one of his others, then? The drinkers?"

"No, ma'am. Not that, either."

"How you come to be looking for Punch, then?"

"Well, I'm married to one."

"A Catholic or a drinker?"

"Both, actually."

She plucked the cigarette from her mouth, stubbing it out in a glass ashtray. Her skin was as tanned and leathery as an old satchel, hanging loose on the backs of her hands, deep folds around her mouth and eyes. "They do kindly go hand-in-hand, don't they? Least it sure seems that way."

"Do you expect him back soon?"

"Punch? Who knows. Those Muellers, they're a tricky bunch. Edwina's cousin, Sis, she hung on to ninety-eight. In and out of the hospital twenty years. Father Norton, he was priest here before Punch come, he must've said last rites over that woman a dozen times before she finally up and died at home, in her sleep. Fooled 'em all, Sis did."

"I guess I should have called ahead." I was feeling a little woozy, and I looked around the room for a chair, but every surface was buried under piles of junk. It didn't look like any church office I'd ever seen. There wasn't one single crucifix or picture of the Almighty on the wall, and the only thing religious at all was the little framed ditty on the door that I'd seen the last time, about angels unaware.

"I could give him a ring on his cell if you want. See how long he expects to be."

I pictured a weeping family gathered around their frail and gasping ancestor as the priest recited the holy words that would send her on to the sweet hereafter, when all of a sudden from the folds of his cassock—or his running shorts—a phone chirped.

"Oh no. Thank you, though."

"Well, you're welcome to wait. There's a couch in Punch's office if you feel like taking a load off."

The idea of turning around and driving back to Mooney seemed beyond my capacity at the moment. "Thanks," I said.

She pointed toward an adjoining door. "Make yourself comfy. There's magazines and stuff if you want something to do. Can I get you a cup of coffee while you wait?"

"I— Are you sure it isn't too much trouble?"

"Nah. Punch drinks it like water. You go on in while I make some up fresh."

I walked into the priest's office, which was just as cluttered as the secretary's, with a heavy mahogany desk and an ergonomic chair, a credenza covered with papers and wilting African violets. Built-in shelves lined two walls, crammed with books and periodicals and a mix of objects both religious and ridiculous: crosses and rosaries, photos of Father Laughlin with an assortment of men in vestments including the recently deceased and much-venerated Pope, antique toy train cars, a battered baseball scrawled with a signature I couldn't make out, a beat-up sock monkey. It reminded me of Aunt Dove's garden, a place where the sacred and the everyday mingled with ease.

Opposite the desk was an ugly plaid couch. I sat down on it, the springs giving under my weight as they must have under the weight of hundreds before me, and leaned back, fixing my eyes on the far wall, where I was startled to see a framed face that looked hauntingly familiar. It was, I realized, the figure from the ceiling of the Sistine Chapel, the woman who months before I'd dreamed was standing in my yard, her head covered by a blue shawl, her eyes glancing warily to one side as she tried to tell me something.

"What?" I said to her. "What do you want? Why are you following me?"

"How's that?" It was Irma, coming through the door with a mug of coffee.

"Nothing. Sorry." I reached up and took the coffee gratefully, lifting it to my face to inhale the rich aroma. #1 GRANDMA, the mug said in red letters. "Thanks. This is very nice of you. Considering I'm not one of Punch's—whatever."

"Oh, I reckon you're one of Punch's, all right," she said. "That man gathers folks like a dog gathers fleas. No offense intended."

I sipped. "None taken. This is great coffee."

Irma smiled, showing large yellow teeth. "It's why Punch keeps me around. For my coffee. That and I'm the only one knows how to work the computer." She seemed about to say something else, then thought better of it. "I'd best get back to work. You holler if you need a refill, hear?"

I thanked her and sat back with my mug. A phone rang in the outer office; I could faintly hear Irma's side of the conversation, something about who was going to pick up Lanny from day care.

On the table in front of me was a stack of books, and I leaned over and lifted one off the top of the stack. *How to Be Happy, Regardless* was the title. I started thumbing through it, looking for the chapter that defined "regardless," but my eyes just skidded over pages of psychobabble until they wouldn't focus anymore. I set down my coffee and sagged back against the couch. Across the room, the woman in the print continued her cagey, sideways gaze, her secret permanently embedded behind her slightly parted lips.

I woke to the touch of a hand on my knee. At some point I'd slumped over on Father Laughlin's lumpy couch, and I sat bolt upright, the blood singing in my ears. The figure kneeling in front of me appeared ringed by an aureole of amber light.

"Sorry," Punch said, his knees creaking loudly as he stood up.

"I didn't mean to scare you, but I couldn't think how else to wake you up."

"Gracious," I said, pushing my hair out of my face, tugging at the hem of my skirt. "What time is it?"

"Four-thirty, give or take a couple minutes. Have you been here long?"

"I don't really know," I said. "Where's Irma?"

"She leaves at four. She called me on my cell on her way out and told me you were here." He shrugged out of his heavy black cassock; underneath, he was wearing chinos and a Motor Racing Outreach T-shirt.

"Oh, no! You didn't— What happened to the lady at the hospital?" I hoped he hadn't left some dying woman's bedside on my account.

I watched him unhook his collar and toss it on the desk. "Edwina Mueller, you mean? Sitting up in bed complaining about the food and the shows on TV to everyone in earshot."

"I thought she was, um, on her way out. So to speak."

"Just between you and me? You couldn't kill a Mueller with an ax." He walked around his desk and starting flipping through a stack of phone message slips. He looked up at me and smiled tiredly. "It wasn't Edwina's time, praise God. Now, to what do I owe the honor of this visit?"

"Maybe I should come back some other time."

"Don't be silly. You've already been waiting a couple hours, at least. Anyway, I've been looking for you to turn up."

"You have?"

"Sure. Ever since your first visit, back in the spring. When you left that day, I said to myself, We haven't seen the last of *that* one." Father Laughlin set down the handful of pink slips. "Are you hungry? I haven't had a thing to eat all day except a pack of Cheez-Its out of the hospital vending machine."

I thought of the half of the perfectly good turkey sandwich I'd tossed into the trash at work several hours earlier. "Come on, walk downtown with me," he said, offering a hand to help me up. "I'll buy you a piece of pie."

He locked the office behind us and we stepped out into the late afternoon. The smell of fresh-cut grass was in the air, and sprinklers hissed in the yards on either side of St. Jude's. It was a four-block hike to downtown in the shade of tall live oaks and pecans arching regally over the wide side streets. Before long, we were strolling up the old-fashioned brick main street. We passed the Hamburger Store, widely famous for its pie, but instead of going inside, Punch crossed the street and motioned me after him.

"Too many tourists in that place," he said. "Follow me."

We went another half-block or so and ducked into the door of a tiny place called Dee's. All the tables were empty, and a woman behind the counter was filling sugar shakers. She looked up when we walked in and her plump face creased into a smile.

"Father!" she said. "Haven't seen you in a coon's age."

"At least since, what, yesterday?" Punch said. "Dee, this is Lucy Farrell. Lucy, Dee makes the best chicken pot pie on God's green earth. Her coconut's not bad, either."

"Coconut's sold out," Dee said. "But I got plenty of peach and lemon meringue."

"Well, I'm having the pot pie," Punch said. "I haven't eaten all day. Been over at the hospital with Edwina Mueller."

"How's the old girl doing?" Dee said as she busied herself behind the counter.

"The good Lord has seen fit to let her live through another day," Punch said.

Dee glanced over her shoulder at him, their eyes glinting as they met. The Muellers' reputation was widespread, apparently. "And what will you have, Miz Farrell?"

"The peach sounds good," I said.

Punch glanced at me. "You sure? You look hungrier than that to me."

I shook my head, and he shrugged at Dee, who reached into the glass case and pulled out a beautiful deep-dish pie, the crust fluted around the edges, with tiny leaves and acorns carved out of the top crust. "Oh!" I said as she set it on the counter. "That looks too good to eat."

"Take my word for it, it's too good not to," Punch said as Dee cut a slice and placed it on a plate.

"You want this heated, honey?"

"Sure she does," Punch answered. "And vanilla ice cream on top."

"Coffee, you two?" Dee asked.

Punch laughed. "Dee. You know me better than to have to ask that."

He beckoned to a table near the window, topped with a yellow checkered cloth and adorned with a jelly jar of daisies and purple cosmos. He held my chair for me, and we sat for several minutes in silence, watching the traffic on Austin Street. Sightseers strolled by in shorts and T-shirts and ball caps, toting shopping bags, and a little pack of Harley-Davidsons roared by, headed toward the bayou.

"Bikers in Jefferson," I said. "I never thought I'd live to see the day."

"We've gotten very eclectic, here in our little burg," Punch said as Dee brought our coffee in thick white cups.

"Mm," I said after the first sip. "This is the second-best coffee I've tasted all day."

"Irma's is hard to beat." Punch took a deep drink of coffee, then set the cup on the table. "So, Miss Lucy. What's on your mind that's worth driving thirty miles and sleeping two hours on the couch in my office?"

"Maybe I just needed a nap."

"You surely could've picked a handier spot. To say nothing of more comfortable. I've spent enough nights on that couch to know."

"That lady in the picture in your office," I said. "Who is she?"

Punch looked confused. "Lady?"

"The one from the Sistine Chapel."

"Oh! You mean the sibyl."

"Sibyl?" The only Sibyl I knew of was in a movie about a woman with multiple-personality disorder.

"The Greeks and Romans believed they were prophets. Seers. The one you're talking about is Delphica, who according to legend lived on Mount Parnassus, in a temple dedicated to Apollo. Among other things, she supposedly told Croesus, the king of Lydia, that by attacking the Persians he would bring down a great empire. Croesus figured out too late that the empire he was destined to bring down was his own. But her main claim to fame was telling Oedipus that he would kill his father and marry his mother."

"But that's mythology! It's pagan, not Christian."

"Well, the early Church Fathers more or less granted the sibyls a place in the Christian lexicon by declaring that their prophecies sometimes predicted things like the Virgin Birth and the Last Judgment, that in so doing, they foretold the coming of Christ. They—the sibyls—were seen as a sort of link between the Church and the pagan world."

Dee appeared and deposited our food. "Have you been there?" I asked as Punch plucked a paper napkin out of the dispenser and shook it over his lap.

"The Sistine Chapel? Three times. Once when I was a prep-school student, and then later when I was in seminary, and finally just a couple of years ago. On that visit I had an audience with the Pope, God rest his soul."

"So you've seen it, then. In person. The ceiling."

Punch nodded, squinting out the window at the street, flooded now with late-day sun. "I always tell people, I don't care what your spiritual beliefs are, whether you're Catholic or holy roller or died-in-the-wool atheist, but I dare anyone to look at that ceiling and deny that they're in the presence of something holy." He cut into his chicken pot pie with his fork, releasing a cloud of fragrant steam. "Have you? Been there?"

"Only in my sleep."

"Excuse me?"

I told him about my dream, about the figures wandering in my yard. When I got to the sibyl's—Delphica's—remark about chocolate, Punch smiled. "That sounds about right. She was infamous for talking in riddles."

"So you think she was trying to tell me something, then?"

"I think our dreams are always trying to tell us something. Unfortunately, dreams are often riddles in themselves. Maybe she was trying to tell you to visit Italy on your next vacation." He gestured that I should eat, and I took a bite of pie. It was delicious, the crust crisp and warm and oozing with fruit, the ice cream melting in a velvety puddle on top. "Good?" Punch asked. I nodded, my mouth full.

Dee walked over and refilled our coffee. "Got everything you need, folks?"

"I think we're set, Dee, thanks." We ate quietly and appreciatively for a while. Maybe this was the quality that had compelled Punch to become a priest, or maybe it made him a good one—he made you feel like you could talk if you wanted to or just sit back and enjoy a piece of pie and the view of a small town on a summer day.

I'd almost forgotten what I was doing there in the first place, so lost was I in the landscape beyond the window and the mélange of fruit and dough and melting ice cream on my fork, when

Punch pushed his empty plate away and said, "So, you still haven't answered my question. What brings you to Jefferson? And don't tell me it was a burning desire to talk about Michelangelo."

I fiddled for a few seconds with the handle of my coffee cup. "If you knew I was coming, then you ought to know why I'm here."

Punch laughed. "I'm a priest, not a seer."

"What's going on with Ash?" I blurted out. "I just—I see him every now and then, and he's building his house, and spending time with our son, and maybe he's drinking but maybe not, he won't say, and, and . . . " I remembered my pledge never to utter the name of Heather Starbird. "And now this Hardy Knox person has turned up from under who knows what cabbage leaf, and I can't tell if he's a savior or a stalker, I mean, he's got it in his head somehow that he's going to resuscitate Ash's career, and at first I thought that was just a bunch of bullsh—of hogwash, but now Audrey, that's my delivery girl, who by the way I just found out broke up with her boyfriend so she can *date* Hardy Knox, tells me that Ash and Hardy are writing songs together! After Ash swore he would never play music again!"

"But that's good news, isn't it?"

"I don't know! I guess I was hoping you could—not betray your, your vows or anything, but just tell me if he's . . ."

Punch set down his cup. "If he's what?"

I bit my lip and turned to face the window. Across the street, in front of some kind of meeting hall, workers were unloading stacks of linens and baskets of artificial flowers out of the back of a van. Two men hoisted a white-painted arbor, which they angled in sideways through the door.

"Bridal fair," Punch said. "Oh, look, there's Missy Connally. I'm marrying her next month." He glanced at me and smiled. "Performing the service, I meant."

"Do you ever wish you'd had the chance? To get married?" I asked.

"There you go, changing the subject again. But to answer your question, I *had* a chance. And I chose this instead." He opened his hands, palms up. They were big-knuckled, scuffed-up looking hands, not soft and pale like you might think a priest's would be. Working hands; fighter's hands.

"Can I offer an opinion? Unsolicited, but then, here you are. Looking for answers."

"Please," I said.

"I think you're asking the wrong question. It's not 'What's going on with Ash?' so much as 'What's going on with Lucy?' "

I gazed down at my hands, wrapped around the bowl of my cup. My head was full of spiraling images: Ash in his sweaty T-shirt standing at the top of the stairs on the open platform of his new house, framed by water and sky; Jude's legs dangling over the side of the kitchen table in Hardy Knox's kitchen, their voices floating heavenward like a couple of angels; Audrey in the cooler in Hardy's arms, surrounded by flowers; the sight of my feet on the restroom linoleum, like they didn't belong to my body anymore. Audrey was right: it was better to feel pain than to live this way, shut off from your feelings, sealed up so tight that you couldn't even recognize your own body. You might as well be dead.

"Do you mind if I ask you a personal question?" Punch asked. "When you left Ash last year, in Nashville—what was it you were running from?"

I had to gather my thoughts for a moment; I'd never told anyone the whole story before.

"We'd been living in Nashville almost five years," I said. "Things had been heading south for a while, maybe two years, by then. Ash was drinking a lot, staying out till all hours in who knows what kind of company, showing up late for gigs, not returning his manager's calls. A couple of times he turned up practically knee-walking drunk onstage, barely made it through the shows—wouldn't have, if it hadn't been for the guys in his band, who were real pros. But even they were getting disgusted, called him out a time or two. It was like he knew he was going down in flames and he didn't give a damn. He tried rehab a couple of times, but he'd only stay for a few days. Claimed it wasn't the way for him—whatever "the way" was, I didn't know. The times I tried to talk to him about it, we ended up yelling, slamming doors, making Jude cry.

"Finally we were just more or less living under the same roof, trying to stay out of each other's way. I thought about leaving plenty of times, even threatened to. 'This is it,' I must've said a hundred times. 'I can't take this. Can't you see it hurts me, too?' But as crazy as it sounds, every now and then I'd catch a glimpse of the man he used to be, the one I fell in love with, and I'd tell myself there was still a chance that we could work things out. And, like I told you before, I wanted Jude to grow up knowing his daddy, the way Ash and I never got to.

"Then, out of the blue, Ash got nominated for some songwriting award. I don't even recall the name of it, but it was something the industry gave out, a big deal. He kept trying to act like it wasn't, but I knew he was excited and scared to death at the same time. He was up against some big shots, and I know it sounds like a cliché, but it truly was an honor just to be nominated. But any fool knows you want to win. And looking back, I think maybe Ash thought it was his last chance. To, you know, give him that push over the top, prove he had the stuff.

"By the night of the awards ceremony, he was a wreck—high one minute, in a funk the next. I remember riding to the theater in the back of the limo just praying out of one-hundred-percent pure selfishness that he would win, because if he didn't, I knew, things between us would finally come to a head.

"I can't even recall now who did win. I guess I don't have to tell you it wasn't Ash. They announced the name, and people started clapping, and I reached over for Ash's hand and his fist was clenched so tight I couldn't have pried his fingers apart with a crowbar. I don't know how we got through the rest of the ceremony.

"Afterwards, there was a party at some hotel. We got in the limo and the driver automatically headed in that direction, jabbering away, asking us if we'd had a good night, if we were looking forward to the party. Ash didn't say a word, and I was afraid to. Finally, a few blocks from the hotel, we pulled up at a light, and Ash just opened the door and got out of the car and walked off down some side street. I climbed out and started yelling at him to come back. The poor driver didn't know what was going on. I asked him to wait and ran after Ash, caught up to him in front of a Chinese restaurant.

"Somehow I managed to talk him into getting back in the car, asked the driver to turn around and take us home. I paid the babysitter and sent her on her way, went upstairs to check on Jude. I remember standing there watching him sleep and feeling lost, just totally helpless. I could hear Ash slamming around downstairs, making himself a drink. I mean, I knew he was heartbroken, I was heartbroken *for* him, but I was so damned tired of it all, too, the way he'd just turned on himself, turned against me. I'd hitched myself to his wagon, after all, and it wasn't that I expected everything to be sunshine and roses, it's just that I knew we didn't have a chance of making it so long as he kept shutting me out. I knew he thought I'd given up on him, but I hadn't. I never have. But he'd given up on himself, and that was something I didn't know how to fix.

"I went downstairs and found him in the kitchen, with a glass and a bottle sitting on the butcher block. 'We've got to talk,' I said, but he didn't answer me, wouldn't even look at me. 'I don't know how to handle this,' I told him. 'I want to help you, but I don't know what you expect me to do.'

"'You want to help me?' he said. 'Then get out of my face. I'm sick of seeing you mooning around here, making me feel worse than I already do. You never wanted to come here in the first place. You never believed I had what it took.' Well, none of that was true, and I said so, but he was wound up so tight, he wouldn't even listen. He turned around and started to pour himself another drink.

"I moved over and tried to get between him and the butcher block, to get my hand on the bottle before he could. We grabbed for it at the same time, and I lost my footing on the tile floor. My feet went straight out from under me, and I clipped my head on the corner of the butcher block at the same time Ash dropped the bottle.

"When I came to, things were swirling. Glass and whiskey everywhere. I tried to sit up and slipped, and cut my hand on a piece of broken glass. Ash was just standing there watching me with the most terrible expression on his face. I remember thinking that he was more upset about breaking the bottle than he was about the fact that I was bleeding and had a knot the size of a goose egg on the back of my head. I remember thinking, *If I don't get out of here, I am going to die.*

"I went upstairs and got Jude out of bed, snatched up my purse and my keys. I didn't even slow down long enough to bandage up my hand or change my clothes, much less pack a bag. I carried Jude out to my truck and buckled him into his safety seat—he never even woke up—and climbed in and cranked up the engine, and that's when Ash came running out of the house, yelling and waving his arms in the air. I thought he wanted to kill me, because everything that had happened was my fault. I just mashed down the gas pedal and took off, spinning the tires on the pavement, Ash running behind us all the way down the driveway out to the road. I'll never forget how his face looked in the rearview mirror, lit up red by the taillights, like a madman's. I didn't know it then, but it was the last time I'd see him for eight months. When we got to the highway I turned south, and by morning Jude and I were in Mooney. But I don't— What was your question, again?"

"I was asking why you left."

"Well, isn't it obvious? I had to protect myself, and my little boy."

Across the street, two men were jockeying a multitiered cardboard wedding cake out of the van. "Did it work?" Punch asked.

"I thought so, at first. Then Ash showed up here—in Mooney, I mean—and the whole mess started all over again."

"Where did things start to go wrong, do you think?"

"We should never have gone to Nashville in the first place. At least I shouldn't have. It was Ash's dream, and I thought . . . I thought there'd be a place in it for me. But there wasn't. I hated it there. Everything was so glittery and fake, everybody all the time grinning at you with these big shiny teeth when they'd just as soon stab you in the back as look at you. I've lived in Texas all my life, and in forty years I never heard so much BS as I heard in the three years I was up there. It was nothing like Ash painted out it would be."

"Did you ever think that maybe it was the same for Ash?"

"How do you mean?"

"That things weren't working out for him any better than they were for you? That, in fact, maybe it was even worse for him, since he was the one who painted the picture to begin with?"

"Not till— He tried to talk to me about it when he first came back, a couple of months ago. About how he felt like he got set up, by the record company and the whole, sort of, industry machine, and when it didn't work out like they expected, they just pretty much dropped him without a net."

"So it sounds as if you were both in the same boat, and you just didn't know it."

"I don't think so."

"Why not? Didn't you both go up there thinking things were

going to be a certain way, and didn't things turn out differently than you expected, for both of you?"

"I guess. But—"

"I see it all the time. Two people go chasing off after something they think they want, and then somehow, without even meaning to, their wires get crossed, and pretty soon they think the only solution is to go their separate ways." Dee walked over, holding the coffeepot, but Punch waved her away. "Let me ask you this," he said to me. "What made you fall in love with Ash in the first place?"

I was surprised—shocked, really—at how hard it was to answer Punch's question. Sometimes I thought there'd never been anything between Ash and me but sex, that I'd been so swept up by our physical attraction that my small-town Baptist raising didn't know what else to call it but love. Then Jude came along and sealed the deal. Sometimes I blamed myself for roping Ash into something he didn't really want, that he wasn't ready for, that Jude and I were nothing but a roadblock on the way to his hopes and dreams. But in my heart I knew that wasn't the answer, that it was cowardly of me to reduce what we'd had to something so stripped-down.

"Not too long after I first met Ash," I said, "he drove me up to this little barbeque spot outside town. Later on, we used to refer to it, sort of joking, as our first real date, though I never would have called it that at the time—my husband had only been dead six weeks or so, and it just wasn't *seemly,* you know? But we ate pork ribs at a picnic table under the pines, and we talked for what seemed like forever, and I remember laughing, really laughing, for what felt like the first time since my husband died.

"And at some point I asked Ash, in all seriousness, if he felt like we'd known each other before, in some past life. This probably sounds like blasphemy to you. But the way I felt when I was with him . . . I mean, I'd only met him—in *this* life—a few days before, but it seemed like we were bound together in some way that had been going on before us and would keep on after we're gone. Oh, I know this is— Am I making any sense at all?"

Punch grinned. "That's a pretty fancy philosophy for a Southern Baptist girl."

"You can see why my mama barely speaks to me."

"So can you honestly tell me you don't still feel what you felt that first day, eating barbeque under the trees? Because I think you do, and I think Ash does, too."

"But we've gotten so far from that."

"Then go back."

"Back?"

Punch turned and motioned to Dee for the check. "Remember that old Beatles song? 'Back to where you once belonged'?"

"But how do we do that? How do we know if it's even possible?"

Punch dug in his jeans pocket and handed Dee a ten, and she carried it off toward the register. "I can't tell you that. I don't think anybody can." I sighed, and Punch nodded. "I know. It'd be nice if there were a pill we could swallow that would solve all our troubles, just like that. Of course, if that were the case, I'd be out of a job."

"My first husband was a farmer," I told Punch. "Just an ordinary man, steady as they come. When I took up with Ash, I knew he was different, that he was going places most folks never get to go. I guess I thought my job would be to stand on the sidelines and cheer a lot. I didn't expect it to be—well, like this."

"Is that how you see yourself?" Punch asked. "As a cheerleader? Because—I hope I'm not betraying a confidence when I say this—but you're wrong."

"What do you mean?"

He toyed for a moment with his coffee cup before answering. "I remember once, when I first met him, Ash described you as his 'light.' The old-fashioned term used to be 'muse.' Meaning—you know—his inspiration. All artists have them, or so the story goes. It seems to me it's no small privilege to be one." I shook my head, letting his words sink in. "Hard, too, I suppose. Considering that it's probably something you didn't ask for. That maybe it, well, implicates you, in a way, in Ash's success or failure."

"You mean it's my fault he's a drunk and thinks his career is over?"

"Of course not. Just that maybe, when he saw things start to fade, it scared him. Made him reckless, trying to find that light again."

"I remember a song he played for me once," I said. "By some other writer, not one of his. But there was a line in it that I thought was Ash to a T: 'I'd rather be a comet than a star.'" I pushed away my coffee cup. "You see, that's the difference between us. He's all dazzle and motion, and all I want is just to stay and shine in one place."

"But that's the way the world works, doesn't it?" Punch said. "God gives us different gifts—none less important than the others, just different. And maybe comets need stars to steer by, to find their way home."

A passing car caught my eye, a flash of sun on chrome, and just like that I was back in Ash's old kitchen, years before it was mine, hearing him say, "Sometimes you just have to cut your losses and go. But sometimes, if you're lucky, you get to go around again." The memory caught in my throat like a copper penny, sharp and cold. Then I swallowed, and it, like my luck, was gone.

I looked at my watch. "I need to pick up my son," I said. "I'm sorry for just dropping in like this, out of the blue. I took up a big chunk of your time, and I'm not even one of your regulars."

"Don't be silly. I enjoyed the company, and I got Dee's pot pie for supper in the meantime." We got up and waved good-bye to Dee, then pushed our way out onto the sunny sidewalk, setting off in silence toward St. Jude's.

"You know, it can be frustrating," Punch said after a minute.

"What's that?"

"One of the drawbacks, I guess you'd call it, of my job is that a lot of the time you never really know if you've helped somebody. All you can do is try to tell them what you feel they need to do and send them on their way. But even priests appreciate a sign now and then."

"A big old lightning bolt, you mean?"

He laughed. "Now and then that'd be nice, yeah. But most of the time, I think God's sneakier than that. Likes to slip things in right under your nose when you're not paying attention. Then all of a sudden you see them and say, 'Hey! What I was looking for was right here, all the time.' "

My Blazer and an old Fiat convertible were the only cars in the parking lot at St. Jude's. I unlocked the Blazer and held out my hand, and Punch clasped it in his big, chapped red one.

"Thanks for the pie," I said.

He held the door for me as I climbed into the driver's seat. "Keep your eyes peeled," he said. "Let me know if you see that lightning bolt."

I DROVE BACK up Highway 59, the sun setting in a gilded blaze in my rearview mirror, the sky ahead over Mooney towering with pink-tipped clouds. I rolled down the windows a crack, hoping to catch a whiff of rain. But by the time I pulled up to the curb in front of Dove's house, the clouds had dissolved and the sky was the flat blue-white of another July dusk: one more night without a chance for lightning.

chapter twenty-one

Every evening for a month, after Jude was tucked into bed or when Ash had him for the night, I laced on my old track shoes and traipsed up and down Little Hope Road, the dogs snuffling in circles around me, then running ahead and loping back as bats swooped in the purple sky and frogs croaked sorrowfully from the dry creekbeds, like they'd given up any hope for rain. I turned my conversation with Punch over and over in my head like a kid holding a marble to the light, thinking that if I could catch it just right, a pattern would shine through.

Instead, I found myself combing back through my old life with Ash, remembering the days when we were courting, the night I'd met him when I'd thought he was the cockiest, most insufferable man on the planet, then the sure but steady way he'd won me over: tilling my garden, fixing my plumbing, singing old cowboy songs under my kitchen window at midnight, till the next thing I knew we were sitting in his pickup at Willie B.'s with rain drizzling down the windshield and talking about knowing each other in a past life. "I want to know you in *this* lifetime, Lucy," he'd said that night. "What if we never get another try?" And before I knew it, I was on my back on a scratchy wool blanket beside Flat Creek with Ash in my arms, moonlight streaming all around us and my heart so full I didn't think my body could hold it. Even now, it was enough to make me search out the rock wall of the old graveyard in the dark and sit a minute and try to untwist the knots in my chest. The ghosts Ash and Denny used to talk about, whispering and dancing among the crumbling headstones, were no match for the ghosts in my head, waltzing thigh-to-thigh to the tunes on Dub Crookshank's jukebox, spending Sundays with the shades drawn and the doors latched, observing their own private, unsanctioned form of worship.

It was surprising how easy the old days were to excavate, once I put my mind to it. I'd sit awhile and close my eyes and the rock wall, the woods, the night would dissolve until I was holding the past in my cupped hands like rainwater, bringing it to my face, drinking it in in long, thirsty gulps. Slowly, painstakingly, I went about reconstructing the past the way archaeologists went after ancient ruins, chipping away on nothing but faith, not knowing what it was yet, this glittery thing I was uncovering, whether it was a single sliver of mica or the gateway to a wonderful secret world below, an entire city paved in gold. Night after night I'd walk and dig, until something—a swallow calling off in the trees, the moon rising fat and as bright as a silver dollar over the pines—would call me back to earth, and I'd turn around, my chest a little looser, retracing my steps with a little more certainty, carrying a little bigger piece of my self in my pocket each night as I headed for home.

IT WAS THE second Monday in July, hot and dry as blazes, but I was in an unexpectedly generous mood and decided to stop by the café for a box of doughnuts on my way in to work.

Carol, the waitress, grinned at me as she slid my white box across the counter and took my money. "Got your ticket yet?" she said.

"What for?"

She nodded toward the cash register. Taped to the back was a plain white eight-and-a-half-by-eleven sheet of paper with block printing, the likes of which customarily begged for loose change for some kinfolk's rare blood disorder or information about wayward pets. This one said,

ASH FARRELL COMEBACK SPECIAL!
LIVE & IN PERSON!
SATURDAY, 8 P.M.
THE ROUND-UP
SPECIAL GUEST HARDY KNOX

I blinked a few times and read it again. Just in case there was any confusion, reproduced beneath the writing was an old publicity still of Ash from his Nashville days, his silver-streaked hair swept back off his forehead, gazing sooty-eyed into the camera.

The room had gone as quiet as a church; I could hear the rustling of a newspaper, a radio back in the kitchen playing an old Roger Miller song. Carol handed me my change, which I made an effort not to drop on its way to my purse.

"You didn't forget the lemon cream, did you?" I said in as steady a voice as I could muster. "Peggy'll kill me if you did."

"Half lemon, half plain glazed," Carol said. "Just like always."

I tried but failed not to cut my eyes one more time at the flyer on the register. The words swam briefly, Ash's face sliding in and out of focus.

"See y'all," I said, raising my hand, my voice full of forced cheer as I headed for the door. I wasn't fooling anybody, I knew, as I pushed my way from the chill of the café into hot air rising in waves from the sidewalk. Money would be changing hands by the time I was halfway down the block.

"YOU *KNEW* ABOUT this? For how long?"

"Only since last night!" Audrey said. "Jeez, could you give me some breathing room here?" I opened the bakery box and plucked out a doughnut and sunk my teeth into it, my mouth filling with glazed sweet dough. "I told you a month ago Ash and Hardy were working on songs."

"There's a big difference between writing songs and getting up on a stage to perform them in front of hundreds of people." It had been five years since Ash had last played the Round-Up. His second record was just out, one tune getting some modest radio airplay, and folks had come from literally hundreds of miles around, camping in the parking lot at daybreak for the 8:00 P.M. show. Dub had had to hire half a dozen boys from the high school football team to handle crowd control.

Maybe he was too much of a has-been by now, I thought. But if the last few months had proved anything, it was that Mooney never forgot a hometown hero. Ash was the one who'd got out and made good, who'd grabbed and held, even fleetingly, the brass ring. His face still hung in a frame behind the bar at the Round-Up, over the back booth at Burton's café. In the town's eyes, Ash would always be slightly above and apart, burnished with the sheen of the wider world.

"Whose idea was this?" I said. "Not Ash's, surely."

"Hardy had to twist his arm a little, I think."

"So how did he do it?"

"To tell you the truth, I'm not real sure. Hardy has this weird sort of mojo about him, you know? I mean, at first glance he looks harmless enough, but spend two minutes around him and I swear he'll have you eating out of the palm of his hand. I ought to know." She bit into a doughnut, wiping her mouth with the back of her hand.

"I swear, Audrey, if this is some kind of scam . . ."

"Oh no! It's honest-to-God for real. They're putting Ash's old band together and everything. One of the guys, Derrall something, is letting them practice in his garage every night this week till showtime." She said "showtime" like an old-time carnival barker, which, it occurred to me, would've been a good occupation for her.

"Something about this just doesn't sit right," I said. "Just a few weeks ago, Ash was saying he'd never play music again. Now he's putting up flyers all over town, getting the old band back together? What I really want to know is, what's in it for Hardy?"

"Can't he just be doing it out of the—you know—the goodness of his heart?"

"I doubt it, sweetie pie."

"You know, maybe you ought to try trusting people for a change. Maybe if you gave them a chance every now and then, they'd surprise you."

I sighed and tucked the flaps shut on the box of doughnuts. "How come we didn't get a flyer? Every window between here and the courthouse has one."

Audrey disappeared into the back room, and returned with a sheaf of paper. "Hardy says it's no big deal if you won't put one up. He said everybody in town would totally understand."

I snatched the flyers from her. "Good Lord, how many copies did he make? You could paper the entire county with these."

"That's pretty much the idea."

I peeled a sheet from the top of the stack. For a minute I stood with my hip against the counter, taking in the words I still had trouble believing, a face I'd known a lifetime ago. Then I tore two strips of Scotch tape from the roll underneath the counter and, taking extra care to get the edges straight, fixed the flyer to the inside of Faye's front window.

After work I drove over to Dove's to pick up Jude. The TV was off, for once, and I found Dove sitting at the kitchen table with Lily, who was bent over a Big Chief tablet, scrubbing like her life depended on it with a green crayon. I glanced over her shoulder at what she was coloring: a castle in flames, something or someone being torn and bloodied by a pair of dragon's jaws. "Where's Jude?" I asked Dove.

"Ash come for him 'bout an hour ago. Said they was goin' to band practice." I dropped my purse on the floor and sank onto a chair. "You look like you could use a drink," Dove said.

For a moment I had the wild notion that my aunt was about to get up and produce a bottle of José Cuervo from the kitchen cupboard, but she just took down a jelly glass and filled it from the tap and handed it to me: lukewarm, as usual, and tasting of whatever the city used to treat its water—nothing like the cool, sweet well water at home.

"What're you drawing, Lil?" I asked.

"The boy was mean," she said matter-of-factly, switching to an orange crayon. "Now the dragon's eating him."

"That must hurt."

"It does. A lot."

Dove leaned over and kissed the top of Lily's silky head. "Your aunt Lucy and me is gonna step in the front room a second," she said. "Don't go anywhere."

I followed her into the living room. She picked up the remote and clicked on the TV, muting the sound of *Jeopardy!* to a dull roar.

"You okay?" she said.

"I don't know."

"It's good news, ain't it? After all that crazy talk about not playin' music no more, Ash is finally gonna get up there and do it."

"I guess so. I just—I can't figure out how Hardy Knox tricked him into it."

"Maybe there wasn't no trick involved. Maybe Ash made up his mind his own self."

"Maybe."

"You ever hear of the benefit of the doubt?"

"Yeah. I've heard of Santa Claus and the Easter Bunny, too."

"Well, it wouldn't hurt you none to open your mind a little."

"It's not my mind I'm worried about." It was my heart, I thought as I walked back out to the car—what was left of it, anyway, tough and stringy, without enough meat or muscle for even Lily's dragon to make a meal of it.

I drove home, changed out of my skirt and blouse into cutoffs and a T-shirt, and fixed myself a supper of cold meat loaf and leftover macaroni and cheese, which I ate standing up at the kitchen counter, gazing out the window at the trailer behind the house. I washed and dried my dishes and put them away, then slipped on my flip-flops and grabbed my car keys.

Dark was falling as I set off up the road, the day's heat finally giving way, grudgingly and by inches, to the cool of pine and clay. At the highway I turned right, toward the Corners, a star or two visible in the span overhead, traces of rose and gold still lingering at the horizon. My headlights caught the sign at the intersection of the two highways: BEER, GAS, GROCERIES. The little store glowed like an oasis in the dusk, and a couple of old men in overalls and feed caps sat on a bench out front under the faded Mrs. Baird's logo, as erect and motionless as cigar-store Indians, watching me go by.

I'd been to Derrall Beeson's place once before, when Ash and I were first courting. Derrall drove a propane truck, and lived in an old farmhouse down one of the unpaved county roads dotted here and there with rusted-out trailers and abandoned deer blinds in thickets of cypress and scrub pine. I slowed as I approached a little girl in yellow shorts picking something, wildflowers or aluminum cans, out of the bar ditch and putting it in a pillowcase, accompanied by a big spotted dog. I raised my hand to wave, but though she straightened up and regarded me as I passed, she didn't wave back. The dog started to bark. I pressed down on the gas and kept going.

I was just starting to worry I might not be able to find Derrall's place when I rounded a bend in the road and saw, up ahead, a cluster of lights and, strung out along the road and across the dirt yard, enough cars and trucks for an old-fashioned country burying. The big-bellied propane truck alone would've been hard to miss, but there, too, were Ash's pickup, Audrey's Charger, Hardy's little blue Corolla, a scattering of other vehicles.

Light spilled across the yard from the house and adjacent work shed, illuminating a hodgepodge of tools and miscellaneous refuse that had evidently been cleared from the shed to make way for microphones and amplifiers. A mixing board had been set up across a couple of spools once used for hauling telephone cable, and the Round-Up's longtime soundman, Jersey Price, sat behind it in a lawn chair with a sweating longneck propped on one knee.

"Miss Lucy!" he called, hoisting his beer. "Long time no see."

"Hi, Jersey."

"Yes, ma'am—this here's the place to be." He nodded toward the shed, where a bunch of guys milled around under a naked bulb, strapping on guitars and twirling drumsticks, talking and laughing. I heard the familiar static hum of amplifiers, someone saying, "Check, check," into a microphone. Off to one side, sitting on a pair of amps, were Audrey and Jude, looking like peas in a pod.

It was Jude who saw me first. So bedazzled was he by the goings-on around him, he must have forgotten his recent indifference to me. He launched himself forward and came running across the yard, yelling, "Mama, look! Daddy's got a band!"

I knelt and hugged him quickly, breathing in his sweetly familiar scent, that Jude-like essence that, no matter how old he got or how far he strayed, would always tie me to him.

He pulled away and studied me, suspicion quickly dawning in his eyes. "You look mad."

"No, I don't."

"Yeah. You do."

I stood and looked into Ash's face, trying to compose an expression appropriate for the occasion: disapproval touched with encouragement, support tinged with wariness. Apparently I wasn't doing a very good job of it; the sight of him wearing his old black Martin guitar over his hip like a gangster's holster momentarily unhinged me.

"Could I talk to you a minute?" I asked.

"Run over there to the cooler, buddy, and bring your mama a Coke."

I didn't want a Coke, but Jude had already taken off.

"What's up?" Ash asked, fiddling with a tuning key on his guitar.

"I just—I want to know what this is about."

"What's it look like? I'm getting ready to play."

"Just like that? After—what, ten months, a year, all of a sudden you've seen the light?"

"Something like that." He shifted his weight to his other hip. "Anyway, it wasn't all of a sudden. It's taken me a long goddamned time to get here."

"Hardy's behind this, isn't he? He's made you some kind of wacky deal—"

"No deal. Just music. Look, I thought you of all people would be glad about this. I haven't had a drink in two months. I'm writing songs again. Isn't that what you wanted?"

The question caught me off guard. *Was* this what I wanted? Was it even what it sounded like—a fresh start, a second chance? Maybe my mistake had been in believing that love was all or nothing: a blush-pink bouquet of roses, fireworks on a blanket next to Flat Creek with whiskey in your veins and a man made of moonlight in your arms, or as black and flat as the highway that ran between Texas and Tennessee. I'd been on that highway a long time; it was the first thing I saw when I got up in the mornings, the thing I dreamed about when I closed my eyes at night. Maybe it was time for a detour, to finally get off the blacktop and find out where the red dirt would take me.

"Ash!" a voice called from inside the shed.

"I'm up," he said. "Listen, why don't you stick around? It'll be like old times."

"No, thanks." To tell the truth, the thought of old times scared me to death; I didn't know what might come welling up in me when I heard Ash strike a chord and put his mouth against the mike and start to sing. "Don't be thinking you can keep Jude out here till all hours of the night," I said.

"I'll have him home by ten. Okay, mama hen?"

I wanted to say it wasn't, but what would be the point? It was clear our son had already crossed over to the dark side. "Okay. But you tell him I said just this once. He can hear you Saturday night, at the show."

"Should I put you on the guest list?" He smiled.

"If it's no skin off your nose."

In the shed the drummer commenced to pummeling, and Derrall's guitar jumped in, playing the opening riff to "Suzy Q." I watched Ash's face as he turned toward the music. I hadn't seen that kind of wattage since last Christmas, when the citizens of Mooney gathered on the courthouse lawn and, on the count of ten, the mayor threw the switch that turned the whole square into an electric, luminous wonderland. He smiled at me, a smile I thought I'd never see again, and turned and sprinted toward the shed, his guitar bouncing off his hip: back to where he once belonged.

"How do I look?" I switched on the dome light and examined my lipstick in the vanity mirror of Geneva's Durango.

"Like you're on your way to the electric chair."

"It's the shirt, isn't it? I knew it! The color's all wrong for me. I should never have let you talk me into it." I tugged at the clingy V-cut neck of the knit top Geneva had picked out for me the day before at Ross Dress for Less in Marshall. The shade on the label said "celadon," but to me it looked more like mental-institution green. She'd claimed it set off my fair skin and red hair, but here, under the pale overhead light of the car, I just looked seasick.

I felt seasick, too. I tried telling myself for the umpteenth time that this evening was no big deal, but it wasn't working. All week long I hadn't been able to stop at the Food King for a loaf of bread, or at Orson's Texaco to fill up my tank, without finding myself the object of stares and innuendo—sometimes behind my back, sometimes straight to my face. "I got two hunnert riding on Ash, Lucy girl!" old Saul Toomey had hollered out Thursday in the café in front of God and a whole roomful of hooting diners. I'd never wanted to give anybody the finger so bad in my life, but I kept my arms at my sides and a big smile plastered on my face as Carol handed me my takeout bag. She wiggled her pinkie at me, and I leaned over the register. "Just to let you know?" she murmured against my ear. "Not too many folks betting on you this time around."

"I'm a mess," I told Geneva. "How can you just sit there cool as a cucumber?"

"Because I'm not about to be made a spectacle of in front of a thousand people. Having Ash Farrell standing up there under the lights begging me to give him a second chance, letting the whole world know what a fool he was to let me go."

I flipped down the mirror again, bending in to examine my eyeliner. "You know what this reminds me of?" Geneva said, slowing to make the turn onto the FM road that led to the Round-Up. "The very first time you went with Bailey and me to hear Ash sing. That was some night, huh? Remember that poor boy Bailey tried to fix you up with? What was his name?"

"Rob, I think. Or Ron."

"He was cute, but he had no idea what he was up against."

"Neither did I. Anyway, that was the second time, not the first."

"What?"

"The blind date. The first time y'all took me to hear Ash play, he had that Misty Potter creature hanging all over him. What an omen that was, huh?" I took my hairbrush out of my purse, then put it back. "I must be crazy. To be doing this, I mean. Maybe I should've just stayed home with a hot bath and a trashy magazine."

"You're kidding me, right?"

"I just feel so—so *out* there, you know? Like everything I'm thinking and feeling is written all over my face."

She laughed. "Like you could hide it if you tried. Come on, admit it—it's not just you and Ash anymore. The whole town's been waiting for this for a good long time. Anyway, if you'd just relax, you'd look like a million bucks. I'd kill for those boots."

"They're great, aren't they?" I was wearing my Rocketbusters, the ones Ash had picked out for me on a trip to El Paso back when he was still feeling flush. They were caramel-colored, with pink butterflies and flowers on a burgundy background scrolling up the sides, a lone pink blossom on a bed of dark green leaves unfurling across the toes. "You don't think Ash will get the wrong idea, do you? Maybe I'm being too obvious."

"You're wearing your wedding ring, aren't you?"

"What if it's a trick? What if he's planning on announcing in front of, of however many people that he's fixing to run off with—" I still couldn't bring myself to say her name or even picture her face; a brown station wagon full of buckets and brooms was as far as I'd let myself go. "With somebody else."

Geneva reached over and closed the mirror. "Get over it, already. You're the luckiest girl in Cade County tonight, and you know it."

I turned and looked into the backseat. "How's everybody doing back there?"

Lily gave me a scowl. She was dressed in a short denim skirt, a flowered western shirt, and miniature red Ropers. "I look like a dork," she said. "I don't see why we can't just wear *normal* clothes, like *normal* people."

"Because tonight is special," Geneva said. "We're going to hear your uncle Ash sing."

"I can hear him anytime I want on the stereo."

"But this is different. This is live and in person, in front of hundreds of people."

"I don't care," Lily said. "I still look dumb."

"Well, your cousin might have something to say about that," Geneva said. "Jude?"

"Don't talk to me," he answered tersely. His hair was slicked back with gel, and he was decked out in a pearl-snap shirt and creased Wranglers and shiny black Tony Lamas. Ash had promised to bring him onstage and let him sing a number.

I turned to face front again. "He's nervous," I whispered to Geneva.

"I'm not nervous!" he said loudly. "I'm just trying to *focus.*"

Geneva and I looked at each other, trying not to laugh. "So, is there anybody in the family who isn't getting a piece of this action?" she asked. Kit and Connie were coming with their kids, and Bailey had gone by earlier to pick up Dove.

"Just Mama. I called her up the other night and asked her if she wanted to come. You can imagine what she had to say to that—five minutes of Bible verses, a big lecture about consorting in the devil's playground."

"I think your mama's lonely."

"Loony, maybe."

"I'm serious. All she does is sit in that house night and day, listening to preachers on the TV."

"Well, whose fault is that?"

"She told Dove she thinks you and Bailey and Kit aren't grateful to her."

"Grateful? For what? Carrying us in her womb so that Dove could raise us? Running around tipsy in her nightgown after our daddy left, so that all the kids at school could make fun of us?"

"She's getting old, Lucy. Her hip's really bad."

"I know that! Dove's been trying to get her to the doctor for months, but she'd rather sit home and ask the PTL Club to take care of it."

"You Hatches are stubborn as mules, every last one of you. I should've known better than to bring it up, tonight especially. Good Lord," she said, as the Durango came up on a line of taillights. We inched forward as a kid in an orange safety vest directed us with a swinging flashlight to a spot in a field at least a quarter mile from the Round-Up. I was sure I'd never seen so many pickups and cars and SUVs in one place in Cade County in my life.

"Whatever happened to the idea of VIP parking?" Geneva muttered, squeezing in between two pickups.

"This isn't Miami Beach," I reminded her as we got out and started to hike up the highway as part of a mass migration, passing beneath the Round-Up's sign—a cowboy with a lasso circling endlessly in flashing orange neon. "Just be glad Ash is putting us on the guest list. I'm betting half these people don't even get in."

Sure enough, there was a long line outside the entrance, and the words "sold out" traveled through the crowd in an ominous buzz. Geneva grabbed my hand with one of hers and Lily's arm by the other; I managed to get hold of Jude's belt loop and drag him behind me as we muscled our way into the throng.

"Coming through, coming through!" Geneva shouted. "VIPs, coming through!" Miraculously, the waves parted. I found myself wondering what we were going to do if and when we finally got to the entrance, where for years Dub had employed an elderly, half-blind man named Arless Cooper to collect the cover charge; I doubted Arless would recognize his own wife without laying his hands on various parts of her, a form of ID I didn't relish submitting to. I was relieved to see Dub's nephew Troy, a handsome, square-shouldered boy who was going off to Texas A&M on a football scholarship a few weeks later, manning the door.

"What the hell you mean, 'sold out'?" a gigantic, red-faced man in a Shania Twain T-shirt was shouting, his nose about two inches from Troy's. "My buddy and me done drove all the way from Blanco County for this, and now you try and tell me we can't get in?"

"I'm sorry, sir," Troy answered with such sincerity that it seemed to me he was more deserving of a scholarship in drama than football. "The maximum capacity of the Round-Up is 480. It's illegal to allow one more— Hey, Geneva. Hey, Lucy."

"Hi, handsome," Geneva said. "How's it going?"

"Hey, kids," he said to Jude and Lily. "Y'all scoot on in. Show starts in half an hour."

"Hey!" the big man hollered as Troy stepped aside to usher us by. "What the hell's this? Women and children first?"

"You got it, sweet cheeks!" Geneva called back over her shoulder. "We're with the band!"

Walking into the Round-Up was like stepping into a time warp, a place that seemed to exist inside a glass case in a museum display, where the songs on the jukebox and the initials carved into the wooden tabletops were the same no matter what was happening in the world outside. The entrance was paneled with planks of cedar weathered to silver and papered with old posters of Roy Acuff and Bob Wills, the air perpetually blue with smoke and neon and smelling of sawdust and whiskey and drugstore perfume. There was something sweetly illicit about the place, an anticipation that set my pulse thrumming. The walls reverberated with Carl Perkins's guitar, laughter, the clack of cues against pool balls.

"You couldn't fit another body in here with a shoehorn!" Geneva shouted in my ear as we edged into the crowd, trying to keep an eye on our kids. "How are we gonna find Bailey and Dove?"

"We're supposed to have a table," I shouted back. "Ash said he'd take care of it."

It took several minutes, but we finally located the rest of our clan at what used to be our regular table, back when Ash's band played here every Wednesday and Saturday night. The cover charge in those days had been three dollars, and a good night was when two hundred people showed up. Now Dub was charging twenty bucks a head, and in spite of the fire code, there had to be six hundred souls squeezed in along the wooden benches, packed shoulder-to-shoulder on the dance floor.

Bailey and Kit had already emptied half a pitcher, and Dove and Connie were sipping bottles of Lone Star. Geneva wedged herself in between the boys and poured herself a cup of beer.

Bailey plucked up Lily and planted her in his lap; she picked up his plastic cup, gave it a sniff, wrinkled her nose, and set it down again.

Jude was tugging at my arm. "Where's Daddy? I need to find Daddy!"

I looked toward the stage, where the instruments sat glistening and upright in their stands, Ash's black Martin acoustic as shiny as a prize stallion under the rose-colored lights. "I don't know, baby," I said. "You sit here with Aunt Dove a minute, and I'll go see if I can find him." I steeled myself and waded off in the direction of the bar.

It took about five minutes to get to the front of the line, another two to catch Dub's eye. "Hey, Lucy!" he called. "How you doin', girl?"

"Good, Dub," I yelled back. "Have you seen Ash?"

He shook his head, jerking his thumb toward the end of the bar, mouthing something I couldn't decipher. I stepped back and looked in the direction he'd pointed, and saw Hardy Knox in conversation with a potbellied fellow in a suit coat and string tie, gray hair combed back in a sparse but tidy ponytail.

"Lucy!" Hardy cried when he saw me. He grabbed my sleeve with a clammy hand. "Where's Ash?" Behind his glasses he was bug-eyed.

"What do you mean? I was thinking you could tell me."

"I haven't seen him since we finished the sound check, and that was"—he checked the Pabst Blue Ribbon clock over the bar—"almost two hours ago. We're supposed to go on in twenty, and, and . . ." He flung up his hands and flailed them in the air; with his flopping hair and narrow shoulders, he looked like some kind of weird bird trying to take flight.

"Look, don't freak out," I said. "He's got to be around here someplace, right?"

"I don't know what to think!" Hardy said. "He seemed fine at sound check, but then he started acting sort of strange. I was trying to keep an eye on him, but what with one thing and another, somehow he just—"

"Strange, how? Was he drinking?"

"Oh, hell, no. He just got real quiet and then his eyes got that, that *look* . . ."

"Yeah." I knew that look.

"So, do you think you can find him?"

"*Me?* This whole thing was your idea, Hardy. I'm just part of the audience."

Hardy stood there white-faced, his jaw hanging from its hinges. He barely looked capable of holding himself upright, much less heading up a search party.

"Wait here," I said. "I'll see what I can do. Meantime, you be thinking about how you're going to thank me for bailing out your ass."

A boy I recognized as one of Troy's compatriots from the Mooney High football team sat guarding the dressing room door with a glazed expression.

"Hi," I said. "I'm Lucy Farrell." The boy stared at me without flexing a muscle, facial or otherwise. I held up my hand, displaying my wedding ring. "Mrs. Ash Farrell?"

"G'hed," he said, jerking his chin over his shoulder. So much for security, I thought as I walked past him and pushed open the door; any woman in the place with the brains or the nerve to flash a gold band could have waltzed right in.

The Round-Up had hardly any backstage area to speak of, just a room about the size of a walk-in closet, with a card table, a few folding chairs, a moldy old icebox. Derrall and the rest of the band, a couple of whom I remembered from the old days, were sitting around drinking Bud Light—the only thing Dub stocked in the icebox besides RC Cola—and gazing at a small TV screen where a miniature wagon train pounded across the desert, pursued by a band of tiny Indians on horseback and accompanied by muffled screams and hoofbeats. A few girls perched in the guys' laps, small-town girls with too much makeup and unfashionably big hair. I could see them scoping me out, ready to pounce if anybody tried to hone in on their action—or possibly hoping to improve it, depending upon who walked in through that door.

"Hi, guys," I said. "Y'all seen Ash?"

"Not since sound check." Derrall grinned at me, the big, easy, no-sweat grin of a guy who drove a propane truck Monday through Friday and got to play Merle Haggard and Johnny Cash covers for the locals on Saturday nights. "Want a beer?"

"No, thanks."

I muscled open the back door. The sky was black behind the dance hall, and reeked of Dumpster. It took me a second or two to get my bearings, another to make out the tip of a cigarette glowing in the dark a few feet away.

"Who's that?" a voice said, thin and shaky and rough as gravel.

"Lucy Hatch," I said. "I mean Farrell. Mr. Cooper?"

It was Arless, all right. Leave it to Dub to give a blind ninety-year-old the job of guarding the back door, keeping potential stalkers and groupies at bay.

"You looking for Ash, he went thataway." The cigarette traced a red arc in the direction of the parking lot. "He's a good boy, Ash," Arless said. "I 'member back when he used to play here reg'lar, he always used to sneak off right before showtime. Then danged if he didn't always turn up two minutes before Dub was about to send the dogs after him."

A long-forgotten image suddenly popped into my head. "Yes, sir," I said. "See you, Mr. Cooper."

"You take care, little girl," he said. "Say howdy to your mama for me."

I hurried down the alley and across the parking lot. There

was still a mob around the front door, and cars and pickups not only filled the lot but lined the bar ditches up and down the highway, even though the boy with the safety vest and flashlight was telling folks not to bother stopping, that the show was sold out and then some.

I waited for a break in the slow-cruising traffic and then sprinted across the blacktop and into the field, weaving my way among vehicles parked scattershot across the trampled grass, like a tornado had struck a used-car lot. At the far edge of the field was a row of loblolly pine leading into a thicket of taller trees and thick underbrush.

The path to Flat Creek was right where it used to be, marked by a lightning-struck scrub oak, split and barren, spectral against the night sky. It was seven and a half years since Ash had brought me here for the first time, had led me through the brushy growth to an open spot above the creekbed, where he'd laid me down on a rough wool blanket and made love to me while the creek, swollen with spring rain, rushed below and the moon bleached our skin the color of old bones.

If memory served, it was only a couple of hundred feet from the edge of the field to the creek, but it felt like miles as I tramped through vines and brambles and over roots. A hot wind had come up, tossing the tops of the pines, sending clouds like ghost fingers scrabbling across the firmament. I stumbled once and got turned around, found myself looking back at the distant lights of the Round-Up through the trees. "Shit," I said out loud. If this wasn't just so typical of Ash, requiring a search party tricked out in two-thousand-dollar boots.

A shrill whistle came from somewhere deep in the brush. It didn't sound quite human, but it didn't sound like any bird I'd ever heard, either. I paused, holding my breath. For the first time it occurred to me that I didn't have any business being here, that no telling what was afoot in these woods at night—snakes, wild pigs, maybe even the legendary but seldom-seen East Texas Bigfoot, to say nothing of beasts of the human persuasion.

I burst out into the clearing. A pale swath of August moon fell on the creekbed, the flat rock where a figure stood, dark against the darker woods behind it.

"Lucy Hatch, girl guide." Ash held out his hand and helped me up onto the rock, where I raked leaves out of my hair and brushed my hands on the front of my Levi's.

"Goddamn you," I said. "I just about broke my leg out here. And my boots! I bet they're ruined." I extended one foot and turned it this way and that.

"Such fine-looking boots, too."

"Some no-account cowboy singer gave them to me."

"Well, maybe he'll buy you a new pair."

"I don't want a new pair. I just want the old ones, the way they used to be."

"Well, now, it's funny you'd bring that up," Ash said. "I've just been out here counting the stars and thinking about the way things used to be."

I put back my head and studied the sky. It never failed to surprise me, the way the earth's course was marked by the movement of the constellations, proof of how even if you stood rooted to one spot, the world went on turning.

"I was thinking about the summer before we went to Nashville," Ash said. "We were sitting out on the back steps one night, and you said you wondered if there were stars like this in Tennessee."

"I remember."

"Well, there weren't. And it was never quiet, either—not like this. Like—listen a second. Hear that?" I shook my head. "My point exactly. Nothing. Just crickets and the wind in the trees. In

Nashville, I always felt like there was this big machine down inside the earth, wheels and gears just churning and churning. It drove me crazy. That, and no stars."

It was true, what Ash said, about the absence of noise, but I could feel a kind of murmur in the earth here that I'd never felt in Nashville, a pulse like a beating heart. It was the absence of that pulse that had brought me back; feeling it now, it was how I knew I was home. I wondered if Ash felt it, too, or if he'd left that part of him forever in Tennessee, or at the bottom of a bottle.

"What time is it?" he asked.

"Just about showtime. There's a whole mess of folks over there across the road all pumped up, ready to hear you sing."

"And only one who knew where to find me."

I took a step closer to him, reaching for his hand. He took it and pulled me to him, lacing his free hand in my hair. I stood on my toes and lifted my face and kissed him gently on the mouth.

"What was that for?"

"I don't know. Luck. Because I felt like it."

"Well, come here, you." He lifted my face in both hands and kissed me for real this time, sweet and slow, our lips parting, tongues exploring the familiar depths of each other's mouths.

"What was *that* for?" I asked, pulling back to catch my breath.

"Luck. Because I felt like it." He smiled, his face half in shadow. "If we're really lucky, maybe you and I can sneak out here later, after the show."

"You never know." With my fingertips I traced the curve of his jaw under the thatch of neatly trimmed beard. "You ready to sing, Cowboy?"

He kissed me again, once, at the peak of my hairline, the way he'd done the first night he came home to East Texas, back in the spring. "Now or never, I guess."

Hand in hand we made our way out of the woods and across

the road. At the edge of the parking lot, he stopped short at the sight of the crowd still loitering around the front door.

"Holy shit," he said.

"We can go around back, if it's easier."

"Nope," he said, tightening his grip on my hand. "Remember what I taught you? Hold your head up and act like you made the rules."

We parted the crowd easily, folks falling aside as we made our way through. *It's the beard,* I thought as a rumble began to build and follow us toward the entrance. *They don't recognize him with the beard.* "Hey!" a man's voice hollered out; it sounded like the same fellow who'd been arguing with Troy earlier. "Hey, it's him! Hey, Ash! We done drove all the way from Blanco County to hear you sing, and instead we're standing in a goddamned parking lot!"

People were starting to shove and shout. "Don't stop," I said as we quickened our pace. "Troy!" I called, and as smooth as glass the future Aggie linebacker materialized and blocked our way, easing us through the door like we were on casters.

Once inside, our progress slowed as one fan or old friend after another stopped Ash to greet him, to say "welcome home," to offer praise or wish him well. It was Hardy who came to the rescue, popping forward from his post by the end of the bar, dragging us out of harm's way. "Where the hell you been, man? I've been about to jump outta my skin here! Thought you'd done gone and bailed on me."

Ash slid over and caught Dub's eye, and Dub reached under the bar and opened a cooler and pushed a bottle of springwater at him. Ash unscrewed the top and took a drink. "We set to go?"

"The boys are backstage," Hardy said. "Just waiting on you, Boss."

He took a swig of water, scanned the room. "Well, let's knock this son of a bitch out of the park, then."

Suddenly his faced tensed, his eyes narrowing to slits. I followed his gaze, landing on the guy in the suit coat and gray ponytail at the end of the bar. You'd think, after all that time in Nashville, I'd have been able to smell a rat, but I didn't even catch a whiff until the man leaned forward and stuck out his hand saying, "Rick Musgrove, Ragtop Music. Great to see you again, man. I can't tell you how excited we all are about what you're doing here tonight." The guy just stood there with his hand sticking out, smiling to beat the band. Capped teeth. I should have known. Everybody in Nashville had capped teeth.

Ash turned to Hardy, whose mouth was open, presumably about to dish out some of his famous mojo.

"You little dick," Ash said. "You lying, ass-kissing—"

"Ash!" That was me. Too late. He spun toward me, his eyes like lit coals.

"Are you in on this?" he asked me.

"No! I never—I had no idea."

Ash turned to the bar, where Dub was occupied at the far end, filling two mugs from a tap. He flagged down the second bartender, a slender young man with a blond crew cut who was pouring out a row of whiskey shots for a burly guy in a creased white Stetson. "Hey! You!" Ash called out.

The boy looked up. "Yessir?"

"Gimme one of those."

The boy glanced nervously toward Dub, busy at his end of the bar.

"Hang on now," Hardy said to Ash. "You're off the sauce, remember?"

"Thanks to you, as of about thirty seconds ago, I'm officially back on it."

Hardy looked beseechingly at me. I opened my mouth to speak, but Ash spun toward me with such rage in his face that I snapped it shut again. He turned back to the bartender.

"He's not my caseworker and she's not my goddamned nanny. Here," he said, digging in his back pocket, thrusting a wad of bills across the bar. "That ought to cover the whole bottle. You just keep pouring till I say stop."

"Yessir." The boy took another glass from beneath the bar and filled it with smoke-colored liquor. Ash reached for it and tossed back half the drink in one shot, then polished it off with another gulp and slid the empty across the bar for a refill. I felt like a wax dummy, standing helplessly by, aware of faces nearby swimming in and out of focus, George Jones on the jukebox inviting us to step right up, come on in, as Ash tipped back his second drink and swallowed it whole, then whirled and grabbed Hardy by the collar. Hardy was wearing a black snap-front shirt with roses embroidered on the lapels, and the top snap popped open in Ash's grasp.

"You and me need to settle a score."

"What?" Hardy's voice was squeaky, his eyes behind the smudged lenses huge and terrified.

"We can do it outside or right here, in front of all these good people. It's up to you."

"Now hold on just a second," the record-company guy said. "I think there's been a little misunderstanding."

"You keep out of this!" Ash said, glaring at Rick Musgrove over Hardy's head. "You Nashville suck-asses are all the same. Take a man's life and just, just put it through the goddamned shredder! Make all kinds of fancy-ass promises, then tie him to the fence and leave him out there for the dogs to lick the bones clean! No, thanks. Y'all had your chance with me, and you see what's left?" His eyes gleamed wetly in the blue light. He let go of Hardy's collar. His shoulders slumped, and he turned and rested his hands on the bar.

Several things happened simultaneously. The song on the jukebox ended. A pool cue cracked against a rack of balls. Hardy slid over next to Ash and laid a hand on his shoulder. A woman laughed, high-pitched and drunkenly, on the far side of the room.

Dub appeared on the other side of the bar just as Ash turned toward Hardy, took a step back, cocked his fist and sent it flying forward, catching Hardy square in his belly. The air went out of him in a loud *whoomph* and he staggered backward, falling against Rick Musgrove, who caught him and set him upright again. Ash's second shot was aimed higher, at Hardy's jaw. Bone met bone in a sickening crunch. Hardy's glasses flew off, into the crowd. The jukebox clicked and whirred and Bob Wills started to play "Cherokee Maiden" as Hardy's eyes rolled back and he slumped to the floor.

Ash turned and waggled his empty glass at Dub. But Dub hadn't been running a country honky-tonk for forty years without learning a thing or two. He came up from under the bar with a wooden baseball bat, a good old-fashioned Louisville Slugger, set it on the bar, and laid his hand over the grip.

"You know I don't allow no monkey business in here, I don't care who you are," he said. "Now get your shit together before I call the law."

Ash lifted the empty glass in his hand, rotating it this way and that, studying the refraction of light in its curves. Then he turned and threw it, straight and hard as a fastball, into the rows of bottles that stood in neat rows against the mirror behind the bar. Glass exploded, liquid flying in all directions. Someone screamed. Dub's wife, Candy, stuck her head out of the office, a portable phone in her hand.

For a man in his sixties, Dub was amazingly nimble. He was over the bar in one leap, the bat extended in front of him in both hands as folks started shouting and stumbling. A mob like this, you never knew if they'd try to save their own hindquarters or if they'd just as soon let their neighbors have a roundhouse punch just for the hell of it, like in some old John Wayne movie or an episode of *Gunsmoke.*

Ash twisted away from the bar, his fists balled in front of him. I saw nothing but pure animal fear as his eyes found mine. *Is this what you wanted?* his expression seemed to say. *Are you happy now?* But before I could react, he was off for the door at a blind run, dodging and weaving through the crowd while Bob Wills's fiddle, as sweet as wild honey, played on.

Dub met my eyes, shook his head. He placed the bat on the bar and squatted, along with Rick Musgrove, over Hardy. Folks were milling everywhere, bumping into each other, trying to see what was going on.

I started to fight my way toward the door. People swarmed one way and another, some trying to get closer to the action, some trying to flee it, as I slowly swam upstream against the crush and sweat of strangers.

Minutes later I reached the parking lot, sucking in gulps of warm, dusty nighttime air. Troy had abandoned his post, along with the couple of dozen of fans who hadn't given up hope of making it into the show. They stood in a loose knot, staring with the same expression of surprise on their faces. I turned, too, in time to see a pair of headlights weaving across the parking lot, headed in our direction. I was dimly conscious of voices shouting behind me as I froze, hypnotized by the bright onrush of glare, glancing off row upon row of glass and chrome.

Time seemed to move on alternate planes, the truck flying toward the crowd and my thoughts slow and liquid and full of the strangest jumble of things: playing with my brothers in Dove's garden while inside our mama wept and wailed over our daddy, Raymond Hatch; walking up the aisle at First Baptist in a white gown toward Mitchell; lying with Ash on the rock at Flat Creek as moonlight fell around us like angel dust; the feel of

Jude's body, solid and fragrant, infant and toddler and little boy all at once, in my arms. I saw myself wandering through the hereafter searching for Ash like a pilgrim, holding the broken pieces of my heart in my hands, asking people along the way: *Have you seen who this belongs to?* Always wandering, never finding him.

A meaty hand grabbed the back of my shirt and jerked me off my feet; I sailed backward, landing hard against the size XXXL visage of Shania Twain, just as the pickup's wheels cut hard to the left, glancing off the fender of a battered red Ford pickup, then swerving hard to the right and smashing nose-first into the side of the building. The front end of the truck folded like an accordion into the cab, metal buckling and groaning, glass shattering, the air bag exploding, steam and water rising in a white plume from the crumpled front end.

Astonishingly, the driver's door opened and Ash staggered out. There was a gash over his eye; his nose was bleeding. He stumbled away from the ruined truck, one step, two, then leaned over and threw up, a thin gruel of liquor and bile.

I slipped out of the big man's grip just as Ash straightened and met my eye, wiping his mouth on his shirtsleeve, dark sockets like empty windows where his eyes had been.

He turned and looked dazedly toward the door of the Round-Up, back at the demolished truck. From far off came the high, thin wail of a siren. He took one unsteady step away from the building, the growing crowd, Troy with Dub now running toward us, shouting. Then he was stumbling away, between the endless rows of trucks and cars, away from the smoke and noise and ruin, the hot August night swallowing him and his crimes and their consequences.

chapter twenty-two

It was almost midnight when Geneva dropped Jude and me at home. Lily insisted on spending the night with us; like a pint-sized bodyguard, she refused to leave Jude's side. Over the past few hours Jude had cried himself into a state of zombie-like exhaustion and dropped off almost instantly, his face mottled with tears and grief-stricken even in sleep. I knelt beside the bed and smoothed his hair off his forehead and kissed him on the nose.

"Aunt Lucy?" Lily's eyes were dark and watchful in the glow of the night-light.

"What, baby?"

"Jude is so sad."

Her eyes dared me to defy her, this old soul in the shell of a little girl. I wondered if she remembered anything of her first two years, if she ever dreamed of walking in a strange green country where everyone else looked like her, whether she understood their soft, musical language, a word resonating here or there: *bird, house, girl.*

What was I supposed to tell her? That I trusted God less than I ever had, that I felt He had tricked me and was laughing right now behind His hand? That happiness was something parceled out like cards in a game of Texas Hold 'Em, that even though you might hold a straight flush one minute, the next hand could cost you every chip on the table? I was mortified for feeling this way, for not having the words to comfort a six-year-old girl, much less my son when he eventually woke up and started asking what had happened to his daddy.

"Yes, he is. But it helps to have you here. Thank you for staying with us tonight."

"You're welcome."

"Do you think you can sleep?" She nodded. "Close your eyes, then."

I stood at the kitchen window, watching the trailer in the dark, my breath catching every time a leaf scuttled by on the hot, dry wind or a cloud passed over the moon, trying to understand this man I'd married who had grown so very strange and far away to me. The evening ran through my head like a broken movie, forward and back, the frames out of order: Ash disappearing, bloody and sick, into the roughly nine hundred square miles of woods and water that made up Cade County. Hardy being borne out of the Round-Up on a backboard by a pair of EMTs in the revolving red and blue lights of the ambulance as Dub hollered about assault, reckless endangerment, destruction of property, breach of contract. Marjo Malone and Dewey Wentzel showing up with their badges and guns, rounding up witnesses for questioning. A tow truck, then another, arriving to dispose of the mangled vehicles. Jude hysterical, inconsolable. I could close my eyes, shake my head to clear it, but always the loop started up again, and it always ended the same way: headlights speeding toward the crowd, then the last-second swerve and crash, Ash limping out of the wrecked truck, reeling off into the night like a wounded animal, in search of a secret place to either heal himself or die.

My eyes flew open at the sound of a motor pulling into the yard. I ran for the door as headlights cut across the front of the house. It seemed I'd been rehearsing this moment since the day I married Ash, in one form or another: the 2:00 A.M. phone call from the hospital, the squad car at the door. *So sorry to inform you, Mrs. Farrell.* I was forty years old, too young to have lost two husbands, though I knew it happened all the time. At the very least, I hoped it was Marjo. She was a tough gal, but unlike Dewey, who was about as sensitive as a garden hoe, she was human.

The driver's-side door swung open and the deputy climbed out. As he stood adjusting his gun belt on his pudgy hips, I heard him belch. I unlatched the screen door and stepped out onto the porch.

"Did you find him? Just tell me."

"Not yet. That's how come I'm here. To have a look around your place. Make sure he's not hiding out somewhere. Or somebody's not hiding *him*."

"Well, you wasted a trip. He's not here."

Dewey laughed a high, nasal laugh. "Like I'd take your word for it."

"I guess you'll have to."

He came around the car to stand at the foot of the steps. I could smell onions and sweat and Aqua Velva, and for a second I thought I would pass out, or throw up.

"We'll get a warrant, you know. Marjo ain't afraid to wake up Judge Poe."

"You're kidding me."

"Oh no, ma'am, I'm not."

"Come in, then," I said, stepping to one side. "But be quick about it. And you'd better not wake the kids or there'll be hell to pay."

I followed while Dewey searched the house. When he came to Jude's room, he flicked on a flashlight, shining it quickly across the bed, then underneath, then crossed to the closet and opened it, closed it again, flicked off the light. A similar check of the guest room and the back porch, including the deep freeze, and he was done.

"What about the trailer?" he asked.

"What about it?"

"You got a key?"

"It's not locked." I knew because I'd checked earlier, moving quickly from room to room, flipping on lights, peeking into the bathroom and the built-in cupboard in the bedroom. I'd paused only long enough to glance at the notebook Ash kept on the milk crate beside the mattress. Mostly nonsense phrases: "Her heaven had cracked open, too." "Successive approximations to goal." And finally, in blurred ink as red as blood, "Without you, I sure do miss me." I'd picked up the notebook and carried it back to the house with me and buried it at the bottom of a kitchen drawer. I hadn't known why at the time, but I did now as I watched Dewey Wentzel pause to give his ass a good scratching and then head up the cinder blocks through Ash's front door.

I stood in the yard until he came back out.

"Okay. All clear for now. But I'm gonna be staked out up the road the rest of the night, just in case he shows up."

"That's the dumbest thing I ever heard," I said. "If he sees your car, he'll sure as hell stay away."

Dewey shrugged. "I just do what the sheriff says. Dub's hopping mad. And I wouldn't be surprised if that boy Ash beat up decides to bring charges, too."

"The whole thing was his fault. If Dub wants to point fingers, he ought to start with Hardy Knox."

"I just got once piece of advice for you, Miz Farrell."

"Spit it out, then, and go."

"Harboring a fugitive's a crime, too. If it comes out that you're in on this—"

"Get out of here, before I call your boss and report you for harassment."

"I'll be up the road, like I said," he told me as he hitched up his belt and swaggered off around the corner of the house. "I'll have my eagle eye on you." Dewey started up the Crown Vic's engine and revved it loudly, then circled the yard and set off up the road the way he'd come.

As I went back inside and locked the door, I heard Lily calling me from Jude's room, her voice sharp with fear. I ran toward it, toward the sound of Jude sobbing.

"What's wrong? What happened?"

"I had a dream!" he wailed. "A man came in my room with a light and shined it in my eyes! A scary man with a gun!"

I crawled onto the narrow mattress and wedged myself between their warm, trembling bodies, gathering them into my arms. "It wasn't a dream, baby. It was— That was me. Just checking to make sure everything was okay. I'm sorry I scared you."

"Is Daddy home?"

"Not yet. But maybe if we all close our eyes and think about him real hard, he'll be here when we wake up."

Things were quiet for a moment or two, except for Jude's soft hiccupping.

"Aunt Lucy?"

"What, Lily?"

"When I think about Uncle Ash, it just makes me sadder."

"Me, too," Jude whispered.

"Think about something else, then," I said. "Think about something you like more than anything else in the whole world."

"Dinosaurs," Jude said.

"Chocolate," Lily said.

"Me, too," I said. "And peonies."

"What's peonies?"

"It's a flower. Keep going. Jude?"

"Disneyland," he said, his voice slurred with sleep. "*Pirates of the Caribbean.*"

"Talladega Motor Speedway," murmured Lily, burrowing into my side.

I was quiet as they settled themselves against me, warm and sweet-smelling.

"Your turn, Aunt Lucy."

"Oh. Okay. Um, peonies."

"You said that one already."

"Hush, now. Go to sleep."

I closed my eyes. *Peonies.* I filled my mind with blossoms, piling them up, bushels and bushels of them, their heavy heads drooping, pink and purple and ivory tinged with blush, until finally they were thick enough that I couldn't see the rush of headlights anymore.

I SLIPPED IN and out of consciousness, and finally woke to a room filled with pearl-gray light. My head was full of scattered dreams, odd puzzle pieces that didn't quite fit. I wormed my way out from between the kids, taking care not to disturb them, and walked across the backyard to Ash's trailer. The morning was overcast, the clouds low-slung and heavy. I went up the cinder blocks and let myself in the front door, moving slowly from room to room. Everything I saw, from the bottle of dish soap on the kitchen sink to the blanket bunched at the foot of the mattress, made me heartsick. The place seemed not just unoccupied but abandoned. I looked into the bathroom cabinet. Nothing but a toothbrush and a tube of Crest.

I walked outside and sat down on the cinder blocks, and I put my head on my knees and sent my prayers up into the gray sky, little unstamped postcards with a barely legible address. Maybe there was Somebody up there, listening. It was, after all, Sunday, the day God allegedly stayed home to reflect upon His creation and accept our praise, at least so long as you'd been raised in the Southern Baptist church. Or maybe God was just kicking back in his hammock and watching pro beach volleyball on TV, like a goodly portion of us sinners down below.

I went inside and put on some coffee, then phoned the county sheriff's office, where after three rings a machine picked up and told me that the office was closed for the weekend and that I should call back Monday morning at eight. I drank a cup of coffee, showered, and put on a dark blue, mid-calf-length dress. I woke up the kids and made them pancakes while they dressed. We brushed our teeth and our hair and buckled ourselves into the Blazer and drove up Little Hope Road toward town.

We arrived at First Baptist just minutes before the start of the eleven o'clock service, rushing into the cool, dim vestibule as the organist played the closing chords of "Wondrous Love." I guided Jude and Lily down the center aisle into a pew behind a group of Lilac Ladies, the oldest of the women's guilds. Skinny, slope-nosed Harriet McNee glanced over her shoulder at us and smiled automatically, then froze. She nudged her neighbor, Bernice Brumley, and muttered something in her ear. Bernice turned and met my eyes with a look that could melt glass. I scouted around for my mama, but didn't see her anywhere.

The choir filed in, followed by Reverend Honeywell in his billowing robes and the brown-suited deacon, Calvin Paynter. The pastor took his place at the pulpit and delivered the invocation and the call to worship. We stood and sang "Lift High the Cross."

Calvin stood to read the scripture, a story from the Old Testament book of Numbers that ended with the verse, "Be sure your sin will find you out." In the pew in front of me, Harriett whispered something to Bernice, who shot another peek over her shoulder at me as Reverend Honeywell intoned from the pulpit, "Let us confess our sins."

I tried. I bowed my head and closed my eyes. But the words jammed up in my head and my heart, bumping against one another like random bits of glass and stone. Alone in my backyard, my prayers had flowed from me as easily as water, but here in God's house I felt a light spreading around me, and it was not the sweet, gentle light of redemption. It was the spotlight of my hometown, aiming its ultra-bright, withering beam on me. God's forgiveness was a piece of cake compared to the whispers and sneaky glances of the old biddies in the pew in front of me.

"Amen," Reverend Honeywell said, his voice echoing throughout the sanctuary. "I ask you now, if there are any among us today in special need of God's mercy, let it be known so that we may ask His favor upon you."

A man down front said that his sister was in the hospital in Waco and the X-rays didn't look good. Leslie Bingham requested prayers for her nephew stationed in the Middle East with the Fourth Infantry Division out of Fort Hood. Agnes Klinger asked, as she did every week, for us to keep her son, Kirk, in our hearts, that the Lord might show him the error of his ways, since the Texas Department of Corrections had not thus far succeeded in doing so.

"Anyone else?" the preacher inquired.

A murmur traveled along the pew in front of me, a row of blue-white heads bent together. I felt a pair of invisible hands closing around my throat. Spots swam in front of my eyes.

Jude began to whimper. I reached for his arm and squeezed. "Ow!" he cried.

Heads swiveled, clothing rustled. I got to my feet, grabbing for Jude's and Lily's hands, pulled them out of the pew and up the center aisle as a buzz moved through the church like the stirrings of a swarm of bees. Jude was sobbing; Lily tripped as she struggled to keep up with me.

I hustled the kids across the parking lot, turned on the Blazer's AC full blast, and sped the half-dozen blocks to Dove's. She was out front in the garden, and squinted up at us from under her broad-brimmed hat as we squealed up to the curb.

I sat paralyzed, both hands gripping the wheel, staring straight ahead through the windshield until Dove walked up and knocked on the passenger window.

Lily unbuckled her seat belt and leaned forward, pressing the button to lower the window. "I don't think Aunt Lucy feels too good," she said. "Maybe we should come in and have some Kool-Aid."

"I think that's a fine idea," Dove said, and reached inside to release the kid-proof locks. Lily scrambled out as Dove leaned across the backseat and lifted Jude into her arms.

"Hey, now, mister bud," she said. "What seems to be the problem?"

"Mama hurt me!" he cried, holding out his arm. "And last night my daddy got in a fight and broke a glass and ran away! I wish I could leave here forever! I wish I never knew *any* of this!"

For the first time since giving birth to my son, I felt shame down to my soles for what I had done. I had brought this boy into the world without scales or armor, to have his tender heart thrown against the rocks, over and over again. We are not equipped for this, I thought. We are too frail for love. And still we do it, and we go on doing it, even when it comes to nothing, even when it cracks us in two.

"Come on inside, Lucy Bird," Dove said. "Maybe you need to lay down a spell."

Five minutes later the kids were in front of the TV with cheese sandwiches and Kool-Aid, watching stock cars zoom around a tri-oval at 180 miles an hour, and I was stretched out on top of the comforter in Dove's guest room, the shades drawn, a cool, damp washcloth smelling of lavender and mint placed across my eyes. She kept them in the icebox in Ziploc bags for just this type of emergency.

"I don't know what happened," I said to Dove as she sat down on the bed next to me, the mattress shifting gently under her weight. "We were saying the Prayer of Confession, and Reverend Honeywell asked if anybody had special need of God's mercy, and all of a sudden I couldn't breathe, and Jude started fussing and when I grabbed his arm he hollered out that I was hurting him. I didn't *mean* to hurt him, I only wanted to— It felt like my heart was about to bust out of my chest, like I was going to pass out from all those eyes on me."

She ran a palm over my hair. "How you feelin' now?"

"Like everything I've ever done in my whole life has been a mistake." I lifted the washcloth and peeked at Dove, who smiled. "I'm not kidding, Dove. What was I thinking, that anything good could ever come of me and Ash taking up together? It's like trying to mix two bowls of crazy stew and hoping it'll turn into some fantastic gourmet dish."

"But that's what happened, didn't it? For a while, anyhow."

"I guess. I don't think I can remember back that far."

"Sure you can. Look here." She reached toward the bureau for a framed photo of Ash and me on our wedding day, my head on his shoulder, both of us grinning like fools, my bouquet of peonies barely hiding the swell of my six-months-pregnant belly.

"Oh Lord," I said. "Look how stupid we were."

"Naw," she said. "Just happy. I was there. I seen it with my own eyes."

"Do you know, that idiot Dewey Wentzel came out and searched the house last night, then spent the night at the end of our driveway? Like Ash was just going to walk out of the woods and turn himself in." Dove reached for my hand and took it in hers, her fingers sinewy and strong. "I feel like I need to be doing something, but I don't know what. I thought he'd have turned up by now. What if he's hurt and needs help? Where's he going to go?"

"Maybe he found someplace to hunker down for the night and let things cool off a little. Can't you think of anyplace he'd go?"

"To the new house, maybe. But—no, not if he knows the sheriff's looking for him. He'd have to find somebody to take him in and cover for him. Isaac King, maybe. I don't know if Marjo would think to look there. Or . . ." I sat up, the photograph falling from my hand onto the mattress.

"What?" Dove said.

"Would you mind watching the kids a little while? I just had an idea."

HEATHER STARBIRD LIVED in one side of a beige brick duplex in a row of them behind the Food King. This Sunday afternoon the street was empty except for a skinny dog who trotted along beside my vehicle for a half-block or so, then fell back, panting in the heat. I cruised slowly, looking for Heather's station wagon, but as I approached her building, the parking area out front held only a shiny new Harley-Davidson and a rusting Chevy Malibu on blocks.

I parked at the curb and sat for a minute with all the air-conditioning vents pointed at me, trying to screw up my nerve. The house was in sorry shape, even by Mooney's standards. What lawn there'd once been had burned to a crisp, and tinfoil covered the front windows, which faced the western sun. On the B side of the building, an assortment of plastic pots on the porch held the withered remnants of plant life next to a kid's Big Wheel, but the A side had nothing to characterize it but a sagging screen door.

I left the motor running and crossed the dead grass in the yard, self-conscious in my church dress, and stepped onto the porch, rapping my knuckles against the metal door frame. On the street, two kids about twelve years old crept past on bicycles, giving me the eye. I waved, and they sped up and disappeared around the corner.

The screen wasn't latched. I opened it and knocked on the front door. It had a small glass panel in it, and I had to fight the urge to stand on tiptoe and peek through it, imagining Heather hunkering behind it, gazing back at me with her flat dark eyes. It occurred to me that I had no idea what I'd say if she answered or, worse yet, if Ash was here: *Just checking to see if my husband survived last night. Have a nice day.*

The door of the B unit opened and a big, sleepy-looking man in boxer shorts and a LIVE FREE OR DIE T-shirt squinted at me through the screen, a can of Bud in his hand.

"Hi," I said. "I'm looking for Heather."

"She in some kinda trouble?"

"Not that I know of. I just want to talk to her."

He gave me the once-over, peered out at the Blazer running at the curb. "You from Family Services? They don't usually come 'round on Sundays."

"No. I'm just a, a friend of a friend."

"Well, she's not here. Took off maybe a couple hours ago. Come over and borrowed ten dollars from the wife for gas money."

"Was she alone? Did she say where she was going?"

The man sipped his beer and considered me warily. "Look, lady. No offense, but I don't know you from Adam. Heather's had a tough time, but she's been doing real good lately, ever since she met that priest down in Jefferson and started going to meetings—"

I took a step backward and nearly fell off the porch. "Heather's in AA?"

"Been, oh, I guess more than a year now."

"Thank you," I said, backing off the porch and across the yard. "You've been a big help." The man continued to gaze at me suspiciously. "Really. You have no idea. Could you do me a favor?" I called out, opening my car door. He shrugged, noncommittal, and sipped his beer. "When—if—she comes home, would you ask her to get in touch with Lucy?"

"I dunno. What should I say it's about?"

"Just tell her Lucy needs to talk to her. She'll know."

chapter twenty-three

When I got back to Dove's, Bailey and Geneva were there, still in their church clothes, spreading out Willie B.'s pork ribs in the kitchen. "Seems to me you oughta talk to this priest fella," Dove said once I'd told them what I'd learned.

I dialed directory assistance in Jefferson and got the numbers for St. Jude's and Father Laughlin's home, but both lines just rang and rang.

"I guess I'll have to go down there," I said. "I can't think who else Ash would trust to take him in."

"Well, you set down and eat somethin' first," Dove said, already fixing me a plate. "It won't do to have you passin' out from hunger on the highway."

"How about Isaac King?" Geneva asked.

"I thought of him. But they haven't got a phone. I'll stop by their place on my way out of town. Maybe run by home first and get out of these clothes."

"Want one of us to go with you?" Bailey asked.

"I'd rather y'all stayed here and held down the fort," I said. "See if you can keep Jude distracted." He'd seemed okay when I came in—sitting glassy-eyed in front of the TV, listening to Lily describe in excruciating detail the NASCAR Nextel Cup points system—but I knew that sooner or later, unless his daddy miraculously reappeared, he was bound to melt down.

Back home, I changed into jeans and a T-shirt and my old track shoes, and went into the kitchen for a drink of water. As I stood filling a glass from the tap, I happened to glance out the window over the sink, and thought my heart would jump out of my throat. Heather Starbird's brown station wagon was parked out back, in front of the trailer.

Wiping my hands on the front of my jeans, I hurried down the hall and down the back steps. Just then the front door of the trailer opened, and Heather stepped out, tossing her hair over her shoulder, wearing a tank top and cutoffs, her limbs long and muscular, her feet bare. We stared at each other across the roof of her wagon. Judge not, that ye be not judged, I reminded myself. Things are not always what they seem.

"He's not there," I said.

She shook her head. She was watching me with the usual veiled blankness in her eyes. But there are all kinds of ways people have of camouflaging their true selves, of keeping their fragile cores intact.

"I went by your place this morning," I said. "I thought he might go to you."

"I've been out looking for him, too," she said, "after I heard about what happened last night. But . . ." She held out her hands, palms up, empty.

I walked over and sank onto the cinder blocks, rubbing my eyes with my fists. She sat down beside me, stretching her legs in the sun. Her toenails were painted a sparkly pale lavender, like a ten-year-old girl's.

"I'm real sorry," she said. "I been where you're at, I know what it's like."

"I didn't know you and Ash were going to AA," I said. She glanced over at me. "Your next-door neighbor told me."

"Charlie? That old blabbermouth."

"I won't tell anybody."

She started tracing a pattern in the dirt with her big toe. "Aw, I don't care. I already been called a witch and a whore and who knows what else. Folks can think what they want, it's all the same to me. But I been sober sixteen months, and I don't fool with married men. 'Sides, Tripp and me is engaged." She held out her left hand, on which a stone barely bigger than the head of a pin winked in the sun. "He behaves himself, he gets outta Hodge in December. We're gettin' married at Christmastime. I'm gonna have me a white dress and those red bushy flowers all over the place—whatta you call 'em?"

"Poinsettias?"

"That's the ones."

"Congratulations," I said. "I wish you the very best. You and Tripp both."

We sat in silence for a while as the sun shifted around behind the trailer, casting a shadow across the yard.

"Look," Heather said. "This is none of my business, but . . ."

"Go ahead."

"Everybody's got a, a dark side to them. Some just has more trouble keeping a lid on it than most." I laughed silently, shaking my head. Ash had blown his lid, all right, right out of the stratosphere. "All's I'm saying is, if you're waiting for everything to line up perfect, the stars or the planets or whatever, then you're gonna be setting by yourself on the front step when you're old and gray, trying to figure out how all the good stuff passed you by.

"It gives me the shivers, sometimes, to hear Ash talk about you. In fact, it's what made me and Tripp finally decide to get serious. Both of us has fucked up plenty, pardon my French. But the thing is, nobody else ever made me feel like he does. Like sometimes him and me are on this little island of our own, and the whole rest of the world can go to hell. He's got my back, and I've got his, you know what I mean? 'You got to hang on to that,' Ash says. 'When it comes your way, you got to grab on to it and never let go.' "

"I have to find him, Heather," I said.

"I know."

"I was thinking about driving down to Father Laughlin's, to see if he's heard anything. I tried calling, but there wasn't any answer."

"You try his cell?"

"I haven't got the number."

She stood up, stretching her arms over her head. "Mind if I use your phone?"

I sat on the living room couch picking my cuticles while Heather Starbird paced up and down my back hall with the receiver jammed between her chin and her shoulder, talking to Punch Laughlin.

"No luck," she said, coming back into the room. "But he'll make an announcement at tonight's meeting."

Before she left, she wrote down Punch's cell phone number for me. "He said call if you need somebody to talk to. And he said to tell you he'll light an extra candle."

She handed me the slip of paper. "What's this other number?" I asked.

"That's mine. Maybe I haven't got a hotline to God, like Punch does, but who knows? Maybe I do."

The numbers swam as I stared at the paper. I remembered feeling this way when Mitchell died, that the smallest unexpected kindness was bound to undo me in a way that my larger grief was too deep to penetrate.

"Listen, I got to run," Heather said. "Today's visiting day at Hodge. Tripp'll be waiting for me."

I walked her through the kitchen to the back door. As she stepped out into the yard I could feel the distance between us growing, our old defenses sliding back into place. She may have walked in my shoes, but the truth was, she'd walked in Ash's, too; she'd ventured firsthand into provinces I'd never traverse. For a crazy second I almost envied her for it.

"I'll let you know if I hear anything," she said as she ducked into her station wagon. "You stay strong, hear?"

I gave her a dopey little power salute, fist in the air, as she backed out of the yard and drove away. After the dust settled, a heaviness began to descend into my eyes, my shoulders. I wanted to go inside and lie down and sleep for five minutes, or five years. But Ash was out there somewhere, needing somebody to get his back, maybe more than he ever had. I picked up my keys and headed back out the door.

ISAAC AND HIS wife and kids weren't home—probably off visiting their family for Sunday dinner—so I left a note stuck inside the screen door describing what had happened and asking him to let me know if he heard anything.

It was weeks since I'd been out to the house site, the wooden skeleton transformed into a near-finished dwelling boasting a façade of log and river stone, a red metal roof like an exclamation against the white-hot sky. I parked the Blazer and got out, picking my way carefully through the staking for the deck onto the porch, and pushed open the front door, gazing up into the rafters of what Ash had called the great room, the stone chimney soaring overhead. I wandered through the unfinished kitchen with its tile floors and marble counters. Some of the interior log walls had been left bare, and others had been dry-walled, ready for paint or paper.

I scaled the staircase. The second story was as hot as blazes, but the vista of the pond through the bedroom windows was as green and peaceful as Ash had said it would be. I turned slowly, remembering the feeling I'd had the first time I stood in this room under the open sky as Ash described the family he foresaw living under this roof, the woman I'd envisioned sleeping here, her head on the pillow. I hadn't been able then, for any number of reasons, to let myself see her clear. Now I stood motionless at the window, watching myself sleep, my eyelids flickering with unexplained scraps of nonsense and grace. I saw myself shaking Ash's shoulder, waking him, making him laugh at how the fifteenth-century Roman Catholic church had managed to invade this Southern Baptist girl's dreams, ancient Grecian sibyls by way of the Italian Renaissance arriving to foretell the future, or just, like Lily, to complain about the dessert menu.

But first I had to find him.

HARDY HAD LEFT the handyman's cottage a wreck: dirty dishes stacked in the sink, fast-food wrappers and newspapers everywhere. The place smelled of dirty socks. The recording equipment, the stereo, his guitars, even the Toyota, all were gone.

On my way across the parking lot at County General, I ran into Audrey coming out. "What are you doing here?" we cried in unison.

"Where were you last night?" I asked. "You missed everything."

"I know. I came here as soon as I heard. But it's too late."

"What do you mean, too late?" For an awful moment I thought she meant Hardy had died.

"I mean he's gone. He checked himself out, the little shitheel."

"Hardy's gone? But I thought Ash broke his jaw!"

"They wired him up and shot him full of Demerol, and some guy with a ponytail drove him out of here at six this morning. I was just about to run by his place and see if I could find him."

"Don't bother. He's not there." I reached out and took hold of her arm. "I'm sorry, honey. But I think Hardy's hit the road."

"Oh, man," she sighed. "What a relief."

"A *relief*? I thought you were madly in love!"

"Oh, that. I guess I got a little swept away, huh, by all that Nashville talk? But, see, I was getting dressed to go to the Round-Up last night, and out of nowhere Joe dropped by, and my mama let him in, and he just started begging me so hard to talk to him. So we went outside and sat on the tailgate and it was just such a pretty night, all purply and full of stars and Kenny Chesney on the radio—you know, the one that goes, 'I can't see how you'd ever be anything but mine'? The whole thing was like a big old flashing neon sign. And, well, the next thing you know . . ." In all the time I'd known her, I don't think I'd ever seen Audrey blush.

"So, you and Joe are back together?"

"When I heard about last night, I just felt so *bad*. I mean, poor Hardy, first getting the shit kicked out of him, and then getting stood up on top of it. I decided I better be a big girl and come to the hospital and tell him myself what happened. But he's checked himself out! And now you're saying he's, like, *gone*!" I pictured Rick Musgrove at the wheel of the Corolla, probably halfway back to Nashville by now, while Hardy dozed on painkillers in the backseat, surrounded by everything he owned that mattered in the world. "So, did Ash turn up yet?" Audrey asked. "I figured he'd come dragging home around sun-up with his tail between his legs."

"No, he didn't. In fact, I've been out looking all day."

"Well, we'll just have to organize a search party. Maybe make up some flyers and post them around town."

"I'm pretty sure everybody knows what Ash looks like. Any-way, he's got plenty of reasons to stay away. The sheriff's got a list as long as my arm of stuff they're ready to charge him with."

"So you think he's hiding someplace? Or that he ran away?"

"I don't know. I've checked every place I can think of. But—I can't explain it. Just a feeling I have. I don't believe he's gone."

We walked toward our cars. "Hang in there," she said to me, giving me a hug. "Tomorrow morning we'll put our heads together, figure something out."

As SUNDAY NIGHT leaked into Monday, Monday dragging into Tuesday, my friends and family closed ranks like the defenders of the Alamo, circling around me with their rifles aimed at the encroaching enemy, who, unlike at the Alamo, never came. For the first time in my life, I was impervious to the judgment of Mooney, Texas, its gossip and innuendo. Peggy and Audrey and Geneva and Dove and my brothers kept it at bay, so that even though I worked at Faye's all day and visited the bank and the post office and the Food King, not one person said "boo" to me, or anything other than, "Hey there, Lucy. How you doin', girl?" "Fine," I answered back, pasting on my best smile. "Real good." My face hurt after a while from keeping a stiff upper lip.

Meanwhile, Lily kept Jude going, shoring him up in ways I simply wasn't capable of. They had only a few weeks left before the start of first grade, and damned if Lily wasn't going to make sure the two of them wrung out every drop. Geneva and I took them to Wal-Mart for new clothes and lunch boxes. Bailey played hooky one day from work and carried them to a water park in Little Rock, where Lily managed to bite open her lower lip on the waterslide, requiring a trip to the emergency room for stitches, which she displayed proudly to anybody who would look. We gathered with Kit's brood at Dove's in the evenings for big, noisy, messy family suppers, sloppy joes or hot dogs cooked on the grill, the grown-ups sitting under the live oaks while the kids ran around in their swimsuits, chasing each other through the sprinkler. It was the beginning of the end of a hot, dry summer, the halfway point of our hardest season. Dark arrived a minute or two earlier every night, the sun gradually angling lower in the twilit sky. Fall was coming, we told each other; relief was on the way.

On Wednesday, the fourth morning after Ash disappeared, I was alone in the shop when Marjo Malone entered in her buff-colored uniform, her hat in her hand. I'd been arranging a birthday bouquet, but I laid down my shears when I saw her, my fingers curling around the edge of the countertop.

"It ain't bad news," she called out. "Sorry if I scared you."

She walked up to the counter and set her hat on it, her lips as glossy as a maraschino cherry, the tiny silver pistols dangling from her pierced ears. "I come to let you know that I had a long talk with Dub Crookshank. He says that if Ash is willin' to make restitution, he'll reconsider pressin' charges."

"Restitution?"

"It means payin' for what he done. With dollars, not jail time."

I cleared my throat. "How many dollars are we talking, exactly?"

"Well, Dub don't want to call the insurance guys, drag them into it. He don't like to operate that way. He figures to do the work himself, him and his boys. So, with the damage to the outside of the building and the bar, replacing the glass and all the liquor and such—well, he says a ballpark number might be eight to ten."

"Eight to ten?" Eight to ten what? Porsche convertibles? Sacrificial virgins?

"Eight to ten thousand dollars."

"My Lord. It's that bad?"

"Yes, ma'am, I reckon it is. To say nothin' of the cost to Dub in man-hours, lost business, and so forth."

"So, what am I supposed to— What would you like me to do about it?"

"I just thought you'd want to know. So that you can tell Ash he ain't lookin' at no time. Or not much, anyhow. There's still the hit-and-run to deal with, the fella whose vehicle he banged up. I'm not sure he'll be as inclined to lenience as Dub, even though the thing weren't much more'n paint and balin' wire holdin' it together."

"But I haven't talked to Ash since that night. I haven't seen him."

"But if you do. It's just that this might make it easier for him to bring hisself in. From wherever it is he's got to."

Late that afternoon, I left Audrey in charge and walked across the courthouse square to First National. The teller, Judy Oliver, didn't bat an eye when I said I wanted to transfer $10,000 from my savings account into checking. I walked back to Faye's and sent Audrey home. I made a quick call to Dove, telling her I'd be late to pick up Jude, then I locked the shop, climbed into my Blazer, and headed for the Round-Up.

It was early yet; the parking lot was nearly empty, and the sign wasn't lit. I parked next to the spot where Ash had hit the wall, where the weathered cedar planking had split and caved inward, exposing framework and pink insulation underneath, and passed through the entrance into the dusky coolness of the hall. Dub and the blond, crew cut bartender were behind the bar. They didn't see me come in at first, and I stood for a moment taking in the room I knew so well, transformed now in a way I couldn't quite put my finger on. It wasn't just the ruined wall covered by a tarp, or that the mirror over the bar was gone. It was, I realized finally, the silence. I didn't think I'd ever been there when music wasn't blaring over the sound system, either live or from Dub's prized jukebox. I could hear the men talking quietly, a woman's voice coming from the office. My footsteps seemed to echo through the vast, empty room as I made my way toward the bar. Dub had been polishing glasses with a rag, but he set them both on the countertop as he watched me come. I couldn't read what was in his face. I reminded myself he didn't owe me a thing, not even the courtesy of hearing me out.

"I'm here about your money," I said.

Dub turned to the young man. "Run out back and haul them kegs in from the cooler," he said. The boy nodded and disappeared.

"The sheriff says you're looking at somewhere between eight and ten thousand," I said as I rummaged in my purse and brought out my checkbook. The check was already written out; all I had to do was tear it loose and lay it on the bar, turning it so Dub could read the numbers. "If it turns out to be less than this, you can pay me back the difference. Or not. It doesn't much matter to me one way or the other."

Dub leaned close to scan the check. "Now hang on just a minute," he said.

"It's good, if that's what you're worried about," I said. "You can call the bank."

"Naw, it ain't that. It's . . . I don't know how to say it, exactly. This here's none of your business. This is between Ash and me."

"I'm trying to help him, Dub. Right now this is all I can do."

"But it ain't about the money, sweetheart. Don't you see? It's about him settin' things right with me."

He turned and looked over his shoulder, to the faded rectangle on the wall where the big mirror had hung. The liquor bottles lined up in front of it were brand-new, full to the brim, the seals unbroken. "Hell, I can replace glass and booze, fix up my wall. What I want is Ash to own up to what he done. I been knowin' him since he come sniffin' around when he was too young to buy hisself a beer, totin' a little ol' Sears guitar. He played here for twenty-some-odd years before Nashville come callin', and all that time we treated each other like family. Candy and me had him out to the house for supper, for Christmas with our younguns. I loaned him money when he didn't have a pot to piss in. He always squared things with me, paid me back when he found work or by doin' odd jobs for me. We watched him come up, and we was as proud as punch when he got the call to go to Nashville. We always knowed he had it in him.

"What I need is for him to march back in here and tell me, how come him to make such a mess a things? Not just my bar, but all of it. Where I come from, you don't get handed no chance like he did on a silver platter and then piss it away, end up screwin' over everbody ever helped you out along the way. It don't set right with me. That's what I need from Ash—to look me in the eye and tell me how he could end up doin' this to hisself, and to you and your boy, and to this town, when all we ever done was treat him like one of ours." He placed the tips of his fingers against the edge of the check and inched it back across the bar toward me. "No offense, Lucy, but your money's no good to me."

"But it's Ash's money, too," I said. "From selling our house in Tennessee."

"Then how come it's your name on the check? How come you to be the one that signed it? No, ma'am, I won't have it. This is something he needs to deal with like a man."

"But I don't know where he is, Dub. I haven't seen him since—since that night. I don't know if he's ever coming back." I pushed the check toward him again. "Couldn't you just take this, just in case? It would be a weight off my mind."

"But it ain't your weight to carry, sweetheart."

"Don't be a fool, Dub." Candy had come out of the office and stood at her husband's side, a tidy little woman with what might have been the tallest beehive in Cade County. " 'Course it's her weight. Ain't you learned nothin' bein' married to me for forty-two years?" She slid the check out from under my fingers and tucked it in the pocket of her smock top. "I'll put this in the safe for the time bein'," she said. "Earnest money, we'll call it. When Ash turns up, you send him on in so him and Dub can hash things out, and we'll tear up your check. Deal?"

I opened my mouth to thank her, but the words dammed up in my throat. "Don't you say a word, honey," she said. "These men, they think they know it all. You ask me, that's why God made Eve, to show Adam what's what."

I nodded and thanked her and backed toward the door, Candy smiling quietly with her hand over her pocket and Dub staring at his wife with a look that seemed to ask, *Will wonders never cease?*

chapter twenty-four

When I got back to Dove's, she was the only one there, drinking iced tea in the kitchen. Bailey and Geneva had taken the kids to a movie down in Marshall, she said.

"How you holdin' up?" she asked as she stood up to pour me some tea.

"All right."

"Well, you could of fooled me."

I pulled in a slow, raggedy breath and then burst into tears. I laid my head on the tabletop and let it all come, everything I'd kept bottled up in me the past four days. Dove pulled her chair over next to me and rubbed me between the shoulder blades, just like she'd done when I was six and too scared of my mama's sadness to sleep. Dove was never one to tell you not to cry. It didn't bother her if it lasted for five minutes or five days. Her mode was to sit by and let it play itself out, and to be on hand afterwards with plenty of sweet tea and washrags steeped in lavender water and stored in the icebox.

"Better?" she asked as I raised my head and reached for the box of tissues she'd placed in the middle of the oilcloth.

"You know, I think I'd almost rather the whole town decided to tar and feather me on the courthouse square," I said. "Everybody's being so nice, it's about to kill me." I blew my nose into a tissue.

"Some gal named Heather come by earlier," Dove said. "Just wanted to know how you was gettin' along. Said Punch sent his regards."

My eyes filled again. "See? See what I mean?"

"You look like you ain't slept in a week," Dove said. "Whyn't you let me fix you some supper and then you spend the night here? Bailey and Geneva can keep the kids."

"I feel like I need to be home," I said. "Just in case—"

"Honey, I don't mean to bust your bubble, but Ash knows where to find you. You 'member what I used to tell you, 'bout settin' with your hand out where them in need can see you, lettin' 'em know you're there when they're ready? In the meantime, you eat, and I'll go run you a tub."

She put a plate of cold fried chicken and potato salad and coleslaw in front of me. I picked at it, listening to the roar of the water in the bathroom, my aunt getting towels out of the cupboard, adding bubbles to the tub. Sometimes all it takes is someone to hand our troubles off to for a little while, to carry part of the load while we're getting back strength enough to pick them up again.

"I laid you out a gown in the guest room," she said, returning to the kitchen. "No, leave them dishes. I'm just gonna run over to your mama's a minute and carry her some a this chicken. I'll be back directly. You get your bath and go on to bed. Don't wait on me."

I let my clothes fall in a heap on the bathroom tiles as I listened to Dove moving around in the kitchen, then the back door open and shut. I'd hardly spent a moment by myself since Sunday, had kept myself surrounded with people and noise and activity. Being alone meant I had to think, and thinking led to feelings that were likely as not to run away with me.

I switched on the little transistor radio on the edge of the tub as I lowered myself by inches into the steaming water. The Dixie Chicks were singing, *This ain't nothing but a heartbreak town,* a tune I'd always taken for granted was about Nashville. But Heartbreak Town, I understood now, wasn't a place on the map, but one you carried inside. I'd thought I could come back to Mooney and pick up where I'd left off, but the truth was, I took Ash with me everywhere, and Mooney wasn't the same place for me that it used to be, with or without him. I had run as fast as I could, trying to stay one step ahead of Ash, but my heart was no safer than it ever was, nothing more than a crude outline of a heart with a jagged tear down the middle, stuck through with crooked cartoon arrows. Love was like God, or the FBI; no matter where you went, if you dyed your hair or changed your name, it would find you out.

I couldn't help but feel a pang for all the time I'd wasted, the ground I'd covered trying to escape that. I tried to think what some older, wiser person would advise me—Punch Laughlin, maybe, or Dove. Or Lily, old soul that she was. Punch would tell me to hand it over to God. Dove would rub my back and feed me cold chicken and draw me a hot bath and sit with me while I slept, the same things she'd been doing for forty years. Lily would urge me to eat more chocolate. But I couldn't ignore the sinking suspicion that it was too late, that I'd let something crucial sail right by me while I was busy trying to shield myself from a thing I was too foolish to see I couldn't shake. I'd been running so hard, for so long, that I'd almost missed the point, which is that you can't make any headway with arrows in your heart. They're there for a reason, to slow you down, get your attention, to remind you with every step you take that love has left its mark.

I let out some of the bathwater and refilled the tub, then lay back with a rolled-up towel under my neck and shut my eyes, which had burned for days, like they'd been steadily blasted by fine, blowing sand.

Down the hall, the phone rang. Six times, eight, ten. Dove had never gotten herself a machine, couldn't be bothered. "If folks want me, they'll catch up with me," she liked to say. "If they can't, then whatever they needed weren't that important in the first place."

The ringing stopped, then recommenced. This time I counted fourteen rings before it quieted. A few seconds passed, and it started up again. This time it didn't stop; it seemed to grow increasingly louder and insistent as I hauled myself out of the tub, wrapped a towel around me, and hurried barefoot into the hall. By the time I reached the phone I'd managed to work up two dozen scenarios in my head, all of them ending in doom. Another thing I'd learned from Ash—to brace myself everlastingly for disaster.

"Lucy Bird." It was Dove.

"What's the matter?"

"I'm at your mama's. I reckon you oughta get yourself over here directly."

"Why? What happened?"

"Just throw somethin' on and hustle yourself on over. Don't bother with the front door. Just come straight on around back." She hung up.

Dear Lord, I thought, blotting myself dry, scooping up my clothes. *Not this, not now.* My mama had been failing for some months, and I'd known it, and had told myself I'd patch things up somehow, make it right with her once my troubles with Ash were settled. As usual, I started praying in earnest for something that was already a lost cause, casting out my pleas and shoddy promises the way you'd cast a fishing line into an unfamiliar river, not knowing what lurks below the surface, what, if anything, you'll snag.

It took maybe three and a half minutes for me to get dressed and out to my car, to drive the six blocks from Dove's house to Mama's. The sun had dropped below the rooflines, the sky ablaze in the gaudy hues of a dime-store postcard, tangerine and violet and magenta.

I ran around the side of the house, past periwinkles and nasturtiums wilting in their dusty beds. For a second I lost my nerve, hesitating with my hand on the gate latch. Why was the house dark? Why had Dove called me instead of 911? The place should have been lit up like Vegas, sirens wailing, trained professionals in uniforms taking charge. Unless, of course, it was too late for all that.

I opened the gate and let myself into the backyard, inhaling lemon balm and fresh-cut grass. On the patio, a citronella candle burned in a little galvanized bucket, though the summer had been so long and dry, even the mosquitoes had given up and moved elsewhere. Music drifted softly toward me, a tune I knew like the back of my hand:

Along the Red River where the sweet waters flow
Where the stars burn bright and the soft wind does blow
There lives a fair maiden, the one I adore
And I'll court my dear maiden on the Red River shore.

"That you, Lucy Bird?" Dove's voice called.

"*Here* she is," my mama said as I walked toward the figures grouped in lawn chairs on the patio, their faces flickering in the long shadows thrown up by the candle. "Be a good boy, Ash, and set her up a chair."

He set down the guitar, the strings pinging as he propped it against the patio table, stood and unfolded another lawn chair. I sank onto it, perched expectantly at the edge of the seat, my hands on my knees. At that point nothing would have surprised me, not a chorus of Ziegfeld showgirls bursting out the back door in sequins and feathers, not Jesus Himself descending on a fiery cloud, surrounded by cherubim and seraphim. My mama poured me a glass of tea from a pitcher and stuck it in my hand. I sipped, registering the taste of sugar and mint. Locusts chirred in the hedges. The candle's flame guttered in a passing breeze and then steadied itself as Ash and I watched each other across it.

"Patsy," Dove said, "how 'bout you and me head on inside?"

"But it's so nice out," Mama protested. "I feel like I've been cooped up in that house for a week."

"We need to let these two have 'em some alone time. They got a few things to talk over, I reckon."

"I guess you're right." Mama stood slowly, stiffly, and began to shuffle off toward the house. As Dove got up to follow, she pinched the back of Ash's arm, hard enough to make him flinch.

"Don't y'all go makin' me call up Marjo Malone," she said. "I done already had enough excitement for one evenin'. Findin' you here dang near stopped my heart."

"Yes, ma'am," he said.

Quiet settled over the backyard as the screen door sighed shut behind Mama and Dove. Out on the street, a car cruised by, a scrambled snatch of song drifting to us from the radio. Ash cleared his throat, scratched at something behind his ear.

"So, do you want to go first?" he asked.

"I wouldn't know where to start."

"Yeah, me, neither."

"Well, hell's bells, Ash. You must have something to say for yourself. How in the world did you end up at my mama's? Do you have any idea what kind of trouble you're in? How many people have been looking for you?"

"Could you maybe scoot on over this way a little?" he said. "I can hardly see you all the way over there."

"I'm fine right here. For the time being." I studied him in the candlelight. "Your face looks funny."

"It's the beard. I shaved it." The newly exposed skin was pale and unfinished-looking in contrast to his tanned cheeks and forehead, and he sported a Band-Aid under one eyebrow.

"I don't get it," I said. "What happened to make you lose it like that the other night? So a record-company guy from Nashville showed up. It could've been another shot for you, a second chance."

"Hardy and I had a deal," Ash said. "I should have known better than to trust that little weasel, but I let myself get sucked into letting myself hear what I wanted to hear."

"What kind of deal?"

"He said we were outlaws. That we could set up a studio and make our own records. He said we didn't need Nashville, that we could do it our way. When I realized he'd sold me out . . ."

"Maybe he didn't," I said. "Maybe this A&R guy showed up uninvited. Maybe he was planning on helping you. Did it ever occur to you to hear them out before you decided to start busting up the place?"

"Oh, so now you're on Hardy's side."

"I was never on Hardy's side. And maybe he did screw you over. What I don't understand is why you couldn't just deal with it man-to-man. Why you had to break his jaw and tear up Dub's bar to the tune of ten thousand dollars."

"Jesus! Ten thousand?" I knew I could tell him about Dub's offer, about the check locked in the safe in Candy's office, but I wanted to hold on to it, to make him sweat awhile. "I don't know what to tell you, Lucy. I feel like I've been walking around with this dark cloud over my head. The longer I stay under it, the harder it gets to come out."

"But things were getting better. Everything was heading in the right direction till Saturday night."

"Yeah, and then I let Hardy Knox get under my skin, knock me backward, take a whole mess of folks with me. That was wrong, and I don't know how to make it right. I just can't figure out where to start."

"You could say you're sorry. Did that ever in a million years occur to you?"

"Yeah. And I am. Sorry. But I'm also not dumb enough to think that it's enough."

Out front, Dove's Lincoln started up and drove away. A light came on in Mama's kitchen, and her face appeared at the window, shaded with her hand as she peered out into the yard.

"Ash, I swear," I said, "of all the folks in the world you could run to, why in the world would you pick my mama?"

"I didn't set out to. I just kind of found myself in the neighborhood, and I figured I'd sleep off my drunk in her shed. What I didn't count on was her coming out at seven on Sunday morning looking for something to spray yellow jackets with. I woke up with her jabbing me in the leg with the Weedwacker. I don't think she even recognized me at first. She thought I was just some bum wandered over from the bus station. Lord knows, I looked it. Smelled like it, too."

"So she just took you in, fed you, and sheltered you, out of the Christian goodness of her heart?"

"Not that fast. First she read me the riot act. Quoted scripture at me until I thought she'd turn blue in the face. Then she started working in her own personal philosophy of life. I admit I got a little confused at times, which was Jesus talking and which was Patsy Hatch." I had to smile at that. "I don't know how long she kept me there, but I do know that more than once I wished I'd gone ahead and turned myself in to the law, or just laid up in some ditch and let the coyotes and the fire ants have me."

"I know the feeling."

"Once she figured I'd suffered enough, she drug me in the house. Stuck me in the shower, fed me coffee and eggs and aspirin and Bible verses till I could barely hold my head up.

Finally, I guess she either figured she'd made her point or she decided to take pity on me, because she took me down the hall to your old room and told me to lie down. Then she covered me up with this ugly old green-and-orange afghan."

"My great-great-aunt Francie made that," I said. "We called it the sick blanket. If we stayed home from school with a stomachache or the flu or whatever, Mama tucked us in with Aunt Francie's afghan."

"When I woke up, my head felt like it weighed two tons, and I had the most godawful taste in my mouth. I sat up and looked around and thought I'd died and got sent to the wrong room in heaven—all those yellow ruffles and cheerleader's pompoms and old Tiger Beat posters on the walls . . . Jesus, Lucy, Peter Frampton I can halfway understand, but Shaun Cassidy?"

"I was never a cheerleader," I interrupted. "I was on the pep squad."

"Here's the weird thing. Even before I remembered how I'd come to be there, I could feel you in that room. I don't know if I can explain it in plain English. It was like I was lying there on your old bed, with all your stuff around me, and you were there, too, the girl you'd been, with your ruffles and your pompoms, and at the same time the girl you grew up into, the one I fell in love with . . . In the back of my mind was everything that happened the night before, trying to fight its way up toward the surface, but for a minute I felt like I'd been blessed, just to be in that room, getting filled up with the, the heart and soul of you. I thought maybe if I could hang on to that long enough I might be able to see my way out of the dark. Oh, hell. Does this make any kind of sense at all?"

He scooted his chair closer to mine and reached for my hand, and I let him take it.

"I know I should've showed my face right then, that day. But I was ashamed of myself, and scared shitless. Not of Marjo or

Dub or any of that business. I've been in enough scrapes in my lifetime; I'm not afraid of paying for what I did. It was knowing how I'd let you down. All these years now, I've been getting your hopes up and then dropping them again. I don't know how you stood it as long as you did. I don't know why you're sitting here right now. Listening to an old fool run on." He stroked my palm with his thumb.

"Where'd the guitar come from?" I asked.

"It was your daddy's."

"What?"

"That's what your mama said. She pulled it out of the attic. The strings were shot to hell, but there were a couple of new sets still in the packages."

"I didn't know he played guitar."

"He wasn't all that good, it seems. She said he only ever learned one song: 'On Top of Old Smokey.'"

"I don't remember him. Just a shape, sort of, in the back of my head. And Mama never told us anything."

"He had red hair—rusty, like your brothers', like Jude's—and he wouldn't go out of the house, not even to pick up the paper, unless his pants were creased and his shirt was ironed and he'd thrown on a splash of bay rum. She loved to stand in the kitchen and iron his shirts, listening to the *Louisiana Hayride* on the radio."

"Mama told you all that?"

"She said she didn't iron a thing for a year, maybe two, after he left. To this day, the sight of the ironing board makes her sad."

"She never even told us she missed him. I mean, we knew at first, when she sat around in her nightgown, drinking and crying. But later on, after Dove took over and Mama straightened herself out and got all cozy with Jesus, we weren't allowed to talk about it. I remember Bailey one time at the supper table—he was mad, Mama wouldn't let him do something he wanted, and he said something ugly like, 'No wonder our daddy left'—and Mama slapped his face. 'You're not to mention his name under this roof,' she said. And that's the last time anybody's tried in, I guess, twenty-five years."

"Well, maybe it's time to try again."

"I don't want to get my face slapped."

"You ought to try cutting your mama a little slack. Maybe she'll surprise you."

"I've had enough surprises for the time being, thank you very much."

"Well, hold on to your hat," he said. "I'm not done yet."

The screen door opened and Mama stuck out her head. "Lucy? Could you come in here a minute?"

"Can't it wait a little bit, Mama?" I called.

"I don't believe it can."

I sighed and got to my feet. "Don't you move," I said to Ash. "I spent the last four days tracking you down, I don't know how much more staying power I've got."

In the kitchen, I found my mama laying out an assortment of cookies, shortbread and chocolate chip and oatmeal raisin, on a lacy-rimmed glass plate. "Carry these out back, will you?" she said. "That boy has a sweet tooth like you wouldn't believe." For the first time I noticed she was dressed in a new dark blue pants outfit, and her hair was neatly styled. More to the point, her mouth was slicked with Fire and Ice. Nothing like having a man around the house to bring Patsy back to her old self.

"Mama, honestly," I said, "Ash and I are trying to have a serious conversation. I don't think either one of us is thinking about cookies."

"Just take them," she said, thrusting the plate at me, forcing me to reach for it. "You might be surprised what a little bit of sugar can do."

"All right. Thank you."

"Do y'all need more tea? I've got a pitcher made fresh."

"We're just fine, thanks," I said, and turned to the door.

"Lucy."

I had to bite my lip from snapping, *What?* "Yes, ma'am?"

"I'd like to have a word with you, if you'll hold your pretty horses a second."

"Yes, ma'am."

She took her time, wiping down the drain board with a sponge, rinsing it out, drying her hands on a terrycloth towel.

"I suppose you've been hearing all kinds of stories about your daddy," she said at last as she shook out the towel and draped it over a hook next to the sink.

"A few."

"I didn't plan—that is, it just sort of came out of nowhere. It started with the guitar and I couldn't seem to stop." She laughed a high, soft laugh. "Believe me, nobody could've been more surprised than me to hear those old tales dragged out after all this time." I wanted to say that I could name one person, easy, but I kept my mouth shut. "I've just got one more thing to say, and then I'll let you get back to your business," she said. "There's something about your daddy Raymond Hatch that I've never told a soul, not Ash Farrell, not Reverend Honeywell, nobody in the world but Jesus.

"Your daddy took off and left us, it's true. Me and you and the boys. His family. He had his reasons. I know what they were, and if it's all the same to you, I'd just as soon keep that between him and me and the Lord."

"For heaven's sake, Mama—what's your point?"

"My point, Miss Twitchy Britches, is that he wanted to come back. And I wouldn't let him."

I set the plate of cookies on the table.

"A few months after he left, he called up out of the clear blue and begged me to see him. Said he'd had a chance to think things through, and that he wanted to come home and try to work things out. Go ahead, call me what you will—proud or stubborn or just plain stupid. But I said no. I couldn't find it in my heart to forgive him.

"For the longest time after, I swore to myself I'd done the right thing. But the older you get, the more the past starts to shift on you—like you're seeing things through a one-way glass, and no matter how bad you want to, you can't reach what's on the other side.

"What I'm trying to tell you, Lucy, is, whether you take Ash back or not, don't make the mistake I did. Don't keep your heart closed up against him out of nothing but pure spite. You might find out somewhere down the road you want to open it up again, and by then it'll be too late." She leaned forward and pushed the cookies toward me. "Now go."

I carried the plate out the screen door and across the yard and set it on the table. Ash glanced at it and lifted an eyebrow. "That's what was so all-fired important?"

"She said you have a wicked sweet tooth. How come in seven years I never knew that about you?"

"It's coming off the booze," he said. "Makes you crave sugar like crazy." He reached for an oatmeal cookie and bit it in two.

"So what's this surprise you were fixing to tell me about?"

He finished his cookie and reached for another before he answered. "Saturday afternoon this guy came out to the new house. City slicker in a big Ford Excursion, wearing brand-new jeans and a polo shirt and fancy-dan boots. Wanted to know if he could have a look around. Said he'd been hunting for a weekend spot for him and his wife, that somebody in town had told him about the place I was building. So I gave him a tour, thinking he was looking for ideas, you know? He asks about a million questions, admires the work, the layout, the view. I'm busy thinking about the Round-Up later on, hardly paying him any mind, when out of the blue he asks how much I'd sell the place for."

"What did you tell him?"

"I just laughed. I had no intention of letting it go." Ash leaned back in his chair and stretched. "But over the last couple days, I admit I've been thinking about his offer."

"I can't believe you're serious."

"Why not? Why not take the cash and get the hell out of Dodge?"

"And go where? To do what? This thing is never going to quit dogging you until you turn around and face it head-on. Haven't you gotten that through your skull by now?"

We sat quietly for a minute before he said, "I can't do it by myself."

"Nobody's asking you to."

"I wouldn't blame you for hanging it up right now, Lucy. I want you to know that."

"Would you just be quiet and let somebody else do the talking for once?" I picked up a chocolate chip cookie and held it in my hand, thinking of the daddy I barely knew, of my mama crying in the dark with her head on the kitchen table, of how something as small as the word *no* could turn out to have such enormous consequences. "I think we should go see Punch," I said. "I think he'll be able to tell us what to do next, where to start. But you have to promise to listen to him, Ash. You can't start hollering and breaking everything in sight if he says you need help. For one thing, he's liable to hit you back. If he says you need to go back to rehab, I think you have to believe him."

"Goddamn it. You know how I hate hospitals."

"Would you rather spend a month in the hospital or the rest of your life screwing up?"

"That depends."

"On what?"

"On what's waiting for me when I get out."

"A house on the water, for one thing. And music. If you're

bound and determined to do it your way, then I believe you'll find a way."

"What about you?"

I shook my head. "I just—I want it to work, Ash. I do. But I think we have to play it as it goes."

"That's not much of a guarantee."

"There are no guarantees. Isn't that what you always used to tell me?"

"Yeah. But I never knew it would come back to haunt me." He stood up. "Come here a minute. I want to show you something."

We walked to the edge of the yard, a spot near the back fence. "Look there." Ash pointed to where, hovering over the last band of rose and gold over the rooftops, Venus and Mars blazed bright against the purple sky. "Supposedly they're closer right now than they've been in our lifetime and will be in the next one."

"Where'd you hear that?"

"I think it was Saul Toomey, over at the café."

I laughed. "We all know everything Saul says is gospel."

"What difference does it make whether it's true or not? It's pretty, isn't it?" And it was, the great expanse of heavens, comets, and stars coexisting like a mirror image of us down below.

"Ash? There's something I need to tell you."

"What's that?"

"I'm going to Rome."

"Rome, Italy?"

"To see the Sistine Chapel."

He reached over and brushed my hair off my jaw with the backs of his fingers. "You think you can wait a month or so?"

In the distance, car doors slammed. A dog barked down the block. I gazed up, feeling the breeze against my face, smelling the damp, dark earth beneath my feet. If I stood still enough, I believed I could feel it turning, one infinitesimal revolution per second, in time to the beating of my heart. I pictured myself, gray-haired and crookbacked, rocking on the porch with Geneva, saying, *I have seen the Sibyl of Delphi. I have walked in the footsteps of Caesar. I have seen the Appian Way.*

Suddenly the patio lights burst on and a crowd came tumbling out the back door, all jabbering at once. Ash dropped my hand and shrank back into the shadows.

It was time to tell him what I knew: that there were only minor charges pending against him, that Hardy Knox had left town, that all Dub wanted was his word to set things right; that nearly all his debts had been paid in full. But before I could get my mouth open, Jude called plaintively, "Mama? Daddy? Where are you?"

"I swear, they were right here five minutes ago," my mama said. "Now, don't tell me, after all I've done for that boy, he's run off and taken her with him!"

"Her car's still out front, Mama," Bailey said. "They can't have gotten too far."

"Hey, you two!" Geneva hollered. "Come out, come out, wherever you are!"

"What do we do?" Ash whispered. His mouth was so close to mine I could feel his breath, smell the soap my mama had laundered his shirt in, his shaving cream, underneath it all the sweet, dark, inimitable scent of him.

"I say we turn ourselves in."

"You sure? No going back, now."

"I'm sure."

He leaned over and touched his lips to the peak of my hairline. "Ready?"

I nodded. "Ready."

"On three."

We counted quietly under our breaths—*one, two, three*—then we threw out our arms and went running, whooping and laughing, out of the darkness and into the light.